TWINNED : BOOK 2

MISSED FORTUNES

TRIS LAWRENCE

DUCK
PRINTS
PRESS

Schenectady, New York

This book is a work of fiction. The characters and events portrayed are a product of the author's imagination. Any resemblance to real people or events is coincidental.

Missed Fortunes
Copyright © 2025 Tris Lawrence

Front cover design by Jade Hallett

Edited by Nina Waters
Print manuscript formatting by Hermit Prints
E-book formatting by Nina Waters

Published by Duck Prints Press, LLC
Schenectady, New York
duckprintspress.com

ISBN (ePub Edition): 978-1-962488-31-0
ISBN (PDF Edition): 978-1-962488-30-3
ISBN (Print edition): 978-1-962488-32-7

Tags:
Genre: Modern with Magic
Rating: General Audiences
Trigger Warnings: cannibalism (mentions of), harm to children (past), microaggressions (homophobic), patricide (mentions of)
Relationships: f/f, f/m, family, friends to lovers, m/m, roommates, siblings, soulmates, twins
Character Features: artist, asexual, bipoc, biromantic, bisexual, child, customer service representative, empathy, gay, lesbian, lucid dreaming, panic attacks, precognition, ptsd, sex averse, student, professor, teleportation, trans man, weather control
Other Tags: break-up, college/university, coming out, dimension jumping, emotional hurt/comfort, estrangement, fraternities and sororities, fraught family dynamics, imprisonment, new york, present tense, restaurant, tarot, third person limited pov, united states of america

To all those haunted by the past, and to those uncertain about their future: remember that "the final outcome" isn't the end.

Keep going.

CONTENTS

THAT WHICH COVERS

FIRST POSITION: COVERS

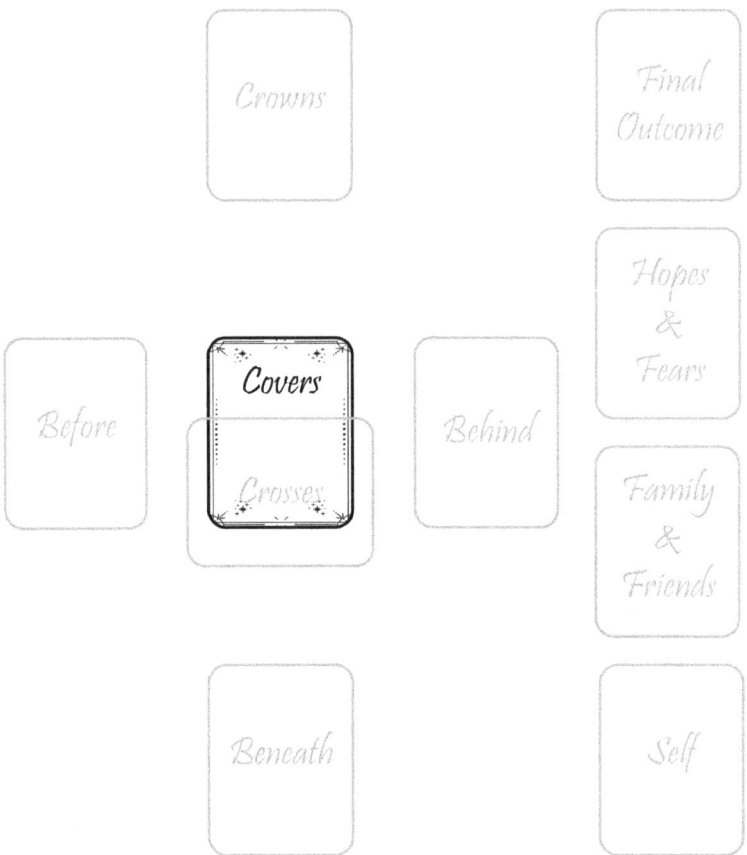

THAT WHICH COVERS...

The first position within the reading indicates the present situation of the querent. It reveals the most important aspect of the querent's life at this exact moment, and it may be positive or negative.

Carolyn's Reading: Three of Pentacles (reversed)

Three men are building a house made of stone. A stained-glass window is partially installed atop a brick wall, three pentacles in place while the structure around them has yet to be built. The house could be perceived as unfinished or as crumbling at the edges where stones have not been placed.

The querent works hard to create a foundation within their life. Their plan is to persevere through all obstacles, yet in the end, despite their best efforts, the querent is surrounded by mediocrity. They are exhausted and broken because they've failed to reach perfection, and now they seek a simpler path. They choose to cut corners, building weakness into the foundation beneath everything they do. While their reputation remains strong, the depth of the work wears upon the querent, and it is possible that even they do not see the cracks that surround them. All they see is the work done, the work in progress, and the work that still must be completed.

Kit's Reading: Six of Swords (reversed)

Six swords lie in a circle, hilts pointing toward the edge and blades pointing toward the center. A dancer stands on his tiptoes where the sword points meet. He has one arm and one leg raised, caught in a moment of perfect balance. He is lit by the moon as if a spotlight shines down on the plain.

The querent stands balanced, all aspects of their life in harmony. They have found the one place—the one moment—where and when everything comes together perfectly. Perhaps they have found a new way of thinking, or their eyes have finally been opened to see the truth. Whatever has changed, it is very public, something that everyone can see: the querent has found their truth.

There are some who associate this card, when reversed, with declarations of intent. A public confession or, perhaps, a profession of love.

Whatever the case, it is always a card of caution, for while balance may have been achieved, it cannot last forever. The swords wait for the querent to fall.

1

"Pawel said he'll meet us here, that Conor'll be happy with scones and his tablet while we talk." Kit holds the door for Teas Please open while Carolyn walks through, then follows her in. He raises one hand; Carolyn follows the motion, catching the moment one of the serving girls spots them and changes direction.

"Hi, Carolyn, Kit," she sings out cheerily. She puts her fingers behind her name tag and shows it proudly. "New year, new job, and all kinds of new resolutions. How are you doing?"

"Hi, Serina," Kit greets her. "I didn't know you worked here."

Carolyn frowns slightly. There was a conversation during rush that she vaguely remembers now: Drea, Serina, Sera, and Trish were talking about crushes. Then, Drea hadn't yet gotten together with Corbin, and she'd seemed uncomfortable discussing the topic. Serina had covered for her by blurting out her own crush, which was on one of the waiters at Teas Please. Carolyn hopes it's not Nate, the waiter Carolyn knows best; if it is, she's pretty sure Serina's barking up the wrong tree.

"I applied in December, just before the semester ended. Nate told me that Jaclyn was graduating and there'd be a spot open. Luckily I snapped it up." Serina grabs two menus and twists to scan the dining room. "Did you want a table or a booth? I don't have any small tables right now, but one should be opening up in a few minutes, and I can get it cleaned for you."

"We're actually meeting someone," Kit says. He stands with his hands shoved into his pockets, rocking back on his heels. He tosses his head, bangs sliding out of his eyes then falling back again. "Pawel should be here."

"Oh, you're who Professor Szczek is waiting for! That reminds me."

Serina darts behind the hostess podium and comes up with a small tin of crayons. "Conor promised me he can fix these, as long as his father says it's okay. You'll be in the back, in Nate's section, but he's on break right now so I hope you're okay with waiting for him."

"We're not going to be in your section?" Kit asks, leaning forward.

Serina laughs softly, gaze dropping. "Not this time, nope, so you'll have to come back another time to bother me."

Kit rubs at the back of his neck and watches her. "I can do that."

That's…new. Definitely different. Carolyn's gaze narrows.

Serina leads them through the restaurant, holding the menus and crayons to her chest. She glances at Kit while she walks, a small smile lighting her lips as they linger over conversation.

Stepping around them, Carolyn spots Pawel and Conor and reaches the booth before Kit and Serina. She slides onto the bench opposite Conor and waits for Pawel to look up from his phone.

Conor watches her quietly, his fingers steady and still on his tablet. "Dad's distracted," he says.

"Just collecting some data. Theories." Pawel locks his phone and shoves it in his pocket. "And now research time is over and advising is beginning. Kit!" he calls out, waving and pointing at the empty spot next to Carolyn. "I had Nate bring out water, but he refused to even consider bringing tea until you got here."

"I have my cocoa," Conor says, nudging the mug forward. "I don't like tea. Why couldn't I go hang out with Alan today?"

"Because Alan's busy. Emily said they won't be home until dinnertime, and they're already coming over then." Pawel touches the top of the tablet. "You know the deal. You get hot cocoa, whatever sandwich you want, and whatever dessert you want. And you get tablet time! In exchange, you sit through this without setting anything on fire, and you clean your room when we get home."

"My room's fine," Conor protests.

"If I let you and Alan go up there to play, I'll lose you both," Pawel says.

"Is that bad?" Conor asks. He sits back, setting the tablet on the table as Serina sets down a tin of crayons. "Oh, wow, you were serious? You're going to let me melt them back together?"

"Only if your dad says it's okay." Serina crouches down. "No actual flames allowed, and you have to be careful because there are a lot of other people here and you never know how someone's going to react if there's a sudden surge of magic. But if you can fix my crayons, that'd be awesome."

Conor straightens his back and crosses his arms. "Of course I can fix your crayons."

Pawel settles a hand atop Conor's head. "Just be careful. Thank you, Serina. Tell Nate not to worry about hurrying back from break; we're not in a rush."

"What are you thinking?" Kit leans over, knocking an elbow into Carolyn.

"Tea," she deadpans. When he rolls his eyes, she opens the menu, even though she already knows what she wants. "High tea with a sandwich, salad, and scone. I'm getting the gobbler…?" Her voice trails off.

"I'll get the buffalo chicken, and we'll split." Kit closes his menu. "I'm getting that vanilla silk oolong again. They've got the chocolate raspberry on the menu if you're interested."

"Why don't you just order for each other?" Conor asks, neatly lining up crayon halves on the table. He seems to be choosing two complementary colors instead of matching halves for each new crayon-to-be. "It's like you're telepathic anyway, right?" He glances up, blinking at them both. "Dad said you're twins."

"We are twins, but we're predictive, not telepathic," Carolyn says.

"She's predictive. I'm not," Kit adds.

"Not possible." Conor flexes his fingers, tiny sparks jumping at his fingertips. He lays his hands across the crayons, his brow furrowed, and Carolyn smells hot wax. When he lifts his hands, there are six awkwardly formed two-colored crayons lying on the wooden surface. "You're twins. You're both predictive or you're both not predictive."

"We're not identical." Kit crowds the table, shifting into Carolyn's space. "Just because—"

Pawel gets a hand up before Kit can keep going. "There's a lot you don't know yet about magical theory," Pawel tells his son. "You work on the crayons and your games. We're going to talk about what Carolyn and Kit are doing for independent study."

Conor mutters something too low to be heard, and his kicking foot catches Carolyn's shin under the table. She winces, and he looks up, apologetic.

She smiles slightly. She gets Conor's frustration, she really does, but she's not arguing the point with Kit anymore. This is her compromise with her twin: working on an independent study that isn't entirely independent.

"I've approached the Dean of Arts and Sciences, and he's fine with your plan for the two of you to complete the same independent study," Pawel says, "as long as you choose a separate final project to present to the department." His gaze shifts from Carolyn to Kit. "I don't think that will be a problem. Kit, what do you want to get out of this independent study?"

"I'm from a predictive Lineage, but the men of our line don't tend to be fully predictive," Kit says firmly. "I'm looking for ways I can start to invest more of my time and attention in ritual, and I want to learn ways to use what little residual predictive Talent I have so I can influence that ritual."

"I want to know how ritual can influence and change predictive Talent, whether I'm working with the cards—my natural inclination—or something else," Carolyn says.

"So the end result for each of you is designing a ritual," says Pawel slowly, "but the impact is different. Carolyn, you want the ritual to improve upon your natural Talent. And Kit, you want your natural Talent to improve upon the ritual. Yes?" His phone is back in his hands, thumbs moving across the screen.

Carolyn glances at her brother and nods when he does. "Yes," they say in tandem.

"Twins," Conor mutters, the smell of warm wax rising again as another half-dozen crayons become whole. He scoops them up, puts them back in the bin Serina brought over, and surveys the litter of crayon pieces left on the table.

"Hey, folks." Nate slides onto the bench next to Kit, nudging him closer to Carolyn. "Welcome back to Unity. Did Serina tell you the special sandwich of the day? What about the soups? Also, we're out of apple crêpes."

"I want a chocolate-hazelnut one." Conor looks up when Pawel coughs, and he adds quietly, "After I have that grilled cheese with the pear slices and all the weird cheeses, and I *said* I'd eat a salad. No dressing, because gross."

"Today, salad dressing is gross," Pawel grumbles. "Last week he ate an entire tub of ranch."

"That's why it's gross now," Conor says. He reaches for his headphones, tucks them in his ears, then says too loudly, "I'm going to watch videos and recharge before I do more crayons."

Carolyn places her order, mixed with Kit as they talk over each other. Nate nods along, then repeats the two orders back perfectly.

After Pawel reels off his own choices, Nate pushes himself to standing. "I'll put that in for you and be back with the tea shortly, and with more cocoa for Conor. It's good to see you, Professor Szczek; I'll see you tomorrow morning in class, too."

"Sucking up to the professor doesn't get you a better tip," Pawel says dryly. "Or a guaranteed A."

"I'm going to be one of the absolutely mundane people in that class, learning about Talent," Nate says. "I just want to get through and see if I can better understand the people around me." He claps a hand on Kit's shoulder. "See you later. Oh, and Serina said she'd be back for the crayons in a bit."

"You have plans with Nate?" Carolyn asks.

Kit shakes his head. "No, I just figured I'd come over here and study later. I have a lot of reading to do for that sociology class I'm taking. I'm supposed to have finished three articles and two videos before the first class tomorrow afternoon. Nothing like starting the semester with a bang, right? Isn't the first day supposed to be syllabus day?"

"You're upperclassmen, and syllabus day is a myth told to freshmen," Pawel points out. "That's not going to be your only assignment this week, you realize."

Carolyn figures that's Pawel's way of saying they'll be starting off with an assignment for their independent study as well. They need to find out when that'll be due. "Kit and I were looking through our schedules, and Kit stalked your class schedule online," Carolyn admits. She pulls out her phone and opens her calendar app. "It looks like our choices for when we can meet with you are first thing on Wednesdays, Monday afternoons, or Thursday afternoons."

"What are you doing at noon on Wednesdays?" Pawel asks, his own phone in his hands. "I want to keep that morning open in case I need a day to go to Conor's class. I'm not done on Mondays until six—the test slot isn't on the standard calendar. Thursdays, I can do something at three."

"That time on Wednesdays, I'm eating lunch." Kit shakes his head, one hand up in a gesture of negation. "I've got a one-hour break between a morning lab and an afternoon three-hour-long lecture. I don't want to miss lunch."

"Fine, then we'll meet on Wednesday at noon in my office, with *lunch* provided," Pawel counter-offers. "We'll go over your previous assignments, then we'll regroup on Thursday at three for new assignments." Pawel raises his eyebrows and spreads his hands. "I'm going to feed you. Don't pass this up. Give me a list of any allergies or dislikes, and expect variety. It won't all be pizza or sandwiches. Do you like your curry mild or spicy?"

"Hot," Carolyn responds for both of them, ignoring the look Conor gives her. "But you don't have to do that."

"If I'm going to demand a lunch meeting time, I'll feed you," Pawel says firmly. "I have a budget that'll take care of it. My department is proving itself to be severely unorthodox, and I don't see that changing. Besides, I have to eat too. And you two will be expected to present work every Wednesday."

"Including this Wednesday?" Carolyn asks, because even though, based on what he'd said before, she'd expected him to give them an assignment, this seems like they're jumping into the deep end. She's not even sure yet what this "class" is going to be.

"Including this Wednesday," Pawel confirms. "No syllabus day for you. Don't worry, it's nothing complex. Since we're branching out from your heritage Talent, I want to start with that. You'll each do a simple three-part Tarot reading before we meet on Wednesday. Do a write up about it, and include all the variables: what was on your mind, what you were doing shortly before you did the reading, who was around you. What deck you used. How the cards responded. Along with looking at traditional ritual, we'll also be looking at the inherent ritual in your personal use of your predictive Talent. We'll explore ritual enhancement and alternative methods of bringing predictive Talent to the foreground. Second assignment, also due Wednesday: outline your goals for this independent study in a clear and concise list. Be specific, and mention at least three other methods of predictive ritual that you are interested in, or at least willing to explore, during this semester. Also, define what 'predictive' and 'ritual' mean to you, and what kinds of ritual might be adaptable to use with predictive Talent."

Carolyn's fingers fly, trying to get everything he says noted in her phone; Kit's doing the same next to her. She glances up to see Pawel watching. Waiting. "Isn't that a lot when we haven't even had a session?" she asks.

"Independent study isn't an easy A," Pawel says softly. "You get my complete attention on your topic of research, but you're both going to work for your passing grade. Are you sure this is what you want?"

"Yes." Kit sets his phone face down on the table and crosses his arms. "I want to understand my options. I want to see what else I can do." Because he thinks he's broken when it comes to predictive Talent—Carolyn can supply the end to that statement without Kit saying it aloud. She inches closer, presses her knee against his, and relaxes when he presses back.

"Yes," she echoes, because if it's good for Kit, it'll be good for her.

That's the thing about twins: they'll always be in this together.

2

MEETING WITH PAWEL is a nice break from polish weekend; as soon as Carolyn's back at the house, she has a paintbrush in hand and fumes to give her a headache. There isn't much left to do because they've been working since the sorority sisters returned from winter break on Friday night. But they're doing a big push to get the paint done in the last of the common rooms while the girls on duty for this week's dinner put it together in the kitchen.

"I'm thinking we go with Italian next week," Soledad muses as she cleans a paintbrush.

"We can't buy from Minnisale's," Drea reminds her. "No ordering in to get out of cooking house dinner."

"We can cook Italian. It's easy, right? Sauce, pasta," Soledad protests. "It makes it really easy to feed a crowd."

"That sounds fine." Carolyn strips off her smock and drops it in the bin Heather offers. She's somehow become the leader of their small group, and she's just happy when one of the other girls takes initiative. "I'll check in with Trish to make sure she's okay with that, Soledad. What do you think, Heather?"

"Italian's fine."

Carolyn's gaze narrows. Heather stands quietly, the bin loose in her hands as she looks at the wall. "You okay?"

Heather blinks, taking a moment to focus. "Of course I'm okay. Everyone's excited to be back—it's overwhelming. You know what it's like."

Carolyn doesn't know exactly what it's like because she's not an Empath. But she has seen Heather falter under strong crowd emotions before; it's a reasonable explanation. "I know," she says gently. "Next week, we five get to hide in the kitchens instead. This week, food is someone else's problem, and it's just about time to eat."

"Speaking of 'us five,' where is my Big anyway?" Soledad wipes her hands on a cloth after she finishes washing the final brush. "I haven't seen Trish all weekend. I thought she was going to get in on Friday with the rest of us."

"She's not arriving until tonight," Drea offers. "I talked to Sera earlier, and they got a late start out of Nashville yesterday and decided to stop at Niagara Falls this morning because they were going through Buffalo anyway. Sera's never seen them."

"Wait," said Soledad. "How did Trish get out of polish weekend, and why didn't she tell me?"

"Music. And she's your Big, so you tell me why the two of you aren't talking," Heather says sharply. She lets out a soft hiss of breath as soon as the words are out, and she shakes her head. "Sorry, that was uncalled for. Still. If you're having trouble with Trish, and you want to talk, my door's open."

That means Carolyn's door is open, but she's used to it. It's part of living with the house Empath-slash-counselor.

How had no one picked up on Trish and Soledad not clicking? Bigs and Littles are matched carefully; Carolyn can't remember a disconnect like this happening before, at least not one that continued past the first few weeks of the school year. Usually by now, Heather would have already noticed and fixed things.

"No trouble, not really. We just don't hang out all the time, I guess. Not like Carolyn and Drea." Soledad gave a soft laugh and a small shrug. "They're, like, perfect. Right?"

"We got lucky." Drea puts her arms around Carolyn, snuggling close and nuzzling her cheek. Coming from anyone else, Carolyn's skin would itch, but it's okay when Drea does it. Easy. Acceptable. "I figure Caro checked her cards and I came up, so she knew I was the right Little. Me, I couldn't have asked for a better Big."

That's not exactly how it happened, but it's close enough. Heather gives Carolyn a knowing smile, and Drea hugs her again. "Strength," Carolyn says, and when Drea looks at her curiously, she explains, "I did a one-card cast when I was thinking of asking for a Little, and it was the Strength card that made me think of you. The woman and her lion."

Drea laughs happily, which is good. Carolyn waited until her junior year before asking, because she knew she wanted just the right person, and that's definitely Drea. But when Carolyn glances at Soledad, her expression has gone sour. Carolyn's no good at smoothing things like that, but she resolves to talk to Trish, see if she can figure out where their relationship has gone wrong. The Big Sister/Little Sister relationship is supposed to be special, and she remembers Trish being excited in the fall. She's not sure why she would let it fall by the wayside.

Drea's right, though. They did get lucky.

After cleanup, they head into dinner, the long tables set neatly with tablecloths and paper plates and plasticware. Several bowls of salad sit on each table, along with pans of macaroni-and-cheese and several optional meats to have with it. There are pans of steamed broccoli and cauliflower, and Carolyn swears she smells chocolate still in the oven.

"We're definitely doing Italian," Soledad whispers as she takes her seat. "And we're using a little less cheese."

They eat quietly and quickly, because with dessert comes an informal chapter meeting.

"Welcome back!" Lauranne calls out as they pass the trash to one end of the table for the bins. Plates of brownies are passed from the table's other end. "We've got a busy spring ahead—oh, thank you for joining us, Trish." Her voice is dry enough to crack wood.

Trish slips into the empty chair next to Soledad, her leather jacket still zippered, black gloves on her hands. "Thank you for not locking the door," she says as she peels the gloves off one finger at a time.

Lauranne's smile is tight. "Weather happens. We understand."

Heather's back is stiff, and Soledad looks at the table. Trish leans back in her chair, balancing it on two legs.

The Five of Pentacles: "Consider your relationship closely before joining forces because working together may not be what you're looking for." A card for the mundane gone wrong between two people when everything should have been right.

Drea looks over at Trish, nostrils flaring. She frowns, opens her mouth, then closes it again when Lauranne speaks.

"As I was saying, we've got a busy spring ahead of us," Lauranne says. "The Paint It Red silent auction is in February, and the Formal is in April. We only have two more weeks to finalize donations for that because we need time to get the programs printed. If you have a donation you've been waiting on, get in touch with the donor to settle it and give the information to Mary. And get those tickets sold! We can't have an auction without people there to buy things. If you haven't had any nibbles yet, go and talk to the businesses around campus. There are always people waiting to help out a good cause, and what's better than heart-health awareness?"

There's a small shiver of pleasant energy at that, a rising urge to get up, go out, and do something positive. Drea wrinkles her nose.

Heather.

Carolyn knocks Heather's knee under the table, and the sensation fades to something less urgent.

"We're also sponsoring the Saturday movie on February 4th; all proceeds will go to the Paint It Red fund," Lauranne says. "We'll need girls at the Madison Center to sell tickets and concessions, and to work security and cleanup. Please see Sherry to sign up for a shift. We'll also have two girls selling tickets for the silent auction and sending flyers home with anyone who might be interested in sending in sealed bids.

"If you want to participate in Outreach this semester, we have four Wednesday events scheduled at the middle school," she continues. "The themes will be 'Music and Dance,' 'Art for All Ages,' 'Chemistry in the Kitchen,' and 'Talent.' Amber's in charge, so see her for details. In other news, we have no need for recruitment this spring." Lauranne's gaze shifts, and Carolyn finds herself meeting her eyes. "No girls chose to transfer to different schools nor were any asked to leave the house." Lauranne's gaze shifts from Carolyn and slides over the others at the table. "For the moment, our numbers remain the same. The final item is that we will be co-sponsoring the barbecue during Spring Festival in April with OPT. Attendance will not be optional."

"I have a schedule of upcoming mixers," Heather chimes in as Lauranne falls silent. "We've gone over the list, and any fraternities who were offensive last semester have been struck from it. At the request of several sisters, we've also added one co-ed frat to the list."

"Sign-up sheets for the events are on the table," Lauranne says. "I expect every sister to help out as needed. If you have to take time off for academics, though, we understand. Your education comes first. We are your sisterhood, and we are here to help you."

Across the room, a chair scrapes loudly, pushing back from the table.

"Sorry," Mac calls out. "I thought that was the final bit."

Lauranne purses her lips, but she nods sharply. "We're done. Don't forget to sign up."

Mac is at the table before anyone else, bending to put her name to paper. Trish touches Soledad's shoulder, and they walk over together. Drea stands and moves closer to Carolyn and leans in to whisper, "How did that happen?"

"What?" Carolyn asks, glancing at Heather as if she might have the answer because she has no idea what Drea's talking about.

Drea gestures at where Trish and Soledad are sifting through papers together at the sign-up table. "That. Isn't there a process for who gets a Little?" Drea asks. "I mean, I had to give the names of three sisters I'd love to have as a Big, and honestly, you were my top choice. Not because we're alike, but because we really get on, and we have a lot of interests in common."

"I thought it was because I remind you of your brother," Carolyn says. She's glad when Drea smiles at the small joke; if she'd had to explain it, she doesn't think it would've come out well. But she sees it, even if no one else does. Drea's twin is quiet. Reserved. Doesn't seem comfortable in a crowd or as if he fully understands social cues. Carolyn understands. Alaric has Drea, and Carolyn has Heather and Kit. The parallels make sense.

"It started off better than it's going now," Heather says. "Soledad was enthusiastic, and she's an art major. She and Trish were working on a project together in the fall. Then…" She shrugs. "It's like they just stopped talking. Neither of them wants to discuss it with me."

"So it's not that there's an intrinsic problem," Drea muses, "but that something's broken. We can work on that."

"No," Carolyn says quickly, and Heather bites back a smile. "We're trying to teach Heather not to interfere with everyone, and you shouldn't either. They have to figure things out for themselves or come to us for help. Heather offered already."

"Who's figuring what out?" Mac asks.

Drea flinches and rolls her eyes. "I hate when you do that."

"And that's exactly why I do it," Mac says easily. "Your brother's even more fun." She hooks her arm around Drea's elbow. "Come on. I was thinking we could all go upstairs and catch up. It's been a while since we've seen each other."

"It was only a few weeks." Heather's brow furrows. "We kept in touch. Didn't we?"

Carolyn had texted heavily with Heather over the break, and often with Drea. She only exchanged a few texts with Mac. "Sort of," she says.

"Mostly," Drea agrees. She glances toward the table again. Trish and Soledad are talking to another pair of sisters. Soledad explains something with wide hand gestures, and Trish laughs. Both seem more relaxed, and Drea exhales softly. She pats Mac's hand where it's wrapped around her elbow. "You're right. Let's go upstairs. Your room, or are we invading Caro's space?"

"My space is a tiny single under the eaves," Mac reminds her as they lead the way out, Carolyn and Heather trailing behind. "Funniest thing I've ever seen is Alaric trying to stand upright in there."

"Imagine if it were Rory." Drea giggles, and Mac makes a face.

"I don't think Rory would like it. Thorne's been up there, but he's short compared to the two of them."

"Thorne, huh?" Drea sways, knocking her hip into Mac's.

"Not like that. No, seriously. It's not like that at all," Mac protests as Drea laughs. "Am I the only person on campus who hasn't slept with him?"

"Drea fits in," Heather murmurs for Carolyn's ears only, "but you're still worried about something."

Carolyn wonders sometimes if she let Heather in because she trusts her, or if Heather simply barreled past her walls. It works for them, though, and Carolyn knows that Heather would never hurt her. She bites her lip, watches as Drea continues to tease Mac and gets shoved lightly for her trouble. "I'm worried about Drea," she admits. "And about Mac. And about everything that happened last semester. I know they both had a lot to deal with over break. Me, I just had to try not to kill my family for being idiots around Kit."

"How is Kit?" Heather's tone is light, but Carolyn doesn't feel like getting into the details of Kit's issues with their Lineage, so she sticks with a surface-level answer.

"He's fine. We're doing an independent study with Pawel this semester, and I think that'll go a long way toward figuring out how to be twins and Talented." It goes deeper than that, but anything more is Kit's to discuss.

When they get to their room, Mac's sprawled on Heather's bed, and Drea sits on the floor, her back against Carolyn's bed. Mac raises a hand and points at the door, and Carolyn pulls it closed behind them.

Heather settles on her bed, nudging Mac to give her some room. Carolyn isn't sure she feels like sitting, so she grabs her bag and pulls it up to the bed, digging through it for her Tarot deck.

"I have good news and surprising news," Drea announces.

Carolyn pauses, one hand on her deck, and looks down. "Is the 'surprising news' good?"

"Surprisingly, yes." Drea grins, stretching back to look up at her. "Alaric's really settling into his whole 'heir' thing. He talked to people during the Conclave, and when they voted a few weeks ago, the decision was that we won't go to war."

"That's good." Carolyn sinks down to sit next to Drea. She pulls her knees up and props the deck on them as she carefully unwraps the black fabric she uses to protect it. It feels good to let the cards fall into her hands as she shuffles them idly.

"Very good. Mac, did he tell you about it?"

Mac makes a noise and does a thumbs-up. "The highlights I heard were that Dax visited, and then Alaric went to kick a tree. Chris visited, and somehow Alaric ended up making an alliance with some girl. The vote happened, and 'no war' won, which is good. Alaric went looking for a

Shadow and failed to find it, Chris left, and Alaric kicked a tree. Oh, and every time he overheard you and Corbin, he kicked trees. Or punched them. I should go apologize to your forest."

"The forest is still standing, so we're fine." Drea picks at the hem of her jeans. "Corbin and I tried to spend a lot of time outside of the house over break. It's funny. I mean, we hear things better than humans, and Ric and I smell things, but Corbin just…notices things. Like a bird does. And growing up, we all knew that people had sex. We knew what it sounded like and smelled like, and we didn't care, but now? I do not want to know anything about it."

Carolyn cringes inwardly. Her body curls in, her elbow moving to give Drea space. "I can't even imagine."

"I bet Corbin thinks this is funny," Mac says.

"He's somewhere between finding it hysterical and horrifying," Drea agrees. "He had fun annoying Ric, right up until the moment that Chris got there. Then he quit."

"Yeah, nope, not something I want to think about," Carolyn mutters. "Moving on. There are some details left out of all that. What happened to that Shadow? Is everything okay at your home? Is your dad okay? Did anything happen when Dax was there?"

"Your brother made an alliance?" Heather leans forward, and Drea's nostrils flare. Heather winces. "Sorry. I'm trying not to; I'm just curious. I know Alaric has trouble making connections."

"You don't need to fix him." Drea's voice is soft but curt. "He's growing into his role. We met a group of people our age—some leaders, some heirs who will be leaders someday. They think like we do, and we made an alliance. Dayton is the ringleader of that group, and she adopted Ric. He told her that—" She stalls out, stops dead on a breath, and exhales rather than finishing.

Mac sits up; she moves to the edge of the bed and looks down at Drea, eyebrows up. Drea nods slowly.

Carolyn flips the card on the top of her deck. The Wheel of Fortune. "Change," she says. "Things are flexible. Mutable. We have to be able to roll with events because change is coming quickly."

Drea's mouth snaps shut.

That was the card that came up for Drea's birthday a few weeks back, when Carolyn offered a one-card draw—just one card to speak to what could happen in the year to come. For Carolyn, it's significant that the same card has shown again.

She bets Drea doesn't remember, though, so that can't be the explanation for the sudden silence.

Mac grabs for her phone, fingers flying across the keyboard while Heather sits bolt upright, hands in her lap, obviously not leaning to look.

The phone chimes a moment later.

"He says 'go ahead,'" Mac says.

"Ric told Dayton that he has a new form," Drea says slowly. "You know how he thinks he's broken? Well, he's not. He can change into a dragon now."

"Dragons aren't real." Heather's voice is high pitched, tight. "What if he does that on the field?"

"You can't say both that it's not possible and that you're worried about it happening," Mac points out, nudging Heather. "And it's very real. I was there the first time it happened. More importantly, the Shadows know that he can turn into a dragon. It was a part of how we captured that one."

Carolyn has never heard the details of what happened that night; events had unfolded quickly at the end of the semester, and she wasn't sure how much Drea knew at the time, either. She turns another card, and the handsome, severe face of the Prince of Cups stares back at her. "Same advice: roll with the punches and don't hold back. But, he's weary and war-torn and exhausted by arguments. He's ready to move on."

"Sounds like Ric to me." Mac pats the edge of the bed, and Drea switches her seat, leaning back against the bed next to Mac's knee. Mac slides her fingers through Drea's hair, and Drea tilts, leaning against her thigh with a soft sigh. "What happened with Dax anyway? Alaric wasn't exactly detailed about that, just pissed off."

"Nothing." Drea makes a face. "Dax went out to talk to Orson, and when he came back, he said that Orson's not happy yet. I don't think it's about the war; I think it's about the Shadows themselves. But we don't know how to chase them. Maybe Rory and Pawel could do another ritual to summon one, but until we know why what we did wasn't enough or what we should do instead, I don't think there's a point." She's quiet for a moment, her eyes closed and a low rumble rising from her throat. "Corbin and I went to the place where she was held. At home."

"Mm?" Heather leans forward, and Drea puts up a hand to keep her from getting too close.

"We went in the house, and it reeks. It smells rotten there, like something horrible happened. There wasn't any sign of the Shadow, and we couldn't stay long." Drea licks her lips and shakes her head. "Not 'didn't.' Couldn't. We both felt like we had to run, so we did. We ended up in the river, even though it was cold. We needed to get clean."

"So that's a dead end." Mac's fingers trail away from Drea, and she falls back on the bed.

Carolyn carefully gathers up her cards and rewraps them. She'd like to keep shuffling, but with those two cards as the first drawn, she's certain that any further advice will be down a similar path: keep going, you're heading the right way, be ready for change. It's good advice, she supposes, but not necessarily immediately helpful.

"How about your trip home?" Heather asks.

Mac laughs dryly. "Awkward. My dad came for Christmas, so it was him, my mom, and my stepdad. Everyone knew that I'd managed to expose myself as the incredible teleporting Emergent girl. Dad's uncomfortable, and my stepdad thinks I shouldn't be telling people." Mac shrugs. "I'm looking forward to practice on Wednesday night. There's a tournament in February and another one in March, so we're going to need to push hard to get those who are qualified to compete ready."

Carolyn translates that as *Mac wants to hit things just like Alaric kept hitting trees over break.*

"It's going to turn out okay," Heather says quietly. "Like Carolyn says, we need to be open to the changes that are coming. Roll with them and accept them."

"It'd be nice if we could see them coming," Drea mutters. "It's all shadows and darkness, and this is one time we can't see in the dark."

Carolyn itches to reach for her deck again, to draw one more card. Just in case it's something different.

Just in case it has the answer.

The problem is, she's pretty sure that won't happen. So she lets the deck lie, and when the conversation drifts from the end of the world to Drea talking about Corbin's antics, she lets that go, too.

3

KIT WALKS IN and drops his bag on the floor by Carolyn's desk. He flops into her chair, slumped against the back, arms crossed.

"I know. You don't want to do this, but it's the assignment. For the independent study that was your idea," Carolyn reminds him. "Being predictive doesn't make you any less of a man."

"Being a man makes me less predictive," Kit shoots back. He reaches for his bag and digs through the front pocket, shoving his hand deep. He pulls out a small royal-blue drawstring bag and opens it, letting cards spill into his palm.

"You still keep the deck with you," Carolyn says quietly.

Kit makes a disgruntled noise. "It's the deck Mom gave me. Of course I keep it with me. I've had it with me since I was little. Remember when we were in kindergarten, and the teacher thought we were bringing satanic tools to school with us?"

"I guess things got a little easier after the Emergence in that respect." Carolyn brings out her own deck and starts shuffling it casually. "Did you ever think that maybe cards just aren't your—?" She cuts off at Kit's sharp look, and she sets her deck down on the bed. "Okay, fine. Do you want to go first, or should I? Do you have your notebook? Pawel had a ton of variables he wanted us to keep track of."

Kit shows a small hardcover notebook with a cover that's almost the same blue as the drawstring bag. Carolyn's is a deep, dusky purple, but other than that, the two books could be twins: the same size, same brand, and both with dots making almost-lines on the pages, so it's easier to sketch out a layout.

Kit might not think he's predictive, but he remembers their early training, and he sticks with it. Carolyn thinks the Talent might still be there, buried under the surface. This ritual work that they're doing with Pawel might bring it out, or it might bury it even more deeply beneath Kit's dysphoria.

She opens her book, reaches for a pen, and labels the first page with the date. She draws three rectangles on the page for the cards, leaving space above them for labels and below for notes. Out of the corner of her eye, she sees Kit doing the same.

She thinks for a moment, the tip of her pen between her teeth, her knee drawn up so she can use it as a desk for her notebook. She writes slowly and carefully, framing her thoughts before she begins.

> *I just came from dinner; Kit and I planned to meet this evening to do the readings together. He's not always here when I read, but I'm often around when he does. At least as far as I know, since he says he doesn't do readings anymore. Heather isn't here; she's left so that we can have quiet and privacy. Sometimes the cards do strange things around her, so her absence is good.*

Sitting nearby, Kit hunches over the desk, curling around the notebook while he writes with thoughtful scratches on the page.

Carolyn continues writing.

> *I know this is an assignment, but it's still a reading, and I hope to learn something about the new year. It seems as if so much is still in flux for everyone I know, while my life continues in the same pattern as it always has. I can see everyone's possibilities, but for myself, there seems to be only one way forward and it is no different than my past path.*

She places the pen at the center crease and closes the book around it, then sets them aside. She shuffles her deck with intention now, letting the cards slip and slide against each other. She waits until Kit lifts his own cards; he taps the deck against the desk and shuffles. Carolyn uses an overhand shuffle, trading the cards from her left hand to her right, while Kit riffles the cards in two interwoven stacks against the table.

Carolyn stops when Kit does, and he glances over at her.

"Same time?" he asks, and she nods.

She lays out the cards face down across the bed—one, two, three—at the same time as Kit does so on the desk. They set aside their decks and flip the cards in tandem.

Kit stares down at his cards. "This is one of those days when I'm really glad that my readings are rarely for me."

"It's not that bad," Carolyn says. Two fives and a nine. Three different suits. It's got potential, if they can figure out what it means.

Kit makes a soft noise. "It's probably muddled anyway."

"Fine. Let's read them. My recent past." Carolyn touches the card of the Magician that lies on her bed. "Opening up to new magical possibilities, letting go of restraints."

"Five of Wands," Kit says. "Competition."

"Or marshaling your resources around your passions," Carolyn counters. "That's exactly what you've done, right? You've changed your life to be honest to yourself, and you're in the process of trying to find a way to be honest with your Talent as well. The only person you're competing with is you, Kit."

"Nine of Swords," Kit says, as if he's not interrupting her. "Time to cut my losses."

"You're anxious. You think everything's out to get you," Carolyn says.

"That could be true, if we were talking about issues with Talent. Which we are." Kit's voice is careful. Flat. "It's a good assessment of my current situation. Yes, I'm anxious. Yes, I'm trying to find a way to stay afloat and a new way forward, and yes, it feels like there will be a bunch of sharp, stabby things coming at my back if I'm not careful."

Carolyn licks her lips and drops her gaze. "For being two entirely different cards, ours are similar," she says quietly. "Three swords piercing something personal. Time to wrap things up and move on."

"If you won't listen to me, will you listen to the cards?" Kit asks dryly. He turns, leaning over the back of the chair to regard her.

She raises an eyebrow. "You're asking me to believe the cards you laid on the table are telling me that you can't predict anything with cards. Irony, Kit. I don't think you're as broken as you think you are, and besides—this card is trying to say something about me."

"You're not broken." He pulls back, brow furrowed. "That doesn't make sense."

"Whatever it means, it leads to a new beginning." She touches the Ace of Swords. "A fresh start and a chance to stay focused and move down a new path. Such as learning to use ritual and predictive Talent. Together."

"Meanwhile, I fall out of love." Kit tucks the Five of Cups back into his deck, burying it somewhere in the middle before he shuffles them again.

"You know that's not what it means."

"Five spilled cups," Kit points out. "I'm all out of love."

"You've lost something," Carolyn counters, "or you're going to lose something. But remember, the cups aren't completely empty. What matters is still inside you, and you can weather the loss. We can weather it together."

"What if it's something I want to lose?" Kit's words fall flat as he wraps the deck and buries it back in his bag. "That's what you have to remember, Caro. I'm not good at predicting things. Maybe I just want to find out what I am good at—find new aspects of magic—because I'm sitting here thinking about the cards, and all I get is a story about how I'm losing things. And I think maybe I'm going to lose the thing I'm actually ready to lose."

Carolyn thinks that can't be it; if Kit needs to lose his predictive Talent, why would the cards be predicting it for him? She's sure there's something else they're not seeing, but she doesn't have the context for the interpretation. She frowns as she looks from her cards to his.

"Write it down," she says. "Everything that Pawel wanted, and anything else that comes to mind. When we're done with this independent study, we should both be more comfortable with our Talent."

"I'm joining Coven," Kit says. He hunches over his notebook, pen scratching quickly until he sets it down, digs in his bag, and brings out a pouch of colored pencils. He spills them onto Carolyn's desk. "If I want to know about other Talents, that's a good place to meet people."

"I'll join, too. I've done a few things with them, but I could do more."

Kit stops, looking over at her. "You don't have to be protective and watch over me. I'll be fine on my own."

"I'm joining to help improve my grade, Kit." Carolyn sketches in the rough image of the Three of Swords, focusing on it as the central card in her reading. The image she sketches isn't exactly the one from the card; it's more a depiction of the way it makes her feel. The standard imagery for the card varies; some decks show a heart being pierced, whereas her deck shows a rose. In the image she draws, the three swords are thrust directly into the ground, a fissure appearing in the earth.

It feels right.

Kit makes a sound of displeasure. "Fine."

Carolyn sets her pen down. "Seriously, Kit, I'm not trying to mother you. You can take care of yourself. I know that."

"You get protective."

"There's a reason for that."

"I don't need it." His voice is flat. He picks up a colored pencil and starts shading something in roughly. "Everything got better when we came to PHU, yes, but I've still been staying in the shadows. I'm done with that, Carolyn. I have friends, but I'm not close to people. I don't talk to them. I'm just that quiet guy, right? The one who got a single his freshman year. The one who hasn't joined a frat, who doesn't play sports, who sometimes goes to the gym. The guy who somehow aced orgo and is a natural at cell bio. I'd like to branch out from that."

Carolyn stares at the page in front of her, at the three shadowy figures standing behind the swords. There are two in the back and one at the front; the central sword has just been plunged into the ground.

He looks like Kit.

She touches it; the ink smears under her fingertip. "I know," she says quietly. "I'm sorry if I've been smothering you. High school—" She stops dead. It's not something she wants to put into words, and not only for Kit's sake. That particular sword has points on both ends.

"High school wasn't great," Kit agrees just as quietly. "But we've moved on, right? And I'm moving on more. Trust me." He glances over at her. "And trust yourself, okay?"

That's easier said than done. Carolyn smiles, but it wavers, and she knows Kit can probably hear that she's holding back. "I did ask for Drea as a Little."

"I like Drea. She's good people. Good Clan." Kit bends back over his work, and Carolyn relaxes. "I'm talking to Pawel this week about partners I can work with to look into developing ritual. People who have more experience with it, but also people who look at it in different ways. There are so many Mages on campus, from so many different backgrounds. Some people are like us, with specific Talents, but there are others who are from broader backgrounds. Who have their own unique, innate abilities."

"You'll follow as Pawel directs, right?"

Kit gives her a dark look. "Carolyn."

She licks her lips. "Sorry. Protective. Sometimes…ritual makes me uncomfortable." It all goes back to high school.

Opening up to new magical possibilities. Letting go of restraints.

That happened, yes, but it wasn't a positive experience for her. She wants Kit to have all the positivity, to love his life.

She must remember that this is now, and what happened then won't happen to him.

She writes *high school* under her sketch of the Magician, then closes the book and sets it aside. It's only Monday evening, and she has until Wednesday to fill in the rest. It can wait. She draws her feet up on the bed and sits, cross-legged and comfortable. "Okay. So talk to me about it. What kind of rituals are you thinking? I know he wants you to use your predictive ability—to see how it can affect rituals. Have you been thinking about anything specific?"

"I don't know enough yet," Kit admits. "I need to get to know people, which is why I need to join Coven. Get to see how my Talent mingles with others'. And I'm sure Pawel will have some suggestions, right? I think it's going to be an interesting semester."

Two readings, two completely different sets of cards. But Carolyn can see how they go together. A major change in the past. A fresh change coming to upset the present. And in the future, new beginnings built out of fresh growth or the spilling of old problems.

"Yeah, it's going to be interesting," Carolyn murmurs.

According to the cards, everything's going to change, but they'll get somewhere when it's done.

She can work with that.

4

"IT WAS GOOD to see you both at Coven on Tuesday." Pawel gestures for Carolyn and Kit to sit in the two chairs in his office. The desk is messier than it had been when they were there on Wednesday to go over their assignments, as if in the absence of Thai curry the paperwork floods back into the space. "I forgot to say that yesterday, but our meeting time was short, and I wanted to make sure we had time to eat and go over your assignments in depth. Do you have any questions about what we discussed?"

Pawel perches on the edge of the desk, and Carolyn scoots her chair back, giving herself more room. Kit leans back in his chair, puts his feet up on the desk next to Pawel, and crosses his legs at the ankle. Pawel raises an eyebrow but doesn't argue.

"About what we discussed at Coven or about the assignment?" Kit asks.

Pawel shrugs and spreads his hands. "Either. Coven's not an official part of your independent study, but given that you're both there now, it'll presumably play a part. It's a good place for you to make contacts among the magically Talented. But let's focus on the assignments first. I've been thinking about what you presented yesterday, and I'd like to do something similar this week, but push your limits in a different direction."

Kit scowls and crosses his arms. "Such as?"

Pawel leans forward and gestures. "The discussion you had yesterday was interesting—you deny your Talent, but by echoing your denial, the cards seem to prove your Talent. And Carolyn, your reading shows a distinct wariness but also a hopeful expectation of a good outcome. You both have some specific things you need to work on."

Carolyn catches Kit's glance, shaking her head slightly. It's fine. Pawel isn't going to tell her to go confront the demons of her past. He just wants her to step out of her shell. She can do that for a grade. She can learn.

"I want you to work predictively again this week, to continue working with the cards for now," Pawel says. He leans back, picks up a folder without looking, and flips through it. "I've been cross-referencing members of Coven with known Talents on campus, and then cross-referencing again for those who are already familiar to you. This week, I'd like you to work with a partner, and I think both of the people I've suggested will be amenable, even if it means extra work for them." He grins. "Neither of them ever minds scoring extra points in general."

"Have you already talked to them?" Because whoever it is will be wondering why they're being dragged into someone else's work, and Carolyn isn't sure she wants to deal with that. From the way Kit sits up at the question, she guesses he agrees with her.

"I haven't," Pawel says. "Doing so yourselves is part of your assignment. I have a proposed study buddy for each of you, but you can go in a different direction if you want. By next Wednesday I want you to have defined who you will be working with for next week's assignment."

"And that's it?" Kit asks, voice tight. "That's all we have to do for next week?"

Pawel leans back again, hitching one leg up and crossing it over the other. "I want you to think about options for rituals. On Wednesday, I also want you to present me options for types of rituals that you can do with a partner—either the one I've proposed or someone else you've chosen—that include predictive Talent. I don't expect a fully designed ritual, but I'd like the skeleton outline of what would be necessary and how you would participate."

"With the partner we've chosen," Carolyn says slowly, wanting to specify.

"Or with another partner, in case your first choice—or my recommendation—doesn't work out. The ritual assignment isn't exclusive. In fact"—Pawel taps his knee for emphasis—"be broad. Design the basis of three different types of rituals, and how predictive Talent could help complete them. For example, one could be working with a Weather Witch, another with someone who is Emergent and has a specific Talent. You choose based on the people you know in Coven. They don't have to be the person you plan to work with, but one of the rituals should be designed around your plan for the following week's assignment."

It sounds complicated. It sounds complicated and messy and time consuming, and Carolyn doesn't want to think about meshing her abilities with someone else's.

"Who were you thinking we should talk to?" Kit asks. He has his notebook balanced on his knee, a purple pen between his fingertips.

Carolyn should take notes, too, but she just wants to listen for the moment.

"Carolyn." Pawel gestures with a pen, pointing the tip at her center. "Your roommate would be an excellent choice. I know she's working on an internship for credit with Bea in Athletics this semester. Bea spoke to me about it since she needed my approval to get it on Heather's schedule as an independent study. You and Heather have already spent a lot of time in close proximity—you've been roommates since freshman year, right?"

"Same floor freshman year, but we rushed SigPsiEp together and have been in the same room for the last year and a half," Carolyn says. She licks her lips and tries to think of ways they could push their Talents together in a single ritual. "She's not a Mage."

"She's an Empath, so she's a Mage that only has one specific line of Talent," Pawel counters. "Empaths are more specific than Weather Witches, less so than someone like you. There are plenty of ways to match your Talents, I think, but you might need to be creative. If Heather doesn't appeal, you could talk to someone like Nikita. You probably remember her from Coven. Although she's not your standard Weather Witch. If you want someone who's more generic, there's Shane. Jeffrey. I'm sure you can find a hundred Mages on this campus easily. We had a great showing of new people last night, and I also know a dozen Weather Witches other than Nikita. Empaths, however, are rare."

And Carolyn has one for a best friend. She knows that Pawel is hinting that she has a unique chance here, but Carolyn isn't sure that pushing the limits of her friendship with Heather is wise. If anything blows up, they'll still have to live together in the aftermath.

He waits, and in the end, she nods. Fine. She'll try, anyway.

"What about me?" There's a tight, defensive note in Kit's voice.

Carolyn taps his chair with her toe, and he lets it fall with a *thunk*. "You want to be someone other than the guy who speaks organic chemistry as a native language," she reminds him. "That means stepping out of your comfort zone."

He glares, and she can't blame him. She's the cautious one. The worried one. But she's trying to be supportive, to help him take steps outside of his usual spaces. Even if it makes her nervous.

"Thorne Baker," Pawel says.

Kit's brow furrows, head tilted.

Wait. "Thorne?" Carolyn leans forward. "Are you sure about that? He can be—"

"—headstrong," Pawel finishes, though that's not what Carolyn had planned to say. "He's gregarious. Willing to work with people. He has more raw ability than many Mages on campus, even if he doesn't realize it. He has an innate Talent that he can call any time he wants, and does, often, sometimes to disastrous effect. But he also has a strong grounding in magical ritual thanks to his upbringing. He has three Mages for parents, and one of his fathers is part of a Mage commune. He has the background in ritual that you're looking for, Kit. He's an excellent choice."

"I'll email him." It isn't a yes or a no, and Kit remains tightly pulled together, hands clenched. "It could work. I could learn a lot from him."

Carolyn's knows that Kit's met Thorne; they were actually sitting on the same side of the room during the Coven meeting. She's also certain that Kit and Thorne are going to be like oil and water. She's seen a lot of Thorne this year because of his association with her Little, and she's not fond of him. He rubs her the wrong way.

"See what you think after talking to him," Pawel suggests, "and don't let him take charge. This is your project. You do it how you see fit. He'll be part of it to help, not to control it."

Kit nods, writing carefully in the notebook.

Carolyn has questions still. She asks for references on ritual, and Pawel provides a list of readings for her to look at, all concerning the idea that rituals can be combined. Kit writes each one down, and Carolyn knows she can get the notes from him later.

It's a quicker session than she'd expected.

"I have office hours, and you have class," Pawel says as he releases them.

"Dinner," Carolyn corrects, although Kit nods. They don't do everything together, just a lot. In the last two years, it's taken a time to get used to the idea that they can have separate schedules and won't work together constantly.

In a way, she supposes, this is the right time for this project. No matter how uncomfortable she feels.

Pawel goes to the other side of his desk and flips open a laptop. Kit shoves his notebook into his backpack, and Carolyn lifts the messenger bag that she never opened, putting the strap across her body.

"We should go over the assignment together," Carolyn suggests. "It might help since we have different perspectives on our own rituals. I'll try to talk to Heather tonight. When are you going to email Thorne?"

"Not until the weekend." Kit fiddles with his phone, a slow smile lighting his features as he replies to something. "I need to get a lab written up tonight, and Friday, I've got a date."

"Date?" Carolyn freezes just outside of Pawel's door. She shifts to the side when a guy approaches, giving him room to knock and go in. Kit takes a step; Carolyn reaches out and grips his forearm. "You have a date?"

His jaw sets. "Yes. A date. Serina and I are going to Albany for dinner and a movie. Why?"

She can think of a dozen reasons why, foremost among them… "You don't date."

"I haven't dated much," Kit corrects her, and Carolyn wonders what she's missed these last two years. What Kit hasn't mentioned. His brow furrows, and he gently takes her fingers off his arm. "You're doing the 'overprotective mother' thing again, Caro. It's just a date. You know Serina—she's friends with Drea and her brother. She's kind of sweet, a little bubbly, and I like her. And she likes me."

"What if—?"

"Don't." Kit cuts her off, taking a step back to put distance between them. "Don't, Caro. Don't tell me why I shouldn't date. Don't give me reasons to second guess this. Just let me date like everyone else dates. She's cute. She's fun. We'll have a good time. We might do something really insane, like go to an escape room together."

Carolyn licks her lips; she purses them when Kit holds up a hand to stop her before she can speak.

He lowers his voice, hand still up between them. "You don't get to tell me what to do," he says sharply. "It's my life, okay? And if you really feel the need to play some part in this? Try being happy for me."

He brushes by her as he stalks off, his shoulder bumping into hers. Bony. Too skinny. All attitude.

Carolyn bites her lips, closes her eyes, and leans against the wall. Shit.

"You okay?"

Carolyn opens her eyes, surprised to see Heather standing nearby with a concerned look on her face. Carolyn's not okay, and she knows that Heather knows it. She likes that Heather gives her the chance to lie about it, though, and she pastes on a weak smile as she looks at her. "Fine," she says. "What are you doing here?"

"I figured that since I just finished class in Thomson, and you were at your independent study here, I'd swing by and grab you for dinner." Heather shrugs one shoulder. "We're going over movie-night plans tonight, right?"

Carolyn thinks she should feel better. She usually feels better when Heather's around, as if Heather can't help trying to fix her. "Why aren't you doing anything?" she asks, following as Heather heads down the hall.

"Because doing something would be rude," Heather says. "It's intrusive, and you should be allowed to feel your feelings, and I shouldn't fix them just because your bad feelings make me feel bad. Besides, do you want me to fix you?"

It's a complicated question, and Carolyn has a feeling there's an entire Pandora's box waiting to be opened here. "Am I addicted to you?" Carolyn asks, wrinkling her nose. "Because that's a really disturbing image." She exhales and gives in. "Yes. Please."

A wave of calm washes over her, and Heather smiles slightly. She puts an arm behind Carolyn's back, and Carolyn puts her arm across Heather's shoulders and leans into her. Heather's shorter, but they move together easily; they're used to it. "Better?" Heather asks quietly, and Carolyn nods.

"I don't think you're addicted to me," Heather adds after Carolyn's had a moment to breathe. "But I think you're used to me. And I'm used to you letting me do this. And you don't like bad feelings."

That's a sour taste. "True," Carolyn agrees.

"Can I say something that you're not going to like?" Heather asks.

She's going to say it anyway, and then she's going to wash it all away so Carolyn only hears the words and doesn't have to deal with the emotions. "Would you ever not?"

The sense of ease never disappears, wrapping around Carolyn like a warm coat, blunting the edge of Heather's words. "When you treat him like he can't handle himself, then you're the one who's acting prejudiced. You're telling him that he can't be trusted, and that he can't trust anyone else. That's no way to live, Carolyn."

There's a swoop in Carolyn's gut in reaction to her words. The swoop fades swiftly, and she nods, accepting the criticism for what it is. She wants to argue, to say that Kit needs common sense, needs someone to remind him of all the dangers around them.

But Heather is right. Carolyn needs to let Kit live his own life, not worry that he's going to fall into the same traps that she did. They are two entirely different human beings, for all that they're twins. She needs to let him be his own person.

THAT WHICH
CROSSES

SECOND POSITION: CROSSES

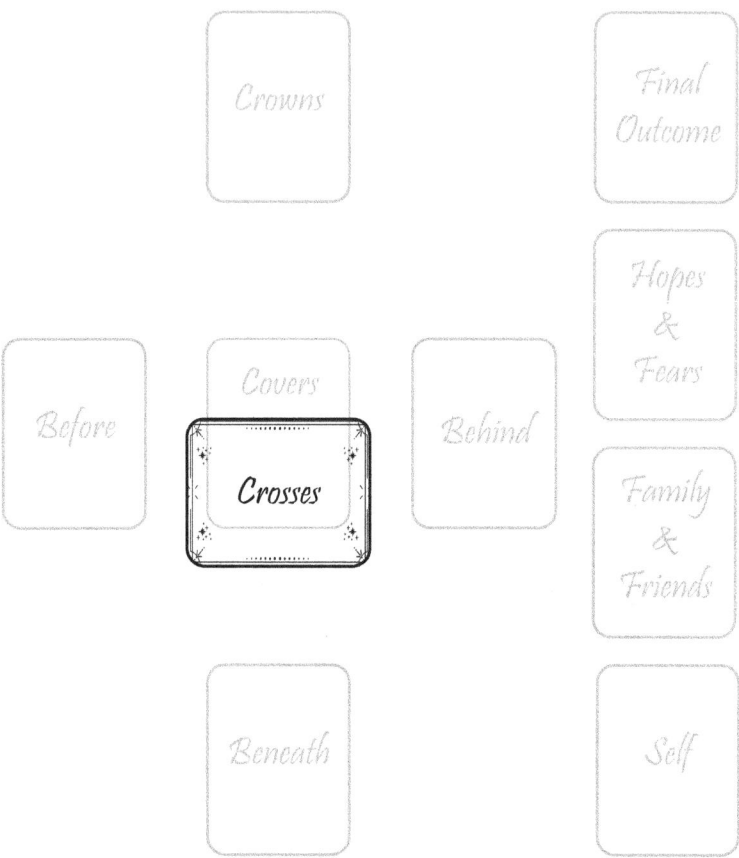

THAT WHICH CROSSES...

The second card defines what crosses the querent: those forces that affect the querent's current situation, whether they are from within or are outside of the querent's control.

Carolyn's Reading: The Tower

A tower crumbles, on fire, set alight by a violent lightning strike. Two people tumble from the tower, flailing and out of control. In the foreground a crown falls, the owner unknown.

The querent is living through a time of great change. The foundation that they have built crumbles, struck by outside forces and burning from within. Arrogance topples that which has been built. Unforeseen destruction takes apart that which was once stable. The querent is in distress, desiring escape from the catastrophe, and they are in a state of desperation such that they are willing to leap without regard for their safety.

However, amidst wreckage, there is rebirth. The crown may fall, and the querent may be temporarily dethroned, but this is a time of liberation. The past is ending. The only way to go is forward. The querent should embrace change, accept it, and move ahead.

Kit's Reading: The Four of Pentacles

A man sits at a table within a well-appointed room. The finery he wears and his demeanor show him to be dominant to the woman he addresses. Her eyes are cast down, avoiding the four pentacles prominently displayed within a luxurious frame mounted upon the wall.

The querent clings to objects from the past, keeping artifacts and memories in the form of property. This is not without merit, as the querent has found and built things of great value. The querent has the gift of legacy, which breeds prosperity and talent.

But within the pride there is warning: if the querent clings too hard to the past, they may never be able to reach the future. The querent should rejoice in the legacy they have been given, but they should also turn an eye to the time ahead, to learn how those gifts may be best used.

At the same time, the querent must learn to listen to those who would provide counsel, rather than believing that they alone know best. They must accept aid when it is offered in order to move forward.

5

CAROLYN TRANSLATES IN fits and starts, Latin words eluding her this afternoon. The piece isn't due this week; she's attempting to decide if this is going to be the source for a project. Thus far, she's not sure, irritated by how complicated the text seems to be. The problem is, she's not sure if the difficulty is with the text or her own mind. Her gaze keeps drifting back to her notebook, her fingers itching like there's a reading she's meant to do. There isn't, not now, and she can't think why she would. But instinct leads her to set down her pen and push her books to the back of her desk. She pulls the cards out of her pack, spills them into her hand, and starts shuffling.

"Carolyn." Heather sits on her own bed, bouncing a little. "Nikita's coming over. Is there any chance we can work up here? It's too noisy downstairs."

Carolyn slides her thumb across the slick surface of the card, shuffles again, and sets the deck down. "Are you working on a project?"

"It's my independent study with Bea." Heather hitches herself up, crossing her legs. "We went over several possible projects for the semester, but a lot won't work. Tuning my emotional resonance to a level that doesn't spill over is going to be nearly impossible while I'm handling social aspects here in the house, so we might try those kinds of projects another semester. When I'm less overwhelmed by the people around me."

That implies that Heather is considering moving out of the sorority house. They've only got one year of college after this; there aren't many other semesters to use for projects. If she does, Carolyn will have to find a new roommate. It's not a thought that thrills Carolyn, and she reminds herself that Heather hasn't actually said anything about leaving yet.

Carolyn toys with the cards, keeping her expression blank. She doesn't think Heather is reading her right now, but in case she is, she'd rather appear neutral.

"Obviously I have control issues," Heather mutters. "At least in the eyes of some people. So, Bea suggested that I work with a single person who is also having control issues with their Talent, and that we might be able to leverage my Empathy to help them. Her." She gestures toward the door and the bed. "That's why Nikita's coming over. She's been doing well since she spent some time with a Dreamweaver, and she's still seeing her regularly, but she's also got more anxiety and a lot more stress. Not to mention sleep issues. So." Heather spreads her hands. "We'll work together."

"I'll relocate." Carolyn stacks her books for the translation project on the back of the desk; if it's too distracting for Heather downstairs, Carolyn's not going to be able to translate there. She grabs her laptop, figuring she'll check the LMS sites for her classes, see what else she can get done over the weekend. There might be some online readings waiting for her.

Oh, right. That reminds her.

"Hey, Heather?"

"Hm?"

Heather's got her own independent study, and this might not be the best idea, but Pawel did suggest it. And it saves Carolyn the effort of trying to find a different Mage who might be a good match. "I was wondering if you'd be willing to work on a project with me as well," Carolyn asks slowly. "Maybe not for the whole semester, and I'm not sure exactly what it will be yet. But if you're interested, I'll come up with some options and pass them by you before I bring them to Pawel."

"I feel like I came in at the middle of whatever you're talking about." Heather slides off the bed and starts picking things up from around the room. Carolyn would offer to help, but Heather's the messy one so it's all her stuff. "Try again?"

"My independent study," Carolyn clarifies. "I need a partner who is a Mage with a different focus than predictive magic. The goal is to work on rituals that combine the two different specialties, and Pawel suggested that since you and I are good friends, you might be a good partner for me. I could design a ritual that uses your Empathy to focus my emotions to change the focus on a reading. Maybe. I don't know yet."

"How much do you think I'd need to—?" There's a rap on the door, and Heather nudges it open. She smiles brightly. "Hey, Nikita. Come on in."

"Am I interrupting?" Nikita makes a face. "I can come back if it's a bad time. I might be a little earlier than I said I would be. Tammy said Mom was going to call me, and I figured that if I happened to leave my phone in my room, I wouldn't have to deal with that."

"Trouble at home?" Heather says sympathetically.

Nikita snorts, shaking her head. She grabs Heather's desk chair and curls up on it. "You don't know the half of it. For one, I'm a good little Weather Witch who can't possibly be Emerging as a Dreamweaver, no matter what the evidence says. So nightmares? Had to spend break pretending those weren't happening. And admittedly, they are better when I'm not on campus. But then there's the whole thing where I finally came out to them. The first half of break, Mom sent me out on blind dates with guys to try to change my mind; by the last week I was home, she was setting me up with nice girls instead. That wasn't bad—I made some new friends—but I think Mom's still thinking I'm going to get it out of my system and come home and marry a nice boy and give her grandbabies. As if I can't have kids without a guy involved."

"I take it she's never heard of sperm banks?" Heather says dryly.

Nikita tilts back on the chair and sets it spinning in place. "Exactly! Tammy actually brought it up over Christmas dinner. Waving a turkey baster. Oh my *God*."

"I think this is my cue to leave." Carolyn doesn't try to hide her discomfort from Heather. She doesn't know Nikita that well and abruptly feels like a stranger in the room. "Are we meeting up later for dinner?"

"Take your phone—I'll text you," Heather says, waving a hand at the door. "I'm figuring six-ish, maybe. Mac'll be back by then, right?"

"Taekwondo should be ending soon." Carolyn gathers up her laptop and bag. "I'm good with eating out or going downstairs." She knows the right things to say, and she turns her attention to Nikita. "We're probably only going downstairs, if you want to join us. If you're not sick of Heather by then."

Nikita spins the chair to face Carolyn. "I probably won't be sick of Heather, just sick of being in my own head. Dinner'll be good, if someone else doesn't try to steal me first." She laughs. "Fortunately, they can't, since my phone's back in the room. I'm in. It'll be nice."

One friendly overture successfully made. There are days when Carolyn wonders how she can possibly be sorority material, but usually it's not diffi-cult for Carolyn to be around here. People like Mac and Heather and Drea make it easy.

But some of her sisters are more complicated.

Like Cass, who's sitting in the middle of the second step from the bottom, blocking the stairs as Carolyn heads down after leaving Nikita and Heather to their own devices. Carolyn coughs, and Cass jumps, turns in place, and scowls.

"I just want to get by," Carolyn says. "You don't need to move."

There's a faint flush high on Cass's cheeks. "No, it's fine. I should get moving. I was just—heading to the kitchen to get a snack before I go into the living room. Trish is playing."

The door slams open, Drea preceding Mac into the house. Drea carries Mac's sling bag, while Mac has her gear over her shoulder. Carolyn wrin-kles her nose; the scent of sweat is pungent, spreading when Mac tosses the bag in a corner.

"Are you going to leave that there?" Cass asks.

Mac raises both eyebrows. "For now. You hungry, Drea?"

"I didn't do anything but watch and still, yes, I am." Drea skips ahead, the energy in her step at odds with the tired way Mac moves. "Watching you guys work makes me hungry."

"She doesn't like me." Cass's voice is low, flat. "It's been two years, and Mac still doesn't like me."

There's a lot Cass could do to make herself more likable, but Carolyn isn't going to try to explain that. Not when Cass is, generally, far more socially oriented than Carolyn is and should be able to figure it out for herself.

"She probably just wants to eat before she takes her gear up to her room," Carolyn says. She hesitates, trying to think if there's a way that she could gently mention that maybe Cass shouldn't berate Mac before even saying hello.

There really isn't a polite way to express that.

"I'll see you in the living room." Carolyn brushes past Cass, leaving her alone in the entryway with Mac's gear. It's Cass's own fault if she doesn't move.

Trish sits cross-legged on the couch, hunched slightly with her guitar on her lap. She's picking at the strings, the sound more strident than usual. Her brow is furrowed deeply as she settles her fingers into a different chord and strums again.

"What are you working on?" Carolyn curls up in one of the two chairs and tucks her feet underneath herself. "It doesn't sound like your usual style."

Trish pauses, glancing up. Her hair hangs long and wavy across her shoulder, half-covering her face. She brushes it back and tucks it behind her ear. "It's just not working," she says, her soft drawl deeper than usual. "Can't find the right sound today. Haven't been able to for a while, now."

"Are you trying to write something new?" Carolyn leans over the arm of her chair, watching as Trish's fingers move along the frets. Pine Hills has attracted a number of young musicians, and Trish isn't the only one, although she's the only professional in SigPsiEp. Carolyn's always liked her quiet folk music with vaguely political lyrics.

"New, old, none of it's behaving." Trish plays a small run, and Carolyn recognizes the opening of a song. She hums along, frowning as the notes seem a little off. Trish thumps against the side of her guitar, grumbling. "See what I mean?"

Cass sets two bottles of water down on the table, sliding one closer to Carolyn and the other closer to Trish. As she settles into the other chair, she says, "I thought you might be thirsty."

Trish licks her lips, sets the guitar aside, and picks up the water. "Thanks, Cass. It's been a tough afternoon."

"You could've come to kick things with me when I left a couple of hours ago," Mac comments, leaning against the wall. Her hair is wet, like she dumped water over her head. Leaning next to her, Drea has a cookie in hand.

"Didn't want to kick things." Trish takes a long swig of water and sets the bottle back on the table.

Carolyn picks up her own bottle and curls back in the chair again. Cass mirrors her position in the other chair, quiet and watchful.

"Come on and sit," Trish offers, patting the couch. "I don't care that you stink."

"I do." Drea drops onto the other end of the couch, leaving space for Mac in the middle. "I was just watching all of them do ridiculous things. Mac kicked my brother in the head three times. It pissed him off, so he kicked Jackson in the head once in his next match. But then Jackson kicked him back twice, so Ric lost overall. It was fun to watch."

Trish points at Drea, her finger shifting to point at Mac's nose. "And that's why I don't kick with you. No kicks to the head. And no worrying about breaking fingers." She wiggles hers. "I need these." When Mac reaches to grab Trish's finger, she pulls away.

"So, what did you do for the new year, Trish?" Cass asks.

Trish runs her hand along the wooden front of her guitar. It's old, burnished in subtly different colors as if the oils from peoples' hands have worn into it. Carolyn suspects it's laden with energy. She's never asked Trish if it was handed down, but it looks like it must have been.

"I was in New York." Trish picks up the guitar again, turning slightly so she can have it across her knee without elbowing Mac. The next chord feels softer, saner, not poking at Carolyn's ears. "TJ Howell had a thing over the weekend, and I hung out with them." She glances at Mac. "Got to meet Jackson's dad, actually. He's pretty cool. And TJ's little sister was there too. And Sera."

Of course, Sera. She almost lives at the sorority house; she's there more often than some of the freshmen who are sisters.

"Was Pat there?" Because Sera and Pat seem to be a package deal some of the time. Not always.

"Why doesn't Sera pledge?" Cass asks, and Trish's fingers trip over the strings, making a discordant jangle.

"Sororities aren't Sera's thing," Trish points out. "Skateboards. Computer programming. But not parties or skirts or makeup or slumber parties."

"She stays here a lot," Drea says.

"She stays at Pat and Jackson's room a lot, too," Trish counters. "And I'm sure she stays in her actual room sometimes, too." It's funny how she says it, like maybe she thinks Sera doesn't. But it's not Carolyn's business to poke.

"I've never gone down to the city for the new year," Cass muses. "It must be fun."

"It was mostly cold." Trish strums again, slowly picking through one of her older songs. Carolyn hums along again, and Trish smiles. "We sat on TJ's roof and drank and watched the ball-drop and the fireworks. Then we went inside and danced until we were exhausted. TJ's a good dancer. He's got this whole studio down there. Sera tried to convince him to let her use her skateboard in it, but he wouldn't go for it. She was pretty ready to get out and on her board by the time we got to Nashville. I think she'd thought it'd be warmer there, but at least there wasn't any snow or ice on the ground."

"Did you guys have a good time at home?" Mac nudges Trish. "I still haven't been down there. Do I get the full tour when I finally make it?"

"My home's open any time," Trish drawls, her accent strong and affected. "It'd piss my momma off and I'm all for that. She was already scandalized by Sera, and we stayed there most of three weeks"

"Why's she scandalized by Sera? Your momma doesn't like tattoos?" Drea asks.

"Sera's ink isn't even real tattoos," Trish reminds them. "It's a printer, just keeps changing on her skin. What Momma doesn't like is magic. Or much of anything that's different than what she thinks ought to be right."

"How does she feel about your music?" Cass asks. She's still curled around herself, but she's leaned forward until she's almost to the edge of the chair.

Trish waves a hand. "Oh, she doesn't mind that. My older sister Patsy—she's been on the road forever and a day, and Momma figures I'm like her. We're the bookends of the family, Patsy the oldest, me the youngest sixteen years and six other kids later. She just wants to be able to say she raised us right, that we aren't doing anything odd or unusual. No drinking. No drugs. No magic. God help us if we meet someone who isn't right in Momma's eyes." She fiddles with the guitar again, smiling; Carolyn thinks it sounds almost like it should.

"Maybe I'll put off that visit to Nashville, then," Mac muses, and Trish leans into her.

"Might be for the best. I don't think I'm going back until summer, and then it's just to get my rig. I'm thinking I'll take fall off to get some tour dates on my calendar, be back for the spring semester."

"Co-op takes on a whole new meaning when you're a musician, doesn't it?" Cass asks. "My mother would be furious if I wanted to take a semester off for a hobby."

Trish's gaze hardens as she levels a dark look at Cass. "It's not a hobby. It's my job. Some of us don't sit around waiting for money to be dropped magically into our accounts."

Cass leans forward a bit more, whispers, "I know who your momma is, Trish. It's not like you need to go on the road to make money."

"I like it." Trish makes a face as her chord comes rough and strident. She stands abruptly, fingers loosely wrapped around the neck of the guitar. "I'm going to work in my room. I'm not getting anywhere down here." She heads up the stairs, silence stretching in the wake of her departure.

"You don't have to be such a bitch, Cass," Mac says quietly, and Carolyn inwardly thanks her for saying what she's thinking.

"I just meant that she doesn't have to leave her education. She could finish, then go perform," Cass protests. "Honestly. It's like she doesn't even want to be here sometimes."

Mac rolls her eyes. "I'm hitting the shower. Drea, you can wait in my room if you want. Dinner after I'm done?"

"Nikita's up with Heather, and they want to come with us," Carolyn says.

Drea glances from Cass to Carolyn. "I'll hang in Mac's room, if you don't mind? I want to call Corbin, and it's warmer up there than it is outside."

Carolyn waves, telling her silently to go. She doesn't need her Little with her all the time, and doesn't begrudge her friendship with Mac, either.

"Why do I feel like they left me with you so you can tell me off now, too?" Cass asks after they're gone.

Carolyn blinks. That's not what happened. At least, she's pretty sure that's not what they meant. "I'm not the person to tell anyone off," she tells her. "But I'll read your cards if you want. They'll have better advice than I would."

Cass pales, skin pasty and gray as she shakes her head. "No. Thanks. I don't like predictive Talent. I mean, it's not you. I just—it weirds me out. Probably has a lot to do with my name."

Carolyn shakes her head, then pauses and nods slowly. "Cassandra. The oracle who no one believed."

"So you get why I'm a bit uncomfortable with it, right?" Cass says.

"Forgiven," Carolyn agrees. "But as long as you're not the oracle, you should be okay." It seems simple to her: Cass is just a normal human listening to a reading. As long as she doesn't try to personally predict the future, everything should be normal. On the other hand, Carolyn's working toward a minor in classics, and the mythology is attractive. She sets the idea on a back burner in her mind to look at later. Maybe, somewhere along the way, she can use it for her independent study.

6

After dinner, Mac heads to OPT with Drea and Cass while Heather follows Nikita back to Douglass Hall. Carolyn takes advantage of the quiet to sit in her room with the door open, sketching out a map of the path of human progress across continental Europe in the days of the Roman Empire.

She pauses, sets her pencil down, and grabs an eraser to change a line.

It's too late a time period to apply to her idea. She's studying sociology and classics; maybe she should go earlier. Maybe she should be digging into the roots of man and the earliest societies. There is more to mythology than the gods of Greece and Rome, after all.

She grabs a notebook and makes a list of materials she wants to request from the library, considering that this could become the basis for her thesis next year. She's focused on the classical myths of Greece and Rome because those are the best-known roots of her predictive Talent, but she wonders what she'll find if she goes back further. Talent is eternal; despite the Emergence, as far as she knows there is no one time when it suddenly appeared.

A knock startles her, and she jerks her head up; she stares at the empty doorway before she calls out, "Come in."

Soledad steps out from the space just beyond the open door. "Hey. Are you busy?"

There are papers spread across her desk, including three notebooks and two texts and her laptop. Carolyn closes the laptop and gestures at Heather's chair. "It's fine. You okay?"

She's not close to Soledad, but she's not not close to her either. She's one of the freshmen who's become a part of Carolyn's little group, mostly because of Carolyn's friendship with Drea and Soledad being Trish's Little. But she's not the kind of friend who stops by randomly.

Carolyn frowns, brow furrowing. "Is it Trish?"

Soledad sits on the edge of Heather's chair, hands clasped tightly between her knees. She's very still, head slightly bowed, long, dark hair spilled forward over her shoulders. Soledad reaches up, tucks it behind her ear, and shrugs one shoulder. "Not exactly."

"Do you want to talk about it?" Carolyn can't offer an ear in the same way as Heather can, but she can do her best to listen.

Soledad winces. "I'm not sure there's anything to talk about. We've grown apart, and I don't know why. I think she's going through something, but she'd rather talk to Sera about it than me. Or maybe she's not talking to Sera, maybe they're just hanging together and ignoring whatever it is. Either way, it's like Trish is avoiding me. It's frustrating, but not world-ending. So." She shrugs again. "It just is, you know?"

It's the kind of thing that would drive Heather mad but seems all too familiar to Carolyn. "I'm probably not the best for advice," she admits. "I've never been good at figuring people out. I've relied on Heather for help understanding people since we met."

"Don't trust your instincts?" Soledad says with a small smile.

"I have terrible instincts," Carolyn says dryly. "When I've tried trusting them, I usually end up in trouble. It's easier to have an interpreter sometimes. There are days when I wonder if I speak an entirely different language than everyone else."

Soledad laughs, twisting her fingers together. "I used to think I was really good with people. I'm a flirt, and that was okay as long as I was up-front about it. No one got bent out of shape, and people were friendly. I'm even friends with Alaric, and he's not the kind of guy who takes to people. But now it's like there's this weird wall between me and Trish, and I don't get it. I don't think I put it there, but maybe I did."

"Or maybe, like you said, she's working through something and doesn't know how to talk about it," Carolyn points out. "Don't blame yourself for everything, Soledad." She turns to her desk, carefully gathers up papers, and puts them away, setting up folders for the new aspects of her research.

She didn't finish her assignments, but she's given herself several new things to look into that have nothing to do with her current classes. She doesn't want to lose track of them.

"I was wondering if I could get a reading from you," Soledad asks quietly. "Maybe that would help me see some direction to look toward, something different I should be doing. Nothing complicated, just…I think I need something to think about. Something other than going in circles."

Carolyn pauses halfway through putting the folders into her desk drawer. She glances at Soledad and takes in the pinched lines around her eyes, the white spots on her dark skin where she twists her fingers together tightly enough to chase the blood away. "Yes," she agrees. "Of course. I can do that."

"Hey, Caro—oh, hey, hi, Soledad." Kit slips into the room without bothering to knock and drops onto Carolyn's bed. "Am I interrupting?"

"Yes," Carolyn replies at the same time as Soledad sits up straight, shoulder tension increasing.

"No, it's okay," Soledad says. "Carolyn was about to do a reading for me."

"I can go." Kit stands up, then sits down again quickly when Soledad shakes her head. He glances between them, adding, "I was hoping to talk about our independent study, Caro. I wanted to see if you'd made any progress and ask what your thoughts are about the assignment."

"Let me get this reading, then she's all yours," Soledad says.

So nice of them both to schedule her, but it's not like Carolyn's protesting their arrangements. She gets out her deck. "So, you want some things to think about," she says slowly. The cards catch on her fingertips, binding when she tries to shuffle them together. "A three-option layout would work."

"Sounds good to me." Soledad relaxes back, shoulders loosening. "Hey Kit, did you go out with Serina on Friday? I thought she said you had a date."

The cards slip from Carolyn's fingers, two of them falling to the floor. She stops shuffling and leans forward to grab the one she can reach. The other has almost slid under the bed; she has to get out of the chair and crawl across the floor to get it. She leans back on her heels and glances at

Kit. He's watching her.

"I haven't seen you fumble a shuffle since we were little," Kit says idly. "Does that mean you're about to go all 'protective mama bear' on me again?"

Carolyn glares at him and pushes to her feet. "They feel slippery today. It's weird."

Soledad hops up, moves to the bed, and nudges Kit over so she can sit beside him. "C'mon," she says. "How'd it go? Serina was so excited. She really likes you. I'm glad she's crushing on a guy who likes girls this time. She had such a thing for Nate, and while he's a total equal-opportunity flirt, he's so very gay."

"And you know that for sure how?" Kit asks.

"Asked," Soledad admits. "I mean, someone had to. I never told him that Serina had a thing for him, that'd be rude. But it's not like he's unwilling to talk about it. He's open about everything, and we're friends."

Carolyn starts shuffling again, then tries to stop. It should feel right, but it doesn't, not yet, so she just keeps shuffling. It's going on too long, her fingers awkward on the cards. She hesitates as they catch on each other, and she has to slow down to keep them from bending.

She finds her rhythm and feels as if she should keep going, shuffling for the next hour. She forces herself to stop; keeping shuffling is definitely not right.

She holds the cards in her hand, thumb resting atop the deck.

"So, the date!" Soledad says. "Did it live up to expectations? I didn't see Serina this morning."

"She didn't stay at my place," Kit mutters. "I dropped her off at Douglass late. I'm not that guy."

"I didn't say you were," Soledad protests. She pets his shoulder soothingly. "I'm a virgin, Kit; I'm not going to tell anyone to go to bed on the first date. I'm not going to tell anyone not to, either. I didn't mean to imply anything; I didn't see her this morning, but she may have left early, or she might've slept in. I haven't been to the dorm all day because I was studying in the library. I just wanted to know if you guys had a good time."

Carolyn slides the card off the top of the deck and holds it between thumb and forefinger. All she needs to do is lay it out, but she's not sure it's the right card.

Everything feels…off.

She glances at Kit as he slides off the bed. "I'll catch you tomorrow at breakfast, Carolyn," Kit says. "Soledad, I had a good time Friday. I like Serina, and hopefully she still likes me, too, and I think she also had a good time. But I'm not comfortable talking about it."

Soledad's expression falls, brow furrowed and concerned. "I'm sorry."

Kit shrugs. "Don't worry about it. Besides, Carolyn doesn't think I should be dating. Wouldn't want to worry my twin."

Carolyn stays where she is, gripping the card, poised to flip it onto the desk. "I'm not worried. You're dating. It's fine." It's not a lie, not exactly. She is worried, and it still makes her far more nervous than it should. But she's trying, and she hopes that Kit gets that.

She's pretty sure he doesn't.

"Read for Soledad." Kit rests his hand on her shoulder and squeezes. Carolyn tilts her head, leaning into his touch. "I'm interrupting." He doesn't wait for a response, shoving his hands into his pockets, shoulders hunching as he stalks out.

"I'm sorry. I scared him away." Soledad shifts back to the chair, rolling it closer to Carolyn's desk. She reaches out to touch the card curiously, and Carolyn finally flips it and lays it on the desk: the King of Wands.

"It's not you." Carolyn knows that Soledad's questions probably didn't help, but maybe Kit would've said something if Carolyn weren't sitting right here. She hasn't encouraged him. She didn't even think to text him and ask how it went.

"You don't think he should be dating?"

Carolyn isn't getting into this. Kit's private life is between himself and whoever he chooses to share it with. "It's none of my business," she says, ignoring how she feels about it and the reasons she feels that way. She slips the next cards off the top of the deck and sets them next to the first: the Ace of Swords, reversed, and the Eight of Wands, also reversed.

She stares at them, tries to construct a story for Soledad, and finds nothing.

"Any advice?" Soledad asks, peering at them closely. "There's a tall, dark, and handsome man in my future?"

"He's strong-willed and possibly domineering," Carolyn responds automatically, the words coming even though she's not finding any meaning in them. She makes a face and shakes her head. "But that's not what we're looking for here. The card probably doesn't mean a person. You wanted cards to give you advice on picking a path forward. Maybe a way of looking at your relationship with Trish, such as a direction to go to either heal it or move on. So it can't mean a person because the only person involved here is you."

Soledad tilts her head, making a face. "Then, what does it mean?"

I don't know.

Carolyn can't say that out loud, but she can't make sense of this. These aren't three paths, or if they are, they aren't valid or productive paths to take. "They're all cautionary," she says with more confidence than she feels.

"Oh?"

Carolyn touches the cards as if contact will enable her to hear their whispers. This is usually easier. This usually makes sense to her; usually, they want her to listen. She inhales roughly and starts talking, hoping that the reading will make more sense the more she says. "The first one indicates that the way through your issues is best forged by being strong-willed, taking risks, and blowing by the obstacles as if they aren't there. The problem is, the King of Wands is domineering. He rolls over people without caring about them, so when you've solved your problems, you may not have anyone left on your side."

Soledad nods slowly, and Carolyn hopes that it makes more sense to her.

"The Ace is usually a great card, but upside down like that suggests a giant failure. This path is all about being distracted. Having someone else conquer you, rather than being the conqueror. It's almost the exact opposite of the first, with no middle ground. And the third card…" Carolyn hesitates, not sure how to explain it.

"It looks good, like I'm flying strongly." Soledad touches the card that shows the man leaping, surrounded by eight wands.

"If it were right-side up, it'd be a card of great success," Carolyn agrees.

"Instead, it's another card of failure. Take risks and fall on your face. Everything's too big, too much."

"So basically, either I'm a domineering bitch, or I'm conquered, or I fail catastrophically," Soledad says slowly.

"That's what the cards say." Carolyn's voice is quiet as she sweeps them up and puts them back on top of the deck. It doesn't feel right, like the reading's trying to say something else. It can't be about Trish and Soledad; it doesn't make sense.

The cards failed.

That's never happened before.

Carolyn neatly wraps the deck up in her cloth, then slides them back into her backpack. "I'm sorry it wasn't clearer. There might not be a distinct path yet."

"I think it's more 'don't' than 'do,'" Soledad says quietly. Her fingers are tangled together again, and tension lines her shoulders. "Or that I'm screwed no matter what I do. I really like her, Carolyn. Not like…I'm not attracted to her. Not like that. But I felt like we really connected as friends even though we're from different backgrounds. Then she just…disappeared on me over break. And I can't get back through the wall."

"Don't try to climb the wall and accidentally jump off the other side," Carolyn says with a small smile. "I think you'll fall."

"And bashing through would be domineering and rude," Soledad counters. "Maybe the cards made more sense than I thought. I just… That's a whole lot of *don't do this* and not a lot of help."

"I'm sorry," Carolyn says again, and Soledad leans forward, wraps her arms around Carolyn's shoulder, and hugs her hard.

"It's totally okay. I'll figure it out."

Carolyn's not sure about that, but she's hopeful.

7

Carolyn reaches out a hand and brushes her fingers against brick; it crumbles under her touch. The floor rocks under her feet, an explosion booming somewhere to her left. She turns, taking a step backward as another brick falls.

The tower. She's in the crumbling tower.

Another *boom*, close by this time. Carolyn runs, not caring where the hallway goes, only that it gets her farther from the next explosion. When it comes, she's thrown forward, sliding as the hallway tilts. She scrabbles against the floor, fingers finding no purchase on the brick, flesh scraped and torn. She screams as her feet fall away, the floor disappearing until she's left clinging to almost nothing, holding on by her fingertips.

Someone falls past her, and she hears the echo of a scream.

Let go!

She doesn't have a choice, brick crumbling from her grasp until she falls, a scream ripping from her lungs. She sees others around her, unfamiliar faces on the bodies tumbling down. A crown passes her, and she reaches for it, grabbing it like the brass ring on an old carousel; it yanks her arm roughly, changing her path.

There's a rocking metal seat below her, and she crashes into it, impact jarring the breath from her lungs. The seat bears her upward, back into the sky on a huge Ferris wheel, moving faster than any fair ride she's ever been on. She clings to the side rails, holds on for dear life as the seat sways back and forth, threatening to tip her free again.

Catch!

She reacts to the thought, the cry, the unvoiced word that somehow echoes in her ears. Carolyn sticks one hand out, only seeing the satin pouch seconds before her fingers close around it, black fabric against a darkened sky. She can't see it, but she can feel the shape of cards inside of it. She grips it tight and cradles it against her chest,

It's a Tarot deck.

She opens the bag and digs into it. Her fingers brush against card after card, sifting through them until they close around one, then pull it out.

Three pentacles are completed in an unfinished stained-glass window atop a half-built wall made of stone. Three craftsmen work to complete the art and the building; it crumbles at the edges where stones have yet to be placed. Carolyn runs her thumb across the card; the slick plastic surface doesn't feel like her deck.

It is the card of the master-crafter, the card of unique talent.

The wheel stops and Carolyn hangs at the top, her car dangling and swaying until it tips her dangerously forward. There is no safety bar; if it sways any farther, Carolyn will fall.

The tower is gone, lost in the distance. The only things left are this wheel and the cards in Carolyn's hand.

She looks down at the card again, the image bright despite the darkness around her.

One of the figures moves.

She tightens her grip on the card, leaning closer as if that will change what she sees.

One of the workmen lifts his hammer and lets it fall with a *clang* that rings in her ears, conflicts with the grinding of gears from the wheel she still rides.

It's impossible.

It's magic. Anything is possible.

Carolyn puts the deck in her pocket, cradling the single card in the palm of her left hand. With her right finger, she lightly touches it, presses through it like it's hardened air, feels the coolness beyond. A smell like old dirt rises around her, thick enough to make her cough.

The image shifts, swirls, and changes. It's no longer a house being built, only a simple, old farmhouse, broken and derelict, thick with dust. She pulls her finger back and the image follows, growing out of the card until it hangs in the air before her.

She reaches forward again, and as her hand crosses the plain between reality and the image, she feels the air change. Cold. Damp. Still and old.

The car she's in creaks, the wheel shifting as if to turn. There's a *clang* in the distance, and everything falls sideways.

Carolyn screams and does the only thing that seems sane in this fragile reality: she leaps forward, out of the Ferris wheel car and through the image that's risen from the card.

She thumps onto the old, tiled floor, knees scraped against the dirt and sand. All traces of the Ferris wheel and tower are gone. The clothes she'd worn are also gone, as is the bag of cards she'd stowed in her pocket. She wears her sleep shirt and shorts, and nothing more.

The floor is cold and filthy, her hands scraped. She scrambles to her feet, trying her best to see in the dark. It's a kitchen, and it looks to have been abandoned for years. There's no hum of electricity, and the scent is rank, the smell of something dead and left to rot. When Carolyn touches the stove, there are still grease tracks there, as if someone left in the middle of dinner.

There's even a pot on the back burner, blackened and burned.

It's frigid, air whistling through the cracks around the windows. She pulls open the door at one end of the room and looks into the darkness at the vague shadows of trees beyond, the thin sliver of a waxing moon hanging above them. She blinks, but there is no light save for that pale hint of moonlight reflecting on the snow.

She crouches down, pressing one hand into the snow.

Cold.

Wet.

Real.

"I was dreaming," she whispers to herself. "I'm still dreaming. I have to be dreaming."

Carolyn stands, closes the door, and pads through the kitchen and into a hallway. There's a bathroom to one side and pictures she can't make out hanging on the opposite wall. The living room at the front of the house is even colder than the rest, the wind whistling through the cracked glass of one window. The room feels wrong, the darkness thick and closing in around her.

She brings her hands together, struggling to remember the ritual to bring light to her palms. It takes her three tries; her teeth knock together as she whispers words until she's holding a small ball of cold light.

It does nothing to keep the shadows at bay.

In the distance, a loud howl breaks the stillness of the night.

Carolyn shivers. "Don't worry," she whispers. "For one, it's a dream. For two, even if it's real, that's outside, and I'm inside, so I'm safe."

Wake up, she whispers to herself several times, but nothing happens.

She pinches her forearm, the ball of light fading as soon as she moves her hand. The pinch bites at her, her fingernails scraping her skin.

It hurts.

Whether it's a dream or not, she's cold, she's scared, and pinching herself hurts.

It feels all too real.

The howl comes again, closer and louder. She stumbles backward, finds the card somehow in her hand again. She cradles it and mutters her way through the ritual until the ball of light spreads across the front of the card.

It isn't the Three of Pentacles, and the picture it shows doesn't match this small, dank farmhouse.

It's her room.

Something crawls up her arm, and she shrieks, jumping, trying to get it off. Her skin itches, aching from being here. She swallows and tries to hold back another scream, but one escapes when the howl sounds once more.

Whatever howled is right outside. It's pacing, making whuffling noises she can hear through the breaks in the window, the cracks around the door.

"I'm safe here," she tells herself. "I'm safe."

The door bursts open, and Carolyn screams again, falls and lands on her back. Her elbow cracks against the floor. The card falls on the ground, the light staying with it, illuminating the peace of her room back at PHU.

A wolf stands in the doorway, huge, towering over her. Its feet are splayed, mouth open in a growl.

"Shit." Carolyn tries to breathe but can't manage to get enough air into her lungs. "Shit. Shit. Shit."

Head down, the wolf takes a step forward, fangs bared as it snarls. There's no place for Carolyn to go; there's a wall behind her.

The card shines on the floor, the ball of light lingering.

It's still a dream.

A nightmare.

It has to be.

And if she's dreaming, then the dream might be consistent. She might be able to make it consistent. Control the dream. Escape the nightmare.

She'd jumped out of the Ferris wheel car and landed in a farmhouse by going through a card. Maybe she can do it again.

She's going to have to leap toward the wolf to do it.

It paces another step closer. She glances at the card, and the light flares, the image springing up to fill the air between them. The wolf growls but steps back, away from it.

It doesn't like magic.

Carolyn gets her feet under her and meets the wolf's gaze. It growls again, haunches bunching.

They leap at the same time.

Carolyn lands on her knees next to her bed. She grunts at the impact and falls forward onto her face, hands and knees stinging brutally.

"Caro?" Heather's sleepy voice. "Did you fall out of bed?"

She wants to say yes, but her hands hurt too much. She stinks of must and dirt, and there's a rip in her T-shirt where she must have caught it on something without noticing. "Am I still dreaming?"

Heather sits up. "You fell out of bed. Unless you're sleepwalking, I think you're awake now."

Carolyn isn't sure she can believe her. The tower had felt real. The wheel had been hard iron under her hands. The wolf… "Shit," she whispers. "The wolf was going to eat me. I'm still in the nightmare. You're not real."

"Hey." Heather slides out of bed, padding to Carolyn on bare feet that look clean. She smells like the lilac hand lotion that they share, that Heather keeps on her desk and sometimes uses on her legs before bed. When she sinks down next to Carolyn and touches her arm, she feels warm.

Carolyn tries not to flinch, pushing herself up to sitting. "The wolf was going to eat me," Carolyn whispers. "How do I know you're not the wolf?"

Heather sits next to her, puts an arm around Carolyn's shoulders, and tugs her close. Warmth floods into her bones, leaving her loose and lax so abruptly that Carolyn feels like she's floating. "I'm not the wolf," Heather murmurs.

"You're soothing me," Carolyn mutters, knowing that her own anxiety hasn't fled. She can still feel it on the edges of her mind, waiting to return. "You're making me feel better."

"Is that okay?" Heather asks.

Carolyn curls closer, sliding down so she can get her arms around Heather's thick waist and rest her head on her chest. "This time, yeah." She inhales roughly and holds her breath for a count of five before letting it out.

When she closes her eyes, she sees the wolf's eyes, narrowed and sharp and full of death.

"You want to talk about the nightmare?" Heather asks.

No.

Carolyn hesitates, letting Heather stroke her arm while she tries to convince herself to do as she knows she should. "Yes," she finally whispers.

Another wave of calm rolls over her, through her, soaking into her skin as she inhales air laden with the scent of lilac skin cream and vanilla shampoo. She holds onto that wave even though she normally gets annoyed when Heather uses her empathy to shift her emotions so strongly. Because this feels real. Heather's Talent is real, and Carolyn can cling to that while her mind shakes free from the remaining fog of the nightmare.

"Can you get the light?" Carolyn asks, and Heather slowly stands up, waiting until Carolyn leans back against the bed before she walks away. Carolyn blinks into the brightness, lowers her head with her eyes closed, and waits to adjust. She presses the heels of her hands against her eyes, and the smell—dirt and decay—brings back the nightmare.

Carolyn smells her palm and finds no trace of metal. But the filth from the house is there. Scrapes, matching the ones on her knees. The rip in her shirt, too; she vaguely remembers, now, how it snagged against the counter when she turned.

"Some of it was a nightmare," she says, and she describes the moment when the tower crumbled around her. She sits next to Heather, her head still pillowed against her chest as Heather rubs circles into her back. The words come easier with every breath, and she tries not to read into the way Heather's touch stutters and stumbles when the story shifts from tower to wheel and then tumbles into a Tarot card.

"Do you think some of it was real?" Heather asks.

There's dirt on her hands, but at the same time, it's not possible. "I'm not a teleporter," Carolyn says. "That's not my Talent. I've been here the whole time. You would've noticed if I'd disappeared, and I obviously didn't cry out until I fell off the bed. That's why I'm scraped up. Someone would have a field day trying to analyze my psyche, even though I know most of it was Tarot imagery."

"Maybe you should write it down for Pawel," Heather suggests. "We're both awake now, and I don't think either of us is going back to sleep any time soon. Write it down, and you can look at it when your head is clearer, see if you can match it up to the cards. Maybe your Talent is trying to tell you something."

"My Talent was feeling pretty fucked up earlier," Carolyn admits. The cards wouldn't behave for Soledad, and the slick feeling was replicated in the nightmare. That makes sense, considering how that sensation had bothered her. She's tempted to get her deck out and make sure they feel normal now. "I don't know what the wolf would represent."

"Don't you have a card with a wolf on it?" Heather nudges her, and Carolyn starts to reach for her pack, stops just short of doing so.

"Lion," Carolyn counters. "It could be strength, inverted. Or it could be Drea, because I associate that card with her. I don't think about her attacking me, though."

"But you were still thinking about Soledad and Trish, and they're pretty antagonistic right now." Heather rubs her hair and pats the side of her head. "Dreams are full of imagery, and Tarot is significant to you. Of course that's what your brain dug up."

"Mm." It sounds plausible as long as she doesn't try to use it to explain the scrapes across her palms. Carolyn curls her fingers, hiding them away.

"I'm going to hit the bathroom, and I'll write up the dream when I get back. You go back to bed. I can work by my desk light, and I know you can sleep through that."

She leverages herself to her feet and turns on the small lamp under the shelf above her desk. On her way out of the room, she flips off the light and pauses in the doorway. Heather is already back in bed, pulling the covers up, almost buried in the shadows.

It makes Carolyn shiver to see the darkness swallowing Heather away.

She exhales with a soft huff. "Thanks for being here," she says quietly, and Heather smiles.

"Of course," she says, a small wave of pleasure sliding across Carolyn's skin. "You're my best friend. Where else would I be?"

Carolyn steps into the hall, the shadows engulfing Heather as the door slides closed. Carolyn pauses there, in the darkness, forcing herself to make her way down the hall one step at a time. This is reality, and there are no wolves.

It was only a dream.

8

"I ONLY HAVE forty-five minutes if I'm going to make it across campus—"

"We'll get pre-made food; it won't take that long," Heather counters, herding Carolyn into the Sunshine Café. There's a long line at the counter waiting to order; Heather swerves to one side where two tall refrigerated cases are filled with salads, sushi, and sandwiches.

"I have a granola bar. I'll be fine." When Carolyn pauses, Heather tugs, and hunger briefly washes over her. "Quit it."

"Pick something out, use your swipe, and we'll go sit down." Heather slides open one door, pulls out a tuna-and-egg sandwich, then reaches for a bowl of fruit and a small side salad.

This wasn't part of Carolyn's planned day. She'd had a big breakfast and intended to eat a big dinner. But if Heather wants to sit, there's nothing Carolyn can do to change her mind. She hunts for a Southwest shrimp salad and grabs a bottle of water and a roll with butter from the side table. She follows Heather dutifully to one of the quickly moving check-out lines and hands over her card when asked.

"Heather!" Nikita waves, beckoning for them to join her at one of the high tables near the window.

"Hey, Nik." Heather sounds too casual for it to be an accident.

Carolyn stows her bag under the table, climbs into the chair, and hooks her toes around the legs. She opens her salad and spills dressing onto it, determined to dig in and eat quickly.

She gets away with it for a few bites.

Her mouth is full of lettuce and shrimp, eyes watering from a healthy bite of jalapeño, when Nikita says slowly, "So, Carolyn. I heard you had a really weird, realistic nightmare."

Carolyn gives Heather a dark look. "Yes, I did. Why?"

"Because I'm an Emerging Dreamwalker," Nikita reminds her. "Because I know what it's like to have weird dreams, even if I don't remember mine. But most Dreamwalkers do, and if you're Emerging as one, too, we're only going to have increasing levels of weirdness."

"If we were both active Dreamwalkers, we wouldn't be able to interact without the world imploding," Carolyn grumbles. "I'm not a Dreamwalker. It was just a messed-up dream about Tarot cards and stinky, old houses. The world didn't twist, and I didn't go into some kind of psychosis."

"I don't do any of that either," Nikita points out. She has a cookie in her hand, the remains of a sandwich off to one side. "I go into the Dreams and I don't remember them at all, but they stress me out enough that my weather witchery goes insane."

"I remembered this one." Carolyn doesn't mean to snap, and she takes a big bite of salad to keep herself from saying anything else, buying herself time to cool down. Besides, she needs to finish lunch to get to class on time. There's a reason why intense discussion and a sit-down meal weren't on her schedule. "Besides, if I were a Dreamwalker, chances are that Kit would be, too. Plus someone in our family would know."

"No one in my family knew." Nikita breaks off another piece of cookie, chewing slowly. It gives Carolyn time to simmer, temper lessening. "Me Emerging is weird, Carolyn. And completely unexpected. But that's the point, it's Emergent Talent, not Lineage. My Talent is changing; I'm not just a Weather Witch anymore."

"I still don't think it makes sense. A person's Lineage doesn't change." Carolyn ignores her brother, ignores that she's still positive he's as predictive as she is even if he insists he isn't.

Heather crumples up the package from her sandwich, a pile of thin crusts all that remains. "Why don't you tell her about the dream," she suggests. "Nik's been training with a latent Dreamwalker, so she's heard a lot about how it should work. She'll be able to tell you if it's even possible that's what it is."

"Fine." Carolyn stabs her fork into her salad, well aware that her chances of finishing it before she has to leave for class are slim. "I started out dreaming about the Tower card. It was crumbling; I figure that was me experiencing some kind of anxiety. After that, I was on a Ferris wheel, stuck at the top, and when I thought that was going to fall, I threw myself into another Tarot card and ended up in an abandoned house. The place reeked like it was full of death and decay, and it made my skin crawl. Complete nightmare. A giant wolf attacked me, and I saw what looked like my room, so I jumped at it, and I fell out of bed."

Heather coughs delicately.

"My hands and knees were scraped up and covered in dirt." Carolyn looks at her palms, clean now but still showing some of the cuts. "The dream wasn't real. But I was real."

"Huh." Nikita pops the last of the cookie in her mouth, chewing thoughtfully.

Carolyn watches her, and when no one objects, she pulls her salad closer again and resumes eating. Salad was not a good plan for eating quickly. At least the roll is portable. And she does still have her granola bar.

"You see what I mean?" Heather asks, and Nikita nods.

"Totally," she agrees. "But I don't think she's a Dreamwalker. There's no way we'd be sitting here like this if she were. We'd both feel weird. Reality would be fraying. We sure as hell wouldn't be having a civil conversation about our sanity."

"So I shouldn't tell you about the pink bunny on your shoulder?" Carolyn points with her fork, and Nikita swivels to look. Carolyn eats another bite of salad, smirking around it.

"Hah," Heather says. She looks between them, and Carolyn only feels the gentle sensation of something wrapping around her because she's used to it. It's as if Heather's Talent slides over her, starting at the top of her head and continuing down her spine, leaving her shivering and comforted simultaneously. "I'm not getting anything bizarre from the two of you right now. You both feel like you're rooted in the here and now."

"What did it feel like after she woke up?" Nikita asks. "We should experiment, find out what it's like after I Dream, too. I could crash at your place, or you could crash at mine if you don't mind dealing with Pels and Jennifer."

"She was afraid," Heather says.

"*She* is right here," Carolyn mutters, but it doesn't stop them.

"There was confusion, too, but the highest emotions were anxiety and fear." Heather twists a piece of hair around her finger, brow furrowed while she thinks. "It didn't feel any different than a normal nightmare, but I also don't have a Dreamwalker sample to compare her to. You're right; we should try having you stay over. Do you Dream every night?"

"Hopefully not, but I don't know." Nikita shrugs. "I've been doing exercises that are supposed to help keep my Talent from manifesting. But also, I don't remember my Dreams. All I know is that I've been sleeping more deeply, so I'm not falling asleep in class. And I haven't summoned any freak ice storms recently."

"Yeah, please don't do that again." Carolyn finishes the salad and pushes the container to the center of the table. "Here's the question. You called weather to you because that's your innate magic to begin with. The cards are part of my innate ability, and that's what I dreamed of, but I dreamed about traveling through them."

"And did," Nikita says.

Carolyn curls her hand around the scratches on her palm. "Possibly." That's the most she'll concede.

She tunes out, letting them talk while she finishes her lunch. A glance at her phone tells her that she has ten more minutes at most before she has to leave; it doesn't matter whether she adds anything to the conversation at this point. She people-watches instead, letting her mind wander.

The Queen of Swords.

Her gaze drifts to a woman sitting alone, her empty lunch thermal and containers on the table beside her. She plays with the straw in her drink while she reads a book. Carolyn can't see the cover from a distance, but she watches as the woman carefully pauses to underline passages. She's not reading for pleasure; she marks the pages like it's her mission to correct every word.

The Princess of Wands.

Two girls in shirts that proudly proclaim them as Tri-Delt stand up and wave, calling out. Three more girls arrive in a spontaneous burst of happy laughter. Tidbits of sound waft over to Carolyn, a name here, a joyous shriek there. One of the girls produces a cupcake from a container, and another sticks a candle in the center and lights it. They sing quickly, letting the birthday girl blow the candle out before security walks over. They wave their hands as if doing so will dissipate the smoke more quickly, but the security guard approaches them, gaze lingering on the freshly burnt candle.

The Wheel of Fortune.

Carolyn hears the creak of the Ferris wheel, turns to see it hanging there in mid-air. If she reaches out, she could touch it, and she starts to do exactly that.

"I thought you were too busy for lunch on Mondays." The scrape of a chair as Kit pulls one up to the table interrupts her; he drops into it.

The Ferris wheel disappears.

"Heather made me." Carolyn fights to keep her voice steady, knows she's failed when Heather's hand falls on her shoulder, stroking gently. "I'm okay."

"What happened there?"

"A flashback to my nightmares." Carolyn makes a motion with her hand, wiping the air clean between them. "I was daydreaming about Tarot cards. Did you ever used to try that, Kit, matching up people and cards? Like those girls over there." She motions toward the Tri-Delts.

"Princesses of Wands, every single one," Kit says around a mouthful of his sandwich. "That's not predictive. That's memorizing the card archetypes. Spontaneous, exuberant young women."

A gentle rush of calm washes over her. Carolyn reaches up and nudges Heather's hand until it falls away.

"I was wondering how you're doing on the assignment for Pawel." Kit nudges Carolyn's knee with his. "I'm meeting up with Thorne tonight to talk through some potential options for rituals."

Carolyn glances at Heather. "We talked about it a little." She'd brought it up, but Nikita derailed the conversation. Not only the first time, but every time since then as well. Carolyn knows that Nikita and Heather being friends is part of Heather's own independent study, but it seems like Heather can't do anything without Nikita these days. "We haven't talked about rituals."

Nor has she confirmed that Heather would help, even for this first assignment.

Heather pulls out her phone and opens her calendar. "I'm busy tonight, but what about tomorrow after you guys go to Coven? I could go with you, and we could get ice cream after and work through some ideas for the rituals. Nik, you could join us."

Carolyn bites her tongue.

"I'll be at Coven, but I don't think you need me for working on rituals, do you?" Nikita sits back, raising both her hands as if to push the idea away. "I'm not going to turn down ice cream, but I don't want get in the way, either."

"We'll figure it out." Maybe Heather is just trying to get as much data on Nikita's emotional state as she can. Carolyn can understand the idea that she's gathering information, working toward her project. She can't resent Heather for that.

"That's pretty much the last second," Kit points out.

"Pawel just wants confirmation of who we're working with, and the basis for some rituals. You know we'll be doing more with this next week."

"Mm." Kit breaks his cookie in half and offers one piece to Carolyn. The chocolate chips are melted, the center of the cookie still gooey, just the way she likes it.

"We'll be fine," Carolyn decides. She licks her fingers, then wipes them on the napkin. Then she slides off the chair and grabs her bag. "I need to go. We'll work on it after Coven. With ice cream. Or pizza."

"Or something," Heather agrees. "We'll get it done."

"It's a date," Nikita says cheerily.

Carolyn almost says "See you later," but she hesitates, standing there awkwardly, the words on the tip of her tongue. She knows she'll see Heather later. She has a feeling she'll also see Nikita, and she isn't sure how she feels about Dreamwalker sleepovers in her room.

She hopes none of this gives her more nightmares.

9

THE DISCUSSION PART of Coven is too short to be considered much of a meeting. Pawel's gaze skims over where Heather stands with Nikita and Carolyn, only glancing at them as he speaks. When he finishes, most of the club members move to the tables to get pastries and coffee. Heather hangs back and touches Carolyn's shoulder.

"We could go to the 'Skeller," Heather suggests. "I haven't had dinner yet, and we could grab a table, get food, and work on the ritual."

"I'd been thinking ice cream, but I'll be happy with a 'Skeller cookie instead," Nikita agrees. "Assuming you don't mind me hanging out with you. I won't interfere."

Kit's in line for food, a few people behind Rory. Carolyn watches as her twin follows and sits with Rory, leaning in to talk to him quietly. She assumes it's about his project with Thorne; after all, Pawel didn't say that they couldn't involve more than one other Mage.

"I could go for a burger or wings," Carolyn decides. "And they have soft-serve at the 'Skeller, so you could get that."

The Rathskeller is in the Madison Center. While the aboveground portions of the center were rebuilt in the 1980s as a student center for clubs, the original foundation and basement were retained, so the old pub hasn't changed since the building was first built centuries ago. While many of the surrounding buildings have connected basements, the only way into the 'Skeller is by exiting the Center, then using the heavy, old wooden door located outside, beside the main stairs.

Heather shivers as she ducks her head slightly, heading down the narrow stone stairwell. Even Carolyn can feel it, as if magic had been worked into the very walls when this was built. Nikita trails one hand along the wall as they go, steps echoing.

They travel down more than a flight's worth of stairs, then emerge into the entryway of the 'Skeller. The room is wide and brightly lit despite the lack of windows, rimmed with benches and racks for coats. The ceilings are high and made of natural stone, the walls a mix of wood and brick. There are cubbies to one side, empty now, although Carolyn imagines that maybe in a more innocent time people dropped their backpacks on the way in.

Nikita wiggles her fingers. "Give me your bags, and I'll claim a table. Heather, get me a double chocolate cookie and a dish of chocolate soft-serve with sprinkles." Parting from them, Nikita threads through the room, heading for a dimly lit back corner where Carolyn can see a couple rising from a table. There are three separate counters for ordering around the front edges of the room: a heavy wooden bar, a counter in front of the grill and wood-fire stove, and a dessert counter.

Heather yanks her lanyard over her head and hands her ID to Carolyn. "Two slices of cheese pizza and a soda, unless you want to do the wings-and-fries deal."

Carolyn's stomach rumbles, and she's suddenly starving. "Wings, sliders, and fries." She waves the ID away. "I'll get it this time; you can get our next surprise dinner out."

The line is long, but it's quick. Carolyn orders a large serving of wings, cheeseburger sliders, and fries, adding a pitcher of soda and three cups. By the time her number's called, Heather's back to help carry everything to the table.

"No talking yet," Carolyn says. They've ruined one meal with conversation in the past few days; Carolyn wants to fill the void in her stomach this time. It's like she hasn't eaten in days, her stomach growling violently as she shivers.

"You okay?" Heather's nose wrinkles as she leans in, concerned.

"Mm." It's the right thing to say even though Carolyn's not actually sure she is. She's starving. She eats two sliders in three bites each, following them up by guzzling half a glass of cola. She pushes fries through ketchup, barely tasting them before she chews and swallows. She has to slow down for the wings, ripping the meat from the bones and discarding the remains on her plate.

"Carolyn."

She stops at the sound in Heather's voice, a strange, twisted note. She looks up, blinks at her. "What?"

"Are you okay?" Heather repeats, her hand on Carolyn's arm, soft, soothing warmth drifting over her. Nikita sits back from the table, eyes wide, arms crossed tightly.

Carolyn blinks and looks at her hands, covered in wing sauce and bleu cheese dressing that drips like blood. There are easily a dozen bones on her plate, and the fries are gone aside from the few on Heather's plate.

Her stomach feels overfull to the point of discomfort.

"I—"

Heather's thumb slides along her skin. "It was like you checked out and just started…eating. Like you couldn't get enough."

"I couldn't." Carolyn grabs a napkin, trying to scrub the mess from her hands. "It was like my stomach was this abyss, and nothing could satisfy it. I didn't realize how much I grabbed. I'm sorry. I'll get more."

"That's not—" Heather cuts off with a sigh, her fingers momentarily tight on Carolyn's forearm. "You scared us. We were worried. It's not about you eating more than your share or anything. It was—"

"—weird," Nikita breaks in. "Like you weren't you."

Carolyn looks away from them, uncomfortable with the concern and pity in their gazes. The room seems brighter now, as if the shadows have backed away from the tables or as if the dim lights have grown, creating larger circles of light. Chatter from a hundred conversations bounces off the walls, echoing uncomfortably in her ears. "I'm fine now, I promise," she says, voice low. She eases off her chair, trying not to touch anything. "I'm going to wash up before we start talking about rituals. You guys finish eating." She carefully hooks her lanyard with her clean pinkies and drops it next to Heather. "Get some more food on my card."

She walks away before Heather can try to reassure her again. As nice as it is to be comforted, right now Carolyn wants to catalog her own emotions— figure herself out.

The gnawing hunger has faded, and what she ate sits like lead at the bottom of her stomach. She makes her way to the restrooms and pushes inside, ignoring the two girls talking from stall to stall. She twists the tap on, waits for the water to warm up, then plunges her hands under the flow and tries to rinse the sticky mess from her fingers.

Her skin is cold, the water hot against it. She holds her hands under the steady stream until they warm up, not budging when the two girls emerge and jockey for position at the other sink. They give her a dark look, but they take turns, then leave.

The room is strangely quiet after they exit.

Carolyn gets soap finally, washes her hands properly, then splashes some water on her face to rinse away the residue of sauce there. She twists the faucet off and leans on the edge of the sink, staring at her image in the mirror, making sure she hasn't left any stray streaks of bright red against her skin.

The lights dim and flicker; she grips the edge of the sink more tightly, blinking as if it'll make the room brighter.

Hunger twists in her gut. She drops a hand to her belly, curls her fingers against the shirt. She can't be hungry. It's anxiety. Fear. Confusion. Something other than hunger. It has to be.

She blinks, and the shadows seem to move out of the corner of her eye.

She remembers what Pawel said, his cautions.

"No," she whispers. She wants to close her eyes, marshal her strength, but she can't. She doesn't dare look away. Instead, she stares at the mirror, at the flared reflection of the single bulb light. There's a halo around the reflection, and the longer she stares, the brighter it seems. She breathes in carefully, focusing on it. It's like the Sun card: bright and shining, green grass around her, the scent of fresh earth filling her nose when she inhales. She can almost hear the chatter of the small child who sits beneath the cheerful, warm rays as the light burgeons forth from the mirror, bright enough to blind her. She steps back, one hand up, blinking before it fades.

The Sun: self. Be true to yourself, see the child within, and seek that which is your roots.

She inhales, then exhales slowly. The room seems brighter now. Her stomach is settled. Her hands are clean. She tugs her T-shirt down, wipes the few remaining droplets of water from her fingers, and leaves the bathroom.

The table is clean when she gets back, Nikita sitting with her elbows propped on it, playing with her glass in a slide of cold condensation upon the wood. Heather is pulling out a notebook and pens, and she gestures for Carolyn to do the same.

"Are you ready to get to work?" Heather asks.

Carolyn is ready for the world to stay steady and stable and in one piece. She glances sideways at Nikita, wondering if she saw anything strange while Carolyn was away, but she seems unconcerned. It's not a Dreamwalker thing. It can't be, or Nikita would have noticed.

It's something else.

Heather touches her shoulder, then slides her fingers down Carolyn's arm. "We don't have to, if you don't want to."

"It can't wait," Carolyn points out, because it can't—it's due tomorrow. She inhales tightly, holds her breath for a moment, and lets it out. Her smile feels tightly stretched, but Heather lets go and withdraws. Carolyn gets out her own notebook and her cards, in case she needs them. "What I need is some ideas for rituals that combine my Talent with yours. Ways to work together, using a more traditional ritual methodology, that allow your Empathy to influence my readings."

Heather wrinkles her nose, sitting back and crossing her arms. "You realize that I don't know anything about traditional ritual, right? I'm a Lineage Empath. We learn how to extend and pull back our Talents, but those are mental exercises, not rituals."

"I've done traditional ritual," Nikita offers. "We're Weather Witches, yes, but I had a lot of talent when I was young, so we worked with some Mages to help learn how to reign me in. I tended to get a little overexcited."

"Maybe you were Emerging even then," Heather murmurs.

"I doubt it. I just got ramped up. Kind of like hyperactivity for weather magic. That's why it was such a surprise when I started losing control again here." Nikita taps the table. "You guys come up with ideas for what you want to accomplish, and I can help you with the 'how.' If that doesn't go against the assignment."

"It's an independent study. I think our main goal is results." Carolyn figures that as long as she gets to the end of the class with some success, she'll pass. Pawel likes research and originality more than he likes seeing people do things the "one right way."

"So, a reading based on a feeling," Heather suggests, "where I try to influence it based on a particular emotion."

"That could be done two ways—either by having your Talent directly influence the reading, or by having it influence me," Carolyn says, writing that down. "I'm not sure if that counts as two rituals, but I'll take it. What about guiding a secondary reading—not throwing an emotion out there, but more trying to say 'what if you want a happy ending?' or something like that?" She scribbles as she continues to talk. "The cards are emotional things already—people have an emotional reaction to them. I'd love to know if the cards could end up lying, or see if they would tell the same exact story in a skewed way. Like two readings done side by side that should be the same, or close enough, but each one has a different bent because of the emotion behind it. Because when it comes down to it, I just give the guidance—the receiver has to do part of the work as well."

"So readings where I influence the cards, the reader, or the receiver," Heather says.

"The latter two sound less like a ritual and more like you being you while Carolyn reads," Nikita says. "But the other one—since the cards don't really have emotions to influence—that's a ritual." She grabs for paper and starts sketching notes next to Carolyn's.

It takes them a couple hours to get it all hammered out, and for Carolyn to write up the notes neatly into her class notebook. The 'Skeller is still busy by the time they're done, but the crowd has changed from people having dinner to grad students there for a mid-week drink.

Carolyn folds up her books and neatly tucks everything into her bag. "We'll walk you back, Nikita," she offers. "It's on the way to our house."

The door to the outside opens as they climb the stairs, letting in a burst of chill winter air. Carolyn tries to cling to one side of the narrow space, passing a crowd as they head down, loud and cheerful. She catches the door as it's closing and pushes it open into the darkness, holding it for Nikita and Heather.

"I'm okay walking on my own," Nikita says. She keeps talking, but Carolyn turns away…and spots Kit.

She takes a step and waves. He's with someone; they're walking down the main stairs from the Madison Center, and they pause at the bottom. His companion stands on the bottom step, which makes her just a little taller than Kit, and he reaches up to tug her down and kiss her.

It's not a chaste kiss.

It's hard to breathe, fear gripping Carolyn's bones in a frigid embrace. She wheezes, sound muffled all around her.

He's going to get hurt. She's sure of it, terrified for him. For her. For the idea that somehow this will rebound against them.

"Hey." Heather's hand is on her arm, Nikita sliding in close on her other side.

"I guess the dating thing is working out for Kit and Serina, huh?" Nikita says. "He looks happy."

"He is. I can feel it from here." Heather smiles. "So's she."

"Then that's a good thing." Nikita hooks her arm in Carolyn's, bumps her with her hip. "Weren't you guys going to walk me home?"

Carolyn lets them bear her with them, shuffling between them until she can get her feet to move properly on their own. "You were going to go on your own," she says quietly. She twists, but Heather stops her from turning back to look at Kit again.

"He's fine," Heather says. "Don't be a mother hen."

"It's totally okay to feel weird about your sibling having a sex life," Nikita says. "I mean, Tammy's married. And she just had a baby, which means I know way more about straight sex than I ever wanted to know. Everything, from practicing for conception to the whole 'gory details about giving birth' part. And we're, like, really far apart in age. But that's never stopped Mom from asking when I'm going to meet a good guy, get married, and make more babies for her to play with."

"Until Tammy brought up the whole 'turkey baster' thing," Heather points out.

Carolyn's grateful for the way they each have a hand on her. For the normal conversation going back and forth around her without requiring her to participate. It lets her float. Not think. Try to breathe.

"Exactly. And that hasn't actually stopped Mom from talking babies, now that she's got her head wrapped around the whole thing. She emailed me today. Her friend from college has a daughter named Gina who happens to be very gay and 'maybe you should meet up and go out sometime!' But she also told me about this 'lovely young man' in her office who has wonderful cheekbones and suggested I could have sex with him once and get pregnant." Nikita's voice shifts, and Carolyn wonders if she's mimicking her mother. "'Pick a good man, have beautiful babies. They can even be lesbians too.'"

That shocks a small laugh from Carolyn and a louder one from Heather. "Your parents are doing their best to be accepting," Heather says.

"They try." Nikita slows, and Carolyn matches her pace, forcing Heather to slow as well. After a few more steps, Nikita stops, turns toward Carolyn, and takes her hands. "Are you still having a panic attack?"

Carolyn inhales slowly and holds the air in her lungs. She shakes her head, rubs her chest. "I'll be okay."

"Do you want to talk about it? Because if you do, I'll listen. I mean, you put up with so much from me 'cause I'm practically stalking your roommate. Or she's keeping me close or something because I'm her favorite project." Nikita's grin flashes, then falls back to seriousness. "I mean it. I'm no stranger to panic attacks, and they really suck, and if you want to talk, I'm here, okay?"

"Okay." Carolyn squeezes her hands, trying to convey that she really does understand. And she knows Heather will always have her back as well. She knows, even though sometimes she struggles to believe it. "Our high-school life had some speed bumps. I'm worried for him."

"It's his life," Heather reminds her.

Carolyn can't argue that. It's Kit's life, and she wants him to be happy. She knows it's going to be okay.

"It's his life," Heather repeats, voice softer than before. "And it has no effect on yours. Let him have his own failures and his own successes. You need to take your own chances, too."

"That's easier said than done," Carolyn mutters.

10

Kɪᴛ's ᴡᴀɪᴛɪɴɢ ᴏᴜᴛsɪᴅᴇ the building when Carolyn arrives for their lunch session with Pawel. There's a faint sheen on his forehead, as if he's run across campus to get there. "Lab sucked," he says, holding open the door for her.

"Sucked because things went wrong, or sucked because it was a struggle to get out on time?" Carolyn asks. The crowds are gone, fled into classrooms in time to attend lectures that start at noon. Kit and Carolyn have been struggling to get to Pawel's promptly on Wednesdays. She can smell Chinese food from somewhere, and she hopes that's their lunch. Her stomach whines.

"It was a longer lab than we had time for, the slides were murky, and my partner is an idiot." Kit wears an unhappy scowl. "He doesn't like to wait or pay attention to anything, so we had to do one part of the lab three times before we got it right."

"Can you switch partners?"

"Probably not." Kit pauses, his hand where the knob for Pawel's door should be. It's slightly open, and voices come from inside.

"Is your family all right?" Pawel asks.

"Mom is." It's Drea's voice, thin and tight. "Dad's…he's Dad. I'm not sure he's ever going to be all right again. He's been off-balance since Orson died."

Carolyn nudges the door open, then steps past Kit. "Drea?"

Pawel blinks at them, a cardboard take-out pint in his hand, chopsticks sticking out. "Come on in. Grab food. We might not get much done today. Did you find partners?" He holds up one hand before they can answer. "Yes-no question, no details needed yet."

"Yes," Carolyn and Kit say in tandem.

"Good." Pawel motions to Drea and Alaric, who stand tight together, Alaric's arm around his sister's shoulder. "Go on."

"He was as good as feral," Alaric says, voice rough. "Our mother had to forcibly call him back from the wolf. He's been spending more and more time as the wolf, too; this is not behavior for Clan as young as he is."

"And usually when Clan get old, they don't get dangerous. Dad's hallucinating," Drea says flatly. "Mom said the place smelled like dust and death, same as always. He claimed that someone had been there, but there was no sign of that. If they were, I don't know how they got in or out, and they didn't leave enough of a scent for Mom to detect."

"The place reeks," Alaric mutters. "She might not have noticed."

"You have a point."

Kit nudges the door closed, pushing the one free chair toward Carolyn before finding a place where he can lean against a bookcase. Carolyn shakes her head, ignoring the chair.

"What happened?" she asks.

"Dad smelled magic and an intruder in this old, abandoned house on our property," Drea explains, hands moving as she speaks. "Mom said it was the middle of the night, and he woke up from a sound sleep, turned into a wolf before he was out of the bed, and raced off. She followed him, but by the time she got there, he was alone, tearing the place apart with his teeth."

"It's the old Berman place," Alaric says; it means nothing to Carolyn. She looks to Kit, who looks back at her and shrugs his confusion. "It's where we took the Shadow we caught so he could interrogate it. And it's where he lost it."

"Oh."

"The family that owned the house disappeared years ago," Drea adds. She rubs at her skin as if she's trying to scratch something off. "It stinks like death and decay. But it was a safe place to put something that wanted to devour us."

"The Shadow loved it," Pawel murmurs, writing something down. "Darkness for a Deathstalker."

"Don't think it liked starving," Alaric says.

"Dad thought maybe it'd come back," Drea says. "Mom thinks he's losing his mind. I think she's afraid she's going to lose him to the wolf."

"He's a wolf," Carolyn echoes softly. Because she remembers the teeth, the sheer anger. She could imagine it ripping through the countertop, pulling up floorboards to get to her. It could easily have torn an entire house apart after she disappeared. She looks at the palms of her hand, the almost invisible remnants of scrapes still there. "I had this really weird dream about a wolf the other night?"

Pawel's gaze snaps to her. "You did?" He gestures at the chair, and when she doesn't sit, he points again. "Tell me about it."

She's aware of their eyes on her, aware that she'd never mentioned this to Drea or Kit. They're probably wondering why she kept it to herself. But it was easier to forget it, to put it aside and let it go. Heather and Nikita are already too interested in it.

"I'd had a rough night—the cards weren't really working for me." She doesn't look at Kit. "So the cards were on my mind when I went to sleep. I was frustrated and confused, and I knew I still needed to get my work done for this project, so that's why Tarot was right there for the dream. It started with the Tower crumbling."

"The Tarot card," Pawel murmurs, writing something down.

Carolyn nods. "The card, yeah. And I was falling, then I caught a deck of cards, and I pulled one out, and it was the Wheel of Fortune, and I ended up on a Ferris wheel. And when I thought that was going to break apart, I pulled another card, and I ended up in this decrepit farmhouse." Her stomach rumbles, but she ignores the bag of food waiting for them to dig in. "I was looking around, and it was creepy. Snowing outside. Wind whistling. Cold. I heard a wolf howling, and I wanted to get away. I was terrified, and I couldn't go anywhere, and I was panicking. So I pulled another card, and it wasn't a Tarot card—it was a picture of my room here at PHU. That's when a wolf—a *giant* wolf—burst through the door and came at me. I fell back, and then it was like I tumbled through the card and fell off my bed and landed next to it on my hands and knees. I woke Heather up."

"That's a hell of a dream." Pawel never stops writing, never looks up. But the others are watching her. Staring at her.

Carolyn curls her fingers around the scrapes on her palm. "It was just a weird dream. A coincidence."

"Mm." Pawel looks over at Alaric and Drea. "Can I contact your mother? I'd like to talk to her about Theobald's condition. I'm concerned that he's been getting worse since he was in contact with the Shadowwalker."

Alaric's watching Carolyn. She bites her lip; his nostrils flare, and she looks away, crossing her arms.

"Yeah. You've got her number, right?" Drea says. "She probably won't be thrilled about talking to a Mage, but she's worried about Dad. I can hear it in her voice. She'll be more interested in him being sane than in worrying about how magic might corrupt her life."

Pawel scratches notes furiously. Carolyn feels like she shouldn't be here, but she can't move because she hasn't been dismissed yet. Her meeting hasn't really begun, either.

"Heather? Thorne?" Pawel asks, pulling over another piece of paper to write on.

"Yes," Carolyn responds. Kit's answer is slightly slower, as if he has to think about it.

"We'll meet tomorrow." Pawel nudges the bag of delivery closer to Carolyn and Kit. "Take the lunch. Go eat and get to your classes. I need to call Alia. Be prepared to go over the outline of the rituals you've prepared." He pauses, staring at a point in the distance. "The outlines you've prepared for the rituals you're considering," he corrects himself. "We'll talk more tomorrow. There's plenty of time for your work." He only gives them a moment before he waves at the door. "Go. Please."

Kit grabs for the bag, hoists it, and is out the door quickly. "There are tables and chairs in the lobby. We can eat there. You guys can join us."

"You went there." Alaric grips Carolyn's hand, twisting it to look at her palm. She tries to pull away, and he lets her. "Sorry."

"It's not possible," Carolyn tells him, fighting and failing to push past her own denial. "I'm not a teleporter. I've never done anything like that before—not the dream, not the potential reality of it."

She follows Kit because she knows she needs to eat, and he has food. She's not actually hungry, she just wants to escape from Alaric's scrutiny.

"You should eat with us," Kit says. "I want to keep talking about this."

"I don't." Carolyn's voice is quiet, but she knows Drea hears her by the way Drea threads her arm through Carolyn's and tucks in close.

"I know," Drea whispers, leaning her head against Carolyn's briefly. "But I think maybe we have to. Because of the Shadows."

They pull two couches close to one low table, then spread the food out. Kit glances at his watch, and Carolyn checks hers as well. They've got thirty minutes before Kit has to be halfway across campus and sitting in a lecture.

"I'll be late. This is more important." Kit squeezes her hand. "Okay?"

Alaric pulls paper plates, chopsticks, and forks out of the bag. They all make their plates, and for a moment, they're silent while eating. It gives Carolyn time to go over everything in her head, try to deal with the idea that if the dream was real, she might have gone to where Drea's from.

"I'd know for sure if I could see it," she says slowly, gesturing with the lo mein at the end of her chopsticks.

"That's—"

"—difficult," Drea cuts Alaric off. "It would be difficult, but not impossible. Right, Alaric?"

Alaric's expression sours. He eats another bite before setting it aside. "Right," he grumbles. "My family doesn't like Mages. You know that. And you're a Mage, whether you think of yourself that way or not. You smell like one. Your predictive Talent is magic. And whatever you did to get yourself there was magic." He stares at her, nostrils flaring again before he shakes his head and makes a disgruntled noise.

"We'd need to make sure Mom keeps Dad clear of the house," Drea suggests.

"I'll go with you," Kit offers. "As long as it's not Saturday. I have a date."

"SigPsiEp is sponsoring the Saturday movie," Carolyn points out, "so Drea and I couldn't go then, either."

"It's not far; if you think you'll be up early enough, we could do a day trip on Sunday," Drea suggests. "We'd just need a car, and Alaric and I don't have one. And Chris's car isn't big enough to get us all there."

"I'll ask Dax if he can borrow his mom's van," Alaric offers. "That'll fit all four of us, plus Dax, no problem."

"So we're talking about bringing three Mages onto the property," Drea muses.

Alaric huffs, jaw set. "And I'm going to distract him while you and Mom go out to the house with them," he says, voice tight. "I've been talking to Dayton about our alliance, and I need to talk to Dad about it. He's not going to like anything I have to say, so he'll spend the whole time yelling at me. I have a proposal from Trey and Joseph; discussing it will take an hour at least before he's calmed down enough to be reasonable. That's not even going into what Aly and Devon want to do."

Carolyn's phone dings, and she pulls it out on autopilot, touching the screen to open her email. She expects it to be something from the house, about the movie or another event, or maybe something from a class.

She doesn't expect to see the name "Shawn Benedict."

She pauses, her thumb over the message, breath tight in her chest.

"What?" Alaric asks. "You're panicking. No one's going to let Theobald hurt you. He's an ass, but I'll keep him busy."

"He's our father, and he's not that bad," Drea says. "Or maybe he is, but we can keep him under control if Mom helps."

"It's not that." Carolyn tilts the phone so Kit can see the name. He inhales roughly, and she touches the message to open it.

Caro—

Hey. It's been a while, hasn't it? Sometimes it seems like we just graduated, other times it seems like a lifetime since we were sixteen. In a strange way, I miss those years, but I know I was an idiot then, so I'm sure you don't miss that me.

I'm sorry. I said that a lot then, and I don't know if I meant it at the time, but I do now. I was an asshole. Hindsight's twenty-twenty.

I don't know if you've heard from Delilah recently, but she's seen some weird things, and so have I, and we were talking and your name came up. It looks like PHU is only a few hours drive away from where I pick her up, so we were thinking we could come out next week to talk to you.

I'm pretty sure you're the only one besides us, and Samson, who'd have any chance at figuring out what's going on.
Delilah says she's sorry, too. And I'm sure Samson would.

Tears spring to Carolyn's eyes. She's shaking, breath shuddering in her chest, and the screen blurs. She rubs at her eyes, takes the tissue that Drea offers, and tries to focus long enough to finish reading the message.

Delilah doesn't have Tuesday afternoon classes, and I'm willing to skip mine, and my Wednesday morning class, so we can come out. It's then or Thursday. I figured you wouldn't want us to come out for a weekend.
Let me know what works for you.

—Shawn

Carolyn locks the phone by feel, drops it on the table, and leans forward, elbows on her knees, head in her hands. Kit slides closer, his hand rubbing her back in slow circles as she gulps in breath, tears escaping in a ragged sob. When he tugs, she goes to him; she curls in tight and presses her face against his shoulder as he continues to soothe her.

"What happened?" Drea asks, worry in her voice. "Is your family okay?"

"That was her ex," Kit says flatly, and Carolyn closes her eyes.

"Relationships," Alaric mutters.

Carolyn doesn't want to see Shawn or Delilah. She doesn't want to think about Samson. But after everything that's happened in recent days, after all the upheaval, she has to wonder at the timing of his message. Coincidences happen, but it's all too possible that her dream and whatever Shawn wants have something to do with each other.

No matter how much she'd like to see Shawn Benedict thrown from the Tower, she's too kind to let someone, even him, hit the ground. She can't refuse to help.

WHAT LIES
BEHIND

Third Position: Behind

What lies behind...

What lies behind the querent has affected their path and brought them to this particular moment in their life. Nothing happens in a vacuum; one's life can be seen as a series of decisions that culminate in the here and now. To consider the future, one must always be willing to look closely at the past.

Carolyn's Reading: The Ten of Cups

A woman sits on the shore of a lake, mountains rising behind her. She is naked except for the scarf that covers her head and drapes across her body. She is surrounded by ten cups, each overflowing.

This is a card for the perfect moment, that one point in time when life is filled to the brim with peace, love, and prosperity, when Talent is perfectly realized. The querent is satiated, replete in heart and knowledge. It may mean that love has come to completion or that a goal has been achieved.

It is also a moment on the cusp of change, the point when completion may become more than is needed, when the cups overflow because there is simply too much. Satiation becomes gluttony. Climax may fall to chaos. There is good for the querent, so much so that the excess spills over and is lost, saturating the world around them. The querent has been stripped bare and must determine whether loss is acceptable in the face of such abundance.

If the querent seeks to know more about Talent, they must beware; while they are rising to the pinnacle of success with their task, this is the moment when the apex may be exceeded, resulting in a spill over into failure.

Kit's Reading: The Eight of Swords

A man and woman stand surrounded—trapped—by eight swords. They are not looking at each other, nor speaking; they do not work together to escape their cage.

The querent is being tested. They face a situation that they must rise above, either alone or by learning to seek those who would help them. They need to find their strength within to succeed; otherwise, they will remain trapped within the cage that binds them to the here and now.

There are disturbances and interferences on the path forward, and the querent must move beyond these obstacles if they are to progress. The querent may be blamed, may be faced with resistance, both from those around them and from their own heart. Beware of internal conflict and problematic thoughts that may be as much of a trap as any physical barrier.

11

CAROLYN DOESN'T WANT to spend the weekend wondering what the hell Shawn's talking about, so she emails him back that Thursday night's fine, but he has to leave before Sunday. Thus, on Thursday night, the living room at the house is full, far too many sisters on hand when Shawn knocks on the door.

He and Delilah stand there crowding into the doorway. The duffle over his shoulder takes up too much space, and Delilah has hers hanging down by her side to compensate. Shawn doesn't smile, but Delilah does as soon as Carolyn opens the door, green eyes crinkling and teeth bright against dark skin as she grins. She drops her bag and pulls Carolyn close, wrapping her arms around her to hug her tight. The weight of her braids falls across Carolyn's shoulder.

Every feeling their presence evokes is familiar, and Carolyn starts to shake.

She steps back quickly, almost bumping into Mac and Heather. She pushes at them, making space, and offers, "Come on in."

Delilah pushes through first, nudging her bag with her toe, leaving it just inside the door until Shawn picks it up. "I never thought you'd be a sorority girl, Caro." Her voice is low, filled with warmth and happiness. "But it suits you. You feel good."

"That's probably Heather's influence," Carolyn says. She glances at her roommate, shaking her head a little when Heather steps closer. She wants to say "I'm fine," but she doesn't want those words to be said out loud in front of Shawn. "They're my sisters."

Shawn nudges the door closed, and the *thunk* makes Carolyn clench one hand tight; she forces herself to relax.

"Are you going to introduce us?" Mac asks.

Carolyn takes stock of exactly who *us* is, giving herself a chance to breathe. Not everyone has crowded into the small space, but Mac and Heather are there, of course. Sera stands with Trish, and Cass is nearby, as is Soledad. Drea seems to be waiting for an invitation. Carolyn smiles weakly at her, then nods to Mac.

"Yeah, okay. These are Shawn and Delilah, two of my best friends from high school." Carolyn's too aware of the way people are looking at her, as if they've never heard the names. Because they haven't; the only one who has is Heather, and Carolyn provided only a minimum of information back in their freshman year. "I dated Shawn. He might be— Are you two together?"

Shawn and Delilah exchange glances. Delilah lifts one shoulder. "Sometimes. When we're bored and it's convenient. There's nothing like being with someone familiar, y'know?"

Carolyn knows.

She ignores Delilah's answer even though she brought up the topic. "These are a bunch of my sisters, except Sera; she's just here all the time." She points to each of them as she names them. Others poke their way into the hall, and Carolyn wonders why everyone's so curious about her guests. She never interferes with other people's guests unless they've come to see Heather. And Heather doesn't usually have guests other than Nikita, and she's only become a regular since they started working on their project.

"And my roommate, Heather," Carolyn finishes. "Say 'thank you' to her, because it's our floor you'll be crashing on."

"So you were friends with Carolyn in high school?" Drea catches Delilah's arm and steers her into the living room. Trish and Sera rise from the couch, giving Drea space to bring Delilah there. Shawn leaves the bags in the hall and follows, sitting in the empty space next to Delilah.

"We've been friends with Carolyn since we were all, what... five?" Delilah looks to Carolyn, and she has no choice but to engage.

"You and I met in kindergarten." Carolyn only sits on the edge of the chair because Heather makes her. "You knew Shawn before that because your moms were friends, right? Then Samson started at Henley in fourth grade, and Kit adopted him."

"Are you seriously named Samson and Delilah?" Mac asks.

Cass perches on the edge of the couch beside Shawn. "Why didn't Samson come with you?"

Carolyn's jaw goes tight, teeth clenched; her fingers curl into tight fists. Heather's hand on her knee is soothing; she knows that Heather is trying to target her specifically, and she carefully sets one hand over Heather's to try to indicate she'll be okay.

She's doing her best, anyway.

Delilah looks at Shawn, and Shawn looks at Carolyn. "He's why we're here, actually," Shawn says.

"They're nicknames," Delilah adds. "My name is Meredith, but honestly only my relatives call me that. Everyone started calling me 'Delilah' in sixth grade because I was Sam's girlfriend. Even my mom calls me Del now."

"And people called him 'Samson' because he was big, and strong, and he had long hair that he was really proud of," Carolyn adds quietly.

"We used to try to see who could keep theirs longer," Delilah says. "His is short now. I think he hates it, even though he hasn't said."

"You've seen him?"

Kit should be here for this. He'd want to know how Sam's doing, and he'd want to see Delilah and Shawn. Even after everything…they were still close. Maybe closer than Carolyn was to them.

"He called me." Shawn's voice is flat. Delilah sets a hand on his knee, and he leans closer to her.

Cass tilts her head, brow furrowing.

"He made it to one of the office phones and called me," Shawn elaborates. "He was really clear when we spoke. He told me that I had to come see you and ask you about the Wheel of Fortune. He made me promise three times. I asked if he had a message for Kit, too, and he said Kit doesn't want it."

"And that's just some of the weird shit we've had going on," Delilah adds. "I've been traveling."

Heather's hand goes tight on Carolyn's knee, and Drea glances at her as well. Cass's attention is entirely on Delilah.

Mac asks casually, "Traveling?"

"It's complicated," Delilah says, her tone shutting down discussion, "but it's not something I did often before. Not really. That it's happening now is weird, and Samson being coherent is even weirder."

"What about you, Shawn?" Carolyn asks. Her heart is thumping hard in her chest, and Drea is staring at her. "What weird is happening for you?"

Shawn licks his lips and exhales softly. "Nothing," he says quietly. "Nothing is happening, and that's weird."

Right. Whatever that means.

Carolyn doesn't know what to say, nor how to say it in front of all her friends who know nothing about this part of her life. She pushes to her feet, shaking Heather's hand from her knee. "I'm going to get something to drink. Anyone want me to bring back water or soda?"

"I can he—"

"Don't," Carolyn cuts Heather off, immediately feeling guilty about being so sharp. "I'll text Kit, too," she says. "He might want to see Shawn and Delilah."

She heads for the kitchen, ignoring the small knot of girls already there. She grabs one of the plastic bins and starts tossing soda cans and water bottles into it, filling it before she grabs her own water bottle and twists it open. She drains half before setting it down, closing her eyes, and trying to think.

"Caro."

She opens her eyes, and Delilah is standing in the doorway, expression soft.

"Del." Carolyn can't find more words than that. She fumbles her phone from her pocket, bringing up Kit's name. *Shawn and Delilah got here*, she texts. *Samson sent me a message by way of Shawn. He said he didn't have a message for you that you'd want to hear.* She presses "Send" and stares at it like Kit's going to text back immediately. He doesn't, of course. They have their own lives here; it's not like high school when they lived in each other's pockets.

"Is Kit coming over?" Delilah takes a step in, and the other girls scatter. Funny how that works. They could always clear a room just by wanting to be alone—any of them—like the energy they produced as a group was simply that strong.

"I don't know. He might have a date."

"He's dating? Oh, that's excellent." Delilah claps her hands together once, clearly delighted. "He never seemed interested in high school."

"Extenuating circumstances," Carolyn points out, and Delilah nods. They've all been friends a long time, and they all remember everything that's happened. There's no point in going into details. "Serina's a nice girl, and Kit's a better choice than the gay guy she had a crush on before."

Delilah snorts, covering her mouth with her hand. "Yeah." She takes another step closer; the counter is at Carolyn's back and there's no place for her to go. Delilah stops before she gets to Carolyn, leaving space between them. "I figured you'd want to hear more about how Sam's doing," she says quietly. "Shawn doesn't like to talk about him, and you don't like it when he talks about him, so I thought maybe it'd be better coming from me."

"A little." It's not easy coming from any of them, but Carolyn really does want to know.

"He's still not in this world," Delilah says quietly. "He has his moments, like when he called Shawn. And sometimes he seems to feel that he needs to communicate something desperately. He fights things no one else sees. He has conversations with ghosts, people who aren't there."

"I've met other people who seem to do that, but they aren't—" She's not sure how to end the sentence. "Insane" isn't the right word, not exactly. At least not for Samson. And while she has friends now who talk to unseen things, Carolyn doesn't think it's the same for Pels or Dax.

"Are they people who are otherwise coherent?" Delilah asks. She leans next to Carolyn, pops a can of soda open, and takes a long swallow. When she leans into her, for a moment it's like being back in high school, like they're still the people who no one else would fuck with. It was the five of them against the world.

"Mostly." Carolyn's not always sure about Pels, but then, they've only really met at Coven. Other than that, she's just heard about her from Soledad and Serina.

"Sam's not. Still." Delilah sighs, shoulders slumping. "He's so not. He won't let me be in the same room as him. I get near and he starts acting out, getting violent. He yells. Screams. I can't even be on the hall when Shawn visits him."

"Do you blame him?" Carolyn whispers, fingers tight enough that she crushes the water bottle.

"No." Delilah presses her lips together, tongue licking out. It reminds Carolyn of a nervous dog, but that's not Delilah. She's not Clan. Carolyn's not sure what she is anymore. A Mage of some kind; that's how they all started out

"Why'd you let us come out here?" Delilah asks.

"Mm." Carolyn drains the rest of her water bottle and shakes the last drops into the sink, then drops it into the bin of returnables under the sink. It's not that she doesn't want to answer, it's that she isn't sure how to explain. "Shawn emailed, and he said there were weird things happening. We've had our share of weird things here, too, and it seemed like we should talk about it. Share information, in case your weird and our weird have anything to do with each other."

"I traveled." Delilah says it again, like Carolyn could have missed it the first time. "Not what happened with Samson. Not like…" She trails off, expression twisted with frustration. "I disappeared, but I didn't go anywhere real. It was like ending up in Candyland."

Carolyn opens her mouth. She's about to say that she traveled too, but she's not sure she's ready to share that, so instead she says, "I know what happened with the freak ice storm last Thanksgiving."

Delilah's eyes go wide. "That wasn't just weather?"

"Weather Witch with her abilities on a major fritz," Carolyn says. "We've been working with her, trying to help her get everything under control so we don't blanket the Northeast in a quarter inch of ice again."

"I think your weird tops my weird."

Carolyn's gaze drifts to the door. She can hear the rumble of conversation, and she wonders what Shawn's telling people. If he's being sweet and charming or is still quiet and as sour as he was when they arrived. If he's telling stories about high school that she never wants anyone to hear, or if he's telling the easier stories, like the time she tried to dye her hair and ended up bleaching it almost orange instead.

She hears a bright laugh.

"Halloween," Delilah says, and when Carolyn's brow furrows, she explains, "he's probably talking about Halloween because he likes to tell stories about the costumes and the stupid things we did when we were little. Because apparently tween magic is funny, and we were pretty ridiculous. It's no wonder the whole school thought we were our own little cult."

"They were scared of us, especially after they knew about Talent," Carolyn says. "I thought it was kind of funny then. Everything seemed so perfect for us."

"Until it wasn't," Delilah adds quietly, because that's exactly what happened.

They were on top of the world, and then they fell off; Carolyn's not sure how far they fell in the end. She knows Samson went the farthest, and he's still stuck somewhere they can't get to him. Shawn never seemed like it touched him, at least not in a negative way.

"What's Shawn—?"

"Take him literally." Delilah cuts her off. "When he says 'nothing's happening,' he means nothing. Sometimes it works, but half the time, it's just…gone."

"Everything?"

Shawn was always strong, and after everything, he was even stronger. Almost unstoppable. He could light a room with a thought, convince mosquitoes to feast elsewhere, and charm bees into giving him honey.

"Sometimes he's normal. Sometimes he's like he was when we graduated. But most of the time…it's like something sucked him dry."

Carolyn wants to be sympathetic. She wants to say "that's awful" and mean it. But she can't. Still, she bites her tongue to keep the words "he deserves it" from slipping free.

"Hey, Carolyn?" Trish calls out, poking her head in. "Hi, Delilah. Do you prefer Delilah or Del? Also, how do you feel about being the subject of a song? Because honestly, I could write an ode to your eyes if you wouldn't mind."

"Are you flirting with me?" Delilah asks, and Trish grins.

"If you want me to be, then yes, I'm flirting. But I don't have to be if it makes you uncomfortable. Up to you." Trish turns her attention back to Carolyn. "Sera and I are going out to meet up with Pat, Jackson, and the rest of the guys. If you want anything from Teas Please, text me. If you need anything in general, let me know."

"I'm good. I'm going to get Shawn and Del set up to crash here tonight. I'm bailing on class tomorrow morning, so don't wake me up thinking I'm missing breakfast."

"Got it." Trish waves at Delilah. "Nice to meet you. Was that a yes or a no on the ode to your eyes?"

"Yes on the ode, no to the flirting, thanks," Delilah says. "Your sisters are nice," she adds as Trish leaves. "I can see why you like it here."

"It's not like high school," Carolyn says. She needs people around her. This isn't how she'd thought to find companionship, but it does work, and better than she'd expected. "I second-guess everything now."

Delilah's silent for a long moment, then whispers, "I'm sorry, Caro. I really am. We didn't know."

"I know." And she does, but that doesn't make it any easier. Any better. "It's not okay, but things are different now. I'm good with moving forward. I've even joined Coven."

"I'd like to hear about that." Delilah looks at her, then leans into her. "I'd like to hear from you in general."

That won't be easy. But when Carolyn thinks about it, runs through the idea of actually opening her email and sending a message to Delilah, she can imagine typing it out.

She hasn't gotten there regarding Shawn yet, but maybe that'll change too. It's been a long time. Life goes on.

12

It's AWKWARD THURSDAY night, but they've found a bit of ease by late on Friday. Shawn sprawls against a bean bag chair that Trish had dropped off without comment earlier that afternoon. Carolyn can't think why Trish thought of it, but it keeps Shawn off her bed, so she's good with the idea.

"Kit looks good," Shawn comments. "He seems happy."

"I'm not surprised. I think Kit's been looking for a chance to get away from his childhood. I've missed him." Delilah glances over at Carolyn, and she hears the unsaid *I miss you*. It isn't the first time that Delilah's implied it, a silent follow-up to their conversation from yesterday.

Carolyn hasn't addressed it. She's not ready to do so with Shawn in the room.

"He's stretching his magical wings, too," Delilah says, gesturing as she speaks as if to mimic flight with her hands. "He was telling me about the projects he's doing, working with those brothers." She leans back on her elbows, lounging on Carolyn's bed. "You go to school with the most interesting people. Pop stars. Folk singers."

"PHU has a lot of strengths, and it's got one of the few Magical Studies programs in the country," Carolyn reminds her. "Plus, it's a good school if you want to combine art and science, like Trish is doing."

"Is she going to be a doctor in her spare time between tours?" Shawn asks, and Carolyn nudges his shoulder with her toe. He blinks at her, and she realizes that she's behaving almost like they used to.

She pulls her foot up and sits cross-legged on her bed so she can't do it again. "Actually, she's majoring in music, and her minor is mechanical engineering," she says blandly. "She does summer classes remotely while touring, and she's designing an experimental engine for her capstone project next year. She does all the mechanical work on her truck, her bike, and her trailer. You probably saw her bike outside. It's orange, pretty hard to miss."

"It looked custom." Shawn sits upright, and for a second Carolyn thinks he's about to get up and hunt Trish down.

"It is." She considers the move before she makes it, letting one foot fall and using it to push dead-center on his chest to nudge him back. "Don't bug her about it now. But yes, she built a bike out of parts, so it's custom. She's good with engines. She wants to make them better."

"All while writing an ode to my eyes." Delilah's elbows slide out; she falls back onto the bed with a soft sigh. "Really, Caro, you have the best people here. But I haven't seen any of the weird."

Carolyn had introduced them to Pawel earlier, had sat through another lecture about shadows and darkness while biting her tongue. "You're one of the weirder things on campus right now," she says. "Maybe you should've told Pawel. He could've helped if it has something to do with—"

"I'm just a Mage," Delilah says, tone flat. "Shawn's just a Mage. You're just a Mage with a predictive Lineage. That's it, right?"

Carolyn's phone *pings*, glances at it, and winces. "It's going to be crowded in here tonight," she mutters.

"Why? Del and I can get a room somewhere nearby if we need to," Shawn offers. "We don't want to put you out."

They're putting her out no matter where they stay. However, it's almost nice having them here. Carolyn's enjoyed sharing her school, her town. She took them on a tour, introduced them to her friends. She showed them her new life, let them into it in tiny ways; she knows she can push them right out again when she needs space. "You're heading out tomorrow anyway," she says. "One more night won't matter. It's just that Nik's crashing here tonight, too."

"Nik?" Delilah glances over, light in her eyes. "Someone new?"

"Nikita. She's a Weather Witch." Carolyn groans at the way Delilah perks up. She answers the question before Delilah asks, hoping she can circumvent explanations that aren't hers to give. "Yes," she says. "That one."

"What happened, anyway?" Delilah's brow furrows. She twists in place, looks at the window, then the door. "Weird," she mutters.

Shawn bolts to his feet. "What kind of weird?"

There are footsteps on the stairs, then the room's door opens as thunder cracks in the distance, lightning bright outside the window.

The house plunges into darkness.

"That kind." Delilah's voice shakes. "Caro…"

"Shit shit shit shit shit," Nikita whispers. "Heather. Fuck. Something's wrong. I can't…" Thunder booms again, louder this time, the crack of lightning almost on top of it. Rain beats against the glass like pellets.

"It's okay," Heather whispers. Carolyn can feel how she tries to soothe Nikita, the sensation bleeding into the air like a thick blanket of calm over a simmering brew of anxiety.

It's not working for Carolyn. She hopes it's working for Nikita.

"Weird," Delilah says again. She reaches out, grips Carolyn's hand, and Carolyn wants to yank away. Delilah is cold, shivering. "Keep me here," Delilah orders shakily. "Don't let me go."

"Why is this happening?" Nikita yells, thunder underlining her words.

And then Carolyn gets it. "It's Del," she says quickly. "Delilah, we've got to get you out of here. Nikita's a Dreamwalker." It's not her secret to tell, but it's important.

Not that they know what Delilah is.

"I'm not," Delilah snaps back at her. "I'm not! I don't Dream. Dreamwalkers Dream. I travel."

"What the hell is she talking about?" Nikita yells.

"You're interfering with each other. The power's out in the house, which means there are shadows." Carolyn looks into the corners of the room, Pawel's warnings fresh in her mind. "There might be Shadows. And you might travel, Del, and Nik might Dream, but if you're something like a Dreamwalker, then separating you should help."

Light blooms, and the room is gone.

They stand in the middle of a meadow, flowers bright around them, the grass as high as Carolyn's knees. There are no clouds to hide the sun, and Carolyn sneezes in the sudden brightness.

Nikita takes a shuddering breath, slowly shaking Heather's hands from her shoulders as she turns to look at where Shawn stands. He's poised as if to run toward her; Delilah clings to Carolyn's hands.

Nikita's smile falters. "This is not how I planned for my night to go. I just wanted to get out of the room and test out that whole 'maybe I'll sleep better around Heather' hypothesis." She raises one hand slowly and wiggles her fingers. "Hi. I'm Nik."

Delilah squeezes Carolyn's hand tightly. "Del," she says. She reaches out her free hand and carefully runs it over the top of the flowers, brow furrowed deeply. "This isn't real."

"This is the first lucid dreamlike hallucination I've had," Nikita says, a hint of laughter in her voice. "Oh, God, I'm going to go insane. It's going to happen. Everything they told me about being a Dreamwalker—about the way we can lose our grip—it's coming true."

"Sam's not a Dreamwalker," Delilah says, and Carolyn shakes her head, following her train of thought: maybe this is what happened then, too.

"I don't think so," she agrees, because it wasn't exactly like this, "but I know someone who can help him find out."

Delilah nods, still looking out over the horizon. "I'm not a Dreamwalker, either. Because this is different than what happens to me. When I go, I go. All of me goes right on in. Can you get into other people's dreams from here, Nik?"

Nikita's mouth falls open slightly. "Um. I've never tried. Like I said, this is the most coherent I've been while Dreaming. And, um, I have absolutely no idea how to get back."

"We need to wake up," Heather says urgently. "You went over this with your mentor, right?"

"What?" Nikita blinks, looks at her. "What do you mean?"

"If you're Dreaming," Shawn repeats Heather's words, careful and slow, "then you need to wake up. We all need to wake up. Is this even possible? You can't take anyone with you, can you, Del?"

Delilah doesn't answer, gripping Carolyn's hand tightly.

Carolyn's never told that part of the story, and she's not going to now. She inhales roughly, then exhales. "Weird. Right?"

"Right," Delilah echoes.

"Wake up," Shawn says, and it feels like an order.

When Carolyn glances over, he's gone; only the four of them are left in the field of flowers.

"Oh." Nikita stands with her mouth slightly open.

"Wake up," Carolyn whispers, trying to order herself to do it. She imagines a Tarot card, tries to think of one in front of her, like in the farmhouse, but nothing happens. No Wheel of Fortune. No picture of her room. Nothing but the soft whisper of wind through the grass, the feel of it on her skin. Nothing but Delilah still squeezing her hand hard enough to hurt.

Carolyn squeezes back harder, forcing Delilah's fingers together. She closes her eyes, clenches her other hand, and digs her nails into her palms. "Wake up," she says again, more forcefully. "Nikita. Delilah. Heather. Wake up!"

When she opens her eyes, her cheek stings, and Shawn stands in front of her. He lowers his hand and shifts his gaze to Delilah.

Carolyn disengages, stepping away from them both. The storm rages outside, and she's certain that hail is striking the side of the house. Lightning slices through the darkness. Girls call out, yelling to each other for candles and flashlights; she wonders how long they were gone. Just a few minutes, probably, even though it feels like a lifetime.

She doesn't want to slap Nikita or Heather, so she grips their shoulders instead, letting her fingers pinch, her nails bite, into the soft muscle. "Wake up," she yells, shaking them once, sharply.

Nikita gasps, and Heather crumples, dropping to sit on the floor before Carolyn can catch her. Nikita follows her down, her head in her hands as she curls in on herself.

The thunder booms once more, then the rain stops abruptly.

The silence echoes in the aftermath, then the shouts begin again.

Heather touches Nikita's cheek gently. "It's okay. You pulled it in."

"I shouldn't have had to," Nikita grumbles. "I don't know what—" She looks up as Delilah approaches and crouches in front of her. Delilah reaches for her, and Nikita scoots backward into the hallway. "No."

"I'm not a Dreamwalker," Delilah says softly. "I promise. I've checked. I don't get lost in my own mind."

"Neither do I, usually," Nikita counters. "You're something, aren't you?"

"I'm a Mage," Delilah tells her. Nikita stares at her, and Delilah's gaze drops. She rocks on her heels, walks back into the room, and starts gathering her things. Shawn is shoving sleeping bags into their duffles. "My innate Talent is the ability to go physically into the Dreamscape. All of me—I don't leave anything behind."

"Just into the Dreamscape, or into other people's heads too?" It's funny how offended Heather looks. Of all people!

"Just the Dreamscape, unless someone else comes to me and brings their dreams along," Delilah says. "It's usually… It doesn't happen often. It hasn't happened since high school. Until recently. That's part of the weird."

"Does Pawel kn—?"

"No," Carolyn interrupts.

Heather is silent while Delilah and Shawn pack and Nikita crawls onto Heather's bed. "He should," Heather finally says.

Carolyn's not sure she can argue that point. She's not sure how to explain.

"Figure it out," Heather tells her.

A knock on the door and Cass is there, a flashlight in one hand, her lit-up phone in the other. "Power's off in all of Townhouse Row, but the rest of campus has power."

"We need to go to a motel or something." Shawn shoulders his duffle, glances at Delilah, then picks up hers as well.

Cass blinks, staring at the two of them. "Did something happen?"

Silence.

"Hey." Mac leans in past Cass. "You guys all right in here? Trish and I are—"

"We were just heading out." Shawn touches Delilah, tries to nudge her to the door.

"We need to get them to a motel," Carolyn says. Nikita and Heather are both on Heather's bed, leaning into each other. Though they seem okay now, Carolyn can't unsee the way they crumpled when they exited the Dream. "How bad is it out?"

"We'll take Trish's truck," Mac says. "It'll be crowded, but at least it has all-wheel drive. You don't want to take a car out right now. The roads around campus are a mess, and I don't know how far the storm stretched."

Cass takes Delilah's bag from Shawn, who blinks in apparent surprise and lets it go. "I know a place that's cheap and decent," Cass says, "and they don't care who you are as long as you're at least eighteen and can pay."

Cass is halfway down the stairs before she turns, bag swinging as she plants her hands on her hips. She glares at everyone who stands there without following. "What? I'm particular. I like nice places, and I hated having a roommate when I was a freshman. No one wants to be sexiled, right?"

"Yet she sexiles Chris on a regular basis," Mac mutters.

"He and Dax have an agreement," Cass says. "Are you coming or not? Trish! We need your truck. Yes, with you in it. How else would we get anywhere?"

"Six people aren't going to fit in Trish's truck," Carolyn says, because someone has to be practical. Someone has to think about reality when the world is crashing down. "If we put everyone in her truck, we'll need to bring Delilah and Shawn back to their car when it's safe out."

"We'll make it work." Mac motions for Shawn and Delilah to head downstairs, closing the door so that Nikita and Heather are locked away. Safe, Carolyn thinks. Or at least better.

They'll make it work. That'll do for now.

13

THE PLACE CASS directs them to is far enough away that it's an uncomfortable drive in Trish's truck; Cass sits on Mac's lap in the front passenger seat, and Carolyn is sandwiched between Delilah and Shawn on the back bench seat. Shawn's thigh against hers is too warm, and Delilah sits stiffly until they're in the parking lot of the motel, a few miles away from the school.

"So you can feel her," Carolyn says quietly. "You and Nikita, conflicting."

"I am under control, thanks." Delilah's voice is tight. When Carolyn holds her hand out, palm up, Delilah grabs it, gripping tightly. Carolyn squeezes, though she doubts it does any good.

The locks on the doors pop open, and Trish climbs down and opens the door for Delilah. Carolyn follows her out, using the running board to step down. It's a big truck with large tires and a rumbling diesel engine. The tow hitch on the back looks too heavy to lift, and like someone could use it to commit murder.

Carolyn stands at the back of the truck, looking down at the hitch, because it's either stay in the stinging, wet rain or follow Shawn into the motel office. She'd rather stay here with Delilah and Mac while Cass and Trish make sure that Shawn's okay.

"It's not bad," Delilah says. Carolyn's not sure whether she means the motel or the way she feels around Nikita, so she just blinks and waits. Delilah crosses her arms tightly, shrugging her shoulders. "This place," she clarifies. "I've been in worse motels. Remember that road trip we did up to Maine? There was that place with the creepy statue outside the office."

It was the summer after junior year, and they'd all been drunk on the freedom of having their licenses and access to a car. "We got two rooms," Carolyn says softly, remembering the faded comforters and the threadbare carpet. "Me and Shawn, and you and Sam. So we could have privacy."

"Then Sam got food poisoning."

"And Shawn ended up in your room with him because Sam said he needed a guy to help him. And you and I snuck into the pool at midnight, swam for an hour, and then passed out in the same bed." Carolyn smiles slightly at the memory of waking up sprawled uncomfortably, her T-shirt still damp and stuck to her body. "My hair was crackling from the chlorine because I didn't wash it right away."

"Why didn't Kit go on that trip?" Delilah wonders.

Carolyn remembers. It was right after they'd paired off, and she'd fought with Kit about the camping trip. He claimed he was a fifth wheel, that he didn't fit into the group anymore. She'd said it wasn't like that, that she wanted him—her brother, her twin—along. She hadn't wanted to go without him.

And if Kit had come, he could have stayed with her and Shawn. She hadn't needed the privacy as much as Sam and Del had.

"There's no creepy statue here." Mac's gaze is fixed on the office door. "There might be something somewhere; I can look around if it'd make you feel more comfortable."

Delilah snickers. "No, really, this place looks pretty nice. I'll be okay." She presses her lips together, smile faltering. "Will your friend be okay? Is that how you ended up with an ice storm last November?"

Carolyn looks at Mac, who looks back at her. "Essentially, yes," Carolyn says, and refuses to elaborate. She's not sure what the protocol is here—by rights, it's Nikita's story to tell.

"I've got the key; we're in room 403!" Shawn yells across the parking lot, waving something he's holding. A real key, maybe, instead of a card. Strangely old school.

Mac reaches into the truck and pulls out both bags. "I'll meet you there," she says, pointing to the fourth floor. There are stairs up the side of the building, leading to a walkway lined by doors, and Mac heads around the truck, hidden from view as soon as she crosses to the other side.

Carolyn's pretty sure Mac isn't taking the stairs. It must be nice.

They meet the others halfway across the parking lot, and Mac's long gone. Carolyn's surprised by the show of Talent in front of Delilah and Shawn, but she supposes this is normal for Mac. Carolyn wonders how many times she's failed to observe what Mac can do because she didn't think about it and didn't know the truth.

"See," Cass says as they open the door to the room, "it's nice."

It is. The room has a clean laminate floor, and the bright white comforter on the bed looks like it's been bleached well enough that no bugs could live in it. The walls are a soft, peaceful shade of blue, and the art hanging behind the bed looks like it was painted in the current decade, not fifty years ago. Delilah pushes through the room, heading straight for the bathroom at the back. She calls out, "Even the bathroom's nice. It's a hot tub with jets, and it's clean."

"I told you. I wasn't going to some dump with Dax just for sex," Cass points out.

"Do you still come here?" Mac asks, adding quickly, "Maybe you should. So Chris can have the room to himself once in a while. Or you could set up some kind of timeshare so that Chris and Alaric can sexile you instead."

"I love you all, and I love living in the house, but this is why I'm getting an apartment next year," Cass says blandly. "Alone. With Dax."

"That's not what 'alone' means," Delilah says.

Carolyn covers her mouth so Cass can't see her smile.

Shawn grabs the bags, drops them on the bed, and starts digging through for something.

Carolyn's phone buzzes in her pocket and she pulls it out. "Unknown Number" flashes on the screen in sync with each buzz. She touches the button and holds it to her ear. "Hello?"

She expects silence or the tinny sound of an autodialer connecting her to an operator.

She gets heavy breathing.

Carolyn licks her lips, aware that everyone's watching her. She cradles the phone in both hands, giving whoever it is one more chance. "Hello?"

"Are you okay?"

Sam's voice rolls through her like an echo of the past. Her eyes go wide, her heart thumping. Her legs shake, and someone guides her to the bed, nudges her until she sits on the edge. "Sam? Samson?"

"Carolyn," he says. "Are you okay? I need to know if you're okay."

"I'm okay," she gets out, and the breath on the other end eases, slows, becoming deep and even.

"You don't like heights," he says. "I worried about you on the Ferris wheel."

Chill twists in her chest. "How—?"

"You got away from the Shadows, right?" he asks, voice still softly urgent. "Don't let the Shadows get to you, Carolyn. They'll come for you, sweep right over you, and take you into them. You'll never get back."

"I'm okay," she says again, as if saying it will warm her, make her feel less like her world has shattered. "Samson. *Sam.* Why are you—? Where are you—?"

"I had to borrow a phone. I still remember your number." There's a thumping somewhere in the distance. Sam yells, but it's muffled by something covering the phone. His voice returns, quiet and clear. "The Shadows are in the house, Carolyn. You got out, right? That happened? It gets…it's confused sometimes. In my head. I don't know what's real. But you and I— we share things, still. We're stuck, Carolyn. You're stuck with me."

A crash, and Sam hisses, "Shit."

The phone goes dead.

Carolyn shivers, and her phone falls through her fingers to the floor.

"Weird?" Delilah says, and Carolyn registers that Delilah's sitting next to her on one side, Mac pressed close on the other. Shawn's behind her, close enough that Carolyn knows she could reach out and touch him, but far enough that he hasn't completely encroached.

She appreciates that.

Cass is sitting cross-legged on the floor. She holds Carolyn's phone out to her, but Carolyn won't take it. Not yet. She waves it away, and Cass edges back, giving her more room.

"The weird got weirder," Carolyn admits. "That was Samson. I think he stole a phone to call me."

They're linked, he said. She wonders what he thinks they share. How he knows about the Ferris wheel and the house.

"I had a dream last Saturday night," she says slowly. "I dreamed about Tarot cards, and I dreamed about a house, and I think maybe I went to the house. Traveled to the house," she clarifies, glancing at Delilah. "I was attacked by a wolf, and Sam seems to think the Shadows are there. I haven't talked to him since high school. I only told a few people about the dream. But I'm going—" She hesitates, because this feels out of control. Like her world is rolling from the past into the future without her permission, and she's just along for the ride.

"You're going where?" Shawn's hand falls on her shoulder, and Carolyn flinches. He pulls away.

"To Alaric and Drea's home," she says flatly. "They're Clan, and their father's a wolf. I might have gone to a house there. I need to know if it was real."

"And somehow Sam knows about this, too," Delilah says.

Carolyn finally takes her phone from Cass, looks at the recent call log. "Unknown Number." There's no way to reach out to him, no way to ask questions. She's not sure Sam would be coherent even if she could actually get to him instead of to whichever administrator owns the phone he borrowed. "Yeah. Somehow Sam knows about this, too."

"So, when do we leave?" Shawn asks.

Nerves coil in Carolyn's gut. "You stay here tonight," she says firmly. "Call me in the morning, and we can pick you up for breakfast at a diner or something. Then we take you to your car, and you go home. I told you, I'm busy on Sunday. I have plans."

"No," Shawn says. He's put space between them again. "Your weird and our weird seem tied together, and if it's all related to that place, then we should go with you."

"Maybe it has something to do with my traveling," Delilah adds. "If you're traveling through Dreams, and I'm traveling into them—"

"Stop." Carolyn raises her hands and pushes everyone away. She gets off the bed, walks to the wall, and wraps her arms around herself. Centers herself. "I'm going outside for five minutes, and you are all going to stop pushing. Because this is too—" The words stick in her throat, and she looks at Delilah and Shawn. "I can't. Not again. Okay?"

She doesn't wait for an answer, stepping around Cass to get to the door.

It's cold outside, but she doesn't care, leaning against the edge of the rail and looking out over the parking lot. It's not a great view. A truck's pulled in and two people lean against it, idly kissing. Carolyn only counts five vehicles in the lot, including Trish's truck; it's not a busy night at the motel. She can't think why they got stuck on the fourth floor unless the guy in the office just wanted them out of the way.

Six college kids coming in during an ice storm. If he's got any ability to recognize Talent, of course he wanted them out of the way. Probably expects to be able to charge for damages to the room once they're done.

Carolyn reaches into her pocket, takes out her phone, and stares at the last call still sitting in her call log. She scrolls past it, finds Drea's number, and presses the button to dial.

"Hey, Carolyn."

"How freaked out would your parents be if there were more people on Sunday?" Carolyn already knows the answer. She's heard enough about Theobald to know that bringing more Mages into his space will only cause trouble.

Drea's silence is confirmation.

"I had this friend in high school." Carolyn hears the door open behind her; she glances over her shoulder to see Trish step out then close the door behind herself. She waits until Trish is leaning on the rail next to her, then shows her the phone and puts Drea on speaker. "And a lot of shit happened. Some really strange, scary shit, and it broke all of us. Literally broke Samson; he's in a facility now because he's not sure where reality is anymore. Someone once told me that he flickers, but that's beside the point. The thing is, he called me. And it just all—it came back around to the dream I had."

"That might be of my home," Drea says.

"Yes. And my friends—the ones who were there when everything went haywire back in high school—have also had some things happen around them. So they want to see this place, too." And they want to see Carolyn see it; she knows how Shawn's mind works. He's gathering data, putting all the pieces in place. Readying information to see how he can use it for himself.

He's changed. She has to remind herself that they've all changed. Grown. Moved on.

"I think it would be good for Delilah to go," Carolyn says quietly. "And if she does, we're stuck with Shawn. They have their own car, so it's not like we need to get them there."

"You could ride with—"

Carolyn laughs sharply. "No. Really. I'd rather ride with you guys in that minivan Dax keeps borrowing. I don't want to be trapped in a car with just Delilah and Shawn. It wouldn't go well."

"Okay."

Carolyn's quiet. She glances at Trish, who shrugs, then looks at the phone. "Okay to which part?" she asks.

"Okay, you don't have to go in their car," Drea says. "And okay, they can come. I'll talk to Alaric, get everything figured out. But you—are you okay right now? You sound…"

"I'm with her," Trish says, raising her voice to be heard as she leans closer to Carolyn and the phone. "Me, Cass, and Mac are with her, and we're leaving Shawn and Delilah at a motel. They can't stay with Heather and her, which is a long story, but the short version is named Nikita."

"That explains a lot about the way tonight has gone," Drea says dryly.

"We're getting ready to leave her friends here and bring Carolyn back to the house if you want to meet us there," Trish offers. "Give us twenty minutes or so. We'll be in my room or Mac's."

"I'll see you there." The call cuts out as a muffled conversation begins in the background.

Trish nods at the closed door to the motel room. "Say your goodnights and make sure your friends are set for now. We're taking you home."

14

THEY END UP in Mac's room under the eaves. It's a tiny space, but every other room has a roommate already in it, and the last thing Carolyn wants right now is see Heather's accusing look because Carolyn's friend triggered Nikita's Talent.

Carolyn sits in the desk chair after Mac pushes her toward it. Mac perches on the edge of the bed, while Drea, Cass, and Trish take the floor. The desk chair rolls slightly but can't go far—there's nowhere for it to go. The place is cramped, and Carolyn is well aware that they are all watching her. Waiting. And she's not sure what they're waiting for.

"Sooo." Drea draws the one word out. "Sunday."

"I want to go," Cass says.

"No." Drea gets one hand up between her and Cass, and Mac leans forward to slap a hand over Cass's mouth. Drea switches to pointing a finger at her. "My father is a really, really big wolf, and he's been on a hair trigger lately, and do you really want to play red riding hood? Because while I am all in for helping my Big figure something out, this plan is getting out of hand. I don't care if your boyfriend is driving; this is not your adventure, Cass."

"Who goes needs to be kept to a minimum." Mac's tone is no-nonsense. She slowly takes her hand from Cass's mouth, and Cass stays silent. Mac sits back on her hands. "The minimum seems to be getting bigger and bigger—is there anyone who can be left home?"

"Kit's going because I'm going," Carolyn says. "And he should go. Because if what's happened is part of my Talent, it might be part of his too. We're twins. Dax has to go because he's driving. Alaric's going to distract his father while Drea takes us out to the house."

"Corbin's going because he's my backup. No offense, but I am not taking you to the Berman house alone." Drea wraps her arms around her knees and hunches her shoulders, shuddering. "That place is creepy, and it's only been worse since the Shadow disappeared. I'm sure you Mages have some way of dealing with things, but I want Clan there. Corbin's not just my boyfriend, he's my brother's right hand."

"That's six for the minivan," Mac says as Trish counts them off on her fingers. "And your two friends in their own car, right, Carolyn?" When she nods, Mac goes on. "So, no Chris for Alaric. No me. No Trish. And no you, Cass."

"Why do your friends need to go?" Cass asks. "I mean, I get what they said, and okay, so they think they're involved. But why do they need to be there? How are they actually involved? They weren't even here when it happened."

And there it is, the question that, if answered, will lead back to everything that happened before. Carolyn jerks when Trish sets a hand on her knee, and she inhales roughly. "They weren't here," Carolyn agrees. "But there's this whole history between us. We did this thing back when we were in high school, like three years ago, and Del's right. This might be similar. Or the same. I really hope it's not the same."

"Because then it would mean this all started three years ago?" Cass asks, and Carolyn shakes her head.

Mac raises a hand slowly. "Pretty sure that this all started a decade or so years ago. When I became the poster child for a magical generation, thanks."

"Because what we did three years ago ended with me sleeping for three days. Sam's been in a facility ever since," Carolyn says quietly. "We didn't get out of that sane, not really. And there are parts of it that Sam and Shawn don't know. Parts our parents don't know. We made mistakes, and it blew up in our faces, and Sam paid the price. I haven't even heard from Shawn and Delilah since we left for school freshman year. And now she's scared. They're both scared. That's why they got in touch with me. And to be honest, I was already freaking out. Now it's worse."

Trish slides closer, rests her head against Carolyn's thigh, and wraps her hands around her leg. She pats her gently. Carolyn touches her head, then threads her fingers through Trish's long hair.

It feels weird, slick. Carolyn glances down, but Mac distracts her before she can get a good look.

"Like I said, I think all of this started when I Emerged," Mac says. "Things got really crazy for a while, right? Then things settled down, and we were able to sort of go back to normal. But now things are getting strange again, like something else is starting to break through."

"Like Shadows," Drea and Cass point out at the same time.

"Exactly." Mac glances at Carolyn, wrinkles her nose. "I know it won't help you to talk about it, but do you think it'll help if we know what we're walking into? Just in case it has something to do with what happened to you?"

There are parts Carolyn can leave out, parts they don't need to know. She's pretty sure that the underlying issues between herself and Shawn aren't part of the story, but for all she knows, they are. Has anyone actually researched whether sexually influenced magic is real?

Thorne, probably, but Carolyn's not going to ask.

"We've all known each other a long time," Carolyn says slowly. "Kit and I are twins, and Delilah's and Shawn's moms are friends. So when I met Delilah when we were five, the four of us got together. And we were those weird kids. We were all Mages, and we all knew we were, but it was before the Emergence. We had to be quiet about it, but there were times when things got out, like when a teacher called Kit 'Satanic' because she found his Tarot deck. But mostly it was pretty good, because we had each other."

She licks her lips; she wants to tell this her way. She wants to leave out the bullying, the psychological damage they each withstood over their younger years. It wasn't easy, for so many reasons, but that's not part of this. She's sure it's not part of this.

"Then in fourth grade, Samson came to town, and everything changed." Carolyn twists her hands together. "Looking back on it, the timing was…is… Maybe it meant something. It didn't feel like it then, just like everything became perfect. Kit met Samson and had a new best friend. Sam became a part of our group. And that spring—" She glances up at Mac.

"Well, then the Emergence happened. Suddenly everyone knew we weren't the *weird* kids, we were the *magical* kids. And it didn't mean much—not right away. It stopped a lot of the bullshit; most groups didn't want us to join them when we were in middle school, and that was okay with us. The Emergence gave us space to just be us. To figure out who we were."

"I'm getting a vibe here," Trish says idly. "Have you ever seen the movie *The Craft*?"

Carolyn ducks her head; she's heard the comparison before. "Right vibe," she says. "We weren't that powerful, but we were *us*, and by the time high school came around, everyone knew who we were. They thought they could get love spells from me, but it was just Tarot readings. Samson and Delilah started dating for real, and Shawn and I started dating, too. Kit figured himself out in middle school, and came out for high school, and we were all…we were powerful. We didn't have any actual power, and we didn't do anything to anyone, but we had a lot of respect. And if you know anything about magic, you know that half of it is—"

"—belief," Cass says flatly. "They respected you and thought you had power over them—"

"We did." The tips of Carolyn's fingers have gone white. "I didn't really care. Kit didn't mind, either, because it meant they didn't pay attention to the details of his past. Sam loved it. And Delilah and Shawn—they kind of got off on it. They loved being popular, loved being in charge. They loved that if they wanted things to go a certain way, they would." And Shawn hated it when things were out of his control. When things weren't perfect or exactly what he expected. Life was supposed to be a certain way. He'd learned to accept some things, but he didn't like surprises.

"What happened?" Trish's voice is soft. Gentle and slow, the drawl easing into the air.

"We tried too hard," Carolyn says. "It was the fall of our senior year, and people wanted more and more from us. They had creative ideas about what magic could do, and we were trying to stay on top. I don't have a good grounding in traditional magic—neither does Kit. Samson's innate abilities were with light, and Del and Shawn didn't have any innate abilities. And we had people asking about so many things, wanting us to do so many different things. And Shawn had this idea that it'd be a great senior prank if we laid an illusion over the entire school. He thought that because Kit and I knew the cards so well, and Samson could bend light, and he and Del could build these illusions…and he got complicated with it. He built in so many levels and layers, spells that would change how people interacted with the world, and it was stupid, but we were popular. We had to make it amazing, right? It was going to be the best prank ever, and, well…it tested our abilities. It was something new and different and, if we could do it, no one would ever forget us."

"And?" Mac nudges.

Carolyn laughs dryly. "I don't even know how to explain it. We… It failed. Kit said afterward that, from his perspective, Samson started screaming, Delilah disappeared, I dropped to the ground not breathing, and Shawn had a seizure. By the time I woke up three days later, Samson was already hospitalized in a facility that could handle his random outbursts and periodic descents into a catatonic state. Shawn had been treated and released. And Delilah was back like she'd never been gone."

"Did anyone see the illusion?" Cass asks. She sits with her knees drawn up, fists under her chin as she props it above her knees.

"Not exactly." Carolyn pushes to her feet, reaches up to touch the low ceiling of Mac's room, and drops back into the chair. "I hate your room, Mac."

"I love it." Mac pats the bed next to her. "Come lie down. Stare at the ceiling and tell it the rest of your story."

"How do you know I'm not done?" Carolyn does as she says anyway, stretching out along Mac's bed, arms behind her head, staring up at the sloped ceiling. At the lowest point, it's almost close enough to touch.

"You don't feel done, and I don't even have to be Heather to know that." Mac rubs her shoulder. "Tell the ceiling."

"Delilah went into…we think it's a Dreamland. Someplace between here and elsewhere. Not somewhere real. Like she said, she can't take people with her, not exactly. And she doesn't go into anyone else's dreams. She just goes there and waits around for things to come to her." Carolyn chews on her lip. "That first time, it was me. I ended up with her. I wasn't inside my own body for a while, we think, until they had me breathing on my own. It was like I was electrocuted at first, and then like someone drained every ounce of magic out of me. So I stayed with her, and she stayed with me, until I was safe. Stable."

She raises a hand and tries to bring out the palm full of fire. It's not her strength, never was, and has been harder since high school. "I haven't had a lot of strength for traditional magic since then, just for my cards. Kit doesn't know about this. Don't tell him. He really wants to work on traditional ritual, and I want to do that with him. Even if I suck at it."

"You said 'someone.'" Cass spreads her hands when everyone looks at her. "I was listening, and that was a specific word choice. She said it was like *someone* drained the magic out of her, not some*thing*. And that's a notable difference. Was it Delilah?"

"Shawn." Carolyn's voice is flat. "That's why it's significant that he's gone powerless now. He's lost whatever he got from me. And maybe from Samson, too; I don't know if that's what drove him mad. And Delilah's traveling again. She only did it once or twice after that happened, and I was never with her." Until tonight, until Nikita walked into that room.

"So what you did is different than what Delilah does." Drea tilts her head back, looking up at the ceiling. "Which is…different from what Nikita does…how?"

"'Dreamwalkers' would be better termed 'Dreamweavers,'" Mac says, lightly tapping the back of Drea's head. "Didn't Pawel give you that speech in the intro class? They're rare, and they fall into Dreams and can take people with them, but mentally only." She touches the side of her head. "It's all in the Dream, with no physical aspect. They weave the Dreamscapes together and create the Dream. So if Delilah goes in physically and is actually inside the Dreamscape, that's different."

"I went through the Dream," Carolyn says, because it's feeling more and more like that's what she did. "I think I started out dreaming, but I ended up going somewhere else. That's why we're going to see the place at Drea's. So we can see if I went there during the Dream. I guess that would make me more like Mac."

Mac holds up both hands. "I can't go that far. A few blocks, maybe a mile or possibly two, sure, but even going that that far gets hard. Worst I've ever felt was trying to get me and another person out of a bad spot in the Mideast, and I was doing these huge jumps. Teleporting all the way to Haverhill? Not happening."

Cass's brow is furrowed deeply, her lips pursed in a moue of concentration. Drea knocks into her with her knee. "What is it?"

Cass smiles then, features smoothing abruptly. "Nothing. I was just thinking about it, and honestly, it's kind of confusing. I thought Emerging Talents were either the same as existing Talents or completely different from them and each other, not just variations on a theme. Like I've only ever known about one teleporter, but Clan are Clan."

"There are variations," Drea says dryly. "Haven't you been paying attention to single-form Clan Lineages, or anything else we've ever talked about?"

"But this is—" Cass cuts off, shaking her head as she gestures at Carolyn. "It's weird. Like Delilah kept saying. It's just weird."

"Everything's weird lately." It's the first thing Trish has said in a long while, and Carolyn realizes that Trish is still sitting by the chair, leaning against it like Carolyn's still there.

And she remembers— "What's up with your hair?"

Trish reaches up to touch her own hair, eyes wide as she looks at Carolyn. For a moment, Carolyn thinks she shouldn't have asked, should have waited until they were in private. Trish's lips press thinly together, the line of her shoulders tense before they sag slowly.

"I Emerged," she mutters. "Over break."

"What?" Carolyn rolls to her side while Mac slides off the bed and pulls Trish into a hug.

"It's this thing, all over me." Trish gestures from her head to her toes. "Like a shield. A forcefield maybe. I must have some autonomic control over it because I can eat, but I can't feel hot or cold in my mouth, and everything tastes flat. I don't feel hot or cold on my skin, either. Nothing burns me, and forces are... Well, Sera hauled off and punched me, and I felt the impact, but it spread out. It didn't exactly tickle, but it didn't hurt, either. And it didn't bruise me." She grumbles under her breath, "And it's played holy hell with my fingers. I can't play anything right."

"Oh, hon." Mac holds on tight, and Trish buries her face against Mac's throat, shoulders shaking. "Why didn't you tell anyone?"

"I told Sera." The words are muffled. "Might've mentioned that my momma's not a fan of magic? That complicates everything, so I haven't wanted to talk about it. I just want to learn how to deal with it. Turn it off. As useful as it might be, I don't plan on getting hit or burned often, and I'd really like to play my guitar and have sex again."

Cass reaches out and gently lays a hand on Trish's shoulder. Mac shifts to make room, and Drea burrows in to join the hug. Carolyn stays mostly out of reach, but she gets a hand onto Trish's head, fingers combing through her hair, and she wonders what it feels like. If it soothes, or if it's nothing, just random contact without any sensation behind it.

The level of chaos seems to be climbing, and Carolyn doesn't like it. Too many people are unhappy, and that's never a good thing.

15

"THEY'RE GOING HOME after this, right?" Kit puts his phone in his pocket and leans over to speak quietly to Carolyn; for this, at least, she's glad they're in the farthest-back row of the minivan. It's worth the squished knees to be able to speak somewhat privately.

Not that Dax is paying attention to anything but the road and his conversation with Alaric. Carolyn thinks they're talking about football, but she could be wrong.

"Shawn and Delilah?" Carolyn twists to look through the back window toward where Shawn's car follows them. "They are. You know why they're coming with us."

"I do, but I don't like it. Are you okay with this?"

It's a valid question. Carolyn shakes her head, aware that Drea's glancing back at them. She shifts from shaking her head to a shrug and a nod. "I have to be. If the things that have happened to each of us are tied together, we're better off having as much information as possible, right?"

"Mm." Kit makes a non-committal noise. "I don't want you getting hurt again. How are things going with Shawn being here?"

"They're okay." It isn't even a lie. "When I think about the messy relationship parts... He was a dick at the end, but when it comes down to it, I don't think we ever really understood each other. He's kind of with Del now, and that works for them. For the magical parts, he's as messed up as the rest of us."

"I'm not sure that makes me feel any better," Kit says dryly, "or any more comfortable with you doing rituals with them. I mean, we had an epic falling out. The kind of epic that can only happen with your childhood best friends, right? It's been a few years, but we're all still the same people."

"Are we?" Carolyn licks her lips and looks out the window at the road going by. "We're changing, I think. Magically and emotionally." She doesn't want to give Kit a chance to point out how much she's retreated, partly because she doesn't think she has. This is who she's always been, it's just that no one noticed before. "I mean, look at you, going on a double date."

"It ended up being more of a triple date. Ish." A smile flickers, and Kit shrugs and spreads his hands. "Me and Serina, Rory and Darrik, and Shane brought his best friend Jessica to round out the group. He didn't want to feel like a fifth wheel, and she seems pretty cool." He chuckles, raising a hand to an inch or so above his head. "She's taller than me, and has broader shoulders. And she laughs a lot. She and Darrik started talking about farming—I didn't know Darrik had ever been on a farm, but apparently he has, when he was younger. And Jessica's family are dairy farmers."

"And Serina?" Carolyn's trying. She's trying really, really hard to be supportive. "How is it with her?"

"You don't actually want to know."

Carolyn wrinkles her nose. "You're right. And you're wrong. If you're into her, I want to see you happy. So how are things with Serina?"

"I haven't told her yet." Kit's voice is low. He touches his pocket, then settles in his seat again after. "Other than that, things are good. We went over to Teas Please and hung out talking until Nate's shift was over. He made fun of Serina for coming there when she wasn't working."

"Hey, Ric." Corbin's voice is loud and abrupt, interrupting their quiet conversation as he leans forward to tap the front passenger seat. Drea glances back at Carolyn and shrugs her shoulders.

Alaric puts the phone down. "What?"

"Will we be back by nine?" Corbin checks his own phone. "Yeah, nine. I need to be somewhere."

"Oh?" Drea asks. "You didn't have to come with us if you already had plans," she points out, although Carolyn knows that's probably a lie.

Corbin gives her a dark look. "I'm with you and Alaric, aren't I? Of course I'm going to be here when you need me. I just want to get back in time for the AKT party tonight. It's the start of rush."

"Wasn't rush back in the fall?" Alaric asks, eyebrows furrowing.

"Not at VIT. Apparently when you're at a technical institute, they think you need a semester to learn how to college before you go joining a frat." Corbin shrugs. "They might be right. I wouldn't have rushed in the fall. I like the people in AKT, but I didn't really know them until we started work on the spring show."

"When does that open?" Drea's posture is relaxed, a contrast to Alaric's tension.

"Spring show?" Alaric asks.

"Theater. Remember, Corbin's been doing theater at VIT?" Drea pokes the back of Alaric's seat. "Keep up."

"You've joined a football fraternity; I'm going with co-ed and theater," Corbin says, leaning back with his arms behind his head. "And yes, they picked the letters because it's pronounced *act*." He pauses. "Apparently STG was already taken."

"STG," Kit muses.

"Stage," Drea whispers, and Kit nods.

"I'll do my best to get you back by nine," Dax says, his focus on the road, "but I'm not making any promises. It depends on how things go."

"If we need to rescue Alaric from Dad, we can do that," Drea offers.

"What's the spring show at VIT?" Dax asks. "Cass and I might get tickets."

"We're doing *Spring Awakening*. Apparently it's rare to get a good group of actors who can actually sing, so we're taking advantage of that by doing a musical. Half the cast is graduating in May, so if we don't get replacements, it's back to plays next year. I'm apprenticing with the house manager, so if you want to get group tickets, let me know. I can get you good seats. Not that there's a bad seat in the house—if you've never been in the VIT theater, we're almost in the round."

"I grew up in Valiant," Dax points out. "I've been in the theater. It was a school trip thing when I was in elementary school. When is it?"

"Two weeks." Corbin cranes his head to look back at Carolyn and Kit. "You guys are included. Get a group together. Just give me the numbers and which performance you want to see, and I'll have the tickets waiting in the box office."

"Serina might like that," Carolyn says.

Kit inhales, nodding slowly. "We could go together. You could go with us."

Carolyn recognizes his invitation for what it is—Kit's way of trying to get her to see Serina as a potential piece of Kit's life, not just a girl who used to wander through the sorority house.

It also sends her back to a time of her life when dating was a thing she did with friends, even if Kit didn't. When relationships were easier.

She answers his slow nod with one of her own. "Sure. If something else doesn't come up, and you want to organize it, you can count me in."

"Kit, if you want to fill the van, talk to me after this and we can figure something out," Dax offers. "Although if Chris and Alaric—"

"I don't like musicals." Alaric cuts him off. "Sorry, Corbin. Not speaking for Chris—if he wants to go, I'm not stopping him, but I don't want to go."

"Not offended at all. I've known you long enough not to worry about it," Corbin says easily. "Are you getting snappish because we're close to home?"

Alaric growls, and the sound shakes through Carolyn. She can feel it more than she can hear it.

"I'll take that as a yes," Corbin says. Drea reaches across the space between them, and they thread their fingers together. "So, what's our plan?"

"Drive in and drop off Alaric," Drea says. "When he runs up to the house, Dad'll come out to meet him. Mom knows we're coming, so she'll make sure Dad and Alaric are behaving, then meet us at the Berman house. We can only drive part of the way, then we'll park and walk the rest. That'll give Mom time to get there. You can fly ahead and make sure there isn't anything unexpected waiting for us."

Carolyn shivers. The wolf had been huge, terrifying. She doesn't want to meet it again.

"That's it?" Corbin says. "That's the plan? That's not much of a plan."

"After that, it hinges on Carolyn," Drea says, and they all look at her. Waiting.

Carolyn's throat is dry.

She coughs.

She fumbles her phone when it buzzes, and she checks her texts.

Are we there yet? Shawn says to tell you that you said it was close.

She quickly types back, *Almost there, just follow the minivan and don't run over the person or animal that gets out of it, okay?*

She's not sure how Alaric plans to do this, but she's positive that Shawn and Delilah need the warning.

"I don't have a plan," Carolyn says. "I just want to see if it looks like the place from my dream. And if it feels like it. And Delilah wants to see if it's part of the weirdness that's been happening."

"So you're saying we should be prepared for things to go haywire," Drea says slowly.

"I'm saying I have absolutely no idea," Carolyn responds, "but maybe. Yes. And if Delilah disappears, we shouldn't worry. She's done it before."

Kit finds her hand with his own, wraps around it tightly, and squeezes. "And if you disappear?"

"I've never done that," Carolyn says firmly. "It was just a dream for me." Maybe if she doesn't remind them how bad that dream was, it'll slip their minds. The look Kit gives her says that he remembers exactly how bad it was. She squeezes his hand back, trying to reassure him.

Her phone screen lights up again. *Are you okay?*

Carolyn runs her thumb across the screen. *Not really, no.* She's past lying to Delilah about this. *Does Shawn get anything out of this other than trying to get his talent back?*

She isn't surprised when Delilah doesn't respond.

"Next turn is our private road," Drea calls out.

Carolyn taps that into the phone, then she keeps her hand in Kit's as she twists to look out the window. She knows they're nowhere near the house, but she wants to see if anything looks or feels familiar. The trees grow close together, thick and dark. She barely spots the turn before Dax takes it, going from the main road onto a dirty pathway into the forest.

A howl shivers through her bones; Alaric's answering snarl echoes loudly inside the minivan. Dax slams on the brakes, and there's a squeal behind them as Shawn does the same and somehow avoids rear-ending them.

Alaric pushes his door open, shifting into a huge bear before he hits the ground. He rears up on his hind legs and roars as a wolf bursts out of the trees, skidding to a stop in front of the van and blocking their way. The wolf is easily large enough that its nose would reach Carolyn's chest if she stood in front of it. The teeth are sharp and bared in a furious growl as it stands head down, feet splayed, ready to attack. Carolyn has no doubt that if Alaric weren't out there, if the bear weren't standing in the way, the wolf would be rending pieces from the van.

The *whir-click* of the rear door sliding open is a shock of electronic sound; Carolyn jerks back as Drea climbs out, her hands up. "Dad!" she calls out.

"That's their dad?" Kit says quietly.

Dax nods.

Corbin's half out the door, but he pauses, turning around. "That's Theobald. You might want to stay in the van until we get this taken care of. Text your friends and let them know too." He jumps down from the van, body language loose and easy as he joins Drea and Alaric.

Carolyn's phone buzzes on cue. *What's going on?*

That's the wolf, she types back, and she hopes they understand what that means. How dangerous this is. *Alaric's the bear. Stay put.*

"What did you say?" Kit asks, leaning close.

Carolyn clings to his hand like a lifeline as she whispers in his ear, "That's it." She knows it's true even if it seems impossible. "That's the wolf from my dream."

What Lies Before

Fourth Position: Before

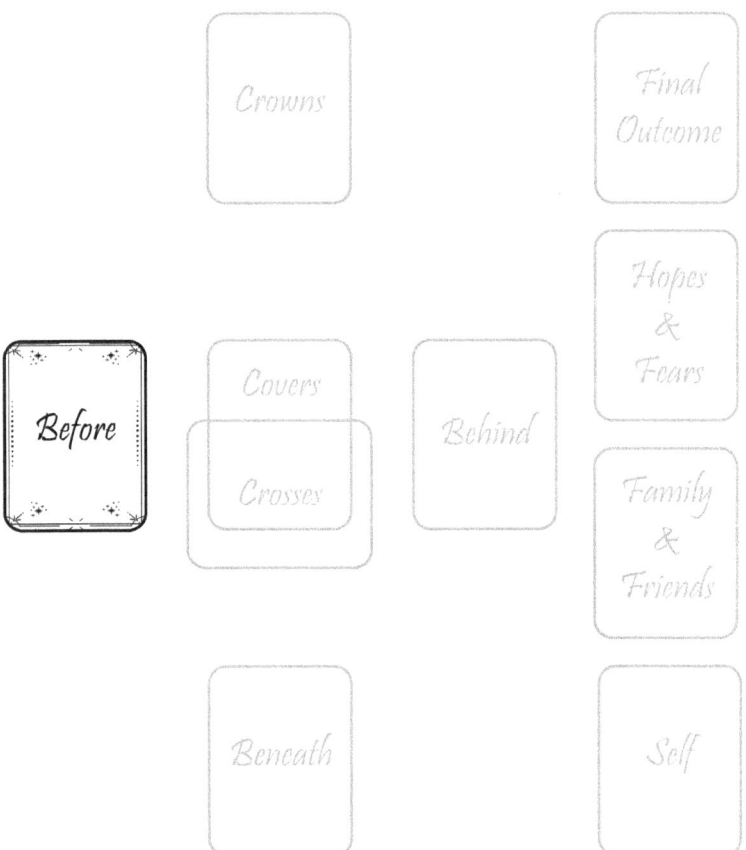

What lies before...

There are two futures that can be viewed at any time: that which lies before and that which will be the final outcome, perhaps years away. That which lies before is the querent's near future, occurring in days or weeks or, at most, months. The querent should be prepared for what's imminent, but even this may be changed if the querent is ready and able to do so.

Carolyn's Reading: Judgement

Three trumpets sound from above, calling all souls to judgement—to the resurrection. People who have been buried are shown breaking through the ground, throwing off their shackles, and rising up to meet a new day.

The querent can see that the past is indeed the past and that the future may be bright. This is a time to rejoice in the renewal that life brings, to accept things that have changed, and to move on. Latent abilities may flower, and transformations may occur. If a Talent is to Emerge, the querent will experience this in the coming days.

The querent should remember the past and look to it for advice, but the querent must learn to move beyond what has already happened: let painful events go and choose what to take with them into the new world that is the days to come. They must remember that there is a fresh, bright path to follow.

If a position is offered, accept it. If Talent grows, delight in it and cultivate it. If unfamiliar people arrive, befriend them and learn how they fit into your day-to-day life. Grow and be renewed.

The querent should trust their heart and know that their instinct will guide them.

Kit's Reading: The Fool

A gaily clad fool dances on the edge of a cliff, poised on the brink of falling. A dog dances with them, by their heels, as sun and moon shine together, bright in the background.

The querent stands upon the precipice, seemingly in a moment of perfect innocence. They dance above danger, heedless of what it might represent. It would only take a moment's inattention for them to fall— the dog might nip, a foot could slide along the cliff. And it is, indeed, a long way down. But the querent does not care; they may not even know.

This is a card of caution. Beware of being too frivolous, of not looking beyond your desires. There will be a cost that comes with them. Mania and exultation can bring about destruction; all it takes is one misstep.

16

CAROLYN HAS HER hand on the seatbelt. She clicks the button, but Kit's hand covers hers.

"Don't," he whispers.

She doesn't like sitting here, the side doors and passenger door to the minivan wide open. Dax is still in the driver's seat, and the engine rumbles. It's easy to feel protected by the walls of the van, but she also feels trapped, vulnerable should the wolf attack.

"Dad," Drea says.

The wolf snarls and sniffs the air. Carolyn swears it looks at her; breath catches in her chest, twisting tightly. Alaric growls, lumbering forward.

She wonders how angry Alaric would have to be to let the dragon out. She wonders if Alaric's parents even know about the dragon.

"Use your words, big guy," Corbin says, patting Alaric's furry shoulder. "You can't negotiate as a bear."

"The same goes for you, Dad," Drea adds.

A moment passes, tension hanging in the air, before the wolf and bear shift back to their human forms. Carolyn can see Alaric and Drea in their father, can find them in the shape of his face and the set of his jaw—Alaric, especially, with the same lines around his eyes.

"What are you doing here this time?" Theobald asks.

"I've come to see you. I have more information from Dayton, and I want to talk with you. Go over it." Alaric gestures at the van. "Dax gave me a ride out."

"And the others?" Theobald looks past Alaric, Drea, and Corbin. His gaze falls on Dax first, then shifts to Carolyn and Kit. He only glances at them before his gaze narrows and he looks at the car behind them. "I know the ghost-talker. I don't know the rest."

"Friends of ours," Corbin says easily. "Nothing to do with you, and nothing that's going to bother you. Dax is going to go talk to Orson, see if he's resting better yet. We're hoping he's finally gone on now that everything is peaceful. Carolyn's here to do me a favor. She reads cards, and I figured that if I want my fortune told, I want it done here, in the place that means the most to me. She'll get the best sense of what it is to be Clan here."

"And the others?" Theobald takes a step closer to the van, head lifted, nostrils flaring.

Alaric gets in his way, pushing him back. "Leave them be. We go into the world to learn how to live among non-Clan. It only makes sense that occasionally we're going to bring our friends home."

"Your brother didn't."

Alaric steps back, Drea's hand on his shoulder as she sidles closer. Corbin, Drea, and Alaric move together, becoming one unit to face Theobald.

"Maybe he should have," Corbin says baldly.

Alaric grunts.

"Stay on the roads," Theobald spits out. "Don't stray. Don't go anywhere without Corbin and Drea. I'll send your mother to you," he adds, and Drea nods.

Theobald melts back into the wolf and lopes away. In a breath, Alaric's an eagle, flying after him.

Carolyn exhales slowly as Drea and Corbin climb back into the car, Corbin taking the seat Alaric vacated.

"He left his bag with the documents," Dax points out.

Should we follow you? Delilah texts.

Carolyn sends back a thumbs-up emoji. *How much did you hear?*

Most of it. We had the windows cracked, but it was muffled. Is there anything we should know?

Carolyn snorts. *Nothing new. Theobald's pissed off, but we knew that would happen. We need to be careful.* She puts her phone back in her pocket before Delilah answers; there's nothing else to say yet.

"We'll swing by the house and pick up Mom," Drea says. "Since Dad played into our plans by showing up so quickly. He's getting more paranoid."

"He met us at the turn," Corbin says sharply. "He was listening specifically for invaders. It's as if he expected someone to come. Does he do that all the time now?"

Drea presses the heel of her hand to the bridge of her nose. "I don't think he was doing so when we were home over break, but maybe we just didn't notice because we were busy with the Gather and no one unexpected stopped by. Or maybe this is because of what happened at the Berman house. I don't know."

It could be Carolyn's fault, if she really came here.

"I'm glad he didn't sniff me," Carolyn says quietly, and Corbin twists in his seat to look at her.

"Keep going that way, you know how to get to the house," Corbin says to Dax, waving his hand at the dirt road ahead. Shawn's car follows them. "Carolyn, he was sniffing for all of you. He didn't recognize you, which may or may not be a good sign. We won't be able to say if you really came here until later, after we've been to the Berman house."

Carolyn can see homes down long drives off the sides of the road. Some are in clusters; some are on their own. The main road they're driving on delivers them to a huge home, mansion-sized, with long wings out to the sides. A tall woman stands waiting, a dog by her side. As they pull up, Corbin hops out and hands the dog Alaric's bag. Clan, Carolyn guesses, as the dog leaves, bag gently clasped in their teeth.

"Blood has not been drawn," the woman says, climbing past Drea into the back of the van. She pauses for a hug as Drea whispers *Mom*, then waves Corbin toward the front when he moves to offer her his seat. "I'm fine here." She turns to Carolyn and Kit, gaze sharp as she holds out a hand. "I am Alia, mother to Andrea and Alaric, and as good as such to Corbin."

Kit takes her hand first. "I'm Kit."

"He's my twin. I'm Carolyn." She takes Alia's hand, a brief, strong clasp. "I'm Drea's Big—her mentor in our sorority," she clarifies, relaxing at Alia's smile.

"I have heard nothing but good of you," Alia says.

The van hits a bump, and Carolyn is jolted, her shoulder bumping against the wall.

"We'll need to walk soon. There's a parking spot here on the right—yes, there, Dax," Corbin directs as Dax stops the van in a small clearing to the side. There's not much room, but Shawn gets his car off the road as well, parking behind them.

The trees look familiar.

Carolyn stands there, arms crossed, shoulders hunched. She inhales, half expecting to taste death in the air, but it's just a cold February day. She pulls her hat down to her eyebrows and her scarf up over her mouth, and she tries not to shiver.

It's just cold, she tells herself. It's not that this place feels wrong.

"Dax, if you want to see Orson, the graveyard's down that path." Drea points to a space between the trees that looks to be a little more traveled than the other paths that branch from this location.

Dax tilts his head and closes his eyes. "I'm far enough away that I don't hear him calling—not more than the usual itch—so I'll stick with you. I don't think Orson and I have anything new to say to each other, and he won't be happy with me yet. I'll come back when I know he can be settled."

"The house is this way." Alia heads in a direction that must be a path, but it's invisible to Carolyn's eyes. Corbin's gone, but a raven sits on Drea's shoulder, eyes bright as it surveys the group.

"Go," Drea says. "I'll bring up the back."

Kit walks with Carolyn, while Delilah stays close. Shawn lags behind, and Carolyn can hear Drea encouraging him to keep up. "You don't want to get lost on Clan grounds."

Carolyn's heard how Drea's family feels about Mages; Shawn shouldn't be left on his own.

"The Berman homestead," Alia says as they emerge into a small clearing.

It's not much of a house. Carolyn wants to label it a one-room log cabin, but she knows better. There's a kitchen, a living room, and a small upstairs that she didn't explore. It's small, but it's more than it seems to be from first appearances. Comfortable, probably, once upon a time. Cozy.

She stares at the trees along the house's side, remembering the way they looked from the inside, through hazy, smudged glass.

"There's nothing dead here," Dax says flatly. "There's no ghost for me to talk to, but it feels like there's something here, like an echo of death hangs over this place."

"That's a good thing, right?" Corbin's human again, and Shawn's nodding along with the question.

Carolyn brushes past them, heading for the steps, only dimly aware that Drea and Delilah are close behind her. She pauses at the door, fingers against the broken spots where the wolf pushed through, then she shoves it wide and stops when she sees the empty space in the dust coating the ground.

That's where she fell.

She crouches and touches the floor. Now she can smell the musty, enclosed scent of the place, the dead air settling around her. "I was here," she says quietly.

"I can smell you." Alia's voice is calm. Clipped. She stands at the door, her arms crossed. "Your scent *does* linger here, faint but true."

"This place is weird." Delilah passes Carolyn, who jumps up to follow her into the kitchen. Delilah opens the cabinets, peering in, then trails her fingers across the countertop. "It feels funny, like the Dreamscape is here. Like it's not quite real."

"It's real," Drea says. There are footsteps throughout the house, echoing from the floors overhead. Someone's gone up the stairs that Carolyn never saw; Drea and Kit have joined Delilah and Carolyn in the kitchen. "The family that lived here disappeared one day. They'd come to us a few years before that, then they were gone. We never knew what happened, but the place smells like magic, so Dad didn't want anyone out here."

"Because you grew up thinking that magic's dangerous to Clan," Kit says slowly, and Drea nods.

Carolyn wishes her senses were better. "It doesn't feel like traditional magic to me. I mean—I'm not a traditional Mage. But it feels different. Darker."

"Agreed," Delilah says. "Like I said, I can feel the edge of Dreams here."

"Or nightmares," Kit suggests.

"Or nightmares," Delilah echoes.

She sits down at the kitchen table, fingers drumming against the top.

There's a stack of plates covered in dust, and shredded remnants of napkins; some animal must have taken what it wanted for nesting. The plates are a dusty blueish gray, and it finally occurs to Carolyn what feels wrong here.

"It's in grayscale," Carolyn says. "It's like someone put an overlay on the place, like everything's been dimmed or covered in shadows."

"Someone was making dinner." Drea picks up the pan from the back of the stove and tips it over, but nothing comes out. She leans in, inhales, and sneezes. "Macaroni and cheese, I think, before it turned to char."

"Mm," Delilah murmurs.

"I was here," Carolyn repeats. "I don't know how, and I don't know why, but I had a Dream, and I traveled here."

"You traveled through a Dream, and I travel into Dreams." Delilah's voice is soft, low…lazy. "Maybe I infected you, and it's finally coming out now. Like a bug with a really long incubation period."

"Talent isn't the flu, Del," Kit says dryly.

"Isn't it? We Emerge. We change. We discover innate abilities we never knew we had. It could be an illness, Kit." Delilah's eyes are unfocused, her finger drawing patterns on the table.

"Don't call Talent an illness," Drea mutters, voice sharp. "There are enough people who think we're a blight on humanity. Don't help them."

"I'm not trying to." Delilah blinks, then focuses on Carolyn. "Come here." She holds out her hand.

It's not a good idea. Carolyn knows this in her gut and from experience. She crosses her arms, shakes her head. "No."

"I'm not going to hurt you."

It had never hurt, not like Delilah means. But it *hurt*. It changed everything, and it left a mark on Carolyn's soul. "Why?" she counters.

Delilah stands, her hand still out. "Because this place is gray," she says. "Because this place is stagnant and broken, like the dreams spilled out long ago. Because this place called to you for help, Carolyn, and you came, and now you're refusing to do what it needs."

"You're not making sense," Drea says.

Kit comes up behind Carolyn and places his hands on her shoulders. It grounds her, keeps her solid.

"She is making sense, to her," Carolyn says. "Delilah sees the world a little differently. She's still here, at least. And she thinks that if I can send her into this place's Dreams, maybe that'll change something."

Delilah's smile quirks. She wiggles her fingers, and Carolyn steps forward.

It's a risk, but she knows what to expect this time. She knows that Delilah travels physically into the Dreamscape, and she knows that there is a possibility—a teeny, tiny probability—that Delilah will take her along for the ride.

"If we disappear, don't go anywhere," Carolyn says firmly to Kit and Drea. "We'll be right back."

Their fingers touch, and Delilah reaches for her, wrapping their hands together, pressing palm to palm. There's a jerk that twists in Carolyn's core, and between one blink and the next, everything changes.

A pot bubbles on the stove, rich cheese melting over warm pasta. Bright-blue-and-white plates rest on the table—three of them, with silverware nearby, and three napkins carefully folded on the diagonal. A girl stands by the stove, stirring the pot carefully, her red dress contrasting with the lemon yellow of the walls and the gray slate of the gleaming, cleaned floor.

Something falls upstairs, but the girl goes on stirring.

Shawn's voice rings out, echoing in the distance. "What the fuck just happened?"

Delilah smiles and drops Carolyn's hand. "Now we're where we need to be."

Footsteps thunder down the stairs as Dax and Shawn push their way into the kitchen.

"What the hell, Delilah?" Shawn yells. Dax stops him at the door before he can get any farther, keeping him there with a hand on his chest.

Carolyn can hear voices in the other room, Corbin's raised and Alia's quiet, both too muffled to parse the words.

The girl stops stirring the pot, resting the spoon on the countertop. She turns to stare at them, eyes wide. "Who are you?" she asks.

"Matteson?" Drea asks slowly. "Mattie?" Her gaze darts to Delilah and Carolyn, then back to the girl. Drea slowly lowers herself, crouching so she's smaller than the girl.

Carolyn flexes her fingers, resisting the urge to reach out for Delilah, to hold on again in case she gets lost. "This is you, right?" she whispers.

"The house still Dreams," Delilah replies softly. "It wasn't hard to step into the Dreamscape here."

"I'm Mattie," the girl says, her head cocked, brow furrowing in confusion. "Who are you?" She pauses, lifts her gaze to the ceiling, then confides, "Mommy and Daddy are taking a nap. I'm allowed to make dinner."

Carolyn licks her lips. She thinks Mattie is maybe nine or ten years old; according to what she remembers Drea saying, this is probably right before the Bermans left.

"I really hope that Mommy and Daddy aren't about to burst in here as nightmare monsters," Kit whispers. He's snuck in close behind her and rested one hand on her arm; it's reassuring to have him close.

"Me too," she whispers.

"I'm Drea. Andrea," Drea says. "We're friends, but I probably look old because you're Dreaming."

"For someone who doesn't like magic, you're very good at following what's happening," Delilah says.

Drea gives her a dark look. "I'm good at rolling with the punches. That doesn't mean I'm happy about this."

Corbin walks toward the door at a swift pace; Dax drags Shawn to one side so Corbin can cut past them and drop into a crouch by Drea. "Hey, Mattie. Do you remember Alia Herne? Drea and Alaric's mom?"

Mattie blinks, wide-eyed, at Alia, who stands in the doorway. "Bedrock," she hisses, then blinks again and smiles sweetly. "Hullo, Mrs. Herne."

"You can call me Alia, Matteson. I have told you that before," Alia says gently. "What do you mean by 'bedrock'?"

"Mommy says I have to be polite, that I'm going to be raised right even though things are a little different here, so I have to call you Mrs. Herne." Mattie turns back to the stove, picks up the spoon, and starts stirring again. "If I don't finish this, it'll burn."

"Pretty sure it's all carbon bricks by now," Corbin mutters, and Drea elbows him.

"Why don't you finish cooking your dinner," Drea says. She rises, yanks at Corbin until he stands and stumbles back a step, and pulls him toward the door with her. "We're going into your living room."

"Don't wake Mommy and Daddy. They don't get a lot of time to nap, and they get really cranky when I disturb them," Mattie says. Her back is to them, and she continues to stir although Carolyn thinks the macaroni and cheese must be done. But it's a Dream, so it's possible they're stuck in this moment.

Carolyn reaches for Delilah, fingers brushing by hers as Delilah pulls away. Kit nudges Carolyn toward the door, but Carolyn shakes her head. "Go with Shawn," she whispers. "I'll be out in a minute. I need to get Delilah. We shouldn't split up here, and we really shouldn't leave her behind."

"If I go into that living room without you, we're splitting up," Kit points out.

Drea, Corbin, and Alia have already left. Carolyn looks between the door and Delilah, who inches closer to Mattie with tiny steps. "As long as we stay in the house, I think we'll be fine," she says. "Delilah said that it's this place, that the Dreams are here. Catch up with them and don't let them try to leave. Delilah and I will be there soon."

Mattie focuses intently on the pot of macaroni and cheese. It bubbles merrily as she stirs it, but there's no scent to go with it, only sight and sound, as if Carolyn is watching a movie instead of experiencing being in this place at this moment.

She supposes that's truly what's happening if this is a Dream. Or the Dreamscape. Or whatever truth Delilah's dragged them into.

"Delilah," she whispers, stepping behind Delilah and reaching out. Carolyn stops with her hand above Delilah's shoulder. "Del."

"That's a pretty dress," Delilah says.

"It reminds me of fire," Mattie replies, looking down at the bubbling pot. "You aren't supposed to be here, you know. Drea's old, and she's supposed to be young. I played with her yesterday. She's kind of nice, but her brother's mean sometimes. I don't like her daddy, and neither does Mommy. Daddy says he's going to do good things for Clan, that we're safe here. The Shadows can't get us."

"Shadows," Carolyn echoes.

"Shadows are nice, aren't they?" Mattie asks. "I like bright things, but shadows are nice sometimes because you can hide in them. They make hiding places harder to find, unless you have a cheating nose like Alaric does. Or bird's eyes. Corbin sees everything. I like Drea best, but they all like each other, so they don't have a lot of time for me. Besides, I'm older."

"Del, we need to go." Carolyn's skin prickles with the idea that something's going to shift. Change. That any second there'll be a wolf breaking down the door or that they'll fall into another place. She checks her pocket, but there are no cards there. She didn't bring them into the house, and she regrets that now.

Not that she believes that she really traveled through the cards.

"Del," she whispers. When Delilah rocks back, Carolyn grips her shoulder, and Delilah finally looks at her. Carolyn smiles slightly, trying to keep her voice even. "Kit and the others are waiting in the living room. With Shawn." She doesn't know if invoking their names will help, but she's willing to try.

"What about Samson?"

Carolyn almost lets go. She catches herself and tightens her grip on Delilah's shoulder instead. "You know Sam's not here," she grits out from between her teeth. "Get yourself into this Dream, not another one, okay?"

"We need to bring her with us." Delilah looks back to Mattie, and Carolyn's stomach twists.

"Maybe," she allows, although she's not sure she agrees. "Let's go talk to the others before we drag pieces of this Dream into reality."

She doesn't ask if Delilah can do that because if Delilah's suggesting it? Then she's probably tried.

Carolyn tugs, and Delilah finally moves. Mattie stays at the stove, humming under her breath while she stirs the pot.

"What the hell is going on here, Del?" Shawn meets them at the door. He gets in her face, and Carolyn slips between them, shoving Shawn back before she thinks about it. When he glares at her, she holds her ground, curling her shaking hands into fists.

"Don't," Carolyn says. "I don't care if you're scared."

Shawn lowers his hands slowly. "I wouldn't."

Carolyn bites her tongue and shakes her head. "Step back, Shawn. Give Del space. She's in charge here, not us, and we don't want her to leave us here."

"It's not like I haven't done this before," Delilah says, tone sing-song and dreamy. "Right, Carolyn?"

She's aware of Kit's and Shawn's attention, of the way Kit glares while Shawn's brow furrows with confusion. "Not at this scale, though," Carolyn says.

Delilah looks from one person to the next, counting them with each nod of her head. "Seven of you. Eight when we bring Mattie back. So no, not this scale. I've taken two before."

Wait. Carolyn frowns; it was her and Delilah in the Dreamscape, and they were alone. She stares at Delilah, tilts her head, and mouths, "Recently?"

Delilah shakes her head and raises an eyebrow in return. She hasn't just traveled with Carolyn, then. Nor with Shawn; he was the only one who was fine then.

That means that somehow, even though Carolyn never saw him, Samson was in the Dreamscape too. And he never quite came back.

"Delilah." Alia says the name as if she's tasting it, testing to ensure she has the right one. She approaches with hands up, her palms out to soothe and calm. "Whatever you have done, we need to undo it. My husband will be here soon. He will have felt the pull of magic, and there is nothing that will keep him from protecting his people."

"We're not in the house," Delilah points out. "We're in the Dreamscape. And when we go back, we don't have to be in the house. We need to be wherever the rest of Mattie is."

"The rest of her?" Drea asks. "Delilah, she looks like a whole—well, I was going to say a whole girl, but this is a Dream."

"Exactly. This is the echo of her from before she disappeared." Delilah's words are clearer now, her gaze sharp. "You said the Bermans disappeared, right? Her parents aren't here, only her. Just as she was then."

"We can't simply jump into a dream and bring a girl out," Corbin protests. "Magic doesn't—" He cuts off, looking at them. "It doesn't work like that, does it?"

"If it's possible to leave a piece behind," Delilah says, "then it's possible to bring a piece out."

There is an entire conversation for another day. They need to have a long, drawn-out discussion about Sam, and why Delilah left him behind if she knew she could travel with people. Carolyn crosses her arms and slides closer to Kit, tucking tight against him when his arm falls across her shoulders.

"I wonder if the echo has been here all along, waiting for me." Delilah runs her fingers along the railing for the stairs. "It calls. Can you hear it, Carolyn? Wouldn't you have gone to it, if it had been calling all along?"

She had, in her Dream. She had come when it called.

"Maybe something changed," Corbin says.

"The Shadow." Drea's voice is tight. She clings to Corbin's hand, fingers white from the tension. "They brought the Shadow here. And it disappeared from here."

Carolyn can't remember the little she'd learned about Shadowwalkers during Pawel's classes, but she's damned sure it's never good when one shows up. "So the Shadow was here, and it—"

"She," Kit cuts her off. "Rory says the Shadow was female."

"Oh." Delilah looks at the door to the kitchen, and Carolyn follows her gaze.

"Oh," Carolyn echoes. "But if she's—"

"—then the Dream may have been here all along, but not active. Or not calling to anyone." Delilah turns, and Carolyn catches her wrist before she can get away. "Carolyn, we have to get Mattie out of here."

"And what will that get us? A Shadow? Something that wants to eat us?" Carolyn asks.

"She called me bedrock," Alia says quietly. "As did the Shadow. I believe you may be right."

Having Alia follow a different path to draw the same conclusion makes it seem more real. More solid. More likely that that little girl somehow became a Shadowwalker when she disappeared.

"We need to get out of here," Shawn mutters. "Now, Delilah. Get us out of here now."

"I can't." Delilah smiles sadly. "You're under the impression that I control this, Shawn. And sometimes, yeah, I do. But not this time. The Dream sucked us in. This is real, not some mental trick like a Dreamwalker does. We're really here. We're not going insane. We're not Samson. We're just—stuck until we figure out what unlocks the path out. I'm pretty sure that girl is at least a part of the key."

"I thought you said we shouldn't leave this house," Kit murmurs, low enough that only Carolyn hears him.

Carolyn bites her lip. "It was a guess. And apparently it was wrong."

Drea has her phone in her hand and is poking at it. "Phones are dead."

Delilah snorts softly. "Are you surprised?" She holds out her hand, palm up, to Carolyn. "Come on. You and I are going to talk a kid into walking out of a Dream."

"Why me?" Carolyn places her hand in Delilah's, even though she's sure it's a terrible idea. She touches Kit's shoulder and whispers "I'll be okay" as she passes him.

"Because this house wanted you as much as me," Delilah says. "Having you with me increases my chances of getting this right."

"I'm not a Dreamer. I'm not like you, and I'm not like Nikita."

Delilah stops once they're inside the kitchen. Carolyn's positive they aren't in private—not with Mattie still stirring her macaroni and cheese feet away, not with sharp Clan ears down the hall.

Delilah leans in and says softly, "I know. You said you started out in a dream, but you traveled into a real place. You saw images, like illusions drawn from Tarot cards. Like Samson's light. If Shawn stole some of your power, maybe Samson's power went to you." She cocks her head and pats Carolyn's cheek. "It's worth a thought. And if your traveling takes you to reality, that may be why we're both here. I got us in. I can reach Mattie, get her to come with us. But you have to get us out."

That's a huge responsibility for someone who isn't sure what she's doing. Or how, or why.

"Mattie," Delilah calls out.

Mattie slows, then stops, twisting in place. "What?" she asks. "You didn't disturb Mommy and Daddy, did you? They're napping." She says it like it's significant.

"We haven't seen your mommy and daddy. We need you to come outside with us," Delilah says.

Mattie takes a step back, shaking her head. "I'm not going anywhere with strangers."

"What about Drea and Corbin and Alia?" Delilah approaches slowly, both hands out. "We can go with them. Alia's as good as having your mom along, right? Because she's Drea's mom."

The Prince of Cups. He'd stood in the place of her family and friends in the last full reading she'd done for herself. It's a card representative of schemers and tricksters, of cunning predators and birds of prey.

Corbin. He's a young man who's cunning and clever, and who prefers a raven form. He's important to Carolyn's Little, so in a way he's part of Carolyn's friends and family.

Then there's Alaric, who's not cunning in the same way as Corbin, but he's still sharp and intelligent, working through the roadblocks that his family has placed. When Carolyn had first heard of the Shadow disappearing from the Berman house, she'd drawn the Prince of Cups, and Mac had likened him to Alaric.

Alaric, who isn't here, and Corbin, who is. Linked in multiple ways.

"I have an idea," Carolyn says. It sounds insane to her in her own mind, but it's the only idea she has.

It's probably not possible. It's certainly not probable.

But, based on her strange dreams, it's the only way out that she can see.

"I'm going into the living room," she says, "and we're going to use the front door. We'll go one at a time, and I need Corbin to go first." Her gaze flicks to where Mattie still watches Delilah warily. "Mattie, will you come with us if Alia asks?"

She's not sure bringing this girl along is the right answer, but she chooses to trust Delilah. Her reading for the new year called for transformation and change, told her to trust the old to bring new.

This would definitely be something new emerging from her past.

"Okay," Mattie agrees, taking Delilah's hand. "I'll go with you."

Time shifts like it does in dreams. No matter how often Delilah says this is real, it still slips past, and then Carolyn is in front of the door. It's complete and whole under her hands, no signs of shreds made by the wolf's claws. She twists the knob and pushes it open, standing in the way of anyone going through.

She closes her eyes and visualizes the Prince of Cups, opens them again with her hands held out, and light fills the space beyond the doorway. She sees him standing there, image flickering. One moment it's the picture she remembers from the card, of a man with dark hair and a goatee, his expression serious. The next it's Corbin, a smirk twisting his lips, merry light in his eyes. Then it's Alaric, his phone in his hands, staring at them in shock.

Carolyn steps back, making space for others to pass her.

"Go!" she yells, and waves at the door.

She doesn't know what they see, but they all rush past her, trusting her order. Delilah goes just before Carolyn, Mattie's hand gripped in hers. As they pass through, the girl dissolves into a burgeoning shadow.

Carolyn's breath goes short, her chest tight. Hands clenched, fingernails pressed into her palm, she leaps into the darkness.

17

Drea's phone chimes.

"What the fuck did you do?" Alaric yells.

The wolf by his side snarls, nostrils flared. It takes a step forward, and Carolyn takes a big step back as Kit comes between them.

"Theobald," Alia says calmly, and the wolf sits.

Carolyn's pulse rings in her ears, thudding loudly. Her knees shake, and she lets herself fall to the ground, kneeling with one hand out to brace herself.

Not ground. Not dusty floor. Wood, polished to a shine. Hard, dark wood. They're in an office. This isn't the house—the now-abandoned cottage—where they found Mattie. This is somewhere else. Alaric and Drea's house, probably, considering that Alaric's here.

It's exactly what she hoped would happen when she dared to think her traveling was real.

It must be real.

Theobald returns to human form; Alia places her hand on his shoulder. Drea and Corbin bracket Alaric, and Kit sinks to sit beside Carolyn on the floor. Shawn is off to one side, arms crossed.

And Delilah stands with a woman wreathed in shadows.

No, not wreathed in shadows. Made of Shadow.

Carolyn isn't sure how to describe her. But she's sure of who she is. "Mattie."

"Yes." The word escapes on an exhale, a sibilant hiss.

"You could have introduced yourself the first time around," Drea says sharply.

"You assume I knew." Mattie disappears in a wave of darkness. The

146

shadows move sideways, sidle up the wall, and are gone, reappearing on the other side. "There's too much light in this room."

Carolyn can't see a mouth, but she still hears Mattie's voice.

Shawn reaches out and flicks the light switch. Sunlight still spills in through the window, but half the room now lies in darkness. A soft sigh echoes off the walls, and shadows coalesce into a vaguely humanoid form in one corner.

"That's better," she says.

"Explain," Theobald growls darkly, "and give me a good reason not to kill this Shadow now."

"I will never forgive it for killing Orson," Alaric mutters. He rocks back, weight settling on his heels with his feet set wide, arms crossed tightly. "But we need information from it more than we need it dead."

"I'm not the same one who killed your brother." Mattie sits, a delicate fold of darkness. She has a form, but it moves constantly. "It was my Shadow, but not my mind. Not the me who remembers exactly who I am. I don't know as much as she did, but I'd also prefer not to be dead." She smiles, sharp and bright. "You're never going to find another Shadowwalker willing and able to talk to you, one able to resist the filling meal that you would make."

"Are you threatening us?" Alaric asks.

Mattie shakes her head. "I'm saying I won't."

A low ache builds in the back of Carolyn's head, cradling the nape of her neck and flowing outwards to her temples. A thud climbs up, settling in to echo her heartbeat with every strike. She presses the heel of her hand against her brow ridge, and Kit reaches for her other hand, tangling them together.

"What did we do?" Carolyn whispers.

"Reunited me," Mattie replies. "A second Emergence."

"As what?" Corbin asks. "Last I knew, people didn't Emerge if they were Lineage to start with."

"We've already proven that's wrong," Shawn counters. "Even before things got weird recently." He gestures from himself to Delilah and Carolyn. "We all changed a few years ago, especially Del. If that's not Emergence—"

"It is." Mattie's voice cuts through his words, shattering them like glass. Carolyn presses on her ears, trying to stop the ringing. "I can taste it on you. The lingering thick, rich taste of Emergence, even now. You continue to change." She glances at Theobald, and her expression twists into anger. "Not you. You're flat. Dark. Dull. I wouldn't eat you even if I were starving. Every bit of flavor has already been sucked from your soul."

Alaric licks his lips, then presses his mouth closed tightly.

"Matteson." Alia's voice is low. Soft and even, each word carefully spoken. "Tell us what happened."

Mattie blinks. She sits back, knees coming up until she curves over them, arms around them, a small, hunched knot of shadow. "Which part?" she asks. "The part where shadows crawled into my vision, surrounding everything I could see? The hunger that consumed me before my soul was ripped from my body as I turned to darkness, when I was split apart and left to starve? That's where it began, for me. For my family."

"Your parents?" Alia says.

The Shadow is motionless. "Dead."

Pain spikes behind Carolyn's eyes. She doesn't want to think about it, but she can see it clearly. That small girl spinning into shadows, her soul dumped into the Dreamscape while she was left hungering for something she couldn't have any more. And her parents, right there.

"You ate them."

Mattie doesn't look up when Drea speaks; she gives her answer to the floor. "Yes."

"You were split." Alaric sounds as if he's thinking something through, words slow. "When you Emerged, your soul split from your body."

"Yes," Mattie says again. "Congratulations, dragon, you've been listening."

Theobald's nostrils flare.

"And your soul went...?" Alaric trails off.

"...into the Dreamscape," Delilah says. "Carolyn reunited her."

Carolyn's pretty sure that Delilah did the heavy lifting by getting them there in the first place. She's not sure what her own role was other than getting them back to reality. And she's not sure she wants to explain to

Alaric that he anchored the return point. That's a conversation better saved for when they have more privacy.

Corbin's looking at her like he can see right through her. Carolyn blinks, turns away, and hopes he doesn't decide to press whatever issue he's thought of. She might have answers to the questions on his mind, or she might be as clueless as everyone else.

"Does that happen to all Shadowwalkers?" Alaric asks. His hands are tight fists by his side.

Alia has her arms around Theobald's center, keeping him standing just behind Alaric. She's smaller than her husband, yet it seems almost easy for her to hold him back. Carolyn wonders if that's the strength of Clan or the strength of their bond.

Either way, she's thankful for it, because murder lies in Theobald's eyes.

Mattie shrugs, darkness rippling out from her. "Probably. There wasn't anyone else there when it happened, and when I saw other Shadows, we had different things to talk about. Maybe we're ghosts. Maybe we're why hauntings happen. Emerging didn't come with a handbook of 'this is how Shadowwalkers are made,' sorry."

"You don't sound like a kid." Corbin gestures at her, and Mattie hisses at him.

"I'm older than you," she reminds him, hissing softly again at the end. "Just because my soul was split doesn't mean I didn't age. Or mature. It's magic. Take it with a little faith."

"Alaric." Alia speaks quietly, firmly. "Your father and I will meet with you before you leave. I recommend that you and your friends finish what you plan to do here and leave."

"In my off—" Theobald cuts off with a snarl, glaring at Carolyn on the floor. "In the kitchen in ten minutes, Alaric."

Because they are standing in his office, Alaric's bag of documents on the desk. They interrupted a meeting about whatever Clan business Alaric brought to distract Theobald. Carolyn bites back an apology.

"You sound awfully human." Corbin continues as Alia nudges Theobald out the door, "for someone who isn't."

"I am human," Mattie says flatly. "As human as you, raven. As human as anyone in this room, maybe more so than some. Shadowwalkers are people who Emerged; do not forget that."

"Is there a Shadowwalker Lineage?" Drea asks.

Mattie shrugs. "I don't know."

"Pawel will want to know this," Alaric murmurs, and Drea nods. Alaric has his phone in his hands and is rapidly typing something.

"I'm not going with you to your annoying Mage," Mattie says. "I remember him. Although I wouldn't mind seeing your Talent-sucking friend again. We have so much to talk about." She pauses, then adds, "And I'm not staying here."

"Don't go yet." Delilah has her hands out, and she crouches close to Mattie. "We're getting answers here. Things are starting to make sense, finally, and I need to understand."

"We," Drea corrects. "We need to understand."

Mattie blinks, slowly unfolds, and flows to standing. She doesn't rise; there is no distinction of limbs moving. She shifts like the shadow that she is, standing in darkness when she's done. "I'm not here to instruct you. I don't even know if I can change anything, if I can reach others of my kind, if I can get past the shadow and into the heart. All I can tell you is that within every Shadowwalker is the seed of someone human and also something that hungers so deeply that it can't control its ravening need to devour its prey."

"And every Shadowwalker is split," Alaric says.

"Yes," Mattie agrees. "That's all." She steps back, fading into the shadows. Carolyn can't see her as a distinct image anymore, and Mattie's voice echoes when she speaks. "For what happened to Orson, I am sorry."

The Shadow fades after that, becoming nothing more than flat darkness against the wall.

"Shit," Delilah mutters.

"At least we've learned things today." Kit remains seated near Carolyn, knees up and feet spread, hands across his bent knees. "Rory's right—the Shadow you caught was a female, and none of the Shadows are indeterminate beings. The ones eating people lack a soul, and that's probably why they're starving. We know that there's a place they go when they're split off."

"I was told, once, to be careful I didn't fall into the split," Alaric mutters. "That might be what she means."

"That you're going to Emerge as a Shadow? No." Corbin shakes his head and wraps his arms around Alaric as if he could hold him back. "Definitely not."

"I think she meant the place, not the state of being." Drea crouches, bows her head, and exhales roughly. "I'm with Delilah. Just…shit. Where do we go from here?"

"Home," Carolyn says. There are too many people in the room, and they're all looking at her. Staring at her, as if by speaking she's demonstrated to them that she somehow knows the answers they're looking for. She holds her breath for a count of five, then tries to explain. "We came to see if I'd really been here. I was. We pulled half a person out of the Dreamscape. Maybe we're supposed to save the rest of the Shadows."

"The split," Alaric mutters.

"We're not doing any of that today," Carolyn says slowly. "I don't know about you, but I've got a lot of things I need to think about before I can even start to work out the bigger picture here. Del, you probably do, too."

"I want your girl Nikita's email," Delilah says, "and her number."

"You think she's important?"

"Never reacted to anyone like that before, so yeah," Delilah says flatly. "It's like you, her, and I are three different ways of looking at the same thing, and maybe that's important, too. But I need to talk to her from a distance, and I honestly don't even trust Skype for that right now."

"I'll get you her info," Carolyn agrees.

Shawn's staring at them, brow furrowed, pupils blown wide for reasons Carolyn can't understand. She coughs, and he meets her gaze.

"Be careful," she whispers to Delilah. She's not sure if Delilah hears her, but she hopes so. Carolyn has issues with Shawn, different issues than most people here have with him. She's never going to trust him again, not the way she used to. But this goes beyond that.

"We need to get the cars," Dax points out, motioning at the door and nudging Shawn to come with him. "Corbin, you're coming with us to give directions, 'cause I'm not sure I can walk back to where we parked on my own."

There's a flurry of wings, and a raven perches on Dax's shoulder, pecking lightly at his ear.

Carolyn leans her shoulder against Kit's. She closes her eyes, but she knows that it's Delilah who sits on her other side, takes her hand, and twines their fingers together.

"It's going to be okay," Kit murmurs.

People move, and there are quiet conversations as Alaric leaves, and Shawn and Dax step outside. Carolyn doesn't want to think about any of what's happening around her. Instead— "What's happening to me?" she asks, and Kit takes her other hand, squeezing tightly.

"I don't know, but I don't think it's bad," he says.

"We'll figure it out," Delilah says.

Maybe.

Maybe they'll figure it out, or maybe it'll be another three years of wondering what went wrong.

Maybe magic is the root of all problems, and maybe everyone with Talent is destined to be split like Shadowwalkers, their souls sucked into some nameless pocket of the Dreamscape.

Maybe things are changing even more, and maybe the Emergence is still happening.

Carolyn just wants life to go back to being simple. Easy. She wants to wake up in the morning and go to class, and she wants to go to bed at night knowing that the same thing will happen the next day. It hadn't been challenging, but it hadn't been heartbreaking either.

She wants to put all the drama back in a nice box and let it be.

She never wanted to be Pandora.

THAT WHICH
CROWNS

Fifth Position: Crowns

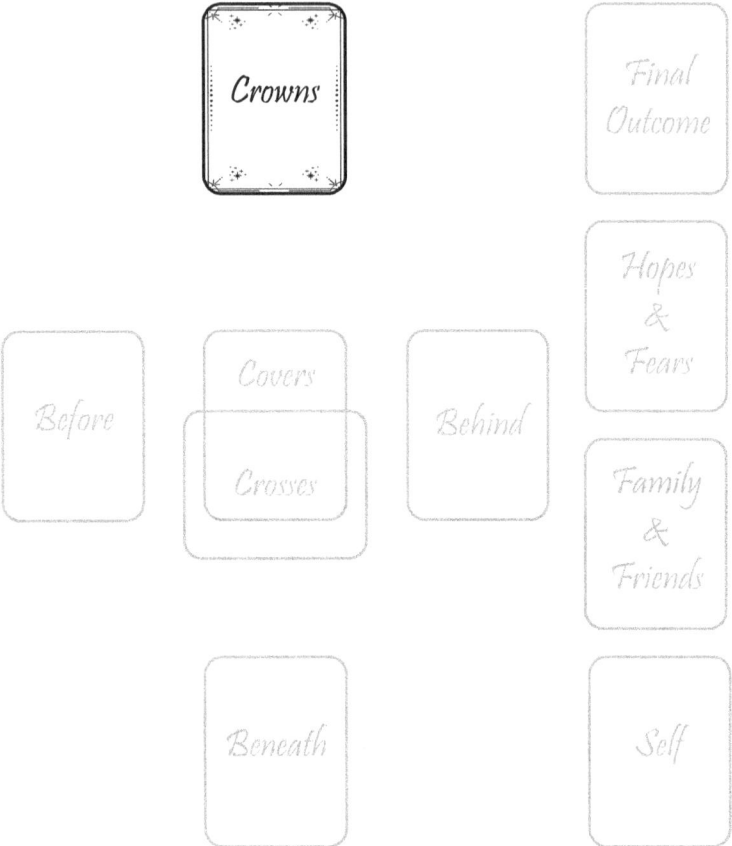

That which crowns...

The querent has goals toward which they strive that may or may not match the possible future awaiting them. Out of all that they hope to achieve, there is always a best possible outcome: that which crowns. The querent will receive guidance about what will help them achieve that outcome, what will lead them to the best outcome for their own life.

Carolyn's Reading: Strength

A woman stands naked, bared to the natural world surrounding her, the sun rising brightly to shine across her skin. She holds a cloth before her upon which is the visage of a lion. She is nude, but she holds the lion's strength, both without and within

The querent's strength is within their heart and it also lies visible, wrapped around them like a shield. This card usually appears for support: strength is a tool to be used, an adjective to describe the situation, or is a reference to the querent themselves. But, when the Strength card is in this position, strength is an achievement, a crowning glory toward which the querent strives.

When all is said and done, the querent will have energy, courage, and success. When they look ahead to the best they have to hope for, they see glory and honor. Strength is not only the tool they can use to achieve success—it is the final goal. With luck, the querent will be able to see their own heart as clearly as others see them. They will achieve their full power.

Kit's Reading: The Two of Cups (reversed)

Lovers kiss, reverence in their expressions as they linger, lost in love. In the background, blooms of all kinds abound, while in the foreground two cups overflow, sharing their abundance.

The querent appears to desire love, but the reversed placement of this card means that the love they desire might not be true. There are competing affections for the querent, choices that must be made. One road leads to affection and harmony, another to unrequited love.

Reversed, this is a card of warning: what the querent strives for may only be an illusory love. This is the querent's opportunity to recognize that, if they continue down this path using the tools they have been given, what they achieve will be momentary. False. Even should they accomplish what they believe to be their ultimate goal, they will not be fulfilled. If the querent can recognize their own contradictory feelings, there is still time to change paths, to look within and make choices that will lead them to the love they desire rather than the illusion of what they think they need.

18

By Tuesday, Carolyn still isn't ready to deal with large groups of people and magic. She knows she won't be expected to conduct a ritual at Coven, but she remains wary of going to the weekly meeting. When Heather leaves to go with Nikita, Carolyn has a chance for quiet and solitude. That feels just about perfect.

She pulls out her Tarot deck and spreads it across her desk. The cards are in a random order, shuffled after the last reading she did, and she doesn't try to divine any meaning from their specific randomness. This isn't a reading.

She's looking for something that feels right. Something she can experiment with.

She pulls the Nine of Pentacles from the center of the deck and lays it in front of herself, then sweeps the rest of the cards into a neat pile. She's not sure how her Talent works—she's not even sure why it works—but she wants to get a handle on it before she finds herself in an emergency again and has to use it.

Most Tarot cards aren't places, and those that are aren't necessarily places she'd want to go. She's had enough of traveling to broken-down houses and the tops of Ferris wheels. While some cards she associates with people, she's not sure if she traveled specifically to Alaric or to his father's office, and she doesn't want to test that. If Alaric had advanced warning of her potential arrival, maybe trying to replicate what she'd done before would make sense. But if he doesn't know she's coming, she doesn't want to interrupt him unexpectedly. And she definitely doesn't want to go back to Theobald Herne's office without someone there to protect her.

The Nine of Pentacles is a decent card. She doesn't associate it with anyone or anywhere, which might be a problem. But it is, at least, a good card: a card of prosperity, of stability. It's a card from the end of the road, when hard work and perseverance have brought peace of mind.

Wherever it leads, it can't be somewhere bad.

The question is, how does she turn this card into an illusion that she can travel through? Does it only work when Dreams are involved?

She stares at it, her gaze lingering on the woman in the image's center. Dark hair and dark eyes; she reminds Carolyn of Serina. The woman is smiling, pleased to be in her well-appointed room, another affluent home in view through the window. She has a plate of delicacies and is dressed in a fine gown; flowers spill over the windowsill into her room. Carolyn inhales and tastes nothing but the stale scent of towels that need to be washed and the perfume Heather used before she left for Coven.

Carolyn has no idea how she's called up illusions before and no idea how to do so now.

Maybe it's the lack of urgency—she's not panicking.

Her phone buzzes, and she reaches for it, tugging it close enough to see a notification for an email from Pawel fading from the lock screen. She should have expected that, for skipping Coven, but she'll see him tomorrow for the independent study. She considers letting it go but thumbs the phone unlocked instead and opens her email.

> *Carolyn & Kit—*
>
> *I didn't see you at Coven, and wanted to let you know that something has come up, and I will be canceling our Wednesday session this week.*
>
> *Please (separately) send an outline of your current project progress and be prepared to discuss further plans for your final project when we meet on Thursday.*
>
> *—Pawel*

At some point, Carolyn needs to talk to Heather about a potential project. The time hasn't felt right yet; Heather has been with Nikita so often. Heather's got enough to do, and Carolyn's had—well, Carolyn's had her own things to think about.

She sets the phone down, nudging it so it slides far enough across the desk that she'll have to reach to get to it again.

Good.

She should probably tell Pawel what happened over the weekend. That they confirmed that she traveled. That they rescued the Shadow. Drea might have already told him, but Carolyn doesn't think Pawel would have canceled Wednesday if she had. Since Pawel probably doesn't know yet, it's fine for Carolyn to wait until Thursday to tell him. And it'll be easier with Kit there; they can offer two views on what happened.

That means she'll also have more time to figure out what to say about the project she hasn't started yet.

Tomorrow is soon enough to deal with how to explain her lack of progress.

The phone pings, but it's just out of reach, and she lets it stay that way.

Carolyn reaches out to touch the card, centering it in front of herself again. She traces the whorls of the flowers, the outline of the windowsill. Her fingers stroke along the strands of hair curling across the woman's shoulders, but it doesn't come to life.

The other images were simply there, bright and bold and abrupt. This lies flat.

There's a rap on the door, and she glances up. "Come in?"

"Hey." Kit nudges the door open, slips through, and closes it again. He drops his bag on Carolyn's bed, then falls back next to it, arms out. "It's been a shitty night."

"You missed Coven," Carolyn says.

Kit pushes up on one elbow, brows furrowed. "How did you know that? I saw Heather earlier and she said you weren't going."

"Pawel emailed. We don't have our session tomorrow, and he wanted to let us know." Carolyn doesn't bother to grab the phone to show Kit the message. He doesn't seem to find it important, either, falling back on the bed again as he takes her at her word. "Are you okay?"

"I don't know."

He brings one arm up to fall across his face as if he can block out the light. The fingers of his other hand twitch, tangling in the sheets and twisting them up.

Carolyn feels out of her depth, uncomfortable with the way his jaw is set tightly and the small hiccup that escapes him. She wishes Heather were there, but this is Kit. This is her brother. Her twin. Talking to him shouldn't be that difficult.

She grabs the box of tissues from her bed and tosses it onto his stomach. Then she moves to the bed beside him, budging up close and drawing her feet up to sit with crossed legs. She nudges him. "Talk to me."

"Serina broke up with me." His words are muffled, and she can't tell if they're tight with tears or not. He hasn't reached for a tissue yet, but he also hasn't lifted the arm that blocks his face.

"Serina broke up with you," she echoes, and this time a frisson of anger slips through her, lighting her spine. "Did she—?"

"It's not because I'm trans," Kit mutters. "Stop worrying about that, Caro. Leave it. Serina doesn't even know, or if she does, it's not because I told her. It's not like I'm in the closet, even if I'm not out yelling about trans pride. It wasn't a topic of conversation."

"Then— But you're such a good guy." Carolyn flounders, and Kit huffs.

"It just wasn't working." Kit lets his arm flop out, bumping Carolyn. He huffs a second time, hiccups, and sits up. She skootches back to give him room to rearrange his limbs. He takes a single tissue and hands her the box, then he blots the corners of his eyes carefully and blows his nose.

He keeps the tissue in his hand, crumpling it tightly as he sits slumped on the edge of the bed.

"Should I be angry with her?" The question is too late; Carolyn's already angry with Serina for hurting her brother. She can feel it coiling in her gut, hot and twisting. When Kit shakes his head, she tries to get the fire to abate, but it only banks. It could reignite at any moment.

Kit reaches over and squeezes her hand; it's strange that he's comforting her. "Serina brought it up, but it was kind of a mutual decision in the end," he says. "There wasn't any spark. We had fun when we went out. I think we'll still be friends; I really like her as a friend. But neither of us was moving into a relationship well. We kissed."

"I saw," Carolyn says dryly. "You weren't exactly subtle."

"We were dating. We didn't have to be," Kit shoots back. He knocks her knee with the back of his hand. "We just—it was comfortable, and that was okay. Kissing was nice. She wants something that's going to be more than that. She's looking for explosions, I think. And I'm not going to be that person for her, and I'm not sure I even want that. And I was looking for…" He trails off. "I'm not sure what I was looking for. Something more than comfortable. But also something where I just feel like me."

"I get it."

"Do you?" Kit catches his lower lip in his teeth, watching her closely.

Carolyn feels like she should shrink back under his gaze, her breath shallow for a moment before she looks away. "I'm not heartless, Kit. I did date Shawn for years, remember? Just because I haven't dated anyone in college doesn't mean I don't know what it feels like."

"How are you doing after seeing Shawn and Del again?" Kit inches closer, and Carolyn leans against him, tilting her head on his shoulder when he offers.

"You're deflecting," she murmurs, and he shrugs the shoulder she leans against.

"Probably," he says. "I'm still processing why it didn't hurt to break up with the first person I've ever dated."

"You didn't love her." It seems simple to Carolyn in that respect. "And you're probably going to stay friends, so you didn't screw up that aspect of your relationship with her. And you didn't need to be closer, at least not to her. There's nothing wrong with being friends."

"Now you're deflecting." His tone is gentle as he presses a kiss to the top of her head.

"I've spent the last couple of days trying really hard not to think about them," Carolyn admits. She twists her fingers together, tight enough that her knuckles are white. "Shawn makes me feel—I still feel this anxiety when I'm around him. I'm angry at him. I'm hurt. It's been years, but I still feel that way, and I hate it. I don't love him anymore, which is a good thing. And it ended in such an epically horrible way, I can't really get past that. Del, on the other hand." She smiles slightly. "I've missed Del. And I really miss Sam."

"So, we're still friends with Del, we're worried about Sam, and it's okay to keep being angry with Shawn for being an utter asshole," Kit sums up.

Carolyn laughs. "Yes, good summation. Although I think it's more complicated than that." She pushes to her feet, retrieves the card from her desk, and shows it to him as she returns to sit once more on the bed. "I was trying to do the illusion thing again. On purpose, this time, when I'm not upset or scared or angry. It's not working."

Kit takes the card, turns it around in his hand, and looks at it upside down and backward as if it will change. "The first time it happened—"

"—I was Dreaming," Carolyn finishes. "And the second time, I was in Del's Dreamscape. Or Mattie's Dreamscape. I'm not sure who controlled that. And both times, the image, or its meaning, ended up being something personal to me."

"Do you think you can do it while awake?" Kit flips the card over and hands it back to her.

She rubs her thumb across the picture one more time, like doing so will change something somehow. "Yes," she says quietly. "I was awake when I was with Del. It was in the Dreamscape, but it didn't happen automatically. I intentionally thought about Alaric, and then we were with Alaric. It worked."

"So maybe you just don't know where this card goes," Kit muses, "or maybe it isn't the cards at all."

"What?" That makes no sense to Carolyn. She lowers the card slowly, leaves it lying on the bed. "It's been a card every time."

"It's been an image every time," Kit points out. "You use cards as the images because that's what you know. You've had these cards forever, and they're in your head. But in the end, they're just pictures."

"They're predictive tools—"

Kit cuts her off with a wave of his hand. "I'm not disputing that they help you. I'm saying, because you're used to them being a focus for your old Talent, maybe that's why they've been a focus for your new Talent."

Okay, that does make sense. "You think I should get a new deck?" Carolyn can't imagine feeling as connected to another deck as she does to this one, although she's had a few that were close.

"Or make your own pictures," Kit suggests.

"I'm not…" Carolyn's voice trails off. Her notebook lies open on the table, her writing visible under the briefest of sketches of the last layout she read. She's not an artist. She can do utilitarian outlines of her readings, make the card on the page the right image to match how the reading felt even if the image isn't identical to the card in her deck.

But Kit's an artist. His sketches are always perfectly done. Complete.

Kit taps his fingers against his knee, not saying anything. It's one of those moments when she is absolutely certain that they are on the same wavelength. Kit will say something when he's ready, and if she pushes too hard before then, he might never get there.

It might be his Talent still peeking through, the link between them, or their natural predictive line.

It puts her heart at ease.

The door bursts open as laughter rings out. Kit slides off the bed, on his feet before Heather and Nikita walk in. Heather stops dead, her hand still on the doorknob, her head tilted and brow furrowing when she looks at them.

"Are you okay, Kit?" she asks; Nikita puts a hand on Heather's shoulder.

Kit blinks, gaze dropping to Carolyn's desk. He reaches past Carolyn, picks up the card she left on the bed, and drops it on top of her deck. "I'm fine," he says, and when Carolyn reaches for him, he holds up a hand. "Seriously, I'll be fine. It's not how I expected tonight to go, but it'll be okay."

Heather's nose wrinkles, but when Nikita nudges, she steps farther into the room, moving around Kit.

Carolyn stands up and hugs her brother, tucking her head into the crook of his shoulder. Kit holds on too tight for a moment, then loosens his grip.

"I've got that thing with Rory and Shane tomorrow night," he says. "The ritual we've been working on."

"Check in with me after," Carolyn tells him. She steps back but keeps her hands on his shoulders. "Are you going to talk to Pawel about this? I thought you were going to work with Thorne."

"This is going better than that was." Kit glances to where Heather and

Nikita are chatting quietly on Heather's side of the room. "I thought you were going to work with Heather."

Again, her lack of progress. "Yeah, well, this semester hasn't exactly gone as planned so far." Carolyn nudges him toward the door. "Text me, okay?"

Kit takes the hint and lets it go, though Carolyn expects he'll bring it up again soon. "Let me know if you need anything for the independent study," he offers.

"I'll think about it." Carolyn closes the door as he goes out. She drops into the seat at her desk, carefully not looking over to where Heather and Nikita are getting ready to sleep. "Nik's staying here tonight?"

"If that's okay," Heather says.

"Being here has been helping with my nightmares."

Carolyn doesn't believe Nikita, and she suspects Heather doesn't believe her either. On the other hand, "helping" doesn't mean "has stopped the nightmares from happening," so it could be true. She lifts a hand and wiggles her fingers while keeping her back to them. "It's fine. Anything to make sure Nikita's okay and we're not going to get plunged into a fresh, new winter hell," she agrees.

She's still idly shuffling her deck when Heather turns off the room's lights, and she keeps doing it for several minutes longer, even after they've climbed into bed and settled quietly. She's got a lot to think about, and the feel of cards in her hands is soothing.

19

CAROLYN ARRIVES TWO minutes late to Pawel's office on Thursday, slipping in and tugging the door closed behind her. Kit is already seated, hunched low in his chair, his bag on the floor. There's a tense line to his jaw, and Carolyn touches his shoulder when she takes her seat. "You okay?"

Kit tugs the sleeves of his henley down over his wrists, covering half his palms. "Fine. It's cold out."

"Mm." Pawel doesn't look up from where he's tapping at his keyboard. "Sorry about canceling yesterday. This year has had its challenges." He stops typing, clicks something, then pushes the keyboard away. "I wanted to be sure you'd have my full attention." His smile seems tight, and Carolyn swears there are fresh lines around the corners of his eyes and mouth. He still seems boyish, young enough to fit in with the college crowd, but he also seems…tired.

Kit pulls at his sleeve again, nods, then shrugs one shoulder. Something's wrong, Carolyn's sure of it. But the best way to get Kit to talk is not to bother him about it.

She pulls out her notebook and waits.

"Tell me about your progress," Pawel prompts, leaning forward, elbows on the desk.

"I'm having better luck working with Rory and Shane than with Thorne," Kit says. He slides farther down in his chair, rubbing at his wrist. "It's not that I don't like Thorne. I just get along better with Rory and Shane. Thorne's—"

"—Thorne," Pawel says, like that's enough.

"Kind of. He backed off," Kit says. "But I didn't feel like we meshed."

"And you do mesh with Rory and Shane?" Pawel prompts.

Kit's breath shudders out, his fingers wrapped tightly around his right wrist. "Yeah," he says. "I guess I do."

Something's definitely not right. Carolyn knows they did the ritual last night, and Kit said everything went fine. Not perfectly, but it was a good start. But this—Kit seems anxious. She can feel his tension.

"Carolyn?"

Her head snaps up, and she blanks her expression as she meets Pawel's gaze. "I don't think it's going to work out with Heather," she says. She expects some kind of response, but Pawel waits, so Carolyn picks her words carefully. "She said we could work together, but she's been busy with Nikita, making sure she doesn't plunge us into eternal winter. And I've been distracted."

Kit darts a look at her. His cheeks are sunken in, like he's biting them from the inside, and he's tugging yet again on the sleeve of his henley.

"Distracted how?" Pawel asks. "Is this about the trip you took to Haverhill with Drea last weekend? I've been meaning to ask how that went."

She's not going to be able to dodge answering him. Her mouth opens, then closes, her chest tight with nerves. "Not like we expected," she finally says. "Not exactly. It was the place from my dream, though. That house where you took the Shadow. That's where I went. And I really, actually traveled there. From here. Theobald was the wolf. And he's pretty damned terrifying."

Kit makes a small noise of assent, nodding.

"Theobald Herne is—" Pawel cuts off, leaving Carolyn to choose her own adjectives. He pulls the keyboard close, sets his fingers on it, and gazes at the monitor. Then he licks his lips and pushes it away again, reaching for a pen and a notepad instead. "Tell me what happened."

Carolyn hesitates. There's a reason she hasn't explained this yet, even though she's sure she should have. "We went on Sunday," she says slowly. "Have you talked to Drea and Alaric?" Maybe she can circumvent the hardest parts if they've already explained the bulk of it.

Pawel shakes his head. "No one's come to see me. I assumed everything went well."

Kit snorts; Carolyn gives him a dark look.

"No one died," Kit deadpans. "In fact, at least one person was brought back from the—"

"She wasn't dead." Carolyn wants that fact on the table, that she and Del didn't resurrect Mattie. "She was trapped, her soul separated from her body."

Pawel sits upright, both eyebrows high. "What?"

"We know what makes Shadows," Carolyn says, twisting her fingers together until they hurt. "They Emerge, and their souls slip into the Dreamscape. Mattie was trapped in that house, and we brought her soul back and put it into what's left of her body. There's a Shadow out there with a soul now. The same Shadow you trapped before."

Pawel is silent.

Carolyn can't remember if she's ever seen him without words before. She waits, and Pawel relaxes by millimeters, slowly leaning forward, resting his elbows on the desk again, steepling his fingers under his chin. Kit continues to shrink in his chair, feet stuck out, both hands cradled against his chest.

Carolyn sits stiffly and doesn't say a word.

"Start at the beginning," Pawel says quietly.

It's not that easy, not without going into far more detail than Carolyn wants to. "Short version," she insists. "My friend Del felt like the house was caught in a Dream, and next thing we knew, we were in a Dreamscape there. A girl was there, too, and Drea recognized her as Mattie, the little girl who lived there before the Berman family disappeared. Del didn't know how to get us out of the Dream, and she said that because I'd traveled out before, I could get us out. I thought of a card that reminded me of Alaric, and then there was an illusion, and we all traveled through it to Theobald's office. He wasn't pleased."

"I'm not surprised." Pawel sits back, steepled fingers still under his chin, gaze narrowed. "So the girl Emerged and…"

"…ate her parents, yes, and then got stuck as a soulless beast eating other people," Kit mutters. "Rory was right, you know. That the Shadow is female. She's also coherent now, but she disappeared."

"Mm." Pawel's gaze shifts to Kit, thoughtful.

Kit pushes himself to sit upright, hands in his lap, tugging at his sleeves *again.*

"Are you okay?" Carolyn asks.

Kit looks down. "I'm fine."

He's not. She can hear it in his voice, see it in the way he keeps playing with his shirt. It's pulled out of shape, and he's favoring his right wrist.

Pawel makes a noise, then leans forward again. "Kit, what's wrong with your wrist?"

Kit lifts his arm and cradles it against his chest. "I want to use this attempt to contact Lora as my final project for this semester. It's not what I'd planned, but I've got a lot of ideas about how to make it work better than it went last night."

Pawel tilts his head. "What happened last night?"

Kit exhales. "I don't know. We were in the middle of the ritual, and it was like Shane fell out of it. Tripped sideways or something, I don't know. I reached Lora for a split second, her vitals went crazy, then it all turned off."

"And your wrist?" Pawel gestures.

Kit's gaze lowers. "Fine," he mutters, tugging his sleeve up to his elbow and shoving his arm out to rest on the desk, his inner arm facing up.

There's a black inked guitar on his wrist. A series of notes stretch out from it, wreathing around it. Something about the way guitar looks is wrong, and it takes Carolyn a moment's study to figure out why: the guitar is facing the wrong direction, as if the person playing is left-handed.

"You keep rubbing at it," Pawel comments. "Is it bothering you?"

"What do you think?" Kit snaps. He tugs the sleeve down and crosses his arms tight over his chest. "It hurt like hell when it happened, and I can still feel it. Buzzing. Like ants or bees under my skin. It's been driving me nuts all day."

"Hm." Pawel scratches notes on his paper, tongue trapped between his teeth.

"Kit?" Carolyn asks, not sure what this means.

"Magic thinks I'm Rory's soulmate," Kit mutters.

"And do you?" Pawel asks before Carolyn can form another thought.

"How the hell should I know? We were just getting to be friends," Kit replies. "I don't like something taking the choice away from me. Two days ago I was dating Serina. She broke up with me, then this happened, and I feel like my world has gone haywire. Besides, Rory's dating Darrik, and he's not talking to me."

Carolyn hears the hurt in his voice, the way his words go tight. "Oh, Kit—"

"Don't."

There are so many things she could say. She could point out that he sounds more frustrated by Rory not talking to him for a day than he has about Serina breaking up with him. She could point out that, just like with the Tarot, he could choose to ignore the mark. "Magic can't make you do anything. It can only suggest a path," she says carefully, and he grumbles.

"Speaking of suggestions." Pawel sets down his pen with a soft *thunk*, then taps the edge of his desk. "Get out your notebooks and decks. One card each."

"I'm not predictive," Kit reminds him, but Pawel points at his bag.

"One card, Kit. That's all I'm asking."

"Fine."

Carolyn has her deck in her hand, shuffling it idly. Kit moves more slowly, spilling his cards from their soft blue bag. He stares down at them warily, glancing at Carolyn as he starts to shuffle. Their movements sync up, and they both stop at the same moment.

"Cut or top?" Kit asks.

"Top," Carolyn decides. It feels right.

Kit lays his hand on the top of his deck, then flinches as if he's been stung. Carolyn times her movement to turn hers over at the same time, and they lay their cards next to each other on the edge of Pawel's desk.

"The Queen of Wands and the Seven of Wands," Pawel says. "Magic for both of you."

Magical influences, yes. Also risk, and high rewards, and people who are willing to push for what they want. Carolyn stares down at the Queen of Wands; she's similar in appearance to the Nine of Coins, but her expression is more intent. More driven. She looks as if she's just spoken, and she stares out at Carolyn as if she expects her to say something in return.

"Push beyond your limits," Kit mutters, arms still crossed tightly. "Leave your comfort zone in order to achieve success."

"Mm?" Pawel gestures as if expecting Kit to continue, but Kit shakes his head.

"I get it. There's no need to keep going," Kit says.

"Carolyn?"

"Be a leader without being a leader," she says. "Look to those around you and follow them, encourage them, help them to be their best. Mother them and lead quietly from the back. Let them shine, and your time will come."

"Are you following Del?" Kit asks, and Carolyn shakes her head.

"I don't think so. I don't know who I'm following. I don't even know what I'm doing right now," she admits. "It feels like everything's gone upside down on me."

"Join the club," Kit grumbles.

"That's your assignment for next week," Pawel says, and Carolyn has no idea what he means. He gestures at the card as if they'll add sense to his statement.

"Write down what you think is happening," Pawel says. "Challenge yourself to look past the minor details and delve into the spaces between them to determine why it's happening now and how you can take hold of it. Don't let this Emergence control you."

"Lineage Talent doesn't—"

Pawel holds up a hand before Kit can finish his statement. "The one thing I've learned in the past few months, Kit, is that everything we know is wrong. I can name several Lineage Talents that have changed; Carolyn's is far from the only one. And you're just figuring out how to be comfortable with your own Talent. So look inside, both of you. Carolyn, I want a detailed report on what happened while you were in Haverhill. Include any outside influences, and your thoughts on why certain pieces interacted as they did. Look at how what happened then is affecting you now. Kit…"

Kit tilts his head, jaw set. "What?"

Pawel's voice gentles. "I want to hear more about the ritual you performed last night. You need to understand what went right, what went wrong, and why. Also, if you intend to use this as your final project, you'll need to revise the ritual, and you'll need to work with Rory and Shane."

"I know."

"You'll need to talk to Rory—"

"I know!" Kit snaps. He grabs the card from the desk, shoves it on top of his deck, and puts the deck in the bag. He pulls the drawstring sharply, then pushes it into his backpack. "I'm trying," he says. "I'm trying to talk to Rory, and he's not answering. You want to say that the mark is like a Tarot card, right? It's predictive, offering an option. Something to think about. Well, here's something for you to think about." He stands, shouldering his bag roughly. "I'm not predictive, and every time I try to be, it goes wrong. I tell other people's fortunes and I get the wrong messages. It's not for *me*. So maybe this is just another missed message, okay? Maybe the magic got it wrong."

He pushes out of the office, the door slamming shut in his wake.

Carolyn remembers to breathe with an awkward cough.

Pawel slumps, head tilted back against his chair. "Please be careful," he murmurs.

"I will be," Carolyn assures him. "I don't plan on playing with shadows," she adds, as if not doing so will help.

Pawel smiles thinly, his eyes closed. "Good girl," he says. "I suppose that's about all I can ask. Think about your project while you're working through what happened. I still need a proposal from you so I can approve it."

"I know." Carolyn rises slowly. She lifts her bag onto the chair and stows her things, waiting for Pawel to continue speaking. When he doesn't, she takes the chance to look at him.

His skin is pale under his freckles. The lines at his eyes seem more distinct than they were a half hour ago. "We're all going to be okay, you know," she says, even though a positive outcome is not hers to promise.

"I know," he replies on an exhale.

Carolyn is pretty sure they're both lying, but it's the best she can do.

20

It's QUIET IN the house for a Friday night. Carolyn thinks that most of her sisters are out, but she has no desire to drink or party or be with a crowd.

She curls up on the couch in the common room and turns on the TV. In the absence of her sisters, there's no need to compromise on what to watch; it's easy to flick through the channels until she finds a mindless cooking show. She slouches down, feet on the table, and daydreams about cupcakes.

They do look good.

She could go find a place to get one.

That would mean leaving the house.

The front door cracks open, and she hears a cheery voice. "Thanks, Soledad!" Footsteps head up the stairs, and Carolyn really hopes that Soledad going up to see Trish means they've made up. She glances up, about to call out, but Serina is standing in the doorway, lingering as if she can't step over the threshold into the common room without an invitation.

"Hey," Serina says.

Carolyn puts her feet down, trying to wiggle her toes back into socks that have gone loose, and straightens up. "Hey."

"So, I..." Serina's voice trails off, and she takes a step closer. When Carolyn gestures at the chairs and the rest of the couch, Serina lets out a soft huff and takes a seat on the couch. "You probably heard," she says. She chews on a fingernail, nerves clear.

"That you broke up with Kit? Yes." Carolyn thinks there has to be more to the conversation than this. "Please don't tell me you want to get back together."

Serina's hand drops, her eyes going wide as she shakes her head. She brings up both hands, palms out. "No. Oh, no. No. I just—he's not answering my texts. I can't blame him, but he didn't really say much on Tuesday. I'm worried about him. It's been like three days since then, and I figured he'd at least send an 'I'm okay' kind of thing back. But he hasn't."

Carolyn licks her lips. "He's had a shitty week. It's not just about you."

"Oh." Serina slumps, shoulders rounded. "I feel—like I should've been there for him. If he needed someone."

"That would have been even more awkward." Carolyn can't imagine being in Kit's position, trying to tell Serina about the soul mark appearing on his wrist. "Give him time. He'll talk to you again, I'm sure. You're still friends."

"We're still friends." She hesitates, glances over. "We're supposed to go to Paint It Red together tomorrow night. So, I'd like to know if he's willing to even talk to me before then. I know it's going to be awkward and weird; maybe I should just pay him for the ticket so we can go separately. But we talked about it on Tuesday, and I thought everything was okay, but then he stopped responding to me."

Carolyn's pretty sure she knows exactly when Kit stopped responding. She pulls her phone out. "I'll poke him. I'm pretty sure he's not going to forget about tomorrow; he's probably just wrapped up in everything else." She texts,

You should talk to Serina at some point to make your plans for tomorrow. She's worried about you.

Dots appear right away, then disappear and don't come back. Carolyn figures Kit will get back to her—and deal with Serina—in his own time. There's nothing she can do to force things.

"I really liked him." Serina worries at her fingernail again. "Like him. I mean. We're friends, and he's really cool, and I had this massive crush before. Like I could barely talk sometimes which, as you might guess, is kind of weird for me. I'd get all blushing and giggly. It's like when I had the crush on Nate, before I found out he's not into girls. But then we started dating—Kit, I mean, not Nate—and we got along pretty well. Like, we could talk, and I felt pretty normal, not like I was going to blush and giggle all the time. And I liked kissing him." She stops suddenly, darts a look at Carolyn. "Is this weird?"

"Talking about you kissing my brother? Yes." It's not something Carolyn wants to think about. Kit never wanted details about her relationships back in high school, either.

"I mean talking about Kit in general. Like, he's your brother. Your twin. So your first loyalty is to him, always," Serina says. "But I figure you and I could be friends, too, and you're probably the only person here who would have any idea what it's like to miss him. Or to be close to him, even if it's different. Because he doesn't seem like he gets close to people. I'm not sure he was even actually getting close to me."

Carolyn doesn't think she can escape the weird and awkward. Serina seems determined to bull onward, and Carolyn doesn't have the heart to kick her out of the house. There's something sweetly earnest about Serina. "Kit struggles opening up sometimes," she says.

"I was willing to wait. I understand having trust issues, and that not everyone is extroverted." Serina waves a hand at her chest. "I mean, obviously I am. But it's okay that he's an introvert. I just— We didn't…"

"Spark," Carolyn suggests. "Kit thinks you're looking for explosions."

Serina flushes brightly. "Okay. Um. Maybe? Yes, probably. Not even really big explosions. I just want it to be more than sweet and nice. I want to feel my toes tingling. I want to be comfortable, but I want to be just a little bit uncomfortable, too. And Kit and I—we're totally comfortable. It was nice. And he's really sweet."

"The relationship just wasn't working," Carolyn says.

"Yes!" Serina relaxes, hands falling into her lap. "He said it wasn't working for him, either. As, like, a relationship thing. I totally want to stay friends with him, and I hope we can do that. I mean. I like him. A lot. He's always going to be super sweet, and I hope we can hang out and stuff. And if he meets the right girl, that'll be awesome, and I'll totally ship it. I just wasn't that girl, I guess." She taps her fingers along her knees. "I don't have a good track record in crushes. I mean, since I got here, there's been Nate and Kit. Back in high school, I either crushed on the unobtainable ones or dated someone for a week and realized it was never going to go anywhere. I think I held the record for 'futile crushes on straight girls' during my junior year."

It's more information than Carolyn can reasonably handle in one blurt.

"Maybe stop looking," she says, and at Serina's stricken look, she realizes that came out wrong.

"I mean—" Carolyn stops, struggling to find the right words. "I dated the same guy for a long time in high school. And have dated no one else since. I'm probably no good at relationship advice. But I remember, after Shawn and I broke up, I talked to my mother about it. She said that if I was looking and finding the wrong thing, then I should stop looking and let the right thing find me. Because trying too hard can push you in the wrong direction. You're driven by all these internal assumptions."

"Oh." Serina sticks the tip of her pinky between her teeth. "You think I'm looking for something unreasonable."

"I was looking for one thing, and Shawn was looking for something else, and I was confused because how things happened wasn't how media had taught me life was supposed to be," Carolyn says. "We were really fucked up. I don't know if my mother was right, but I realized that I didn't want to look for something solely because I've been told I'm supposed to have it. I want to find something, eventually, that's the right thing." She remembers Kit's card draw from Thursday, and adds quietly, "Even if that means I have to go outside my comfort zone."

Serina chews on her pinky nail aggressively, brow furrowed. "Okay. So. You mean like how every movie and book says we're not complete unless we're with someone."

Not exactly.

"Sure," Carolyn says, "if that's what it means to you."

"Mm."

Carolyn worries for the health of Serina's fingertip. She can see the break in the nail; it's peeling away at the top, but Serina's obviously using it as a soothing mechanism while thinking.

Maybe what Serina needs is a distraction. A break-up-appropriate distraction.

"We should get ice cream," Carolyn suggests. At Serina's startled look, she says, "Sweet Scoops is open, and it's February, so it won't be packed. You're suffering the heartbreak, so I'll treat."

Serina's brow remains furrowed, pinky still caught between her teeth.

"You need to chew on something better than your own hands," Carolyn says. She wraps her fingers around Serina's wrist and nudges her hand down.

"You're probably right." Serina looks down, then her smile comes back, bright and happy. "Okay. Ice cream it is. Are we walking to Sweet Scoops, or do you have a car?" She turns her hand in Carolyn's, clasps her firmly, and squeezes. "Thank you."

Serina's palm is warm, her grip tight. Carolyn's ears go warm, and she tries to smile back, to be supportive. She's not sure what response would be correct, so she nods to acknowledge the thanks and says, "Walking. If you don't mind the cold."

"I forgot gloves, but I'll be okay." Serina waves it off, and they head to the door together. Serina grabs a jacket from the floor where it lies next to a backpack. "Is it okay if I leave my bag here?"

"You can grab it later." Carolyn's jacket is in the closet, her boots stored nearby. She waits while Serina tugs on a hat and wraps a scarf around her neck. She pauses once she's ready, then offers the only way to help she really has. "Do you want me to bring my deck and do a reading for you?"

Serina's eyes light up, and she claps her hands together. "Yes, definitely. Thank you."

It only takes a moment for Carolyn to run upstairs and grab her wrapped deck and notebook, tucking them under her arm before they head out into the cold.

Serina shoves her hands deep in her pockets and she tilts her head back, sending puffs of condensation into the sky. "Spring is going to come eventually," she says, voice light.

"It always seems like winter lasts forever around here," Carolyn says, each word visible as breath upon the air. "But it comes up fast, too. One day we're buried in snow, the next the sun's beaming down and everything green is poking through the dirt."

"Do you think it'll be different this year?"

The question sounds simple, but it's not. "I think Nikita's doing better," Carolyn says. She considers her next words carefully, but before she can continue, Serina hunches her shoulders, shivering. Juggling her deck and notebook, Carolyn strips off her gloves and hands them to Serina. "You're colder than me."

Serina takes them, slipping them on and rubbing her hands together. "Thanks again. And I'm sorry." She glances at Carolyn. "Nikita doesn't sleep on our floor much anymore. She tried this thing with Rory—he said he could help her using his Talent." Carolyn wonders if Rory realizes how many people know about that now. She nods, motioning for Serina to go on. "So, it sounds like Nikita is staying at your place a lot?"

"Heather's helping her." It's later in the evening than Carolyn had realized, but as they turn onto the right street, Carolyn can see that Sweet Scoops is still brightly lit, a few intrepid people sitting on the stone wall outside eating their ice cream, a few others inside. She moves ahead quickly, pulls the door open, and holds it for Serina. "I'd planned to ask Heather about helping with my independent study project, but she's busy with Nikita. Except for the storm when my friend came to visit, it's been good." Serina gives her a look; Carolyn wishes she hadn't mentioned it. "Del's not a Dreamweaver, and neither am I. But things are weird for all of us, and our weird interacted with Nikita's weird. That storm…"

Serina nods like there's only been one recent storm that Carolyn could mean.

Carolyn touches Serina's shoulder and points at the board listing the day's flavors. "Get whatever'll make you feel best."

"I think it's the company more than the sweets, but I'm not going to turn down free ice cream." Serina grins at her and heads straight up to order. "One scoop of double chocolate with pretzels and salted caramels, and one scoop of dulce de leche with chocolate chips and peanut-butter cups. Hot fudge and whipped cream on top, please."

They wait for her toppings to be mixed into each scoop and her bowl to be topped off. Carolyn's is a simpler order—vanilla bean with gummy bears on top—and she pays quickly.

Serina pauses as they look for a seat. There are plenty available, but Carolyn follows Serina's gaze to where Cass sits alone to one side, tongue poked between her lips as she reads something on her phone.

"Should we—?"

Carolyn shakes her head. "This is for you. And she looks like she's busy."

Cass glances up at the sound of Carolyn's voice, and Carolyn raises her hand in greeting. She does tilt her head, a silent offer that Cass can choose to join them if she wants, but Cass goes back to looking at her phone.

They pick a table off to the side. It's meant for four, but the place is empty enough that Carolyn doesn't feel guilty taking the extra space, and it allows them to sit on the same side together. Carolyn lays her notebook and deck on the table, setting them aside until she's had a chance to eat her ice cream.

"So." Serina jabs her spoon into the paper bowl and comes up with a blend of ice creams and mix-ins. She gestures at Carolyn. "Do you actually want to read for me, or was that you being nice? Or do you want to talk about how it's weird having Nikita in your room like an extra roommate? Or about any of the other weirdnesses going around?"

"Are things weird for you?" Carolyn counters.

Serina laughs and pops the bite of ice cream in her mouth. She swallows and murmurs softly, "I forgot how good the ice cream is here. Why don't we always come here? Why did we stop coming here?" She stops, gestures between herself and Carolyn. "I mean, not 'we,' we, but 'we as a whole,' like students at PHU. Why did we stop eating ice cream when it got cold out? But we"—she gestures again—"can definitely come here together again."

"Because the weather's been so cold it was like hell froze over a few times," Carolyn says drily. "We'll have to plan to come back."

Serina gestures between them again with a happy smile. "Yes. We will. And my life isn't weird. Unless you consider starting to work at Teas Please, starting to date your brother, and then promptly breaking up with him again to be weird. Oh, or going out with him tomorrow because we already have tickets. At least. I think we are. I do have a red dress. We're supposed to wear red, right?"

"The sisters have to, but you don't," Carolyn says. She's trying to eat her ice cream rapidly, but the rush of cold is quick, leaving the roof of her mouth aching. "But it's nice if you do."

"I'm not Talented." Serina nods as she speaks, answering the current conversation and the prior question simultaneously. "So nothing really high-level weird happens to me. Maybe if you do a reading, I'll have an idea what's coming next?" There's a bird-chirp sound, and Serina fishes her phone out of her pocket and lays it face down on the table. "If you were serious, that is."

"I was serious, but some of my weird is the cards not always behaving," Carolyn admits. "Sometimes they're doing things they shouldn't."

"Like what?"

Carolyn ignores the question, shuffling her deck. "So, I'm going to do a three-card draw, which is one of the simpler layouts, to give you some things to think about. Sometimes we do a one-card—it'd tell you just your potential. But I like the three-card because it gives you a kind of past-present-future look at things." She finishes shuffling and slides the deck toward Serina. "Cut it," she instructs, opening her notebook so she can record the reading.

Serina considers the deck. She chews on the end of her plastic spoon, then carefully removes the top few cards and sets them aside. She removes another stack of cards, puts them on top of the first set, then puts that pile on top of the deck and pushes them back to Carolyn.

"Like that," she says.

It wasn't the weirdest cut Carolyn has ever seen, but it was definitely methodical. Hopefully the cards were paying attention.

She lays them out from left to right: the Five of Pentacles, the Three of Cups reversed, and the Prince of Cups. As she sets the last down, something unpleasant twists in her gut.

It must show on her face. "What?" Serina asks. "The first card looks dark, but the others don't look awful."

"So, in your past, you were in the dark," Carolyn says, and draws in breath. "That fits with what you were telling me, if we're talking about relationships. You had a lot of tension, and a lot of want and need, but not a lot of resolution. And it's a continuous path: you keep trying, you keep not getting what you need, and you keep moving on. You have to keep moving on to try to resolve that tension inside of you."

She taps the second card, depicting two lovers, their cups overflowing but upside down. "That brings us to now, and this card, which is usually a good one. It's about being perfectly in tune—in synergy—with another person. But because it's upside down, so is the relationship. You think you've finally found the right person to be with, the right place to be, but everything's awkward and every note is out of sync. You're probably trying too hard."

Serina huffs. "We already talked about this." She leans forward and touches the last card on the table. "So what does tall, dark, and grouchy have to do with my future?"

"The Prince of Cups is both a good sign and a warning sign. See the scorpion? And the wand in the background?" Carolyn touches both, and Serina's finger moves with her as they brush together across the surface of the card. "He's a trickster. He's holding out the cup, so he's supposedly all about love, but there's also risk, and a bit of illusion, involved. On the other hand, he's about potential. If you take the risk, you could get a reward. A really big one. Cups are about love, and emotion, and finding resonance with someone else. The question is, is he who you're looking for, or do you need to dig deeper and look beyond the surface and take a chance on someone else?"

Serina sits back. "Oh. Well. I guess that makes sense."

"Does it?" Because Carolyn could come up with ways for it to work, but it seems muddled to her.

Serina nods once, a quick, abrupt motion. "It does. I think it does. I mean. Take risks. But like you said, don't just do what I think I want. Because maybe I think I want something because the world told me that's what I want, so I need to get past the illusion." She gestures at the card. "I don't want to get bitten by the scorpion, but I wouldn't mind a bit of magic."

None of that made sense to Carolyn, but Serina seems satisfied, which is good. Carolyn carefully notes the cards and interpretation in her notebook before sweeping the cards up to put them away. By the time she's finished, Serina's mostly done with her ice cream.

Serina reaches for Carolyn's cup and slides it in front of Carolyn. "Eat. Your gummies are going to drown in vanilla soup at this rate."

"You say that like I don't like melted ice cream." Carolyn sticks her tongue out, then quickly slurps the melted vanilla from her spoon.

She likes how it sounds when Serina laughs, as if some of Serina's tension has slipped away.

Serina nudges her with an elbow. "Okay. Now that we're done talking about my horrible attempts at having a love life, do you want to talk about your weird stuff with the cards? They seemed pretty good to me."

Apparently Serina isn't going to let Carolyn sidestep her problems. That's probably good. Normally, Heather would keep track of her, make sure that Carolyn didn't feel emotions that made Heather's skin prickle, but because of Nikita…Heather's been busy.

It's funny how Carolyn misses Heather's interference now that it's gone.

"Sometimes the readings have been off," Carolyn admits slowly, "but it's been better since I traveled."

"When you went with Drea and Alaric?" Serina asks.

"Yes. But no." Carolyn pulls her cards out again, finding comfort in shuffling them idly as she talks. She tells Serina an abbreviated version of the story—the Dream first, then going to Haverhill and confirming that the Dream was real.

Serina furrows her brow and tilts her head as she listens. She taps her spoon against her mostly empty bowl, then knocks into Carolyn's. "Eat your vanilla soup," she says.

Carolyn sets down her deck again, slides it to the side, and tries not to think about it as she finishes her ice cream. They both push their cups away at the same time, and Serina turns her chair to face Carolyn's.

"Okay. So. In your Dream, when you were in the house with the wolf, there was a card on the floor behind you, right? That took you back to your dorm," Serina says.

Carolyn nods.

"Which card was it?"

Carolyn opens her mouth, then closes it. She frowns and shakes her head. "I don't know. I remember seeing my room on the card. I saw it, focused on it. It opened up into a life-size image of my room, and I fell into it. That's definitely not a card in my deck."

"Do you have any pictures of your room?" Serina asks. Of course Carolyn has pictures of her room. She and Heather have been living in the same room at SigPsiEp for a year and a half now, and they've taken dozens of selfies and pictures of friends in that room. But images like that don't feel like the right answer to Serina's question.

Photographs aren't the same as Tarot.

Carolyn reaches for her notebook and flips through it to the beginning. She started this notebook a long time ago, and she thinks…maybe… She skims through pages until she finds one that isn't drawn in her own hand. It's Kit's work, and it stands out from her own art. It's better. More real. He drew it when she and Heather first moved into the room, and it shows only the barest outline of how their room looks. It has little symbols, though, like an emoji poster near Heather's pillow that isn't there in the real world. That was Kit's way of saying that an Empath lived there. Carolyn's Tarot deck is scattered across her bedspread, along with a smattering of photos of herself and Kit. The lamp shines brightly, and the room is welcoming.

Carolyn touches the page of her notebook, and it feels right. She shows it to Serina. "Kit drew this."

"And that's the card you saw," Serina says.

Carolyn nods. It may not be exactly the same, but it's pretty close.

Serina covers Carolyn's hands and makes her lay the notebook flat in front of her. "You have to try it! Maybe not the traveling thing, but can you make an illusion out of this? It's something you have resonance with, and you did it before, right? And it's Kit's art, so it's like it's a part of you."

This is a really bad idea. They're sitting in the middle of Sweet Scoops, although it's late enough that most of the tables have emptied. There's a couple in one corner, more attention on each other than on the room at large. One boy sits studying at a large table, his ice cream melting nearby. And Cass is still there, watching them over the edge of her phone, expression inscrutable.

"A small illusion," Carolyn agrees, even though she doesn't have that much control. Or any control. She's not even sure she can do it on demand.

She settles her fingers on the image; that feels like the right thing to do. It's a little cool, and the page feels slick under her fingertips. She's aware of Serina leaning into her, a line of warmth against her shoulder.

Carolyn pulls back, sitting upright.

"What?"

Carolyn chooses her words carefully. "I don't think you should touch me while I do this. In case something happens."

Serina blinks at her and cocks her head. "But touching you other times is okay?" she asks, and warmth floods Carolyn's cheeks.

Carolyn nods, and Serina throws her arms around her, yanking her close for a quick hug. "I want to be friends," Serina whispers, breath tickling Carolyn's ear. She pulls away, brushing Carolyn's shoulder as if cleaning away any remainder of her touch. "I'll sit back," she promises.

Carolyn's skin tingles, and when she sets her fingers against the picture once more, it feels like a small shock. The paper seems to have changed to something smoother, slicker, and colder. She presses her fingertips down against it, and the images come to life in three dimensions, like a pop-up from the book.

"Oh," Serina whispers.

It's so easy. So right. Like this is something that's been inside of her all along, just waiting to come out. And it's so much simpler with this picture. Maybe Serina's right, and it's because it's Kit's work. Because he's her twin.

She exhales, and the image grows. It expands until it takes over the tabletop.

Oh, shit.

It's too big. Too much.

Carolyn tries to lift her fingers, but they're stuck to the page. She manages to free one hand as the image expands; she grabs onto her deck, fingers curling against the edge of her notebook.

"Carolyn?" Serina asks. She sounds far away.

She can hear whispers in the distance. Voices. Murmurs.

Carolyn tries one more time to step back, but the image sucks her in, and she tumbles forward into her room. She lands by her bed, her knees slamming into the floor. She cries out at the pain and curls her fingers tight, body hunching. "Fuck."

She looks up as Nikita and Heather push back from each other. Heather's ponytail is askew, Nikita's fingers still tangled at the base. Heather's lips are wet, and a smudge of Nikita's lipstick stains the side of her mouth. Nikita blinks at Carolyn, and there's a rumble in the distance.

"Carolyn?" Heather pulls back, and Nikita's fingers slip free of her hair.

"What are you doing here? What happened?"

Carolyn can't quite catch her breath. "I didn't mean to interrupt you," she mutters, ducking her gaze away.

"You're always here," Nikita grumbles, almost too softly to hear.

"Nik," Heather says, and there's another rumble outside.

Carolyn curls her hands tighter, rocks back on her heels, and stands unsteadily. Her knees are throbbing; the heel of her hand aches from hitting the ground. "Traveled," she says. "Illusion. Again. Didn't mean to."

"No, it's fine. I'll go." Nikita slides off the bed and searches until she finds her jacket.

Heather's eyes are wide, brow furrowed. "Nik."

Carolyn shakes her head, puts her hands up. "No. Seriously. I'll go. I didn't mean to interrupt. I didn't know there was anything to interrupt. I mean. You're—" She falters because she can end that statement any number of ways based on the information she has.

Nikita shoves one arm into her coat and twists to try to get her second hand into it. "I mean it. I'll go. You two—whatever." The rumble grows louder.

Heather's gaze skates to the window. She inches forward and lays a hand on Nikita's shoulder only to have it shaken off. "Nikita, you—"

"I told you," Nikita says. She manages to get the second arm in, then buttons exactly one button before giving up. She turns toward Heather, and her expression softens. "I'll see you."

There's nothing kind left when she glares at Carolyn and storms out.

Carolyn swallows hard. "I didn't know."

"That was our first kiss," Heather says softly. "Probably our last."

"I'll fix it," Carolyn tells her, and rushes out the door before Heather can realize that Carolyn can't fix her own life, let alone anyone else's.

Everything lately comes down to relationships. And everything is a mess.

And shit. Her deck and notebook. Either they're on the floor of her room or she left them with Serina at Sweet Scoops. She doesn't have the hang of traveling yet, although she's beginning vaguely to understand it. She thinks.

It's a pity that she doesn't have a way to get downstairs faster. Her sisters watch as she takes the steps two at a time, then yanks open the front door.

"Are you okay?" Mac calls out, and Carolyn waves before stepping through.

"I'm fine!" she yells.

"Oh, good." Nikita's still there, just past the front steps. Her words punctuate the slam of the front door behind Carolyn, but she doesn't turn to look. "I wouldn't want to think you're not fine."

"Nikita, why are you so angry at me?" Carolyn knows why she should be upset with Nikita, but she can't understand why Nikita is this upset.

"Why?" Thunder cracks, closer now. There's a hint of ozone in the air. "Because I finally worked up the courage to ask my crush if I could kiss her, and then you land in the middle of the room interrupting us! I like her! I really like her, and every time I turn around it's all about you."

Carolyn shivers in a stiff breeze, and she crosses her arms against the cold. "You shouldn't get so involved with her." She knows the words aren't kind, but they're true. "It's not—" She halts as the first drops of sleet hit her face, sliding over her nose.

"Why?" Nikita asks, spreading her hands. "Because you think she's not pretty enough? Because she's not skinny enough, or maybe she's not gay enough for me? Or maybe it's because you think I'm stealing your best friend and you're jealous."

"It's not that." It's not just that, anyway. Yes, maybe Carolyn is a little jealous. Nikita's always there. She comes first right now, but Carolyn understands why. "She's trying to help you," Carolyn blurts. "You have a semi-professional relationship. You're working on a project together."

Nikita's gaze narrows, her lips pursed tightly. Lightning streaks through the sky, thunder booms, and the skies open up. It's too cold for rain, but too violent for snow; water falls in icy droplets, beating against Carolyn, melting as soon as they hit her skin.

"Are you saying I'm just a project to her?" Nikita asks, voice dark and low. "Are you trying to say that what I'm feeling aren't my own emotions? That she's manipulating me? Because she wouldn't do that."

"Of course she wouldn't." This conversation has slid out of control, and Carolyn has no idea how to get it back on track. "I'm just saying that maybe, while you two are working together, you shouldn't—" She stops at the next bolt of lightning and crack of thunder.

"I really like Heather." Nikita carefully enunciates each word. "I love her hair, and her eyes, and her mouth. I love her style, and how she always tries to make sure everyone's happy. I want to help her be happy, too, because she deserves it. She's an incredible person, and everyone here takes advantage of her. This whole sorority"—Nikita waves a hand at the front of the house—"you all assume she's going to be there to pick up the pieces. None of you know how to emote on your own anymore."

"I was broken long before I got here." The words fall flat between them, and Carolyn flinches at the sound of her own voice. "Heather offered to help me. I never asked. And I try not to ask. I try not to lean on her, and she is an amazing best friend. And I do miss her, and I'm probably jealous, but I just—I don't want to see her get hurt."

Nikita blinks, laughs sharply. "I'm not the one hurting her right now."

"Then you should go back inside," Carolyn says quietly. "I'll leave."

Nikita shakes her head. "Mood is officially broken. I'll text her, and I was already planning on going to Paint It Red with her tomorrow."

"Will you be coming back to the room afterward?" Carolyn's positive that it's a stupid question; Nikita's been there most nights lately, and they weren't even dating yet.

Maybe Carolyn should've noticed before.

Maybe she should have talked to Heather.

It's too late; she can't go back in time and fix it.

Nikita tilts her chin up. "Probably." She takes a step back as thunder and lightning crack again; this time the flash comes a little before the sound. The storm is receding as Nikita moves away, although the sleet still falls hard.

"I'll see you then." It's meant to be an offer. An olive branch. Carolyn hopes Nikita understands it as she walks away, past where Cass's car sits idling by the sidewalk.

Great.

The car stops, and Cass hops out, her jacket tugged close around her body as if she's holding something in. "Go inside," Cass orders. "Unless you want to stick around out here in the cold rain."

"Sleet," Carolyn says, but she follows when Cass motions at the open door.

Carolyn peels off her wet coat and hangs it on a hook. Her hair dangles around her face, dripping over her shirt, and her fingers are frozen. She hops, trying to warm up, blowing on her hands.

Cass stows her coat in the closet. When she turns around, she holds out Carolyn's notebook. "I gave Serina a ride home since you left so abruptly, but when I got here, I didn't want to interrupt what was obviously an argument."

"I took my deck?" she asks.

"You must have. Neither Serina nor I saw your cards on the table." Cass frowns. "You don't know?"

"I traveled into my room, and Heather and Nik were kissing. Then Nik stormed out, and like you saw, we were arguing." Carolyn chooses to leave the description simple, though she has a feeling they'd have done more than kiss if Carolyn hadn't interrupted.

Maybe she should talk to Heather about tomorrow night. Make different arrangements.

She has no idea where she would go. She doesn't have the energy for another complicated, emotional conversation right now.

She's done.

Cass catches her elbow, guides her into the living room, and sits her down on the couch next to Mac. Somehow they're the only ones there now, though Carolyn swears there were more sisters around when she stormed out.

"You don't look okay," Cass says.

Now that she's inside, the sleet clicking against the windows, she's cold. Carolyn exhales roughly and tries to control her shivering. "I'm not okay," Carolyn agrees. "But I'll be okay. I mean, it's nothing bad. Just. It was a surprise. That's all. And I don't think…" She trails off because both Cass and Mac are looking at her. Just looking, but Carolyn can feel the weight of it. "What?"

"I'm not even going to pretend not to know what's going on, because the whole house heard you," Mac says drily. "And Carolyn, I love you, but maybe what you think doesn't matter right now. Maybe what Heather and Nikita think is all that matters."

"I know Mac and I don't always see eye to eye, but I agree with her on this one." Cass leans forward and touches Carolyn's knee. "Would you want someone to tell you who you could date? Or, like, how you can use your Talent, and who you should hang out with? To dictate who you can talk to about your life?"

Carolyn licks her lips; she shudders as a deep chill rolls through. "Of course not."

Cass smiles slightly. "You looked like you were having fun tonight."

"Really?" Mac's eyebrows go up.

Cass rolls her eyes. "Not now. Earlier. She was at Sweet Scoops with Serina."

"Getting ice cream seemed like the right thing to do. She broke up with Kit." And Carolyn just leapt out of the place and abandoned her there. She's a great friend. "Thanks for getting her home."

"I almost brought her back here, but I wasn't sure if this was where you'd gone. I kind of saw the illusion you made, and it looked like your room?"

"Yeah." Carolyn pats her side and feels the shape of her phone in her pocket. "I should text Serina. See if she's okay. Let her know I accidentally traveled back to the house." She looks up to find Mac still watching her with concern. "I'll be fine," she insists. She stands up slowly, hair still hanging limply in her face, creating cold puddles on her shirt. "I just need to go dry off. And talk to Serina. And apologize to Heather."

But when she gets upstairs, her room is empty. The purple bag with her deck lies on the floor near her bed; seeing it unwinds a tense knot in her gut. Carolyn shuts the door carefully behind herself and quickly strips, pulling on dry pajamas. She has to walk down the hall to hang her clothes in the bathroom to dry, but once that's done, she puts her deck away, curls up on her bed, and finally looks at her phone.

I heard from Kit, Serina sent a few minutes ago.

Will you be there tomorrow night? Carolyn doesn't ask her if she's okay. She's had that conversation too many times in the last ten minutes.

He's picking me up, so yes. We're still going together, as friends. I think we're on our way to figuring things out.

Carolyn smiles slightly at her phone. *Good.*

She sets the phone on her bed and pads on bare feet to the door. She stands there for a long moment before she opens it cautiously and peers down the hall.

Nothing. No one.

She grabs her notebook and a pair of scissors on the way back to the bed. She drops both to pick up her phone and send a text to Heather: *I'm sorry.* She doesn't expect an answer, but she hopes that if Heather doesn't come back tonight, she's somewhere safe, and she's happy, and she's not just hiding from Carolyn.

They've never fought, and Carolyn doesn't know how to feel about it.

Carolyn opens the notebook, flipping through it until she finds Kit's sketch of the room. She hates to do it, but she neatly cuts the image out of the page, staying as close to the outer edge of the picture as possible. She's left with an image that's maybe six inches wide and a few inches tall. She touches it, but it's just paper now, and she doesn't want to think about what would happen if she tried to travel to someplace where she's already sitting. Hopefully, it just wouldn't work, but sometimes Talent does strange things. It's best not to chance it.

Instead, she carefully folds the picture and tucks it into the plastic holder that holds her student ID. It could come in handy; Carolyn wants to make sure she always has this escape route on her. She wants to rely on what she knows works, not what she dreams.

21

ACCESS TO SPECIAL collections at the library requires authorization, but one perk of being an upper-level Magical Studies student is that Carolyn's pre-authorized for the part of the collection that contains texts related to Talent. They're kept in a separate room, the walls lined with glass-fronted bookshelves that are filled with books of all shapes and sizes. Not a one of these tomes has ever been mass produced, although several, dating from as early as the seventies, have been printed from computer texts, and some from before then were reproduced by mimeo.

It's like mixing texts hand-copied by monks with old-school zines.

Every single text is a first-hand account of Talent. They have, to a point, been cataloged and organized, though Carolyn wishes they were cross-referenced under more in-depth topics. She knows that Pawel hopes to digitize them, but for now, collecting them in one place is his primary goal.

The room is smaller than the main special collections room, but there's still enough space for two large wooden tables, each surrounded by a half-dozen chairs. Carolyn leaves her bag on one chair, her laptop open on the table and ready for notes. She can't take photographs of any of the texts, but she plans to type up notes on what she finds.

If she finds anything.

The texts are organized by geographical location first, then by year. Carolyn is positive that there's a logic behind that, given how different specialties tend to group together, but it's not helpful right now. It takes Carolyn hours of searching, starting in the Northeast US and spreading from there, before she has managed to find a handful of texts. She steps away from the wall and stretches, pressing her hands at the base of her back as she arches.

There's a knock on the door; Carolyn turns as it creaks open. She flushes, realizing that she's been on display through the glass door and large windows. The librarian smiles slightly as she pokes her head in, and it's almost reassuring. Carolyn wishes she could remember her name.

"I'm doing fine," Carolyn tells her. "But I'm probably going to be at this for hours."

"We're looking for a student hire to help us cross-reference the works," the librarian says. "If you happen to know anyone in the Magical Studies program looking for work."

Carolyn suspects there are plenty. "I'll ask around with my sisters and classmates," she tells her. "Don't worry, I'm being careful with the texts. I'm looking for some fairly specific information."

"Isn't everyone who uses this room?" The librarian waves a hand, a silent signal to go on, and backs out, closing the door carefully.

Carolyn sits down at the table and picks up the top book she found, a slim volume handwritten in the late 19th century. It looks like a cross between a diary, a list of recipes, and an old-fashioned spell book. On the first page, the script begins, "This is the story of one Josephine Adams, and her sister Clara, and the things they saw in the cards."

It sounds promising.

Carolyn brings up a fresh document and begins to read and type notes. Josephine was fifteen years old when the volume began, and Carolyn flips to the end to note that, according to the date, Josephine was seventeen by that time, and her sister had just turned fifteen. The time can affect a reading when it comes to interpreting the cards, so tracking it is important. She has the advantage of being able to look back and see a greater picture than the girls could.

She skims through the book, pausing whenever the cards are mentioned. Both Josephine and Clara were being raised in traditional ritual, but they'd received a hand-drawn deck from their maternal grandmother a year before the book began. While there are periodic sketches of cards from the deck, none of them are detailed enough for Carolyn to find more than hints of symbolism or get more than a feeling for what the card was like. She wonders if the deck itself has been preserved in special collections as well, or if the family still passes it on.

She pauses on a day that shows the Wheel of Fortune at the top, Strength next to it, and the Hanged Man beside that.

> *We met a family of wolves today. The grandfather could no longer change, his wolf aged and grey about the muzzle, his breath sour and some teeth missing. He curled by the fire, while the mother and father sat with our elders and spoke. We children were sent away.*
>
> *The eldest son of the Clan family—Bernard—argued that he was adult enough to remain, but he was sent with us outside. Clara, of course, peppered him with questions. She has never met a Clan boy before, and made him shift to show his claws, and his teeth. He was gentle with her; for that I am thankful.*
>
> *She insisted that I Read for him, and he agreed. Even though he snarled and bared his teeth when I brought forth the Cards. He whined as each was laid upon the table, and refused to come to his human form.*
>
> *I have never laid a Reading before that was entirely of Trump. This family looks to outside sources, both for strength and for leadership. They have nothing within. When Death was the final card laid, I gathered them all up and told him to be ready for Great Change.*
>
> *They only stayed through dinner, then left, running on four feet through the woods as if the very Shadows hunted them down. I asked Mother what brought them here, and she refused to answer.*
>
> *She said that dark times are coming, and that Clara and I should not Read. It is not true Talent.*
>
> *Grandmother disagreed. Clara and I have hidden the deck so Mother cannot take it from us.*

The cards are drawn more carefully than the other illustrations in the diary, and the passage ends with an image of Death. Carolyn pulls back from it, fingers resting lightly upon the image.

This, she knows.

It's a Shadowwalker. There is no cloak, no scythe, no rose—none of the traditional symbolism for the card that means change. This is a woman made of darkness, with another in the distance, almost hidden in the shadows that lie around the edges of the card. Death points toward the shadows with one hand, the other beckoning the viewer closer.

A shiver rolls down Carolyn's back, and she pulls her fingers away.

She should see if these images have enough of whatever power her Talent seeks. Should see if she can raise up an illusion from them. But not that card. Not that shadowed Death. She knows change is coming; she doesn't need to invoke it in the library.

The image of the Wheel of Fortune looks as if it's dry paint against an old wooden wall. Carolyn brushes her fingers over it—just paper, nothing more—then presses her fingertips closer. She glances at the glass windows and door, hoping no one is watching, then ducks her head to focus on the picture.

It's a good image, one that she instinctively feels a kinship toward, but it doesn't come to life under her touch. The paper remains paper, with none of the slick, cool feeling that signals the beginnings of an illusion. She slumps back and looks down at the images again.

She's not sure she'll be able to shake that image of Death any time soon.

As tempting as it is to snap a quick photograph, she won't let herself break the rules again. Instead, she pulls out her notebook and quickly tries to copy the sketches. They don't have the same vibrancy that the originals do, so Carolyn adds a note to ask Kit to take a look at the book.

Another brief rap against the door, and Carolyn snaps her head up, thankful that she's not doing anything wrong at this moment. Cass wiggles her fingers, then opens the door and slips inside.

"Hey, I was walking by and saw you in here," Cass says. "I'm probably interrupting, sorry."

Carolyn's only managed to make it through one book so far, and she can't borrow anything that she's found. Having an ally might make the work go faster. She nudges one of the remaining books toward an empty chair.

"You can help if you want. I'm looking for anything related to predictive Talent that also references illusionary work and traveling. I've pulled everything I could find from the eastern states that appear to reference Tarot cards."

Cass drops her bag on one chair, takes another, and opens the book. She wrinkles her nose and coughs delicately. "Dust," she says.

"Things get a bit musty in here sometimes." Carolyn carefully closes the one book and picks up her next. "I've spent an awful lot of time in here for someone who isn't actually majoring in Magical Studies."

"But Kit is, isn't he?" Cass says easily. She tilts her head as she runs her finger down the first page. "It's my minor. I haven't had to do a lot of independent research yet, but I expect I'll start in the fall. I have to talk to Pawel about my options."

"Are you Talented?" Carolyn asks, then looks away. The question is rude, but it seemed logical in that instant. Almost everyone Carolyn knows in the program is Talented.

There's silence, and when Carolyn looks back over, Cass is nodding. "Emergent," Cass says. She fiddles with the pages, flipping forward and backward through the book slowly. "I don't like to talk about it much, if that's okay."

"It's fine." Carolyn lifts the book she's holding. "So, are you up for helping me out today? Oh, and if you ever need a job on campus, they're looking to hire a student in the program to work on cross-referencing the resources in here."

"That might be a fun project." Cass stops several pages in and holds it up so Carolyn can see the images. "This isn't the same as your deck, right?"

The images are stiff and extremely traditional—the deck that every non-Talented person knew long before Talent became a household word. Carolyn huffs; more than likely, that book won't be about true predictive Talent. "No. It's a mass-produced deck—the Rider-Waite Tarot. See if there's anything about true prediction or guidance, or any unique images."

"Mm." Cass bends to her work, and Carolyn does the same.

Carolyn works her way through a history of a Lineage of Healers as told through Tarot. Three generations of women authored it: Prudence, her daughter Patience, and her granddaughter Tempest. Each Healer has a two-page biography, in which the birth is recorded along with a card cast on that date for the infant's fate. Notes are made throughout the years and cards cast every decade until the death is noted.

There is no explanation how this line of predictive women intertwined with the Healers, and Carolyn makes a note to look for further texts from this geographic region, hoping they might provide more explanation. It may not help her project, but it's interesting and a little different.

"I thought all the texts in this room were from Talented families and communities," Cass says. "This boy seems to have grown up in a completely mundane household."

"He could be Emergent," Carolyn murmurs, then pauses. "Wait." She carefully marks the page she was reviewing, sets the Healer's book aside, and reaches toward Cass. "Let me take a look."

"Sebastian Edwards Smith," Cass says. She slides closer to Carolyn, sharing the book between them. "There's a photo tucked into the book with his name on the back. It's interesting—his parents moved in the 1950s and he found the deck in their new home. Like you said, it's just a standard deck that was available at the time. But after he worked with it, he claimed to be able to talk to spirits and to be able to tell the future. He talks shit about the ghosts in the book. The cards really do seem to have guided him, and he started drawing his own and got even better at it."

Sebastian. A predictive Talent named Sebastian, and literally the first reference to a male of predictive Lineage who holds the Talent. Carolyn dashes off a quick text with the name of the book, its storage location in the room, and a note that Kit should take a look at it.

She goes to set her phone down and pauses, adding, *If you get a chance, can you do me a favor? I would really really love if you could sketch the special collections room for texts concerning Talent. I want to see if I can use it to travel.*

Carolyn has a theory, and if she's right, she and Kit will need to work together.

"How is the search for illusions going?" Cass releases the book to Carolyn, putting a little space between them.

"Still struggling to figure out how it works, but I've got a few ideas. Some things seem to work better for me than others. I wish I could just use any picture. It'd be nice if I could open my phone and look at a picture of a place and go there, right?"

"It sounds both amazing and convenient," Cass says, sighing. "Very different than what Mac does. She can only pop around line-of-sight."

"As open of a secret as that is in the house these days, we probably shouldn't talk about it," Carolyn says. Mac is careful and doesn't want the world knowing that she's Kenzie Davis, the first girl who Emerged on national television. Carolyn doesn't blame her. It must be awkward and uncomfortable to be in that public a position.

Cass nods. "You have a point." She drums her fingers on the table but makes no move to take the book back.

She wants something. But she's not saying what.

There isn't much that people come to Carolyn for. Relationship advice lately, but she can't imagine Cass wanting or needing that. She's been with Dax for a long time, and despite occasional arguments, they seem solid.

Cass must want a reading.

Carolyn takes notes on which research books she's reviewing and her places in them, then carefully closes them and returns them to the shelves. Once the books are away and her laptop closed, she reaches into her bag and draws out her Tarot notebook and deck. She spills the cards out and shuffles them a few times, then holds the deck out to Cass.

"Are you sure?" Cass asks, and Carolyn nods.

"Shuffle a few times, until you feel ready, then cut the deck. I'll give you a reading," she offers, even though Cass never actually asked.

Cass shuffles the cards, moving slowly like she's trying to read the cards with her fingertips.

Cass finally sets the deck down without cutting it, then nudges it toward Carolyn. "I was thinking about the challenges I'm facing right now," she says. "Not romantic ones. Familial ones, and social."

"Okay, we'll do a three-card spread, but a little differently than the past/present/future that I usually do for quick readings." Carolyn lays out the top three cards from the deck, face up, then points at them in order from left to right. "The Four of Wands: this is your current situation. The Ace of Pentacles, reversed: this is the challenges you face. The last—the Fool—offers guidance to help you get through them."

Cass tugs her braid loose, finger combing her hair as she sits back. She pulls her hair away from her face, redoing it into a high ponytail. It's a nervous gesture; Carolyn might not be good at people, but she's picked up at least a few things from Heather.

"You're balanced," she says, touching the Four of Wands, on which a girl dances joyfully between four wands and four roses. "You've figured out how to balance everything. Your family. Your sisters. Dax. Schoolwork. It's pretty delicate, but it's a good feeling. The thing is, anything that perfectly balanced has a way of falling."

She picks up the next card—reversed and therefore upside down—and turns it right-side up so Cass can better see the pentacle surrounded by ruins, awash in the glowing light of a new day. "An ace is a good card," she says. "Aces are about new beginnings, but your ace is reversed, so the new beginning may not be something you want or need right now. It has the potential to go really well, but it's also a challenge. Challenges don't always go as you hoped. This particular card is usually about money coming in, or it may have something to do with creativity and talent. Or Talent." Carolyn trusts that Cass understands that difference between those two words. "It's a card of success."

Cass leans her elbows on the table, shoulders tense. She touches the third card of the reading. "Okay. So I'm balanced, and it sounds like this new beginning is going to toss me off balance and onto my ass. Why does it look like my guidance is going to walk off a cliff?"

"Remember that the Tarot is symbolic. Just like Death means change, this cliff isn't literal, either," Carolyn says. "The Fool is about innocence, about trusting those around you and being spontaneous. The Fool is, in some ways, almost the direct opposite to your current situation. You are so tightly balanced that you could fall. The Fool encourages you to open up, play a little looser. See what happens when you let chance in. You can't plan for everything in your life, and if you follow the Fool, it might be easier to handle the unexpected."

Tapping her fingernails on the table, Cass sits tautly, her jaw set. "Okay.

So. Stop being a control freak. That's what it says, right? Because I can't actually control what's happening, and if it gets out of control, it'll be okay."

"And trust your family and friends. Don't let anyone push you off that cliff," Carolyn taps the dog that nips at the Fool's heels. "Remember that there are people who would warn you away from danger. Listen to them."

She gathers the cards and carefully puts them back in the bag. Cass remains silent while Carolyn sketches the layout and takes notes on her reading. When she's finished, Cass is still staring at the table, drawing one fingernail along the grain of the wood.

"Cass," she says quietly, and Cass's head snaps up. "I know that you're really reserved. You can be bubbly, sure, but you keep everything important all knotted up inside. Maybe you need to undo some of those knots and let people in. Not just Dax, but your sisters, too."

Cass licks her lips, then nods. She smiles slowly, although it never reaches her eyes, and she touches Carolyn's hand. "Thanks. You've given me something to think about," she says. She glances down at her phone, then shows the time to Carolyn. It's a lot later than Carolyn thought. "We'd better go back and get ready for Paint It Red."

"Yeah. Shit." Carolyn finishes packing her things. "We have to hurry."

Cass tilts her head and holds her hand out, palm up. "You were able travel to that illusion of your room. Think you could take someone through it?"

Possibly. Probably.

Maybe.

But if she can't, it could be an epic disaster.

"I don't want to chance it; it doesn't exactly work on demand," Carolyn mutters, ignoring that the picture is easily accessibly if she wants to test her theory. "Let's just walk back. We'll make it in time."

She'll test it eventually. She has to. She just wants to be a little more certain that it's going to work. And she's not sure she wants to test it with Cass.

22

Paint It Red is one of Carolyn's favorite events.

She loves that they're raising money for research into women's heart disease and to help fund treatments for Capital Region women. She loves seeing the area community come together and knowing that SigPsiEp has brought them there, united against the number-one medical problem facing women. They get to dress nicely, without the stress of it being a formal; every sister wears a red dress. There's no competition, and they work together to make their guests welcome and encourage them to be generous during the silent auction. It's social, yes, and that isn't one of Carolyn's best skills. But she can smile and enjoy the party; she's not the one who has to chat up the local dignitaries in attendance.

And now that dinner's cleared, she's looking forward to dancing.

There's a soft tapping at the microphone as the quiet dinner music goes silent. Heather stands with the DJ, a cheerful smile on her face. Her red dress is wonderfully retro, with a pleated skirt and princess neckline. Heather's hair is caught up in a twist at the back of her head; Carolyn's never seen her best friend shine so brightly.

From the way Nikita is looking at her, Carolyn thinks she's not the only one impressed.

"We've reached everyone's favorite part of the evening!" As she speaks, Heather gestures at the dance floor, then to the sides of the room. To the left are the tables laden with desserts, and to the right are the tables for the silent auction. "It's time to enjoy dessert, spend some money, and get your dance on! Please enjoy our fabulous sweets buffet, with treats so spectacular you won't realize how healthy they are. We hope that you've had a chance to look at the wonderful donations for our silent auction; remember, every dollar spent in the auction goes directly to our chosen charities. And if you'd like to read about those charities, we have information about the research we've chosen to support and the families who've been helped this past year by your generosity."

Heather pauses for the smattering of applause. There's a quiet whoop from one corner, and when Carolyn glances over she sees Drea smack the side of Corbin's head.

"Once you're done eating and spending, please join us for some all-out fun on the dance floor," Heather continues. "Our DJ will offer up the best music from across several decades, guaranteed to keep you moving. And of course, the DJ will happily take requests. If you have a dedication, be sure to let us know."

There's louder applause this time, and when the music returns, it's loud enough to shake Carolyn's bones. It's meant for dancing, for letting loose and having a good time. And she intends to do just that as soon as she can find someone to dance with.

Drea waves, and Carolyn threads through the crowd toward her. As soon as she's close, Drea grabs her shoulder, pulling her in so she can be heard over the music. "I love it!" Drea shouts. "These are the same people I've seen on the local news my whole life! And look." Drea squeezes Carolyn's shoulder and points at the dance floor where news anchors from competing stations are dancing, their high-heeled shoes abandoned, their hands raised as they bounce to the music. "I expected this to be so much more serious. I'm so glad my parents aren't here."

"I'm glad I'm here," Corbin says, grinning. "Hey, Carolyn. Can I drag Drea onto the dance floor? Or wait, better yet, think I can get Ric out there?" He turns away, shouting over the music even though Alaric isn't far away. "Ric! Dance with me!"

Even Carolyn can hear Alaric's low answering growl.

Chris holds Alaric's hand. He tugs, and the growl cuts off abruptly as they walk over to join Carolyn, Corbin, and Drea. Alaric's outfit complements Chris's and matches Corbin's and Drea's. His charcoal suit is the same color as Corbin's, and Alaric's deep-red shirt is a similar shade to Corbin's tie and Drea's cute red dress. Chris is in black, his shirt in a lighter shade of gray, and a red and black tie. Drea reaches for Alaric's free hand, but Corbin gets in the way.

"Wait. Picture time." He hands off his phone to Carolyn. "Take one of me, Ric, and Drea please."

She frames them against the wall, a light overhead projecting a backdrop onto the wallpaper. She takes a picture of Alaric and Drea together next, then one of Corbin and Drea. When Chris insists it's his turn, Carolyn misses the shot, blushingly distracted by the intensity of Chris and Alaric's kiss, but Corbin retrieves the phone and gleefully takes several shots.

"Twins," Drea says, touching Carolyn's arm. "Where's Kit? I want a picture of the four of us."

Carolyn spots him with Serina, Soledad, and Mac. She can't seem to catch his eye, but Serina looks over and waves. Carolyn motions, and Serina waves again, and a moment later the four of them walk over.

"Hey." Serina hugs Carolyn, kissing her cheek. She's in heels and almost as tall as Carolyn, her dress lower cut and shorter than what most others there are wearing. Serina tugs at her skirt, warmth staining her skin. "I swear, it used to fit better. I think I gained weight and it got shorter or something."

"It looks good." Carolyn's not lying; Serina looks fantastic. She can get away with wearing something that's clingy, unlike Carolyn, who is in a simple, sleeveless sheathe dress that's cut just below the knees, like something from the roaring twenties. "Mind if I borrow Kit?"

"Not at all." Serina steps back, giving Kit space to approach.

He seems…quiet. Quieter than usual. His sleeves are pulled down, buttoned tight at the wrists, and Carolyn wonders if he's told Serina about the soul mark or if he's ignoring it. Serina's going to find out eventually, and it's probably for the best if she finds out from him.

Kit tugs at his sleeve and meets Carolyn's gaze with a rueful smile. "I'm fine," he says. "What's up?"

"Twin pictures," Drea says cheerfully. "Me, my Big, her twin, and my twin. Since we're all cleaned up and nice looking. Who knows the next time we'll get Alaric in a suit?"

"Team pictures at the end of summer," Chris deadpans. "And those only take a half hour, so it might be hard to catch him."

"He looks so nice in a suit." Soledad has one arm curled around Alaric's free arm; she presses close and pats his chest. "My safe, fake boyfriend. Would you dress up to take me out?"

Alaric blinks at her, bemused.

"Chris could come," Soledad decides. "We should do a group outing. Dancing. I trust you, Alaric."

"Why is she allowed to hang on you when no one else is?" Corbin asks.

Alaric shakes his head. "She's safe." He gently sets Soledad aside. "Be nice to Soledad, Corbin."

"Pictures." Drea grabs Alaric's hands and pulls him away from Chris and Soledad. "Come on, come with me." She rearranges them until she and Carolyn stand flanked by their brothers, all four squeezed close together against the wall.

Kit stands stiffly, tense where Carolyn has her arm behind his back. When she glances over, he's smiling, but it looks awkward and vaguely pained.

Corbin gathers everyone's phones to take pictures, then hands them back after he's done. While Soledad tries to convince Alaric and Chris to join her on the dance floor, Carolyn catches Kit's hand.

"Serina, do you mind if I borrow Kit for a bit?" she asks. "Go on and dance. We'll be out later."

"I'm not really in the mood for dancing," Kit says once they've reached the hall outside of the ballroom and he can speak without shouting over the music.

"I can tell." Carolyn wants to tug him in and hug him, but Kit's notorious for refusing affection when he needs it most. She keeps them moving until they're out of sight of the main room. "I figured you needed a break. Besides, I was wondering if you'd had a chance to—"

"Oh, right." Kit reaches into the pocket inside his jacket and pulls out his tablet. When he opens the case, there's a paper tucked inside. "Here. I did the best I could from memory."

Carolyn had just been in the special collections room that morning, and she'd say he did pretty well. The books aren't perfect, but the colors pop and the room feels inviting. The two heavy tables sit at the center of the image, one chair cocked as if waiting for someone to drop into it. There's a small pile of books on the end of the table nearest the chair, and Carolyn recognizes the titles as books they've used for past projects.

"I think it's perfect," she says. "The picture you drew of my room doesn't look exactly like my room, either, but it worked."

"I drew a picture of your room?"

"Over a year ago, when Heather and I first moved into the house." Her clutch is sitting at her table in the other room, or Carolyn would show him to remind him. "I traveled from the ice cream shop using it. Almost on purpose." She leaves out that she abandoned Serina there. There's no point in rubbing salt in the wound.

"Hm. So my art works as your focus," Kit muses.

"It has once. I tried it because—" She hesitates because the thought had been inspired by Serina. "I remembered that when I traveled back from Haverhill, I dreamed of an image of my room, not a Tarot card. And then I remembered the drawing you did in my notebook, so I tried focusing on that."

"We should experiment with this more," Kit says. He still has his tablet out, and he opens up a notepad app to jot ideas down. "What do you think of trying to use a picture of a person?"

"I'd be really wary about it depending on the person," Carolyn admits. There are very few people she'd like to reach directly.

"Me?"

Carolyn nods. "Of course you. Probably Heather and Drea. There are people I trust. But I also have a phone to call you. It's not like this is going to give us a psychic phone line."

"But if you could create an illusion and travel to me, no matter where I am…" Kit's voice trails off, distracted as he types with his thumbs.

"It could be either really convenient or intensely awkward," Carolyn points out. "So far, I haven't been able to peek through first to see if it's safe. I touch the illusion and I go through. There's no chance to back out." And there are definitely things she does not want or need to see.

"We're twins and literally grew up in each others' shadows," Kit mumbles.

"I can't think you interrupting me is going to be any different than you barging into my room at home, or me barging into—" He cuts off, the ink on his wrist peeking out from under his cuff.

Carolyn smiles ruefully; that would be exactly what she doesn't want to intrude upon.

He slowly stops typing, closes the case of his tablet, and puts it back in the interior pocket of his jacket. "Rory and I are still working things out. You aren't going to interrupt anything there, believe me."

"We all deserve privacy," Carolyn says. She opens her arms, and Kit steps closer and lets her draw him into a hug. His hands grip her, and she can feel some of his tension ease. "How is it with Serina tonight?"

"We're still friends, but it's awkward," he admits. "I'd rather be in a group than just with her."

"There are enough of us that we can keep you company on the dance floor, if you think you can take it." She almost laughs at his horrified expression. "You like dancing. I know it and you know it. You just don't want them to judge your lack of skill."

"That's a 'privately in my bedroom' kind of thing," Kit protests. "Not for a crowded dance floor at a formal event."

"Do you think anyone will be looking at you? Or me?" Carolyn lets go of him, and he takes a step back. He smooths the vest under his jacket. "Join us. It's a large enough crowd that no one will care. Just let go and have fun."

"Maybe."

It's the closest she'll get to agreement, and she'll take it.

Carolyn has to stop at her table first so she can drop off Kit's art. Once it's tucked safely in her clutch, she leaves the purse on her chair and heads to the dance floor. The current song is from the '80s—something she remembers her parents playing while they danced around the kitchen. It's not slow, but there are couples slow-dancing on the dance floor's fringes anyway. Carolyn spots Heather and Nikita together, Nikita's head bowed so they sway forehead to forehead.

"Carolyn!"

It takes effort to figure out where Drea's voice is coming from, and by the time she does, Mac, Cass, Soledad, and Serina are yelling as well. The group has grown; Mac has joined them, as have Cass and Dax. Serina catches Carolyn's hands, and she gets pulled into the group. Carolyn laughs as the song shifts, and they all start screaming the lyrics while jumping up and down with their hands up. It's far from elegant, but it's fun and energetic. Dax is a good dancer; Corbin appears determined to put him in his place, and the girls cheer them on while they show off. Corbin takes Carolyn's hands, an unspoken invitation for her to be his partner; she willingly goes, letting him dip her in exaggerated motion, but when he goes to pick her up and swing her around, she laughs and pushes him toward Drea.

He lets her go, and she stumbles into Serina, who catches her with hands on her arms.

"Dance with me!" Serina shouts, and Carolyn embraces her automatically as the song changes. It's slow this time, soft and dreamy. Carolyn falters as she starts to sway, tripping over nothing; Serina just smiles and says, "That's okay. I'm okay."

"Did I step on your feet?" Carolyn asks, and Serina laughs, shaking her head.

They end up spinning in almost a waltz, moving through the crowd. Serina sings along, her voice cheerful and light, and Carolyn can't stop laughing. Carolyn spots Kit at one point; he's sitting at her table, his tablet in his hand and his feet up on a chair. He glances up as if he senses her looking his way and waves one hand, flicking his fingers as if to say *go back to what you're doing*, so she does.

When the song ends, Serina bows with exaggerated motion. It seems like the only proper response is to curtsey deeply, so Carolyn does, tugging the narrow skirt from her thighs as she dips low. Serina claps, color warm and bright in her cheeks.

A thumping bass beat shudders in Carolyn's chest as a new song begins. Mac is at her elbow, drawing her back into a circle with Soledad and Drea. Out of the corner of her eye, Carolyn spots someone whisking Serina away; Serina's laughing.

Kit still sits at the table, and a small smile tilts the corner of his mouth.

Maybe everything's going to be okay.

23

CAROLYN ISN'T DRUNK. She hasn't had a sip of alcohol, nor has she taken any other substance that might alter her mood. But she's happy. Giddy. Silly from dancing for hours and spending time with her friends, and perhaps a little punchy. She slips off her shoes as soon as she's inside the house, then picks them up, straps dangling from her fingers, as Mac laughs.

"You don't have to take off your shoes. We don't have to sneak in," Mac whispers.

"Then why are you whispering?" Carolyn whispers in return.

Mac laughs again, the sound echoing off the walls in the small entryway; Carolyn presses a finger to her lips as she slowly climbs the stairs with Mac behind her.

It's late, but not all that late. Some of the SigPsiEp sisters are still at the event, cleaning up or doing press with the local celebrities. Most left earlier, heading out with family members or significant others, disappearing to enjoy their lives outside of the gala.

Carolyn had stayed because her friends were there and she was having a great time. Unsurprisingly, Cass and Dax left early, but Drea and Corbin stayed, and as long as they were there, so were Alaric and Chris. Carolyn had eventually persuaded Kit to come out on the dance floor, joining Mac, Soledad, Serina and the others. They'd danced until the DJ played the last song; when silence fell, it was finally time to go home.

Mac hisses "Shhhh," and when Carolyn turns around, Mac opens her eyes wide and tiptoes past her and up the stairs exaggeratedly. Carolyn giggles, the sound loud in the strange silence of the house. She can't remember having ever felt this silly while completely and utterly sober.

A door opens on the second floor, and a girl calls out, "What are you guys doing?" The door slams again, and Carolyn laughs loudly while Mac hushes her equally loudly.

"We are sober!" Carolyn insists.

"We are totally and completely sober," Mac confirms, laugh fading to a quiet giggle. She nudges Carolyn. "Come on. We should get to bed. You've got a case of the sillies, and so do I."

"We're punchy from lack of sleep."

"It's been a long week," Mac agrees, smile disappearing. "A long few months." She takes a deep breath as they reach the top of the stairs. Carolyn echoes her, the urge to giggle ebbing with a long exhalation. It really has been a long few months. One good night doesn't erase the stress, but it still makes Carolyn happy that they had this one good night.

"I love how, despite all the work that goes into it beforehand, Paint It Red always somehow ends up being fun," Carolyn says quietly.

"Did you hear Alaric shouting a time limit when Cass dragged Dax off the dance floor to leave?" Mac asks.

Carolyn winces. "I tried to ignore that. Is it just me, or does Cass seem oversexed?"

"She's got a healthy sex drive, and you prefer that people around you be private, which is fine." Mac tugs, and Carolyn goes into the hug, letting Mac pat her on the head. Carolyn's tall enough that Mac comes up to her nose, so she has to hunch over. It's uncomfortable, but at the same time, it's kind of nice. Besides, she's used to hugs with people shorter than her; Heather is short.

Oh. Right.

Heather.

Carolyn looks at the door of the room she and Heather share. "Um. Do you know when they left?" She keeps her voice down even though she knows that if Heather's awake, she must know that Carolyn's there. It's not like they've been quiet.

"Last I saw, they were slow dancing, then you dragged Kit away from the table and I lost track of them." Mac gestures at the stairs. "You're welcome to sleep on my floor, if you need to."

"No." Carolyn puts her hand on the doorknob and turns it without opening the door. "Nik's already here most of the time. It's not anything new tonight."

Except it is new, because Heather and Nikita are officially dating now. Carolyn's not sure what that means for the room. They've both been single since they moved in together; they haven't had to worry about this before.

"The offer stands. Knock if you change your mind," Mac says. She waves as she heads for the stairs that lead up to the third floor.

Carolyn pushes the door open slowly. She figures that if they're in the room and awake, she's given them plenty of warning by turning the knob and waiting before she entered. But more warning can't hurt, so she calls out a soft "Hey" before she gets the door open all the way. As light spills out, she moves more quickly, stepping into the room.

"I'll be back in a minute," Nikita says, catching the door before Carolyn can let go. Nikita's already wearing a sleep shirt and shorts, her feet bare as she pads down the hall.

Carolyn closes the door slowly. "Hey," she says again.

Heather's hair has come loose from her earlier twist, frizzed and curled around her face. Abandoned semi-formal attire lies crumpled on the floor, and Heather's also dressed for sleep. She sits on her bed, cross-legged, her expression soft. "Hey," she replies, smile blooming.

Carolyn feels calm wash over her, soft pleasure in slow waves. "Um. Do you realize that you're leaking happy all over the place?" she asks with a small laugh.

"I'm not the one who sounded drunk and could've woken the dead coming up here." Heather slides off the bed and stretches. Her shirt rides up, and Carolyn can see a red mark on her side. For a moment Carolyn is concerned, then Heather tugs the shirt down, and Carolyn flushes with embarrassment. Carolyn really doesn't want to think about the specifics of how that mark got there.

"Still leaking all the happy and uncomfortable emotions," she mumbles. "Also, I didn't interrupt something, did I? I mean, is this sleepover a 'girl-friend' thing, or a 'Dreamwalker' thing? Do we need to start doing some kind of 'sock on the door' warning? Or you could text me. I'll read my texts before coming home."

"It's both a 'girlfriend' and a 'Dreamwalker' thing, but you didn't interrupt," Heather says. "Is that okay?"

"As long as you're done having sex and I don't have to see or hear it," Carolyn says, because she knows Heather will value the bluntness. Carolyn sighs heavily. "I barely saw you before the gala today. And we all had a great time during it. You guys are really cute, and I can see that she likes you. A lot. I just…I'm sorry we fought last night."

Heather licks her lips, her gaze darting toward the door. Her skin is stained with red. When she pushes a hand through her hair, pulling it back from her face, it lifts her shirt again. Carolyn stares at Heather's face to avoid seeing any other signs of their intimacy.

"I'm sorry we fought, too," Heather says. "I was going to tell you, but it wasn't actually a 'girlfriend' thing before you interrupted us last night. She kissed me, and I—"

"I didn't even know you liked—" Carolyn stumbles to a stop. She didn't mean to interrupt Heather, and she waves for her to continue. Or respond. She's not sure exactly which.

"Nikita?" Heather says, breaking into low giggles.

"Girls," Carolyn says quietly. It feels like something she should've known already.

"I hadn't really come to terms with that myself," Heather admits. "I've had crushes. I just never thought about acting on them. I thought it was an aesthetic appreciation, or some kind of emotional spillover from somewhere. You know how sometimes it's hard to tell what's internal and what's external?" She touches her head and waves as if to suggest that emotions can come from anywhere, and for Heather, Carolyn supposes they can. "I didn't think of it as 'me,' and now I'm wondering how many opportunities I missed because I haven't gotten past *she's cute* and into *oh hey I should ask her out* before."

Carolyn glances at the door and lowers her voice. "This isn't an 'experimentation' thing, right?" At Heather's dark look, she continues, "I just—I don't want you hurt. And Nikita summoned a hailstorm on my head. She really likes you, and she has universe-destroying Talent. I don't want her to get hurt, either."

"I don't want to hurt her. I really like her. Emotionally, aesthetically, and physically." Heather grins and wiggles her eyebrows. Her bright cheer would have been infectious even if her emotions hadn't been leaking. She's happy, and Carolyn's happy for her.

Carolyn holds out her arms, hugs Heather hard, and says, "Gross. No details." She digs in the closet, pulling out a fresh T-shirt and shorts. "And stop thinking about missed opportunities. In the end, you make your own fortune, right? And it seems to me like you've made the one you want most. You like Nikita, she likes you, so you're where you need to be. Nothing's been missed at all."

"When you put it like that…"

"…I almost sound like the smart one about relationships." It's a joke, and Heather laughs, as Carolyn meant for her to do. The change in tension gives Carolyn a chance to step back and change out of her dress, hanging it over the edge of her chair so she can send it off for dry cleaning tomorrow. Then she picks up Heather's and Nikita's clothes as well, draping them carefully.

By the time she looks at Heather, the serious expression has returned. "We didn't get to talk last night," Heather says. "About what you did."

Carolyn stops cleaning, confused. "I thought we just did."

"Not about you barging in and interrupting. About how you did it." Heather gestures at her, then at her backpack lying on the floor. "Was that your traveling Talent? Like in your dream? Did you do it on purpose this time?"

"Oh! That." Carolyn grabs her discarded clutch and pulls out her phone and the two pictures now tucked in the pocket on the back. She motions for Heather to join her, then carefully unfolds them both on the desktop. "Do you remember when Kit did this sketch of our room? Serina and I were at Sweet Scoops, and I told her about the illusions. She asked about the card I saw that got me back here when I had the nightmare, and I remembered this sketch. So I brought it out, and I tried to see if I could create an illusion for it—I could, and it sucked me in. I disappeared from Sweet Scoops. Cass had to get Serina home, and she brought me my notebook when I left it behind."

Heather's smile blooms even wider, a tiny squeal of pleasure as she claps her hands. Sensation washes over Carolyn, infusing her bones with Heather's delight. "You did it! What next? Was it because it was Kit's sketch? I thought you were using your cards?"

Carolyn's not sure she's as excited as Heather. "This is still kind of terrifying and new," she admits. "Kit's art felt good. I had the cards in that Dream, and I thought about a card for Alaric when I was desperate to get out of the Dream with Mattie. But I hadn't been able to do it on purpose. With this picture, it worked when I wanted it to."

"So you can control it," Heather says.

The door creaks open slowly, thunking closed after Nikita slips in. "Don't mind me," she says.

"Carolyn made an illusion and traveled on purpose yesterday," Heather says.

Carolyn winces. "'On purpose' and 'control' are really big words for how I feel about this, Heather. I'm not sure either one really applies yet."

Nikita huffs. "I completely understand that feeling," she mutters. "'Control' and 'on purpose' are things people say when they think you've figured everything out. Then next thing you know it's hailing, and you realize that it all means shit."

Their situations aren't exactly the same, but Carolyn appreciates the sentiment.

"What's the picture of the library for?" Heather touches the new sketch on Carolyn's desk.

"That's my experiment for tonight." Carolyn inhales slowly, holds the breath for a moment, and counts. Tries to center herself and calm the nerves she can feel pricking at her skin. "I've only done it more-or-less on purpose once. I need some kind of controlled practice. So I asked Kit if he could sketch the library Talent special collections room for me. I'll be spending a lot of time there this semester."

Nikita slides up behind Heather and wraps her arms around her center. She's tall enough to hook her hands together just below Heather's breasts; the shirt bunches up as Nikita presses her cheek to Heather's. It's intimate in an emotional way rather than a physical one, and Carolyn ducks her gaze away. She can't figure out how she missed noticing their growing affection. Probably because she's not good at understanding how people fit together, no matter how many people seem to be coming to her for advice lately.

"You think you can use that picture to get to the library?" Nikita asks.

Carolyn's heart trips. This seems like that moment to test her theory. "Yeah. I like the way my cards feel. They work for me when I do readings. They feel like a part of me. But when I want to reach out for an illusion, when I want to try to reach that new Talent, Kit's art feels right. So I guess the trick is seeing if it'll work, and making sure I take everything with me when I go."

"Are you going now?" Heather's brow furrows, and Nikita presses a kiss to her cheek.

Carolyn looks at the pictures on the desk, her phone lying next to them. She carefully folds up the picture of her room, tucks it back in the pocket, then shoves her phone into her bag. She has her notebook and a book she needs to read. "Sure," she says, not feeling as certain as she sounds. "Why not? I'm not tired, and you two probably wouldn't mind privacy. And, um…" Her smile wavers. "As cute as you are together, this is awkward. I really wouldn't mind giving you that privacy. Text me when you're going to sleep?"

"You could just walk over to the library," Heather points out. Her lips are pursed, and Carolyn knows a lecture is coming. One that begins with *you need to do things the right way* and won't be stopped by anything Carolyn says until Heather is done delivering it.

So Carolyn shoulders her bag, then picks up the picture and holds it in both hands. "The only way to know is to try. And I need to know if it works before I can talk to Pawel about it, right?" She wiggles the picture, the paper rustling. "So, I'll head to the library and do some more research. And if you text me when you're going to bed, I'll just…pop back here. Hopefully without tripping over things and landing on my knees this time. Practice. Control." She breathes slowly, tries to project a far more calm presence than she feels; her heart hammers in her chest.

It's impossible to lie to an Empath.

Heather stares at her, and Carolyn is positive that she's reading her.

Weighing the lie against the way Nikita's hands press flat against Heather's belly as Nikita kisses her cheek.

Heather covers Nikita's hand with her own, squeezes lightly, and Nikita straightens up to look at Carolyn.

"Show us the illusion?" Heather asks.

Carolyn nods as if she has any control over it whatsoever.

She holds onto the paper tightly, determined to take it with her when she goes through. She stares at the picture, thinking about the smell of the room, the order of the books on the shelves. She imagines it coming to life, and it does, springing up into a tiny image just a few inches across. Carolyn inhales roughly, and the illusion expands over the edges of the paper. It takes up the space between herself and Heather and Nikita; they step back as if it's chasing them.

"Text me," Carolyn says.

"I will." Heather nods.

And that has to be enough. This is going to work. She is going to do this on her terms, taking the picture with her, and she's prepared to come back the same way. Carolyn holds onto the picture with one hand, reaches forward with the other. The illusion ripples as her fingers break the surface, and she resolutely steps forward and through.

What Lies Beneath

Sixth Position: Beneath

What lies beneath...

In order to achieve their goals, the querent needs tools to work with. The querent has a natural instinct and inclination that can be leveraged to reach for the crowning situation. If the outlook is positive, these instincts will help the querent achieve success. If the outlook is negative, it is possible that the querent's natural instinct drags at the querent's heels, pulling them down and leading them to the negative outcome. The querent should take heed and look closely at what lies beneath.

Either way, the querent must dig deep and discover their inner talents in order to move forward.

Carolyn's Reading: The Six of Pentacles (Reversed)

A man stands atop a rocky cliff beneath a partial eclipse of the full moon. He spreads his arms, joyful, as six pentacles arch above him.

This is a card of great stability and success. It is a card of gifts and perfect timing, of generosity and kindness. However, when reversed, the good can become unstable, the success illusory. This instability drives the querent forward to the crowning situation and could breed either success or failure.

If the illusions can be mastered, if the instability can be wrangled, this can be a positive force. But take care, as the querent could lose themselves in the illusion.

Kit's Reading: The Princess of Wands

A woman stands, her wand melting in the heat of a sunny day. She wears a tiara to show her rank, but she is still young and new to her position. She stares at the querent, waiting, one hand on her shoulder as if to disrobe.

This is a card of passion and energy. The querent has strong beliefs and is ready to accept risks and impulsively leap ahead into new territory. It may mean that a man enters the querent's life, one with dark hair and dark eyes. If the card refers to a man, he will be loyal to the querent, loving and faithful, and will aid the querent in achieving what crowns them.

The querent should be willing to take risks if what crowns them is desirable. If there is something negative waiting, the querent may wish to weigh their options carefully and rely upon family and allies before proceeding with caution.

24

CAROLYN GLANCES UP at the knock on her door, her brow furrowing when it opens without whomever is on the other side waiting for her to call out. Kit stands there, his bag over his shoulder, his arms crossed, and his beanie pulled down over his ears.

She blinks at him.

"We have projects. I figured we could work on them tonight," Kit says. He steps in, not quite closing the door behind himself as he shrugs out of his jacket. He drops it on her bed along with his bag and leans over it to pull out his notebook. He flips through the book, his back to her and his shoulders rounded.

"You do realize it's Valentine's Day, right?" Carolyn looks past him. She hadn't expected to be interrupted tonight. Of all nights, this is the one time she figured that everyone else on campus was paired off—either permanently or temporarily.

Kit turns around slowly, shoulders going stiff as he straightens. "So?" He grabs the chair from Heather's desk and drags it over. "We just had a long weekend, and you and I haven't discussed about anything for our meeting with Pawel this week. So I figured we should talk. I can catch you up on where we are with helping Darrik—which isn't much further than the last time we talked. You can use me as a sounding board for whatever you're working on."

If Kit's making progress on his project, that implies that Kit's been working with his project group. The group that includes Rory. That circles back to why Carolyn hadn't expected to see Kit tonight. "Shouldn't you be on a date with your soulmate?" she asks.

Kit freezes, drops the notebook on Carolyn's desk, and sits back abruptly.

He starts to cross his arms again, then pauses, lowering his hands to the desk carefully. "No. We both agreed that we're nowhere near the 'epic romantic Valentine's date' level yet." He yanks off his beanie and tosses it on the bed; his hair sticks out in all directions. Carolyn leans forward and finger-combs it for him.

"Want to talk about it?" she offers. As nonchalant as he sounds, Kit's body language is wary and stiff. She's not sure if he's upset about how things are going with Rory or just avoiding thinking about it.

"We talked."

Carolyn stays silent, waiting to see if he'll elaborate.

"It's complicated," Kit finally says. "There's so much going on in this one potential relationship. Soulmates. Me being trans. Me trying to figure out if I'm bi or pan. Or was I just ignoring liking guys because it seemed easier? Sexuality. Like, he doesn't do sexuality. And I don't think I care about that, but I have to figure that out for sure because it wouldn't be fair to lead him on if that's going to turn out to be a big deal. It's all this new stuff when we were just getting to be friends. And I really like having him as a friend. We're nothing alike."

Carolyn laughs before she can stop herself. Kit is so wrong; she laughs even harder at his offended expression. "You are," she tells him. "You're both quiet. Prickly. Untouchable. He's a music geek, and you're a science geek. I bet the two of you could fall into complete study fugues sitting next to each other and be fine with it. In all the details, you're different, but when it comes to your base personalities, you seem very similar to me."

"Don't people usually date opposites?" Kit counters, his cheeks faintly flushed. "Heather and Nikita. Chris and Alaric. You and—" He cuts off, shifts gears. "Del and Sam."

Carolyn doesn't want to follow the thought that he'd cut away from. "Del and Sam are more similar than not," she says. "Like Corbin and Drea. Del's outgoing and kind of abrasive. A little dreamy sometimes. Sam had his illusions that were as real to him as reality, and he was loud and soft and sweet, like a cheerful rumbly teddy bear. And Drea and Corbin are similar, too, both as outgoing as Alaric isn't."

Kit's gone quiet, picking at a thread from a tear just above the knee of his jeans.

"What?" Carolyn asks.

Kit makes a face. "If I ask this, are you going to run away from the conversation? Because the last six times we talked about this it turned into a conversation about how I felt too awkward to date in high school."

"That depends on what you're going to ask," Carolyn says, even though she's pretty sure she knows where this conversation is heading. Maybe not the exact destination, but the direction. She reaches for her deck, spilling the cards into her hand so she has something to do with her fingers. She looks down at them, shuffling them with a sliding motion.

"Have you been okay since Shawn visited?" he asks, voice low. "You haven't dated anyone since him. I don't know what happened—" He cuts off when she looks up.

Carolyn shuffles through answers like cards in her mind. "I'm not hung up on him, if that's what you're worried about," she says, and Kit makes a noise. "You don't believe me?"

"No, I knew that." Kit leans forward. "I'm your twin. You hated Shawn after everything happened. It's cooled since then. You don't talk about him. As far as I know, you don't talk to him, but you've talked to Del since they visited. You worry about Sam."

"Yeah, well, he and I were the ones who got screwed," Carolyn mutters. She worries about Sam so much that she's even sent an e-mail to his mother, hoping for more information about how he's doing. She'd not received a response yet.

Kit's silent.

"It's not a big deal," Carolyn lies. "Shawn and I were broken long before the ritual. That just—it was the nail in the coffin. What happened to Sam, what happened to me, those were the icing on a really gross cake that had been baked months before."

"That is the strangest metaphor I can think of anyone using for a messed-up relationship," Kit says, his nose wrinkled. "It implies you were sweet."

"We weren't." That's easy to say, her voice flat. "We were messed up. We had different views on what we wanted out of our relationship, and Shawn…" She trails off because she doesn't want to put it into words. There was a reason they ended, and it's better to leave it in the past.

"That definitely complicates things." Kit's tone is light. He leans back, his body seeming at ease, as if he's trying too hard to relax. Carolyn catches her cards, holds them for a moment, and he smiles at her. "Do I need to kill him next time he visits?"

Carolyn huffs. "No. He didn't get what he wanted, and that broke us. Also, if you want to feel better about everything, think about this: Shawn kisses like a wet noodle."

Kit blinks. "What? Have you been kissing noodles?"

She nudges him with her toe, a laugh bubbling up. "No. Just. All wet, and all tongue, like he's trying to swallow you whole, or maybe get you to swallow him instead. I hated kissing Shawn."

There's no point in mentioning that Shawn's the only person she's ever kissed.

That first time they kissed more deeply than a brief peck on the lips is still vivid in her mind. Shawn had been eating kumquats, popping them into his mouth like popcorn, chewing them and swallowing them down skin and all. Carolyn never understood the appeal; to her they were bitter little citrus packets, and there were plenty of other fruits she'd rather eat. But Shawn loved kumquats.

In the distance, she'd heard the door close. Shawn had set down the bowl of kumquats, grabbed the remote, and paused the movie they were streaming. "Mom's gonna be out for a while," he said.

Carolyn couldn't see why this was a big deal, but Shawn had a plan: making out on the couch with his tongue in her mouth, surrounded by the smell and taste of bitter citrus. She couldn't figure out what to do with her tongue, how to kiss back without feeling like she was choking.

She hadn't liked it.

But Shawn had, and she couldn't find a way to say that she'd like to go back to the easy kisses. The soft presses of lips that made sense to her and only tasted like lip balm.

"Caro?" Kit says, and Carolyn pastes a smile back on her lips.

"He really was a terrible kisser. Would not recommend." It occurs to her that Del's apparently with Shawn now, for some definition of "with," and she wonders what Del would say about his kisses. She'd better not ask. There were a lot of things that were broken between her and Shawn, and Carolyn's had a feeling that most of them were her fault. It wouldn't help if Del confirmed that.

"The upshot is that I'm the only one who had a relationship in high school, and it was bad," she says firmly. "You're handling the relationships for college, but other than breaking up with Serina, you're not doing too badly. You two weren't epically horrible, just wrong for each other. And now you have Rory."

"How did you circle back to that so easily?" Kit mutters.

"If you get to quiz me about Shawn, I get to poke at your relationship trauma," Carolyn says. She doesn't expect him to give in and talk about it, but they are twins, and everything is equal between them in the long run. Even the hard stuff. "How's everything with Serina?"

Kit relaxes and leans back. "We're okay. We're talking again, and we're still friends. I don't think it's going to be awkward to run into her at Teas Please when she's working. She's been sending me recommendations for movies and books she thinks I'd like. I'm going to meet up with her to help her with Orgo 2." His expression is rueful. "I really thought it was going to be more awkward, but honestly, it's just like we were before only without the cuddling and making out. And it feels better this way. So you don't need to worry about me being broken-hearted. It was weirdly easy to get over."

"Because of Rory?" Carolyn's amused by the quick flush that rises to Kit's cheeks. "You said it's complicated."

"Is there a word for romantic attraction?" Kit asks. "Because the word 'attraction' always implies sexuality, and yes, that part is complicated. But if it's just about cuddling, that's less complicated. Easier."

"You're saying you'd hug Rory," Carolyn says, trying to feel her way through Kit's explanation. "You seemed fine getting close to Serina. That was a pretty big statement of trust for you, I know."

Kit's expression softens, and he touches the guitar on his wrist. "Definitely fine with it. I was at Thorne's on Sunday night—Rory's band apparently needed to pass judgment on me. We watched movies and held hands. It's comfortable being with him, Caro."

"Then be with him."

A door slams upstairs, and Kit's out of his chair and halfway to the door before she can react. He gets it open as Mac storms by, yelling, "Cass!"

Kit glances a question at Carolyn.

"I don't know," Carolyn says, pushing to her feet and joining him, "but I think we should find out."

By the time they get to the bottom of the stairs, Cass and Mac are facing off in the entryway. Trish stands in the doorway to the living room, blocking anyone else from getting close, and Soledad stands in the door to the hall to block that route. Serina is pressed back against the front door, as close to it as she can get, her eyes wide. Kit crowds in behind Carolyn as they form a barrier at the base of the stairs.

Cass tucks a strand of hair behind her ears, twisting it around her finger. "Is there a reason you're screaming my name?"

"I thought you went home this weekend," Mac says curtly

Cass's gaze narrows. "I did. I came back Monday morning. It's none of your business if I left the next day."

Mac inhales, mouth open, but nothing comes out. As soon as Mac returns to staring at Cass, Serina darts past and joins Kit and Carolyn on the stairs. Carolyn has never seen Mac this angry, and she can't think why she is. Cass has her moments, yes, but nothing that deserves this level of fury.

"What?" Cass bites out, arms crossed and head tilted. "Get whatever it is out of your system. If you've decided that I'm—"

"My father thinks you're charming." Mac drops the words like small bombs, each one slower than the last.

Cass furrows her brow, leaning back. "Your father—" She stops, mouth slightly open. "Oh," she exhales. "Oh."

Serina leans in close, one hand on Carolyn's shoulder, her side pressed against Kit. "What did I walk into?" she whispers.

"No idea," Carolyn whispers back.

"Why didn't you tell me they knew each other?" Mac asks, voice low. "Didn't you think that might be important information?"

"I didn't know." Cass's words are too quick, and Mac shakes her head, dissatisfied. "I didn't know," Cass repeats firmly. "This was a work event. A big one. There were people there who I've never met, including Sen—" She stops as Mac's hand comes up between them.

Silence. Then—

"You brought it up," Cass points out.

"We've been sisters here for a year and a half," Mac snaps. "You know exactly who I am."

"I didn't know everything until last fall," Cass replies sharply. "It's not like it matters. I don't understand why you're so angry. So I met your father. So what?"

"It's that your father was there, too," Mac says. "It's SD."

Cass goes pale. "I don't know what you're talking about." Cass is too sharp, her lips pursed, words bitten angrily before she crosses her arms and tilts her chin defensively. "I was only there to keep my mother company."

Carolyn is no Empath, but she swears she can feel anger rising in the air around Mac, spreading through the house. Mac looks away, her gaze dropping. "I can't trust you," she says.

"No one asked you to."

Mac's head comes up quickly, gaze pinning Cass. "We were sisters, Cass. You asked us to trust you, and I'm not sure anyone can. I sure as hell can't."

"Mac." Trish's voice, soft and even. Low. Lyrical as it lilts when she speaks. "Maybe we ought to step aw—"

"Not in the mood for an intervention," Mac snaps. She looks at Carolyn. "Don't get Heather involved. I want to be angry. I want to remember how I feel about this."

"I don't know what you're talking about," Cass protests.

"Lie," Mac says, and Cass looks away, her arms crossed tightly over her chest. Mac smiles thinly, repeats, "Liar. Heather would smell it on you."

Carolyn bites her tongue from the instinctive desire to correct the assessment, to remind Mac that Heather's an Empath, not Clan.

"Are you okay?" Serina's breath is a warm whisper against Carolyn's ear.

"I don't care!" Mac yells, and Carolyn flinches, not sure what she'd missed. She's never been scared of Mac before, but now, she swears she sees death in Mac's eyes. Anger. Fury. Disappointment. "I don't care," Mac repeats, softer now. Sadder. "Fine. Keep lying. I'm not going to believe a word you say anymore. I know better, Cass."

"I'm not hurting anyone," Cass insists.

"I think you believe that," Mac says, "and I think you're wrong."

And then she's gone like she was never there.

Soledad darts forward and puts an arm around Cass's shoulder as she sags. "Are you all right?" she asks.

"I'll be fine." There's a distance in Cass's voice, a polite veneer as she smiles. She's definitely lying now.

"I've never seen Mac be so blatant," Trish muses. "She's always so subtle when she teleports."

Kit's staring at Cass like he's trying to figure her out. "Mac's not the kind of person who lashes out like that. Not without reason."

"I assure you, her reason is all in her head," Cass mutters. She shrugs, pushing Soledad's arm away so she can stand, her arms still crossed across her chest. "I'm fine. Stop fussing."

Serina slides her hand down Carolyn's back. It tickles as it drifts along her spine, and she isn't sure Serina knows she's doing it. It gives Carolyn something to lean into, to take comfort from, so she does.

"What was she talking about?" Kit asks. "It looked like you knew."

"I have no clue."

"Kit." Carolyn tries to cut him off before a new argument can escalate. "It's over. Let it go."

Kit looks at her, then to Serina. "Hey," he says like he's just noticed her there.

"Hey," Serina replies, her fingers going flat on the small of Carolyn's back. "I was bored and thinking about ice cream, so I came over to see if anyone here wanted to brave the heart-shaped crowds to get some with me." She shrugs, and Carolyn feels the motion against her back. "Interested?"

Kit takes a step down, reaching the bottom of the staircase. He shoves his hands in his pockets. "If it weren't Valentine's Day, maybe. But right now? Definitely no."

"It's not a heart-shaped question, only a heart-shaped crowd," Serina says. "I just want ice cream."

For a moment, Carolyn thinks Kit's going to blurt something, but he looks at the others around them, stops himself, and shakes his head. "Just no," Kit mumbles, and he heads for the door.

"Your hat and jacket," Carolyn calls out. Both are still on her bed upstairs.

"I'll get them tomorrow. I'm not going to freeze," Kit calls back, and then he's gone.

"Stubborn," Serina observes.

Carolyn makes a face. "Sometimes very," she agrees. She shifts to the side as Cass approaches the stairs, reaching out to touch her arm. "Cass," she says.

When Cass looks at her, there's no pretense in her gaze. Conflicting emotions leave her shoulders hunched and tight, her jaw twitching while her lips press thin. "What?"

"Ice cream," Serina says with a small smile. She moves away from Carolyn, making a circle on the stairs that includes only the three of them. "I want it. You guys should come with me." She pauses, adds, "My treat."

"I can afford my own ice cream," Cass retorts.

Carolyn glances over to where Trish and Soledad are motioning at the door. Trish points upstairs, probably at Mac's room. Carolyn inhales deeply and tucks her arm in the crook of Serina's elbow. "It's just ice cream," she says, echoing Serina's words. "After that tension, we all need some. Right?"

Serina smiles brightly, eyes crinkling in the corners. She reaches out, waiting until Cass offers her elbow before tucking her hand there. "Right," Serina says cheerily. "We need something to chew on other than these toxic emotions. Carolyn took me out, so I'll take you guys out. Cass, it's your turn next time."

Cass hesitates, and for a moment Carolyn thinks she's going to pull away. "My jacket's upstairs," Cass finally says, tugging her arm free. "I'll meet you outside."

Serina's eyes are wide. She blinks, and Cass huffs.

"I mean it," Cass says. "I'm not trying to run away. I'll meet you outside, and you can take me to eat my emotions over some fight I didn't even start. Fine. Soothe me." She turns on her heel and stalks up the stairs.

"Good luck with that," Trish says quietly. "You're going to need it."

"We'll be fine." Serina hugs Carolyn's arm, leaning in close as she smiles. "We've got this under control."

25

"You got that last time," Serina says, gesturing at Carolyn's bowl as she slides onto the bench next to her, blocking Carolyn into the booth. They're tucked in the back of Sweet Scoops, in the last empty space in the entire shop. Every other table and booth has been claimed by couples, and there are more outside, eating and cuddling for warmth in the Valentine's night chill. Carolyn isn't sure what magic happened for them to get this space, but she's grateful not to be outside.

"That's what Carolyn likes for ice cream," Cass says dryly, taking the other bench. "We have a big bag of gummy bears in the pantry, and she and Heather are the only ones who eat them. Carolyn puts them in ice cream. I've seen Heather drown them in vodka. I think once they put the ice cream in the vodka with the gummy bears."

"We made a vodka caramel sauce for the ice cream, then added the gummy bears on top," Carolyn admits. "It was really good. And I like vanilla ice cream like this. Did you get something complicated again?" She leans closer to Serina, peering at her bowl; she can't see the ice cream under the fruit.

"Mixed berries and hot fudge on top of double-fudge chocolate and double peanut-butter-swirl ice creams, and my cinnamon whipped cream's on the side like a dip," Serina says. She dips her finger in the whipped cream and holds it out to Carolyn. "Try this. It's better than plain whip."

Carolyn stares uncertainly at her finger.

"Go on," Serina says, wiggling the tip.

Cass coughs. When Carolyn looks at her, Cass waves her spoon. "Chocolate with bananas and cacao nibs for me," she says. She gestures at where Serina's finger still waits. "Are you going to try it? Now I'm wondering if it lives up to the hype."

Carolyn nods, and Serina reaches out as Carolyn opens her mouth. The spice of the cinnamon explodes on her tongue, enhanced by vanilla and cream. She licks it from Serina's finger, savoring it as Serina withdraws, her cheeks flushed. Carolyn's tongue tingles. "It's good." That doesn't seem like enough to say.

"It's the best," Serina corrects her softly, licking the last of the cream from her fingertip before she picks up her spoon and digs in.

Cass coughs. "Sorry. Something in my throat."

"You've had a rough night," Serina says, smiling down at her ice cream.

"And you think ice cream's going to make everything better." Cass pokes at her own, laughing dryly. "You sound like my sister."

"You have a sister?" Serina asks.

A flicker of something crosses Cass's expression, as if she didn't mean to say that. "One sibling, and she's older," she says, tone curt. She clearly means to shut the conversation down. Carolyn's fairly certain Serina won't let her.

"How much older?" Serina asks. "I'm the oldest in my family. I have two younger sisters; one's a freshman in high school, and the other just started middle school."

Cass lowers her spoon and stares at Serina, who keeps eating. "Older," she repeats slowly. Softly. "Her name's Minerva—yes, our parents like mythology. She graduated from high school when I was eleven, and she went to college and never came home again."

"I didn't know," Carolyn says. It feels like a huge omission, as if she should know this about her sorority sister. Family is important. But then, Cass, as outgoing as she can seem, is hard to get to know.

"I don't talk about her much," Cass says. Her spoon clinks against the side of her bowl, the sound sharp in Carolyn's ears. "I did tell Allison." At Carolyn's silence, Cass adds, "Allison Maven. My Big, remember? She graduated last year."

"You have an abandonment complex," Serina says.

Cass huffs. "I do not. I don't care that Minerva left; I knew she wanted out of our town. I thought she'd at least come home for Christmas, but she and Dad fought through the end of high school, so I wasn't exactly surprised when she didn't. She got scholarships; she could afford to leave. Whereas I'm Daddy's little girl, and he pays for anything I want. Personally, I think I've got it easier than her. I'd hate to have the kind of loans that come with this education if my parents weren't paying for it."

"You realize that makes you sound as selfish as everyone thinks you are." Carolyn meets Cass's sharp gaze, refusing to back down.

Cass smiles, thin and sharp. "I'm pragmatic, yes. I've chosen to trade familial stress for a lack of debt. She chose otherwise." She's stopped eating; her spoon rests against the side of her bowl, sliding into the melting ice cream.

"Have you ever thought about trying to find her?" Serina asks. She digs into her ice cream, scooping out a big spoonful.

Carolyn makes a mental note that nothing gets in the way of Serina and ice cream.

"Would you?" Cass props her elbows on the table, chin on her hands as she regards Serina. Her gaze is even, her mouth a careful line. "Think about it. You're just starting middle school, and your big sister decides that she's never coming home again. She doesn't care that you have questions about growing up, that you want someone to lean on. She disappears. Why should I bother caring about her? She didn't care about me."

Serina looks down, but Carolyn swears she whispers "Abandonment complex" under her breath.

Silence for a moment, then Cass picks up her spoon. She digs out a bite, has it raised to her lips when Serina comments, "I'd still look."

Cass drops the spoon. "Really."

"Really." Serina quickly eats her last two bites, wiping her mouth with the back of her hand when she finishes. She gestures at Carolyn. "Like. I have little sisters. I love them both, but oh my God, it can be so much drama sometimes. When I packed to leave this year, they each told me they hated me. They told me they were taking my room, that they didn't care if I came home." She smiles, bright and big. "And when I got home for Christmas, they wouldn't let go of me."

"Are you Talented?" Cass asks abruptly.

Serina shakes her head. "None of my family is."

"I am. Emergent. It complicates things," Cass says. "So don't assume that, just because your little sibling story has a fluffy, happy ending, mine would too. I don't miss Minerva like you miss your sisters. My life has enough pressure in it without dragging her back into it."

Serina cocks her head, brow furrowed. Carolyn's not sure why she seems so interested in what Cass has said, but she can see the wheels turning as Serina processes. Then Serina shakes her head, smiling as she turns to Carolyn. "Do you have any epic twin-sibling stories?" Serina gestures at her, fingers falling against Carolyn's forearm. They're warm, and Carolyn feels as if she's suddenly been reconnected to the conversation, included rather than observing.

"Kit ran away when he was seven, but I went with him," Carolyn says.

Cass picks up her spoon, stirs the melted ice cream, then scoops some up.

Carolyn keeps speaking, trying to hold Serina's attention and give Cass a break. "He'd had a fight with our mom, I don't remember about what, exactly, but it probably had to do with his name or his clothes. There were a lot of fights until we had a better understanding of who Kit is. At that point, all I knew was that he was throwing things into a backpack and yelling that he was never coming home. I couldn't let him go alone, so I packed quickly and followed him out the door."

"Where did you go?" Serina asks.

"We made it all the way to the train station," Carolyn says. "There was a bus that stopped at the corner of our block—it went down the main street of our town. So we walked down to the bus stop, and when we got on the bus, Kit paid because of course he'd thought to bring money. I think the driver thought we were with the woman who got on ahead of us. We snuck off when he stopped at the station. We were arguing with the ticket person, trying to buy our tickets, when security asked us to sit down on the bench to the side."

She licks her lips, fingers flexing; Serina covers her fingers and squeezes lightly.

"Kit and I sat there and held hands. Our feet didn't hit the floor, and I felt so small, and I thought security officers were the same as police and that we were going to be arrested. When we got bored, we started going through our backpacks to see what we'd brought. Kit had all the money from his piggybank and from mine. He had three T-shirts, a pair of jeans, and a second pair of sneakers. I'd been rushing, so I had a backpack full of underwear and six books to read on the way." Carolyn smiles slightly. "And we both had our Tarot decks. He tried to give me his while we sat there, but Mom arrived and convinced him to put it back in his bag."

"You must have gotten in trouble." Cass drops her spoon again and dabs delicately at her mouth with a napkin. Her lips purse, and Carolyn wonders what kinds of trouble she's remembering.

"We didn't. There are only the two of us, and Mom was so grateful to have found us." Carolyn makes a face. "What's funny is that Kit forgot. I mentioned it to him last year, and he didn't even remember the bus ride, or the way he got angry at me for being the one to be practical enough to remember to pack underwear. Or the way he laughed when he realized I hadn't packed anything else."

"My parents are really strict," Serina says quietly. Her fingers stay atop Carolyn's, holding on lightly, while she gestures with her other hand. "There are a lot of expectations because I'm the eldest. In high school, I had to get good grades, do at least three extra-curricular activities—one sport, one art, and one to prove I was smart—and I had to help with my little sisters. My parents are paying for college because they think I shouldn't have any debt, and my dad's working two jobs to do it. I hate that they won't let me get loans. I did get scholarships, but not enough to help as much as I'd like to. I'm worried that by the time my littlest sister gets to college, my parents will be bankrupt."

"I'm angry at Minnie." Cass's words are sharp, blunt. They don't match up with what Serina has said, but at the same time, they lay her just as bare. And the name has shifted, Carolyn realizes. Cass refused to think about Minerva, but Minnie's loss upsets her.

Serina makes a soft noise and, as if she hasn't been interrupted, motions with her free hand for Cass to go on.

"She had a boyfriend," Cass says, her jaw tight. She stares down at the table, shoulders tense, fingers twisted together. "She got pregnant her freshman year, and my dad told her she couldn't come home if she kept it. She never told me about it. I mean, I knew she and Drew were together; they'd met in high school and went to school together on purpose. Dad hated him and hated that Minnie picked her school partly because Drew was going there. But I overheard Mom and Dad talking about them, and I pieced it together. I don't know if Minnie tried to talk to me and Dad blocked her somehow, or if she just walked away from us because of what he said. I have a niece or a nephew, I think, and I've never seen them. Or maybe Minnie's dead, and Dad's been lying. But I have to be the good girl. The nice one. The one that does everything right and lives up to every family expectation, because Minnie didn't. And I'm pretty sure he still doesn't love me as much as he loved her."

"Oh." Serina's mouth makes a perfect oval, tongue peeking out when she licks her lips. "Oh. Cass. He loves you."

Cass smiles tightly and makes a small huff of a sound. "No. He doesn't. But he needs me, and I'll take that for now."

"I bet if there's any trace of Minnie or her boyfriend online, Sera could find them." Serina wiggles her fingers next to her temple, her other hand squeezing Carolyn's. "If you really wanted to know, that is."

Carolyn can understand the difference between wanting to know and needing to know. Sometimes it's easier to let the past stay safely in the past. Cass glances up, and for a moment she looks achingly vulnerable, then she blinks. The shutters slide back into place, and her expression goes politely blank.

"Maybe," Cass says.

Carolyn looks down at her almost empty bowl, then fishes the last gummy bear free from the melted ice cream. She pops it in her mouth and carefully cleans her fingers. "We've had dessert," she announces, "and I don't know about you, but I'm in the mood for more comfort food. Cass, order one of those big containers of mac and cheese from Gepetto's, and I'll order wings from Fire and Fry. We can pick both up on the way back to the house, then eat ourselves into oblivion."

For a moment she thinks that Cass is going to resist, that she'll walk away after laying her soul bare. Then Cass fishes out her phone and starts tapping on the screen. "Okay."

Serina lets go, leaving Carolyn's hand cold but free to pick up her own phone. Serina starts doing something as well, waving her phone as she says, "Cannoli from Minnisale's because we are going to need a second dessert when we're done eating."

Carolyn can't argue with that, and Cass doesn't, so she orders the wings as promised. It seems like a good night to sit around with friends and gorge on comfort food until they're sated.

26

"Cass says you're surprisingly good to talk to, without the emotional overhead that goes with talking to Heather." Trish drops next to Carolyn on the couch in the common room and puts her feet up on the coffee table.

The cowboy boots are new, or at least Carolyn hasn't seen them before. The stitching looks custom, and she leans forward, trying to identify the pattern. The swirls don't make sense, and the color of the thread isn't Trish's usual orange. Instead, on the outside of the leg, the stitching shades from pink at the top, through a narrow purple band in the middle, to blue at the bottom. On the inside of the leg, the pink shades to yellow, then to a brighter blue.

Trish has them placed prominently enough that Carolyn suspects she's supposed to say something. She's not sure what to say without sounding awkward, which goes entirely against Trish's comment that she's good to talk to.

Or maybe it's good that Carolyn doesn't talk back. Maybe that's what they like about her.

Trish straightens up, dropping her feet to the floor. The boots disappear, no longer a part of the conversation. "Want to go over to Teas Please?"

Carolyn frowns. Her homework is spread out on the table, her deck near where Trish's boots had been. She needs to get her project together for the independent study; Pawel had let it go this week, but she knows he's waiting. "Why?"

"For tea," Trish says blandly. She stands up, reaches for Carolyn, and tugs her up as well. "Clean up here. Drop your stuff in your room. I'm getting you out of here."

Carolyn's certain Trish has an ulterior motive and equally certain that she won't find out what it is until Trish is ready to explain. She gathers her things and takes them to her room, where Heather and Nikita lie curled on Heather's bed. She mutters "Sorry for interrupting," and tosses everything on her desk. She picks up her deck again, throws the bag into her purse, and puts it over her shoulder. Just in case.

"Going out?" Heather asks.

Carolyn glances at her. Heather's hair is still half in a ponytail, the rest wisping around her face and curling along her neck. There are red marks on her throat, bruises and lipstick. Nikita lies back on the bed, her shirt rucked up and wrinkled, a smile lifting her lips.

Carolyn coughs. "Yeah. Tea. With Trish. I don't know how long we'll be, but I'll just—" She motions at the door. "Go ahead and lock it. I've got my key. Text me when it's okay to come back."

"We will," Nikita calls out, wiggling her fingers. "Go have fun, Carolyn. I'll take care of Heather."

Take care of Heather.

Right.

Carolyn ducks out, closing the door with more force than is needed. She's still standing there when she hears someone throw the bolt on the other side, locking the world out.

Maybe Carolyn needs a single next year.

Trish is waiting downstairs when she gets there, Carolyn's jacket hanging from her fingertips. Carolyn shrugs into it quickly, pulling on gloves and a hat before venturing out into the chill.

"It's so much colder here than in Nashville." Trish has a scarf in front of her face, muffling her words. "Feels like I ought to be used to it by now, but I'm not." She walks with long strides, quicker than Carolyn. The cold air bites into Carolyn's lungs as she rushes to keep up, and she wishes Trish had suggested taking her truck. It feels like a waste to drive such a short distance, but at least it would be warm.

Carolyn doesn't recognize the hostess who meets them at the door, but she spots Serina waiting tables in the front, and Nate's working in the back. Nate waves, and Serina rushes to their table as soon as the hostess seats them. She plunks down two empty glasses, then brings out a pitcher and fills the glasses with water.

"Welcome to Teas Please," Serina says cheerfully. "Are you here for tea or dessert tonight?" She leans in closer, asks quietly, "Are we eating our emotions again? Should I be worried about you, Carolyn?"

"I just wanted to get out of the house, and I dragged Carolyn with me," Trish says. "I'll have a smoothie with coconut milk, honey, mango, pineapple, carrot, and bee pollen."

Serina writes it down quickly, then turns to Carolyn. Her brow is still furrowed, smoothing when Carolyn does her best to smile.

"I'd like the vanilla rooibos," Carolyn decides.

Serina bites back a laugh. "I don't think we have any gummy bears," she says.

"That's ice cream; I don't need to drown them in my tea," Carolyn replies. Trish makes a bewildered noise, but Carolyn likes the way Serina is smiling, as if this joke is just for them. "Honey on the side would be nice, though."

Serina finishes writing with a flourish, then tucks the pen behind her ear. "Got it. If you need anything before the tea is out, give a yell. And be nice to Nate; he's moody tonight."

"Will you be offended if I don't talk your ear off in front of Serina?" Trish asks, leaning on the table. "I know you and she and Cass have been doing the 'going out' thing, but I don't know her as well."

"I don't think Cass knows her well, either, and she seems to be doing fine." Carolyn feels like the conversation has shifted and she was supposed to follow along. "What is this about, Trish?"

"I talked to Cass at outreach last night," Trish says. She leans back, and something pokes Carolyn's foot. Carolyn adjusts, giving Trish room for her legs.

"And?" Carolyn asks. She slides her pocketbook off, pulling out her deck before she hangs the pocketbook from her chair. She lays the card bag on the table, noting the way Trish's gaze drifts to it. "Did you want a reading?"

"That wasn't what I had in mind, but it's not a bad idea," Trish admits. "I wanted someone to talk to. Cass said she's been talking to you. And we all know Cass hates talking to anyone, so I figured that meant you have a good ear."

"I'm not good at advice," Carolyn says. She lays her hand on the bag, then carefully opens it, pulling her deck out and setting it on top of the soft fabric. "The cards might help. I don't always know what to say without them."

"Maybe I just need someone to listen," Trish mutters. "You already know about me Emerging." She touches the side of her face, her finger sliding along her own cheek like it's skating over a barrier between the touch and the skin. "But there's this other thing that's driving me nuts. And it shouldn't be. I mean, it really, really shouldn't be. Because I'm poly, okay? I don't need to have one person and keep them to myself, and I never wanted that. I've dated a lot of guys and a lot of girls. I've had one-night stands because they seemed like fun, and I've had longer relationships. But they were all open, and that was fine, and I didn't mind. It's what I like."

Carolyn blinks, unsure how to handle that explanation. "What's wrong, then?"

"It's Sera." Trish's voice goes flat, and somehow, Carolyn isn't surprised. Of course it's Sera. Trish and Sera have been inseparable since Sera first showed up at the house during rush. Sera's not in SigPsiEp, but she's at the house more than most of their newest sisters.

"I thought you two were still living in each other's pockets," Carolyn says. "She was with you over winter break, right?"

"Yeah, and we're going down to New York for spring break in a month," Trish says. She lifts her napkin, picking at it. "We're staying with TJ. She and TJ are—flirting, I think. Or more. I'm not sure. Sera's not talking about it. And I honestly thought TJ was gay, but he's flirting back."

Carolyn's gaze flicks to where Nate stands at a table, laughing with the three girls and one guy sitting there. "Gay guys flirt," she points out. "With girls."

"TJ is flirting with intention," Trish mutters. "I'm jealous, and I hate it."

"Does Sera know you like her?" It seems like the obvious question, but Trish flinches. "For all you know, Sera's pan and poly, too."

Trish holds a hand up, one finger in the air. "That I know the answer to. She's not poly. She's confused about what it even means and thinks that

I'm promiscuous. She's also pretty sure I've slept with Thorne because we're the only poly people she knows. I haven't. She thinks we have a rock-star attitude, and she's looking for something more stable. That doesn't seem to match up with the whole 'skater girl' thing, but Sera's actually kind of a marshmallow on the inside, behind the outer 'fuck you.'"

"Is this the other thing that's been bothering you?" Carolyn asks when Trish lowers her phone again. "Because you've been absent as a sister. A lot."

"I was at outreach on Wednesday."

"We all had to sign up for one, and that one was music related. Of course you were there," Carolyn says. "What about Soledad?"

Trish leans back as Serina sets a pot down on the table in front of Carolyn, a timer clicking away next to it. Serina slides a glass to Trish, the straw sticking out. "Nate says to tell you that he'll be over for his break because he wants to say hi," Serina says. "Do you need anything else?"

"I think we're good," she says as Trish noisily sucks at her smoothie.

Serina touches Carolyn's shoulder. "Wave if there's anything else you need," she says before leaving.

Carolyn waits. She asked the last question, and if she leaves it long enough, Trish will either answer or change the subject. When her timer dings, she takes the little basket of leaves out of her teapot, sets it aside to drain, and pours a cup for herself.

"There's nothing wrong with me and Soledad," Trish says quietly. "I just haven't been spending enough time with her. And we didn't get close, not like you and Drea. I don't feel comfortable talking to her about things like Emerging and relationships and sex."

"I don't know what Cass told you, but I'm probably not the best person to talk to about Emerging or relationships or sex, either." Carolyn picks up the teacup in both hands, sipping the tea cautiously. "I haven't had a relationship since high school. And that one was not good, as you may have guessed after meeting Shawn."

"I get that you don't think you have any experience to offer. But you listen. You pay attention to people. And you have your cards, which means you're always thinking about how people fit together, about the consequences of actions."

Maybe she has a point.

"You still need to get your shit together and fix things with Soledad," Carolyn says. "She thinks you hate her."

"I will." Trish takes a long slurp, her smoothie almost gone already. "Hey, Nate. You're on break." She pushes one chair out with her foot.

"I'm on break. I'm exhausted. I'm stealing your chair," Nate announces as he slides into the seat. He sinks down, the back of his hand against his forehead in an overly dramatic gesture. "I am wiped out. Absolutely wiped out."

"Are you all out of flirt? I don't think I've ever seen this," Trish tells him.

Nate swats at her. "It's been a long week. I worked Tuesday because I don't have any regular romantic prospects, and no, you don't get to ask why. He is beautiful and unattainable, and I have accepted that."

"Is he straight?" Trish asks, and Nate sighs. Trish lifts her glass in silent toast, and Nate knocks it with his knuckles. "Never crush on the straight ones."

"Amen."

Trish finishes her smoothie with the next long pull through the straw. Carolyn watches her, waiting for the conversation to shift. Nate closes his eyes, crosses his arms, and tilts his head back.

"One card draw," Trish finally says slowly. "I'm crushing so hard I'm actually jealous. Nate's crushing on someone unattainable. And apparently, your taste in relationships is shit. So. One card for each of us. What do you think?"

Carolyn thinks she could do with being left out of the equation, but it doesn't sound like Trish is going to allow that. "Okay," she agrees, setting her teacup down and moving it carefully out of the way. She spills her cards into her hands, shuffling them quickly before setting them in the middle of the table. "Whichever one of you is going first, cut the deck and turn over the card that appeals to you most."

Trish reaches for the deck, neatly picks up almost all of it, sets that pile to one side, then flips over the card on the top of the small remaining stack.

The Eight of Pentacles. A smiling, dark-haired woman looks down at a rose that is surrounded by pentacles.

"I know there's a rose, which would make you think this is about love, but this isn't a relationship card," Carolyn says. "It's a card about workmanship. About trial and error, and about perfecting a craft. This is more likely to be about your music, or about—" She stops, not wanting to refer to Trish's Emergence in front of Nate.

"I get it," Trish says. "Deal with the practical and let love fall where it may. What about Nate?"

Nate opens his eyes and sits up as Carolyn shuffles the deck and sets it in front of him. Instead of cutting it, he fans it out across the table, closes his eyes, and fishes a card out of the center of the deck. "This one," he says, laying it face up on the table. "Seven of phallic symbols," he deadpans. "How appropriate. Why am I fighting them off?"

"It isn't necessarily about fighting off dicks, Nate," Trish says, clapping a hand on his shoulder. "You've got one in the hand, after all."

Carolyn's cheeks heat. "The Seven of Wands is about valor and taking risks," she says before either of them can continue. "This is your moment, so seize it and act. But don't get conceited; if you're an ass about it, you may fail. Figure out what risks are worth taking and take those, then move on."

Nate sits quietly, fingers touching the card. "Yeah. I—I'm not sure I'm ready to take risks right now. But I'll keep the advice in mind."

"Maybe when you're ready, the risk will be worth taking," Trish counsels, rubbing his back lightly as Nate leans into her touch. "Maybe your unattainable man isn't so unattainable after all."

Nate huffs, a disbelieving sound. "I'm not so sure about that. What about you, Carolyn?" He tucks his card back into the center of the deck, neatens the pile of cards, and hands them to her.

Trish watches, waits. Carolyn isn't going to get out of this, so she quickly shuffles the deck and splits it neatly in half, then places one card on the table.

"The Devil," Trish says slowly.

It's a terrifying-looking card. "He enslaves people," Carolyn says. "Exerts dark magical forces. Pushes people into being who they aren't. He keeps people in the dark. When this card shows up in a reading, it means someone important is lost, and that the querent should take risks to get them back."

"The querent is you?" Trish asks.

Carolyn's phone vibrates, and she looks at it, sees an unknown number, and picks it up immediately. "Hello?"

"Carolyn." A familiar voice, strong and steady. Calm.

"Sam."

"I'm ready to get out now," he says, the words coming faster with each breath. "I keep trying to get out, and I keep going back. But I'm ready to get out now. I need you to help me."

"How?" Because Carolyn knows he's still in the facility, still not sane most of the time. "Sam, how?"

"Come talk to me. I'll be here for you," he promises.

"Sam, I'm—"

"You know how," he cuts her off. "You know how to get here. Promise me, Carolyn. Promise me you'll come. As soon as you can."

She looks at the card on the table, the devil's chains wrapped tight about the throats of his prisoners. "I promise," she says quietly. "Give me a day, Sam."

"I trust you," he says, and the phone goes dead.

"Was that the devil?" Nate asks. He goes silent when Trish presses a finger to his lips, shaking her head.

It's not the wrong question.

"Something like that," Carolyn says. She gathers up the cards and carefully puts them away. Her hand shakes when she lifts her tea, sipping at the brew gone cold. Just for a moment, she needs to pretend everything's normal. Then she needs to figure out what to do.

27

Kɪᴛ's ʜᴇʟᴘ ɪꜱ provided reluctantly at best.

"I thought you didn't want to try to travel to specific people." He holds paper in his hand, the image facing away from Carolyn. She only asked him for one picture, so she knows it has to be a picture of Sam as they remember him. The Sam from high school.

She holds out her hand, wiggles her fingers. "He asked me to," she says plainly. "He made me promise to. And since he's stuck somewhere I can't get to easily, and I don't know what his visiting restrictions are, this seems like the easiest route." She can admit that it's against several rules, but if she does it right—if it even works—no one but her and Sam and Kit will know.

Kit keeps the paper close to his body, his lips pressed together in a sour expression. "And you think this is safe?"

Not really, no. Safe is a relative term. She hopes she'll be able to get there, and she knows Sam believes she can. But she doesn't know what traveling to a person instead of a place entails, nor where she'll end up. And there's still the possibility that it won't work. "It's new territory for me, and I may end up just sitting here for an hour staring at Sam's picture and going nowhere," she admits. "Kit, I'll be fine. I have my phone. I have the picture of my room and the one of the library, so I've got multiple places I can travel back to. I'm not defenseless, and it's not like Sam's dangerous. He only wants to talk to me. And I want to talk to him."

Kit huffs. "After we brought Mattie back, I was thinking about Sam. And Del and I had a really interesting conversation. Because you guys never said that he went into that place. That he's lost there. That's what happened to Mattie, too, which makes me wonder if that's what happens when Shadowwalkers are made, if it's how you make Shadowwalkers. If that's true, Sam might not be as safe as you think."

"Sam's not a Shadowwalker." Carolyn doesn't think he is. She trusts Sam. More than she trusts Shawn, these days.

"Maybe you should ask Del for help," Kit says. "I'm talking to her tonight."

"You are?" Carolyn's gaze narrows. That's twice that Kit's mentioned talking to Del. She can't think why they're suddenly so chatty; they've been ignoring each other since everything went upside down.

"Rory," Kit says, shrugging one shoulder as if that explains everything.

In a way, Carolyn supposes, it does.

She could ask Del for help. But she doesn't want to. Things have a way of going sideways around Del, taking a left turn instead of staying steady. She's not sure Kit understands that.

Carolyn shakes her head slowly. "Maybe. If it turns out to be something I can't handle. But I think I'll be fine."

Kit hesitates, then lowers the paper. No, papers: it's a small stack of them, each about 3 inches by 5 inches. Carolyn takes them from him, riffling through them like a deck of cards. Sam's is the first, and the rest are other faces. People who she knows and trusts, like Kit and Heather. Some of her closest sisters, like Drea, Trish, and Mac. One new friend: Serina. And one old, familiar face: Del.

"Just in case it works," Kit says. "I figured I might as well make them since I was already spending the day drawing."

Carolyn pulls him into a hug, careful not to wrinkle the pictures. "They're perfect, Kit. You're perfect."

"If this traveling thing is going to be a big deal, we should work together," Kit mutters against her shoulder. "I draw, you travel. But we can plan it out better than this. Make the pictures more stable, so a rainstorm doesn't destroy everything."

"I don't plan on getting them wet," Carolyn says.

"It's just one example of how things could go wrong," Kit says dryly. "Do they still work if they get smudged? Ripped? We need to think about things like that." He pulls back and picks up his things. "I have to meet Rory and the others at the Madison." He hesitates, reluctance obvious. "Let me know when you get back safely, okay?"

"I will."

As soon as Kit leaves, Carolyn sinks down to sit on her bed. She folds the pile of sketches neatly into her wallet, keeping only the one of Sam in her hand. She tucks her wallet into her bag, putting it over one shoulder, the strap crossing her body securely. She doesn't want to risk dropping anything by accident. Then she holds the picture of Sam in her hands, trying not to hold it so hard that she crinkles the edges. She stares at it, imagines it expanding into an illusion.

Nothing happens.

"Going to spend an hour thinking of Sam and going nowhere," Carolyn mumbles. "So what's different...this is a person, not a place. I'm not a Telepath. Normally I make an illusion of a place—the one in the picture—and go there. But that's not happening."

Yet. It's possible that it's just not happening yet.

Carolyn has a sinking feeling in her stomach, however, that it might not work at all.

She picks up her phone and looks at the unknown number listed in her call log. Calling Sam isn't going to work; she knows that the number he used is from a facility phone. Hearing his voice might help, but they're not going to put a patient on the phone because she asks.

She has to do this herself, and if she wants to keep her promise, she has to make it work tonight.

She carefully smooths the paper against the top of her desk and settles into her chair. She makes herself comfortable, her bag resting on her lap, and she lets go of the tension in her shoulders. Then she places her fingers along either side of the image, holds it flat against her desk, and thinks about Sam.

How tall he was, and how his head tilted when he looked down at her. How broad his shoulders were. The way he'd smile so broadly, with such joy and enthusiasm. The life he had. The way he laughed. When any of them were down, he could lift them up with a few words and a strong hug.

His voice seems quieter now, less booming. But he still commands attention, and she closes her eyes, calling their last conversation to mind: *I'm ready to get out now. I need you to help me.*

"Let me help you, Sam," she whispers, and slowly his image comes to life.

Unlike the rush she's experienced with the image of her room, this illusion builds by inches. It grows out of the picture, increasing in size until he sits in front of her. He's leaning back in a vinyl recliner, his eyes closed, his hands clasped across his stomach.

"Sam," she whispers, and in the illusion, his eyes open wide, staring straight at her.

She reaches for him, and as soon as her hand breaks the plane of the illusion, she's somewhere else.

Carolyn rocks back on her heels as Sam stares at her. Her bag bangs against her hip, but the picture of Sam is gone, probably lying on the desk in her room.

Sam blinks and pushes himself to sit upright. "Are you real?" he asks quietly. "This is my room, and there are no paths to bring you here. I have to know: *are you real?*"

Carolyn exhales roughly. "That's a really good question, and I'm hoping that the answer is yes and I haven't just catapulted myself into the Dreamscape where the rest of your mind is."

He makes a low noise in response, reaching for her as he stands. When he pulls her in, envelops her in his arms, it certainly feels real. Steady and solid, her head against his shoulder because he's still broader and taller than she'll ever be.

She pats his back, smooths circles over the soft cotton of his T-shirt. He almost smells right, a woodsy scent beneath the starkness of the detergent used by the facility. "Sam," she whispers. "Are you okay?"

"The forest is dark and deep," he replies. When he pulls back, he frames her face with his hands, his gaze intent. "Roads diverged into infinity, and I have taken every single one, and none lead home."

Carolyn doesn't know if this is him being coherent or incoherent. It's not how he sounded on the phone. "What forest, Sam?"

He doesn't respond, staring past her shoulder. When she looks, there's nothing there on the wall, not even a shadow.

"Sam?"

He walks away and settles into the recliner again. He's silent, and Carolyn gets the feeling that his mind is somewhere else.

The only other place to sit in the room is the bed. Her gaze flicks to the door, and she wonders if the staff come around regularly. Will they freak out to find her there? She perches on the edge of the bed closest to the recliner and keeps her voice low. "Sam. You wanted me to come here so you could talk to me. You wanted my help."

Nothing.

Patience is essential. Carolyn wishes she'd brought her deck, and lacking her cards, she shuffles through the pictures Kit gave to her. There's a new place picture tucked in among the people—Kit's room on campus. Carolyn touches it lightly, looking at the bright blue of Kit's notebook lying on the bed next to his deck. He might reject his heritage, but it's there in this picture for Carolyn to connect to.

She appreciates that.

Maybe she should text him to let him know that everything's going okay. She pulls out her phone and is halfway through typing a message when Sam says, "Carolyn?"

She shoves the phone back in her bag without hitting "Send." "Sam."

"I'm here," he says. "For now. It's like…" He raises both hands, clenching at the air. "I can't hold on. Like this is the Dream and everything else is reality. Like I don't fit in my body anymore."

"We'll get you back," Carolyn assures him.

Sam looks around, peering into the corners. "We?"

"They aren't with me, but you know Kit and Del will help." When he flinches at Del's name, Carolyn slides off the bed, takes his hands in hers, and crouches in front of him. "You called Del and Shawn for help."

"I needed to reach you," Sam says firmly. "Del can't help. It's her forest, and it doesn't lead home."

"What forest?"

He leans forward, expression gentle and solemn. "The dark one. You don't know what it's like, how far it goes. There are meadows, yes, but the forest—it leads to elsewhere. And there are so many paths, more paths than

I can count. And I can't find the one home. That's what I need you for."

"You want me to find you in a forest and get you out," Carolyn says slowly.

Sam touches her face and nods. "Yes. Because Del's the one who put me here."

"After the ritual."

He nods again. "Yes. All three of us were there, and everything else went to Shawn. I saw him—you didn't—when he exploded inside. It was too much, and he was never truly stable, so everything leaked out again. We've all changed, haven't we?"

That's putting it mildly. "Sam, I have no idea how to get inside your head, find this forest, and get you out," Carolyn says. "Del goes into Dreamscapes. And I can use my new traveling Talent to get us out again. But I can't get in there on my own."

He stands up, walking away to look out the window.

"Sam?"

He ignores her, standing framed by the light from the fading moon. He doesn't turn when her phone pings.

Carolyn slips the phone from her bag, her half-written message to Kit still on the screen. She finishes it quickly and presses "Send." *I'm at Sam's and he's not dangerous. We're talking, for what it's worth. Sort of. I'm safe, and I'll text again when I'm back.*

She switches to her email, expecting a message from Pawel. Instead, it's a response to a message she sent to Sam's mother days ago.

He's doing well, all things considered, she's written. *He's never been as bad off as they thought he would be. He was simply gone for a while, as if his mind had fled. But he would eat, sleep, and move as if he were fully conscious. He was never catatonic. He's been healthy, physically, just rarely available mentally. It's strange that both you and Delilah contacted me recently. He's been agitated, sneaking into the nurse's stations at Pelham. But he can't explain why when they find him. We're worried about him, Carolyn. If you'd like to visit him, I can try to make arrangements.*

Carolyn glances to where Sam stands silent by the window. She shouldn't tell Sam's parents that she can make her own way in to visit. She doesn't want them to think they can't trust her.

"It's funny," Carolyn says quietly. "You're lost in a forest somewhere—probably Del's Dreamscape. And Kit's trying to help his soulmate's ex-boyfriend reach a friend who's been in a coma, and I think they're doing about the same thing. Except she's not up and walking around and functioning. She was attacked by a Shadowwalker. They aren't just legends, Sam."

"The shadows have teeth," he agrees.

Wait. He's already mentioned the darkness once before. "Are there Shadowwalkers where you are?" she asks.

"When you walk the paths, you have to be careful not to fall into the split," Sam says seriously. He turns back to face her and smiles slightly. "Carolyn. You came."

Carolyn's heart twists, aching at the innocent pleasure in his expression. "I came," she says, "but you have to stop calling me. I'll come if you need me. I'll help you. But stop trying to get to the phone. You're worrying people, your mom included."

"I'd rather come home than be safe," he says mildly. "Can you tell Shawn something for me?"

Apparently it's her turn to pass messages. "Of course."

He approaches quickly, wraps her up in another firm hug, and murmurs against her hair, "It's all out there. Everything we've lost. All we need to do is find the right path. He's going to be scared as shit to walk it, but we need to walk it together. All of us. Kit, too."

A shiver goes down her spine. Some things, she'd rather see stay in the past.

His grip tightens, then goes lax. "You have to go. They won't understand how you're here."

Carolyn can't hear anything, but she suspects Sam is in tune with the nurses' schedules here. "I can do that. I promise I'll come back."

"I know." He releases her and takes his place on the recliner again. He puts his feet up and leans back, eyes closed.

Carolyn pulls the pictures out again and looks through them. The one of her room is on top; she hopes that Heather and Nikita aren't there. She's starting to stare at it when there's a soft knock, and the door to the room immediately opens. Carolyn startles, takes a step back, and the papers rustle in her hand.

The nurse wears purple scrubs with cartoon cats all over the top. Her dark hair is pulled back in a twist of braids, and her dark eyes narrow. "What are you doing here?"

"Just leaving," Carolyn says. She closes her eyes, praying that it'll work, and calls up the illusion.

It's not her room.

She has a moment's surprise to realize that Serina is looking at her, mouth ajar in confusion as Carolyn reaches toward her and falls into her arms.

"What...?"

Carolyn still has the stack of papers in her hand, crinkled from the strength of her grip. She untangles herself from Serina, quickly shuffling through the pictures to ensure she hasn't left any behind. The only one missing is Sam's, and she's pretty sure it's on her desk in her room. She shoves the papers into her bag and looks at Serina, who stares at her, openmouthed and unusually silent.

"I traveled," Carolyn says.

"I guessed that," Serina replies, gesturing at her. "You just...stepped out of nothing, and then you were here. It's not every day that I get to catch a swooning damsel." She pauses. "Not that you're in distress. Are you in distress? Because I can do more rescuing if you need it. But how did you get *here*?"

"Kit made me some new pictures—"

"Of my room?" Serina squeaks. "He hasn't even been here, has he? Unless he was visiting Rory and stopped in. But I don't think he has. We didn't come up here when we were—"

"It's okay," Carolyn says hurriedly. "He didn't sketch your room for me. He drew me a picture of you."

Serina's stunned silent.

Carolyn tries to find the right words. She licks her lips, looks away. "I trust you, I guess," she says.

"Oh." Serina's voice is small. "Thank you."

"I visited Sam. My friend who..." Carolyn trails off. She can't remember if she's told Serina this story, doesn't know if Kit's told her. And she's tired, wavering on her feet, the world fuzzing at the edges. "Can I sit down?"

"Yes." Serina grabs her shoulders, rotates her, and nudges her back until there's a bed behind her knees. It's the lower of the two beds in the room; the other one is on a loft, the space beneath it hidden by curtains. Carolyn sits on the floral comforter when Serina nudges her.

"Do you want to lie down?" Serina asks.

No, but...yes. "Please." Carolyn goes as Serina tugs her, shivers building from the insides of her bones outwards until she's shuddering hard. Serina wraps her arms around her, and it's so different from Sam's hug that it's jarring.

It's soft and familiar and comfortable.

Carolyn hiccups, and she doesn't know why she's weeping, but she is, her face pressed against Serina's shoulder. It strange to feel so stable and steady; this is just Serina. Carolyn's taller than her, broad enough that Serina has to burrow close to curl around her; Serina seems small where she's pressed against Carolyn. But somehow Carolyn feels safe here, and this is good and right. As Serina's fingers comb through her hair, Carolyn can't seem to stop crying.

Her eyes ache when she finally stops, her nose full of snot and Serina's shirt soaked. "I made a mess on you," Carolyn mutters.

Serina's fingers stop in Carolyn's hair, scratching softly against the base of her skull. "It's okay. You need cuddles, and I have cuddles to give. And if you want to talk about what made you cry like that, I can listen."

"It's not—it's not any one thing," Carolyn manages. She has no explanation. The tears felt like they had to happen, like they were exploding out of her. "If Heather were here, I'd be fine."

"You can't use Heather as a crutch."

The words would hurt, except Carolyn knows they're true. She's spent so much of her college life coasting along, knowing that when things got overwhelming, she could rely on Heather to suck the pain away, smooth it over with a sweet, happy, light mood. "I know." But owning her emotions—every little thing that's happened in the last few years that she's tucked away—that's not easy. "When I'm ready to talk about it, I'll talk to you. I promise."

"I'll be here when and if you're ready," Serina says softly, fingers combing through her hair again. "Becky went home for the weekend, if you want to crash here. Just tell Heather the room's all hers, and you don't have to worry about being sexiled or about bothering her and Nikita."

"I don't want to put you out."

"Pfft." Serina waves away Carolyn's objection. "I invited you. You want company and cuddles, you stay. Text the people who need to know things, take off the bag you're carrying because that can't be comfortable to lie on, and then we'll stream something silly and cuddle until we sleep. Okay?"

All Carolyn wants to do is close her eyes and relax into the closeness that Serina offers. She nods slowly, then manages to get the strap of the bag over her head. It only takes a moment to text both Heather and Kit that she's crashing at Serina's; Serina takes the phone and bag and puts them aside.

By the time Serina manages to set up her laptop to stream, Carolyn's floating in a haze, half asleep. She doesn't remember what they watch, only that Serina's soft, and her hands feel good where they lightly rub her arm.

28

CAROLYN HAS WRITTEN pages and pages of notes. She should be typing them, but while surrounded by stacks of handwritten books, it feels more natural to scribble into her journal. It's strange to think that once, this book was only a log of her Tarot readings, lists of cards and meanings and thoughts on how she'd interpreted them for the querent. Now, it's full of her musings about every time she has traveled, and she's started lists comparing different interpretations of Dreamwalkers and Shadowwalkers. Her has charts are drawn across two pages of her journal, another reason it's easier to write longhand.

She doesn't think they're separate Talents. Dreamwalkers are acknowledged as real, and Shadowwalkers are treated as legend, but she thinks that they are different aspects of the same ability.

She's certain that teleporters, like Mac, belong on that same axis.

She's been awake since six; she sneaked out of Serina's room and traveled back to her own, then dressed quietly while Heather and Nikita still slept. She's thankful for her picture of the special collections room; she was able to get in a few hours before the library would have usually opened on a Saturday morning.

This new traveling aspect of her Talent definitely has its advantages.

There's a knock against the door shortly after the library opens at 10 a.m. She glances up as Pawel opens the door and ushers Conor through. He shoos Conor to the other table, then sits at the end of the table closest to Carolyn.

"So," Pawel says. Her message wasn't filled with information; she can't blame him for giving her a look that says he's waiting, that he's disappointed and curious.

"Thanks for coming," she says. She starts to close the journal, but he stops her by placing a hand on the pages.

"You're not one of the students I expect to have troubles that require a weekend intervention," Pawel says. "When you email me, I know it has to be bad. I'm worried that you waited longer than you should have to get me involved."

That rankles. "With all due respect," she says tightly, "I don't think you'll have any better idea how to deal with this than I do. I'm in uncharted territory, and I'm working out some brand-new theories."

"You're not a Magical Studies major," Pawel says. He withdraws his hand and sits back, fingertips steepled under his chin. He's scruffy, like he's still not shaving regularly, and his hair, longer than usual, has started to curl at the ends.

Conor makes a small sound, but when Carolyn glances over, he's focused on his game.

"I'm not, and I'll definitely figure out a way to look at this from a sociological viewpoint," she replies. "But right now, I'm neck deep in theories about how Talents interact and what that means for someone like me."

Pawel nods and gestures at the notebook. "Talk me through it. And tell me where you want to go with it."

It simpler to start with the end. "I want my final project for the independent study to be reuniting my friend Sam with his body," she explains. "He's lost, and while he's functional in some ways, he's incoherent. He wants to come back. Investigating his situation has led me down some strange paths regarding Dreamwalkers, Shadowwalkers, and people like me and Del."

His gesture says *go on*.

"Okay. So." She flips to a notebook page where she has people's names written across the top and abilities listed in a column beneath each name. "I started thinking about this because there are definite similarities between myself and Del, and between Del and Nikita, and it got really complicated when we brought that Shadowwalker back."

"Mattie," Pawel murmurs.

"Nikita's abilities aren't like those typical for Dreamwalkers, either."

Carolyn slides her finger down the column. "Nikita keeps falling into Dreams, but she doesn't remember them. When she's lost in a Dream, weather happens. And she's been assuming that things happen here because things are happening there. I think that's true. The thing is, when Nikita's stressed, she loses control." Carolyn can't help her wry smile. "Nik will tell you she's perfectly in control, but she's not. She gets upset, weather happens. Even though she can't remember her Dreams, some pretty horrible things must be happening to her in them. Most Dreamwalkers remember their Dreams, and sometimes they drag other people into them, like a shared delusion. And Nik doesn't do that, for which I'm thankful."

She slides her finger to the next column. "Then there's Del, who actually, literally travels physically into what we call the Dreamscape. That might not be the right name for it, and I want you to keep that in mind because it's possible that Dreamwalkers aren't actually walking in Dreams, either. Anyway. My point is, while Nikita's mind travels, Del's body travels. She slips into this other world, and sometimes she can take people with her. When we were in high school, she took me and Sam there; she went in physically, us mentally. Sam never came out; he's still trapped in that place. When we were in Haverhill at Drea's place, Del took us all in, and it was completely physical for everyone involved. That's when we found Mattie's—for lack of a better term—soul, and I got us all back out. Del had no idea how to transport us out. I'm not sure she even knew what she was doing when she took us in."

She inhales roughly, on a roll now. "Then there's me. I bring up illusions and I go through them, without visiting anywhere during the transition from one place to another. Or to a person."

Pawel's eyebrows rise. "Really?"

She nods. "Yes. Really. Tested twice now, both last night."

Again he motions for her to continue.

"When we see Shadows travel, they go in and out of darkness," Carolyn says, moving to the fourth column. "Mattie said that the Shadows live in the split, but her mind was in the Dreamscape. And—this is where it gets really complicated—when I spoke to Sam last night, he implied the two places are linked."

One of Pawel's eyebrows arches.

"Sam's in a forest cut through by paths. He said some of the paths lead dark places, and some don't, and he can't find the one that'll lead him home. And he mentioned the split, too. That you have to be careful not to fall into it." That was the phrase that sent Carolyn down this train of thought. "It made me wonder—we all travel in some way. What if we have the same Talent, and what if everything we do involves passing through this Dreamscape—this place between? What if Shadows go through the darkest place, and people like me and Mac never really land in it? We kind of…fold it and hop across. But Del goes in and can't get out, and Nikita enters it mentally. Because I'm not actively linked to it at all times, it makes sense that Nikita and I can interact. However Del's version of the Talent works, maybe it's like this gravitational force pulls Nikita toward the Dreamscape, like they're both Dreamwalkers."

"Makes sense to me," Conor mutters, still staring at his game.

Pawel glances over at Conor. "You should never experiment with this. The Shadows are dangerous."

"You've said that before," Conor replies, thumbs moving quickly on the buttons of his device. "I know, Dad."

Pawel reaches for the notebook, and Carolyn lets him take it. He reads silently, finger tracing over the words. He turns the page, reads through her more detailed notes about accounts of Dreamwalkers and Shadowwalkers and Deathstalkers. Then he flips back, reading her written account of her visit to Sam yesterday.

"Side point," Carolyn says. "I remember Drea telling me the story of the Deathstalker and the lemon, and Alaric says that Heather smells like citrus. Heather is also able to keep Nikita's Talent under control; her ability to keep Nikita on an even emotional keel helps Nikita not slip into Dreams. If all of these Talents are somehow linked, then it makes sense that Shadowwalkers would be afraid of lemons. They don't mean literal lemons. They mean Empaths."

"Mm."

His tone doesn't give her a hint what he's thinking. She starts to speak, but Pawel holds a hand up, then touches a finger to his lips. Fine. She can be quiet and let him read.

Carolyn feels like she's laid bare there in the pages of her journal. He doesn't seem to be reading in depth, but he's engrossed, reading and rereading, paging back and forth.

She gets up to put books back and pulls out a new one about a woman who claimed to have met a Deathstalker. The name on the book's front page isn't familiar, but the fact that it was transcribed from the account of a 120-year-old woman who believes herself to be immortal does sound familiar.

"I met with her." Pawel waves at the book. "Her family donated that diary to the collection. One of her grandchildren took the transcription. It's lengthy. How does a woman who stared death in the eye, refused it, and never saw it again fit in with your theory?" He glances up. "She's still alive. I correspond with her regularly. She's adapted well to technology, all things considered."

"I don't know," Carolyn replies. "It's a theory. Proving it will require collecting a lot of data, and I want to look at it from different angles. Psychological, because the history of Dreamwalkers is tied into the history of psychology as a whole and institutions specifically. Sociological, and how Talented societies grew around these particular Talents. And classical, looking into history and myth." Carolyn meets his gaze. "This is thesis material."

"In a subject that is not your major," Pawel points out.

"Sociology, Psychology, and Classics," Carolyn says firmly. "Those are my majors. If you don't think I will find something to fit this—"

"I can see it." He nudges the notebook back toward her. "I want a copy of your notes so I can review them again. And I want you to think about exactly what you're asking to do, and how you'll do it. I'm not going to approve this project until you can provide me with a more definitive plan."

"I haven't given you any plan yet."

"Exactly." Pawel's smile is tired, and he pushes his hair back from his face, fingers tangling in the strands. "Carolyn, you've been pushing the limits of an Emergent Talent that you know nothing about. I understand that you think you know what you need. I appreciate that you've learned a lot working with Kit, and I am relieved to see the two of you bonding again over magic, even if it's not the same predictive magic you originally came to me about. But you've put yourself in danger repeatedly. You haven't kept control, and you haven't always had a failsafe."

"I'm not five," Carolyn protests.

"I'm not saying you are, but as your advisor on this independent study, I need to make sure that your project isn't endangering yourself or others." Pawel leans forward on his elbows, head bowed for a moment before he looks at her again. "The world changed once, drastically, and now it's changing again. And I would be lying if I said that didn't scare me." His voice is low. Carolyn's aware of how Conor sits quietly, like a tiny Szczek shadow, focused on his father's words.

She presses her lips together. "I haven't always been given a choice in what I'm doing," she mumbles. "Things happen."

"I know, and that's part of the joy and terror of magic," Pawel says. He lays one hand atop hers, then withdraws. "All I'm asking is that, when you do have control, you think first. Lay out a plan, ensure that others know exactly what you are doing, and do not operate alone. If you cannot have a friend with you—Drea, Heather, Kit, anyone from your house—then contact me."

There's something in what he says—in how he says it—that makes Carolyn furrow her brow. "You aren't responsible for what's happening," she says. "You aren't responsible for the Shadows attacking people, or for Nikita or any of us Emerging. This isn't something you can control. Or stop."

"I'm not?" Pawel asks. He sits back again, legs stretched out, fingertips steepled under his chin. "Carolyn, when I Emerged, I decided to study Talent—not just study it, but to create an entire academic discipline related to it. I was conceited enough to believe that I could become the one person who knew everything there was to know about Talent. After all, I was new to magic, but the signs of it had always been around me. I had always believed. And I was strong, and stubborn. I was the perfect person to create the study of magic.

"And it worked. I'm considered a national—if not international—expert on Talent and magic," Pawel says. "PHU created a department for me. I'm not even thirty years old, and I'm a dean. People come from all over the world because PHU is a welcoming university, and because if you come here, you can study Talent as well as living it. Because of me, people like you are here. A lot of people like you." He lowers his hands, fingers splayed flat against the table. "There is so much power at PHU now. So much creativity and ability, and you are all changing. And most of you are here because I'm here. So in what way am I not responsible for creating a nexus where this can happen?"

He slumps back, and Conor looks up, watching. Pawel rubs at his eyes, pressing the heels of his palms into his eye sockets. Carolyn looks past him and waits until Conor meets her gaze before she says, "You may not be wrong. But you're not right, either." Conor tilts his head, and Carolyn continues speaking to him because Pawel isn't paying attention. "We've always gathered. It's in our nature as humans and as Talent. We build societies around our similarities, and we bond, in some ways, based on our differences. You know this. You know this possibly better than any of us because you did go out and talk to people. You interviewed Clan and Mages from all kinds of social backgrounds. You've met people who were solitary and gone places where Talent intertwined." She smiles slightly when Pawel finally looks at her. "See, I do remember the readings from the intro class."

Pawel laughs under his breath.

"You did exactly what we always do," Carolyn says. "You worked to create a stable, safe space. And you did. We feel safe here, and we're working with non-Talented people, side by side, in ways that we didn't pre-Emergence. If this means we've created a space that's also attractive to the Shadows, you couldn't have known that would happen. No one thought they were real."

Pawel's gaze drops.

"She has a point, Dad." Conor's back to his game. Carolyn can hear faint music as he plays.

"It doesn't change that you need to tread more carefully and be aware of the larger picture." Pawel crosses his arms, expression strangely young and mutinous.

"Fine. But stop feeling guilty about it," Carolyn replies. She tucks her notebook in her bag. "Do you have a copier at your office? I don't want to pay the library to copy the pages out of my notebook."

"Better. I have a scanner." Pawel unfolds slowly. "Conor, text Alan—see what time I can drop you off."

"Because you're going to be too distracted when you start reading Carolyn's notes?" Conor mutters. "Okay, sure. Hey, do I still have a babysitter tonight or can I stay at Alan's?"

"Emily and I discussed it. Alan will be staying with you tonight, and Alex will take care of both of you," Pawel says. He exhales, straightening as he does so, seeming to purposefully relax. "And no, you are not yet old enough to stay home alone without a babysitter. You'll like Alex."

Conor makes a dubious sound.

It seems like a good time to wrap things up, so Carolyn finishes packing, then puts the books away. She jots down the information about the ones she wants to look at next, nudging Conor's chair on the way by. He sighs loudly before putting his device away in a pocket.

"I'm ready," he announces.

Pawel pulls the door open and ushers Conor through. He waits until Conor's halfway down the hall toward the stairs before saying, "Don't forget what I said, Carolyn. None of us are immortal."

Carolyn's pretty sure she can't forget that. "That one lady is," she says, just to be contrary. "She stared death down, right?"

"Do you really think that'll work twice?" Pawel pulls the door closed after they're both through, the *thunk* a heavy ending to his statement.

No. She really doesn't. But it's still data, still something to keep in mind. Carolyn has a lot of research to do.

THE VIEW
OF SELF

SEVENTH POSITION: SELF

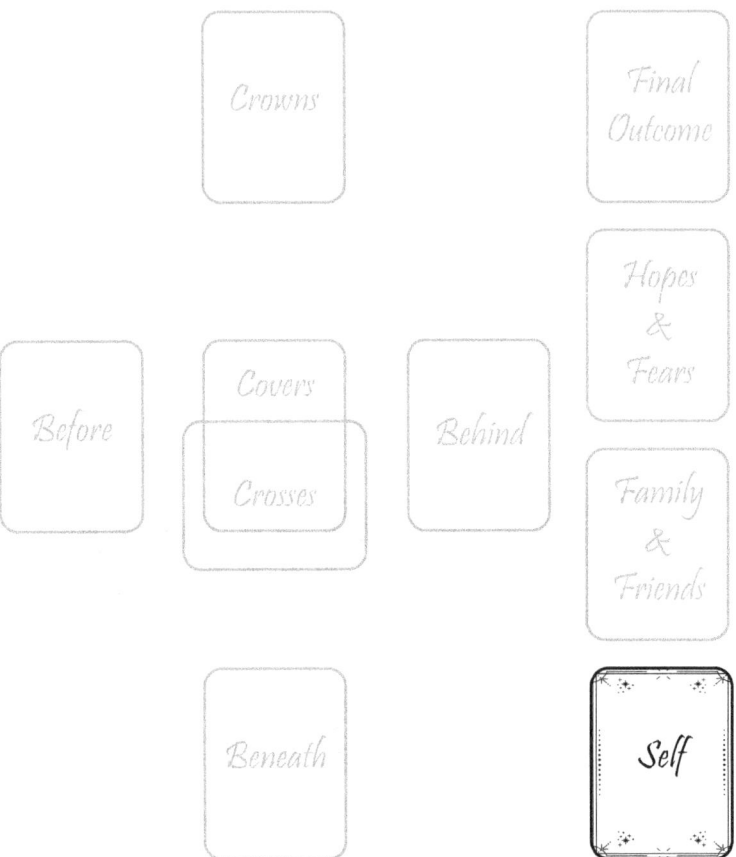

THE VIEW OF SELF...

When a querent casts their gaze within, they see certain truths about themselves. They also see fallacies: fantasies about who they wish to be, about who they try to present themselves as to the outside world. The card that lies in the "self" position represents a chance for the querent to contemplate their place in the world and how they might affect their own future. It is not a definitive statement that "this is how the querent is," but rather this card reflects the querent's self-perception. While this card may be viewed alone, it is best viewed within the context of the entire reading.

Carolyn's Reading: The Four of Cups

A young man reclines next to a pond as his horse waits nearby. A castle is visible in the distance. Four full cups and four lotus flowers rest atop the surface of the pond, waiting. He smiles slightly as he ponders his choices. The cups are full and the flowers are in bloom, but the man's ribs show through his gaunt torso.

The querent has a lot to think about, and they believe that they have enough time to rest and relax while doing so. However, time moves on around them, and they will need to make a decision soon. There is pleasure in reach should the querent seek it instead of daydreaming. The querent shouldn't let uncertainties hold them back lest they waste away.

This is a card of refusal. There is wine just out of reach. There are blooms and new beginnings there for the taking should the querent desire them. If the querent hungers, there is sustenance. But this card suggests that the querent has chosen to ignore everything around them and stay in place. It is a warning that the querent should move past indecision and reach for that which awaits.

Kit's Reading: The Queen of Pentacles

A woman stands in front of a palace on the shores of the nearby lake. A lotus flower blooms, offering a pentacle to her: magic and success for the taking. She is serene, smiling; the world is hers.

If this card were part of a draw regarding a specific situation, it would represent success. As it is, in the "self" position, this card suggests that the querent sees themselves in a positive way. They are good-hearted and gentle, quiet and friendly, and they know themselves to be thus. They are generous with their talents, though they may be shy about taking credit for their generosity. The querent is at a point where they feel comfortable sharing what they know and what they can do.

29

"I LIKE THIS theater."

Serina tangles her fingers with Carolyn's and leans against her shoulder. She's warm and soft and smells like ginger and spice. Carolyn isn't sure where the smell comes from—maybe it's shampoo or something Serina ate before they headed for VIT—but it's clouding Carolyn's mind in strange ways. She exhales slowly, her gaze settling on the row of seats on the opposite side of the theater where Kit and Rory have settled in at the end of one row.

Serina squeezes her hand. "We're here to enjoy the show," she murmurs. "Why do you seem so worried?"

"She's not worried," Heather says idly. "I can't really classify what I'm getting off her as anything other than low-level anxiety, which isn't unusual for Carolyn."

Carolyn should tell Serina not to think about it and tell Heather to stop reading her. But they both mean well, and she's leaned on Heather's Empathic abilities more than she should have over the last years. By now, it's probably automatic for Heather to keep an eye on her.

"Worried," Serina counters. "Anxious. Whatever it is, if there's a reason for it other than brain chemicals messing with you, you can let it go, Caro." Her tone gentles. "And if it's just brain chemicals messing with you, I'm still here and am happy to play anchor."

An anchor is a thing that can weigh you down, tug you under the water until you can't breathe.

It's also a thing that can be carefully placed to keep you from floating away on dangerous currents.

It's strange how one word can be both positive and negative.

"You're the good kind of anchor," Carolyn muses. "Like Heather is for Nik." When Serina squeezes her hand, Carolyn squeezes back. "And I'm not worried. I'm just..." Her gaze drifts to where Kit and Rory sit, Kit's head tilted against Rory's shoulder. "I keep thinking about everything going on with Kit."

"Protective," Heather says.

"Worried," Serina says again. Her voice is low and fond, and she leans into Carolyn, a soft weight against her shoulder. "You don't need to worry about Rory. He's sweet. He's shy and quiet, and he's really helpful and adorable."

"I like him," Nikita adds, leaning past Heather. "He's one of guys I trusted when I was talking to people about coming out. He's level-headed."

"I'm not worried," Carolyn says again, even though she's certain none of them will believe her. At least Nate, Dax, and Cass seem otherwise occupied, Nate leaning away from Nikita so he can chat with the other two. Carolyn doesn't need anyone else to weigh in on her state of mind.

Nikita continues leaning against Heather, shifting to direct her talk toward Carolyn. "It's like a weird double date, isn't it?" she says.

Serina's hand twitches in Carolyn's, and Carolyn loosens her grip in case Serina wants to let go.

"Kit and Rory," Nikita says, looking across the way. "Drea's being a third wheel with Alaric and Chris because Corbin's working the show. Cass and Dax. Me and Heather."

"Nate," Carolyn says before Nikita can finish her thought. She wiggles her own fingers, and it's Serina who lets go, withdrawing into her own space. "He's not dating anyone here."

"Nate has a crush on someone, and he won't say who," Serina whispers quietly enough that Carolyn and Nikita have to lean closer to hear her. "Be nice to him. And don't say the word 'date' around Alaric. He gets cranky. I think he's still working on vocabulary."

That's something that Carolyn can understand. She's never sought the right words to explain herself, although she's getting the idea that she could. It sounds complicated, and she's shied away from learning more.

"I think they're cute." Nikita finally settles in her seat. "As cute as two gigantic football players can be together." She blows a kiss when Alaric looks over, his brow furrowed into a glare.

"Don't antagonize the bear," Heather murmurs as the stage lights flash.

Carolyn's happy to let the subject drop and enjoy the show. Doing so would be easy—the cast is good, and the story is engrossing—if it weren't for her companions. Heather sits with one arm around Nikita's shoulders, but she keeps glancing in Carolyn's direction. And Serina sits with her hands pinned between her knees, her shoulders tense.

Oh.

Carolyn leans toward Serina, reaching out to lightly touch her knee. When Serina jumps, Carolyn withdraws quickly. "Sorry."

"It's okay." Serina's voice is soft, like she's trying not to disturb the people around them. "I don't want to invade your space."

"I don't mind," Carolyn says. When Serina presses her lips together and doesn't move, Carolyn carefully places her arm on the armrest between them, her hand palm up. "I really don't mind."

Serina relaxes slowly, knees first. Carolyn waits, not moving, as Serina moves closer. Serena's hand tangles with Carolyn's, then she tugs, and Carolyn lets her pull her hand close so she can cuddle it. By the time Serina's done, she's tilted entirely toward Carolyn, curled up in a way that would have her pressed against Carolyn's side if there weren't an armrest between them.

Serina exhales softly, her shoulders at rest.

Carolyn doesn't look to her right, not wanting to see Heather's expression. She can feel her regard; Heather is probably wondering what's going on. And Carolyn doesn't have an answer other than that this is more comfortable and far less awkward. She doesn't want Serina to be uncomfortable.

As the show's story rolls forward, Carolyn is engrossed. The performance makes her skin prick, the themes sticking in her mind. By the time the play ends, Carolyn is in tears, droplets slipping over her cheeks while Serina digs in her bag and comes up with a small wad of napkins. Carolyn blots at her eyes and waves Heather away.

"We're meeting the others in the lobby," Heather says, lingering. "I'm sure Kit will find us there."

"We'll be there in a minute," Serina says quickly. "I don't like crowds, and it'll be easier to find each other if there aren't as many of us. Right?"

Carolyn exhales slowly, waves at Heather again. "I'm good. Go. I'll wait here with Serina."

"You didn't know what the show was about," Serina says softly as soon as they're alone. The crowd thinned while they were talking.

"I knew the name," Carolyn protests. "It was a group thing, and everyone seemed so excited. I didn't think it was going to try to rip my heart out."

Serina catches her hand in both of hers and squeezes it. "It's about how children learn, about how they—we—move beyond what our conservative parents have done. It's about growing stronger."

"If it were about Talent, it would've been a *Romeo and Juliet* with Clan and Mages," Carolyn mutters. Her next inhale fills her lungs, and she blots the remaining tears from her face. "I'm good to go. Let's get out there. I was hoping to talk to Rory a little. I don't really know him."

"You didn't try to make sure I was good enough for Kit," Serina says lightly.

"I already knew you," Carolyn protests. "More than I know Rory." She realizes that she still has Serina's hand clasped in her own, but when she flexes her fingers, Serina holds on tight. They stay close until they reach where Drea stands with Corbin off to one side in the space near the stairs.

Rory and Kit are already there, Kit's hand between Rory's shoulder blades. It's a casual touch, easy and comfortable.

Serina drops Carolyn's hand, turning away to talk to Cass and Dax.

Corbin's got some plan to go out as a group—Carolyn remembers Drea talking about it before they arrived at VIT. Carolyn likes the idea, because it'll give her a chance to get to know Rory and see him interact with her brother. She hadn't wanted to see the public displays of affection between Serina and Kit, but at least, because she witnessed those, she knew where they stood. She can't tell where Kit stands with Rory; she wants to know that Kit's happy.

He looks happy, leaning slightly against Rory, smiling when Rory drops his hand to the small of Kit's back.

This could be good.

She blinks when Corbin pulls away from Drea, slips between Rory and Kit, and slings an arm around them both. Kit goes tense, and he and Rory pull away at the same time.

"Sorry," Rory says, his hands up. "We'll just take the bus back. Maybe walk around a little first."

"But—"

"Let him go," Drea whispers loud enough for Carolyn to hear. And that's it; Kit and Rory escape the lobby before Carolyn can say anything. Corbin's chased them off somehow, and while Carolyn missed most of the actual exchange, she's not surprised.

"I wanted to spend time with my twin," she says quietly, and Corbin gives her a sharp look.

"Are you blaming me for—?"

"Yes," Drea says, her hand over Corbin's mouth. "She is. So hush. Let's head for that dessert place you mentioned and get a table, and then we can get caught up on home news."

"There's home news?" Corbin asks. He motions and Alaric drifts closer, Chris in his wake. "You've been holding out on me."

Drea glances at Carolyn. "It's Shadow-related. I'd kind of hoped to talk to Rory, too."

"We can talk while we walk. Let's get out of the crowd," Alaric mutters. He moves away, and the crowd parts around him; Carolyn's not sure if it's his size or his attitude, but whatever it is, it works to get them out quickly.

Their large group gathers on the sidewalk. Dax stands with his arm around Cass's shoulders, and Serina is chatting with Nate. Corbin's fingers are linked with Drea's, and Chris has one hand at Alaric's back. Heather and Nikita are off to the side, their heads bent close together. Carolyn suddenly feels awkward and alone. She crosses her arms against the chill air.

"Lead on," Drea says.

Corbin starts walking, and the group follows in a mixed knot of not-quite-couples. "I'll walk, you talk," he counters. "What fun drama is happening at home now?"

"Dad's on a hunt for the Shadow," Drea says. "Still."

"We're not telling him she's in Vermont," Alaric mumbles. "I wouldn't mind seeing her dead for what she did, but she's helping us best she can. Besides, Rory would kill me if I did anything to her."

"We need her," Drea says, "and the thing is, I think Dad gets that she's important to understanding what's happening. And he knows, intellectually, that she got out and that things have changed, but he hasn't fully parsed it yet. Mom understands."

Carolyn frowns. "Does she know the Shadow is in Vermont?"

Drea nods. "She's not helping Dad hunt, though. Things are…complicated at home."

"What you're saying is that dear Theobald is in a rut and stuck in the past while your mom is moving forward," Corbin translates.

Alaric growls softly. "He's going to get himself declared unfit."

"Will you have to—?" Chris doesn't finish the question before Alaric growls again.

Carolyn glances at Drea, trying to convey her sympathy. "We'll find a way," she says, even though that's not a promise she can deliver on. In the silence, she realizes that Serina's looking at her in surprise and Drea is smiling. "I'm studying the—" She's not sure how to explain what she's been working on. "I'm trying to understand how the Shadows and everything else that's happened recently relate to my new traveling Talent. Once we understand how things fit together, we can try to keep Shadows from attacking anyone else."

Serina slips her hand into Carolyn's, then leans against her shoulder. Something in Carolyn's back unwinds.

"I'll talk to Mom, see if we can get Dad calm enough to think about properly leading our community," Drea says.

"Instead of leading us into disaster." Corbin twists, walks backward, and motions with grand gestures. "Okay, folks, come along. Time for your tour of VIT. This is the hill, and we'll be climbing a few staircases, so be ready for a workout. It's impossible to attend VIT and not end up with buns of steel. Let's cut through the crowd over here, and we'll take these stairs— they're steep so hold the railing—and we'll be there soon!"

"Stairs," Serina groans theatrically. "At least it's a good workout, and it'll warm us up."

Nate's already sprinting up, Dax close on his heels. A moment later Alaric and Chris take off, like they're participating in some kind of impromptu sports drill. Nate outpaces them all.

Carolyn's happy to follow at a slower pace. There's only a rail on one side, and Serina is holding that, but Serina's got Carolyn's hand as well. That's good enough. Serina won't let her fall.

30

THEY GET BACK from Valiant late; Nikita follows Heather and Carolyn into the house and up to their room. It's no longer as awkward to have Nikita with them, although Carolyn still wonders if they want more privacy than they can have with her there. On the other hand, once it's dark in the room and they have semi-privacy, it's possible they don't care that she's there. If that's the case, Carolyn doesn't want to know.

Heather kisses Nikita's cheek and heads down the hall to take a quick shower before bed. Carolyn turns away from Nikita and digs out PJs for herself, giving her a chance to change. By the time Carolyn's in her sleep shirt and has turned back around, Nikita is sitting cross-legged on Heather's bed, fidgeting with the edge of the blankets pulled half into her lap.

Carolyn starts to climb into her own bed, but a small noise from Nikita attracts her attention. She glances over; Nikita is watching her.

"Are you still doing that independent study with Heather?" Nikita asks.

"Not really." Carolyn isn't sure how to explain that she didn't want to distract Heather from Nikita. "She's seemed busy," she says, deciding it's the simplest explanation, and Nikita nods like it makes sense.

"I threw a wrench in everything, didn't I? With my storms and weird dreams and invading your room like this," Nikita says. She gestures at the room, and there are things that belong to her everywhere: her clothes lying on top of Heather's dresser, her backpack nestled against Heather's by the wall. Heather's hamper is filled with a mix of their clothes, and Nikita spends laundry day at the house rather than in her dorm, wandering around in sweats and an oversized shirt as they wash their things together.

Heather says it's cost-effective.

It's not a problem, so Carolyn doesn't really care.

Her issue isn't with the laundry.

It is, just a little, about the way that Nikita has invaded every aspect of their lives.

Nikita's smile fades, and her hand drops. "And Heather's doing her own independent study."

Carolyn has been silent too long. "I'm not angry at you," she says. "If Heather's happy, then I'm happy for her. I'm adjusting. Everyone has this happen, right? Friendships change. Relationships change. And it's okay about the project, too. I didn't have a solid idea in mind when I pitched to Heather that we could work together. I've gotten a better idea since, and I'm mostly working on my own right now. I'll probably need help from my old high-school friend Del."

Nikita wrinkles her nose. "The Dreamwalker."

"She's not," Carolyn says. "Not exactly."

"Close enough," Nikita mutters. "If you need her to come here, let me know when and I'll go home for the weekend. We probably shouldn't be in the same place; I don't want to blanket the Northeast in a blizzard or something."

"I'll be going to see her," Carolyn says. "I mean, we need to be somewhere else to do the project. But you might be interested in the research I'm doing." She pulls her bag onto her desk, withdraws the purple notebook, and flips to the pages where she worked with Pawel. "I'm trying to figure out how you can be a Dreamwalker and how she can go into the Dreamscape. There're also people like Mac and I, who travel to places— how do we get to where we go?"

She touches the parts of the chart that she hasn't filled in. "I've got a long way to go. I think, sometimes, the explanations we have about how Talent works aren't scientific or comprehensive. They're social. They're psychological. We take Talent almost on faith because humanity has spent lifetimes upon lifetimes trying to explain things that didn't seem to be explainable. So we put things in neat, separate boxes, even if they don't actually fit in those boxes. Like a Weather Witch who Dreamwalks."

Nikita works the tip of one finger into the corner of her mouth, chewing on her nail. She makes a small noise, and Carolyn isn't sure if she's agreeing or indicating "go on."

"Dreamwalkers can bring the Dreamscape out into the real world, right?" Carolyn's thinking out loud, looking at the column labeled "Control"—the list of information that everyone knows about Dreamwalkers or, at least, as much as Pawel's been able to gather. "When two get together, they can create a Dreamscape so vivid that everyone around them experiences it. Or Dreamwalkers can be lost in their own mind, absorbed by the Dreams."

"According to what Professor Szczek said, yes," Nikita says, still chewing on her fingernail.

"And you're already different," Carolyn says, tapping Nikita's column. "When you sleep, it's obvious you're stressed because you lose control over your Talent and affect the weather." She pauses, but Nikita doesn't protest, simply nods agreement. "You don't bring any of those Dreams out, unless the storms are what you're Dreaming about. And you don't remember your Dreams."

"Actually..." Nikita mumbles around her finger.

Carolyn lowers the book, but Nikita doesn't say anything else. Carolyn sets her book carefully on her desk, then moves to Heather's bed. "Nik—"

The door nudges open as Heather walks in. She stops as soon as the door is closed, her head tilted, then rushes forward, squeezing between Carolyn and the bed. "Nik," she says, and calm floods the room.

"You're leaking." Carolyn steps back and turns around, giving them space. "I don't need to be calmed right now. Focus on Nikita."

"It's worse when I worry," Heather says. She hitches herself onto her bed, one arm behind Nikita as Nikita leans closer to her. "Better?"

The sensation of being wrapped in Heather's calming empathy fades. "Yes," Carolyn says. She pulls out her desk chair and drops into it. "Are we in danger of an ice storm?"

Nikita shakes her head. "No. There's just something I was going to talk to Heather about, and it hasn't been a good time, and now you're here and—"

"Do you need me to leave?"

"No." Nikita bites the word out quick and sharp. Her tone softens. "No. You should get your notebook out, though. I have some new data points for you."

"Data points?" Heather's gaze shifts to Carolyn, brow furrowing as she opens her notebook.

"I'm trying to figure out the commonalities between Talents that aren't exactly alike but are too similar not to be related," Carolyn says.

"I've started remembering things," Nikita says.

Oh. Yes. That's definitely a new data point.

Carolyn flips to a new page, tugs the cap off her pen with her teeth, and writes "Nikita's Dreams" at the top. "So you know what's been stressing you out enough that we get storms?"

Nikita nods slowly. When Heather tugs, Nikita goes with her until they're sitting with their backs against the wall; Nikita tips until she's lying with her head on Heather's chest, her arm resting on Heather's stomach. Heather gently combs through Nikita's hair, and they seem to finally relax.

Carolyn feels on edge.

"It's not always bad there," Nikita says softly. "I say 'there,' like it's somewhere else. I know it's a Dream, but I'm always in the same place. It's like I'm watching a movie or reading a book, and when I come back, it's a little further along in the timeline."

"How long have you been remembering?" Heather murmurs.

Nikita hesitates. "Only a few days. Kind of."

Heather's fingers stop where they're tangled in Nikita's hair. "'Kind of'?"

"There've been hints," Nikita whispers. "Like, I'd be sitting in class, and I'd remember something, but it had nothing to do with me. It was like I was remembering someone else's memories. But that's Dream-me. Which is weird, because Dream-me is a guy. But he's Nik, too."

"How in-depth are these Dreams?" Carolyn asks, busily taking notes.

"It's a completely different world. Dark. Terrifying. We're always on the run. Something's chasing us, but I'm not sure what. Like I think the darkness is going to eat us alive."

Carolyn hesitates writing mid-word. "Nikita. Shadows. The darkness probably is trying to eat you alive, or at least suck out your soul."

Nikita shudders. "Lovely image. Thanks."

"You said 'we,'" Heather says gently, and Nikita nods.

"There's two of us, me and Seth," she says. "It's like the world has ended, only I get the feeling that, for most people, the world's still out there. But we can't go there because we're Talented. Dream-me's only Talent is being a Dreamwalker; Seth's an Empath." Her gaze flicks toward Heather. "He's not you, although he reminds me of you. He's short. Brown hair. He has glasses that are always slipping down his nose because they've been broken so many times. His hair is wavy and a little long and ragged. I don't think he gets to cut it very often. And Dream-me is scared all the time. Seth and I are scared together. Seth is my anchor in the Dream, and I need him as much as I need you."

Carolyn carefully writes down "Empaths anchor Dreamwalkers," because that seems significant. She doesn't know if Nikita's Dream is based on her relationship with Heather or if it's something else, but it's obvious that the parallels are important to her.

"It's not only Shadows hunting us," Nikita adds. "It's people, too. There are these places—hiding places set up by other Talent. There are places where Talents gather, but they have to hide from everyone else, and I think we're trying to get to one of those places. To be safe again. Because people with Talent who get caught disappear. I don't know where they go. Dream-me doesn't know, no one knows, and Dream-me is terrified. And Seth—he's terrified that Dream-me will go insane. Because that's what Dreamwalkers do."

"What do you think it means?" Heather asks. She presses a kiss to the top of Nikita's head, and Nikita makes a small, pleased noise.

Carolyn feels like she shouldn't be watching, like she's intruding on their moment.

"I don't know," Nikita whispers, "but it feels real. I see why Dreamwalkers get lost in their Dreams. It feels like I'm really there. Like I'm him. And when I get scared—"

"—we get storms." Carolyn underlines the word "real" three times before she sets her pen down. "Nikita, I've been talking to Sam—my friend who's stuck. He's unresponsive generally, unable to hold a conversation. But he may be in the Dreamscape. He told me about this forest, and paths, and that he can find all these realities but can't find his way back home. What if Dreamwalkers—when they do Dream—are actually seeing these other realities? If that's the case, then what you're seeing doesn't just feel real. It is real."

"Oh." Nikita pushes against Heather and sits up. Her mouth is slightly open. "You weren't kidding when you said you were relating Dreamwalking to teleporters."

Carolyn shakes her head. "Not joking at all. I think several abilities we thought were completely separate may be really mixed up. And when we start combining Talents, things get unpredictable. Like with you."

"Like with me."

Carolyn carefully closes the notebook and slips it back into her bag. She'll have to do more research, send more information to Pawel. "I need to sleep on this," she says, leaving the bag behind so she can climb into bed. It occurs to her that the light's still on, and she wishes telekinesis was her Talent.

Heather's bed is closer to the door; Carolyn ignores the brightness and slides under the covers.

"Hey, Caro." Heather's voice is soft. Carolyn peeks out; Heather is moving to get the light.

"What?" Carolyn keeps her voice just as low.

"How's Kit? He and Rory left really abruptly earlier. Are things awkward with Serina?"

"Neither of them is big on crowds," Carolyn reminds her. "They went for a walk around campus; Kit texted me when he got back here. He's got a surprise planned for Rory tomorrow."

"So they're good?" Heather asks. Carolyn can barely see the movement across the room as Heather and Nikita slip beneath the covers, curling close together. "I was worried about him." Heather's voice is muffled.

"I think Kit is comfortable with Rory," Carolyn muses. "He and Serina are friends again, and she and I are friends now too. It's not as awkward as it could be."

"You were holding hands," Nikita mumbles, and Carolyn can't deny that. But she doesn't want to talk about it right now.

So she makes a low noise and rolls over to face the wall, dragging the blanket over her head.

"If you Dream, wake me up," Heather whispers. "I'll be here for you."

"I know."

Carolyn can't see the kiss, but she can hear it. She closes her eyes tightly and tries to summon sleep. She hopes Nikita sleeps peacefully, not just for her sake, but for the sake of the entire Northeast. Winter's been bad enough already.

31

SUNDAY IS PEACEFUL, and Carolyn's thankful for a little quiet. Mac leaves the house early in the morning for a taekwondo tournament. Carolyn doesn't remember where they're heading today, she just knows that a layer of tension seems to lift from the house once she's gone. No one has to worry about Cass and Mac butting heads again. They haven't been arguing constantly, but things haven't been normal between them either. It's like living in a cold war; everyone's waiting for another explosion. And while Mac has assured Carolyn that none are coming, Carolyn doesn't read the situation that way.

She could be wrong.

She hopes she's wrong.

With Mac gone, Cass spends the day in the living room, her feet tucked under herself as she reads through a book for class. Carolyn brings her own work down to join her, and the morning passes in a haze of studying her notes and trying to collate her data in a way that gives her more points to research.

It's tempting to travel over to the special collections room and come back with a book so she can work in the comfort of the house, but Carolyn doesn't want to be that person who uses her Talent to get around the rules. Getting into the building early is bad enough, but removing books would just be wrong. Instead, she and Cass walk over to the library after lunch so that Carolyn can work there while Cass keeps her company. Carolyn has no idea what project Cass is working on, but it doesn't matter as they both work silently.

When they head back to the house, Cass nearly walks into Soledad as she comes out, Trish close behind.

"We're heading over to Teas Please to get something to eat," Trish calls out. "Since we don't have a formal dinner this weekend, we figured we'd do something fun."

Serina's on-shift. Carolyn knows because Serina pauses to text periodically, sending funny stories about the things people order or the strange anecdotes she overhears in the restaurant. But Trish and Soledad…Carolyn isn't sure she wants to barge in on any Big/Little bonding time. She glances at Soledad, uncertain.

"Come on! It'll be fun," Soledad encourages. "We'll make notes for ideas on what we can cook next time it's our turn."

"None of us are good cooks," Carolyn points out. "That's why we eat a lot of pasta for house dinners."

"It's always Teas Please, isn't it?" Cass says dryly. "But it sounds better than ordering pizza. I'm in."

Trish glances at Cass, then at Carolyn, and shrugs. "Let's go."

There's a light snow falling as they walk over, and Soledad holds out her hands, catching the flakes on her mittens. "I know you all hate it, but I still love snow. I wish it snowed more."

"Nikita's accidents aside, it's been a mild winter," Carolyn agrees. When they've had anything more than flurries, the storms have been bad, but she's fairly certain that every one of those was caused by Nikita.

"And they say global warming's a lie," Cass mutters. She pulls her phone from her pocket, swipes to look at something, then shoves it away again.

"You okay?"

Cass smiles sweetly. "I'm fine. Trish, Soledad, did you have a good weekend? I've been buried in reading for my women's lit course. It's a good class—we've been learning about female-identifying authors writing during the last hundred years, and comparing and contrasting tropes and ideology."

"I was looking at that class, but it's so popular I heard you have to be a junior or a senior to get a seat." Soledad's brow furrows. "How did you get in as a sophomore?"

"I explained that I wanted to take it early for my psychology major," Cass says. Her voice is lighter now, warming to the topic rather than simply being polite. "The way the class looks at how women write—and how their work is received—means it's about more than just literature. It's a sociological and psychological examination of how we perceive and present our views differently." She glances over and gestures at Carolyn. "You'd probably love it."

Carolyn probably would, but she also can't think when she'd fit it in her schedule with only one year to go.

"I'd hate it," Trish says mildly. She pulls open the door as they arrive at Teas Please. "I love looking at how people think, but I hate dissecting things people have written. I mean, I write music—I know that writers put meaning into their words. But I don't think we can know what someone else meant unless we ask them. It's like how sometimes I write a song, and I know what I mean it to be about, and when it gets popular, everyone thinks I meant something else entirely. Readers and listeners find what they want in words, not necessarily what was put there."

"That's one of the things we talk about, as well as how perceptions of literature differ depending on who's reading and when," Cass says. "That's why it's so interesting. If I read a book now, with modern eyes, I'll get something completely different out of the story than someone who read it fifty years ago."

Carolyn tunes them out as their conversation goes on. There's a short wait at the hostess station, but Carolyn doesn't mind. She scans the restaurant, spotting Nate in his usual section toward the back. He waves and ducks into the kitchen, and a few minutes later, Serina emerges and waves cheerfully.

She is carrying a tray of drinks, and she pauses at two tables to drop them off and reassure her customers that she'll be back momentarily for their orders. Then she approaches Carolyn, smiling happily. "Did you come to break up the monotony of my shift?" Serina asks. "I get a break soon. I could come visit you, if you don't mind."

"I don't mind," Carolyn agrees. She'd ask the others if it was all right with them, but the conversation has shifted to discussing some book that she's never read, and she doesn't want to interrupt.

Serina looks away, then reaches for menus. "Come with me. Nate's pointing to a booth in his section, so I'll put you there."

Carolyn taps Trish on the shoulder, and the other three girls trail after, still discussing. When they arrive at the booth, Carolyn waits to let Trish and Cass slide into each side so she can get an end seat.

Serina drops the menus on the table. "Nate'll be over to get your order soon, and I'll be back with water in just a minute when I take my break. Do you want to give me your tea orders?" They give them, and Serina writes down their choices quickly, grinning as she taps the pad with her pencil. "Perfect, I'll be back!"

"Writing songs," Trish says. She's apparently returning to an earlier conversation, but Carolyn isn't sure what she's responding to. "Or, well, one song, and some music. I was with Thorne today because he wanted an opinion from someone other than Rory for some reason. Plus, we decided a while back that we should do some collabs, so we were working on those, too. We want to blind-drop an EP of the two of us singing about completely random stuff—totally innocuous things, like ice cream or flowers—and see what people think of the lyrics. It goes back to that whole question of interpretation versus intention. We've got reputations. It'll be interesting to see how that affects what people hear in our music."

"Aren't you afraid everyone will think you're sleeping with him?" Soledad asks, and Trish brushes off the question with a wave of her hand.

"Everyone here already does. I'm pan and poly. He's pan and poly. People figure that means we've had sex. Which, no." Trish wrinkles her nose and leans on her elbows on the table. "He's not what I'm looking for. I don't know what I'm looking for lately."

Carolyn meets her gaze, and Trish looks down. Carolyn's fairly certain that's a lie, but she figures that Trish isn't ready to talk about Sera to anyone else. It's strange being the only person who, to the best of Carolyn's knowledge, knows about something. This is not normal for Carolyn.

Serina returns, Nate right behind her. She sets down four pots of tea, nudging the correct one in front of each person, and keeps a fifth for herself. Nate pushes mugs and silverware across the table.

"Is it okay…?" Serina gestures to the bench next to Carolyn, and Carolyn squeezes closer to Cass to give Serina room. "Thanks," Serina says, cradling her mug in her hands.

Carolyn smells chocolate, and there's a thin sheen of cream on the top, as if Serina's already licked away a mound of whipped cream. Carolyn was hungry when they started walking over, and her stomach growls at the scent. When Serina grins, Carolyn flushes.

"It smells good," she admits.

"Taste," Serina orders, holding the mug up to Carolyn's lips. "It's not searingly hot; I like my cocoa a little cooled."

It's as rich as it smells, the consistency thicker than Carolyn's used to. "There's melted chocolate—"

"—blended in, yes." Serina presses her knee against Carolyn's, looks over at the others. "I didn't mean to interrupt. I mean, I'm just sitting here while I'm on break. I get like fifteen minutes, and I spent a few making cocoa. I still need to eat a snack, too, unless Nate's nice enough to bring me something." She cranes her head, tilting back as she looks for him. "Nope, he's busy. So don't worry, I'll be gone soon. Thanks for coming to visit me."

Cass snorts.

"Any time one of us decides to head to Teas Please, it turns into a party," Trish says. She pours her tea and offers the cup to Soledad to taste, and Soledad offers her own in return. They seem to be getting along better, and Carolyn wonders if that's because Sera has been spending time with TJ instead of Trish.

"I got a care package from my parents," Soledad says, leaning on the table, her voice low. "It's four bottles of homemade wine. I was thinking I could bring it over to the house, and we could have a wine tasting one night with the sisters. My aunt and uncle are really proud of these four batches, and I'd love to be able to share."

"I take it your parents aren't worried about underage drinking?" Cass asks, fingernails tapping against the wooden tabletop.

"Are you going to tell?" Trish counters, and Cass pulls back, affronted.

"No. That was conversational. Most parents don't give their kids alcohol."

"My aunt and uncle own a vineyard, and we grew up tasting wine since we were little," Soledad explains. "My father wanted to work with them for a long time, but he has a talent—not a Talent, we don't think, but who knows—for working with computers. And he doesn't have any kind of a nose for wine, so my uncle encouraged him to follow his passion. We help there when we can, so we have their wines at home all the time. I've been missing it, and I asked at Christmas if I could have some so…care package."

"Never did understand why more parents don't teach their kids how to handle alcohol," Trish says, her accent thickening. "My friends never had a drop unless they stole a six pack from their folks, and they all thought it was this big deal to get hammered and drive around like fools. Momma said she didn't raise her kids to drink or do drugs, but that hasn't helped—" She cuts off abruptly.

"What?" Serina asks, her smile falling away when Trish looks at her.

"My older sister Patsy's an alcoholic, and Momma doesn't know," Trish says quietly. "She's on the wagon now, but she says sometimes it's hard, especially after she's been home. Momma's got a strict 'no alcohol' policy at home, though. Just like her strict 'no magic' policy." Trish turns her hand palm up, as if they'll be able to see her Talent plays across her skin.

Soledad's brow furrows. "Trish, can I ask a weird question?"

"Sure. Might not have an answer," Trish admits.

"Are you and your sister both named Patricia?"

It's funny, because Carolyn's never thought of that even though she's been friends with Trish since freshman year. Cass laughs into her drink, and Serina's eyes go wide.

"Whoa, really?" Serina asks. "I thought that was, like, this total fictional stereotype, having a family with the kids all named the same."

"It's just me and Patsy sharing the name," Trish says easily. "Patsy was already a teenager when I was born, and there's six other kids between me and her. She was all rebellious, so Momma asked what she had to do to get Patsy to help out around the house instead of leaving. Patsy said to name the baby after her, so that's what Momma did. Then Patsy left anyway, went out on tour without even graduating high school."

"You don't sound upset by that." Soledad sounds bewildered. "Why aren't you angry?"

"Because sometimes family leaves," Cass mumbles. She pulls her phone out, looks at it, then turns it upside down on the table.

"She came back," Trish says firmly. She reaches for Soledad's teapot and pours herself a cup. "She was there more than not once I got to be a teenager, then when I started high school, she stuck around and made sure I graduated instead of being stupid like her—her words, not mine. I was already writing songs, and I'd sent her some, and she helped me start recording. But she said I had to get my high school diploma first, and when she found out I liked engines and that I was good at working with them, she said I should go to school for that, too. She pays my tuition, even though I could afford it, and like I said, we're close. She didn't abandon me. She just needed to grow up a bit away from Momma. I think maybe she had the right idea with that one." She smiles ruefully. "I love my momma, but sometimes I don't like her all that much."

Nate comes by the table, setting down two baskets of crispy breadsticks and two ramekins of dipping sauces. "Serina, you're needed in the back. Your section is filling up and people are going to want service, and I can't do it all."

"Gotcha." Serina downs the rest of her hot cocoa, then glances at everyone. "Anyone need a refill?" Cass raises her hand. "I'll put that in and bring out more tea shortly."

"I'll bring out their tea and you'll go back to your section," Nate repeats. "Go earn your own tips." He stands tall until she hurries away, but as soon as she's gone, his shoulders slump. "She was excited to see you come in, but we're too busy tonight for much socializing. Even for me." He takes their orders and pockets his pencil and pad. "Carolyn, have you got a minute?" His voice is strangely formal.

Carolyn rises, following when he motions for her to head toward the narrow hall leading to the back where the restrooms are. "I'm not good at advice," she says when they are out of sight. "No matter what anyone else might say. I'm really not."

"I'm not looking to get advice," Nate says. "I'm looking to give it. Anyone with eyes can see that Serina's fallen hard, and I don't want her get hurt again."

Carolyn blinks. "What?"

"First she had that crush on me, and I had to let her down easy because as much as I adore her, she's not my type." Nate ticks points off on his long fingers as he speaks. "Then there was Kit, and she was over the moon, and then suddenly they were done. And she didn't seem all that upset, and I wasn't sure why, but then I saw you."

"Me?" Carolyn's still not following.

"If you're not interested, you need to let her know," Nate says.

Oh.

"I don't know if I'm interested," Carolyn admits. "I mean, I think I am. But there's—" She doesn't want to get into the details with Nate, doesn't feel like he belongs that deeply in her psychology. "I don't want to hurt her, either. I like Serina. A lot. And I'm comfortable with her; when I needed someone to flee to, she's who my subconscious chose." She shrugs, wrapping her arms around her center before any other words slip free. "Take that as you will."

Nate regards her for a long moment, then opens his arms and gestures for her to come closer. She does, and he wraps her in a hug, holding on tight as he pats her back. "Don't let her hurt you, either, Carolyn," he murmurs. "Remember that you're as important as she is."

Carolyn disengages slowly. "Weren't you just giving me the shovel talk on her behalf?"

"You're both my friends; I can give you both the shovel talk," Nate says seriously. He keeps his hands on her shoulders, watching her. Carolyn isn't sure what he's looking for, but he eventually drops his hands and steps back. "I need to get back to my shift."

"Have you had any luck with your risks?" Carolyn asks. She follows him out until he stops at the end of the hall, and she does the same.

At the table, Heather and Nikita have arrived and are standing nearby. Cass slides out of the booth, pushing past them roughly as she leaves the dining room. Nate turns slightly, brow furrowed as he watches her go.

"Nate?" Carolyn prompts him again.

"Hm?" He glances at her. "Risks? Oh, you mean fighting off the dicks in pursuit of valor. No, sorry, he remains gorgeous, straight, and absolutely unattainable. And to be honest, if I could stop thinking about him, I would, but there's nothing sensible about crushes. I have a thing for a human stats machine. He isn't even my usual type. But don't worry, I'll get over him soon enough. Summer's a great time for flirting with tourists trying to get away from the city."

"It's February," Carolyn points out.

Nate pats her cheek. "Don't lose hope; spring is coming. Let me get your food orders in before you all starve waiting for me."

They part ways, and by the time Carolyn makes it back to the table, Heather and Nikita have taken over the other side of the bench where Cass had been. Rather than squeeze in, Carolyn grabs an empty chair from another table and makes her own spot at the end. "What happened to Cass? She was all over her phone tonight."

"She got a text and stormed out," Soledad says, looking at the door as if she can still see Cass. "She was really upset."

"Dax?"

Trish shakes her head. "Not Dax; we asked if he was okay and she said she had no idea. Whatever the text was, she didn't want to talk about it, froze us out like Cass does."

But it's not like Cass does, not anymore. Carolyn's begun to think of Cass as someone closer to her, sometime who trusts her, someone whom she can trust in return. She pulls out her phone as Nikita and Heather pore over the menu and flag down Nate to add their orders and cancel Cass's.

You okay? She sends the text to Cass, not expecting an answer.

They have their food by the time Cass replies. *I'm as okay as I'm going to be. It's nothing major. Just family drama again.*

For a moment, Carolyn wants to ask if it's about her sister, but she doubts that would be it. Not now, not after all these years. So instead she says, *If you want to talk about it, I'm here.*

She figures that Cass will understand how rare an offer that is coming from Carolyn. And how truly she means it.

32

"CAROLYN."

Drea catches her as she's about to open the door to SigPsiEp, and Carolyn turns, her hand still on the knob. Drea stands on the sidewalk next to a small sedan; Alia Herne stands next to her, wearing a long woven wool coat, her mitten-wrapped hands clasped before her.

Carolyn swallows. Alia Herne at PHU can't be a good thing. "Hey, Drea. Mrs. Herne. Is everything okay at home?"

"Call me Alia," she says, tone gentle. "And yes, all is as it has been, which is not necessarily well, but I can assure you that things have not grown worse. I worry for my husband's health."

"His mental health," Drea corrects. She touches her mother's shoulder, then gestures at the door. "Why don't we go inside? Caro, can we talk in your room?"

"You're here to see me?" Carolyn can't imagine why Alia would spare a thought for her. She figured Drea's family would want to forget that anything outside their settlement existed. "I haven't been back, I promise. I'm getting better control of my traveling, and I don't want to go back to that house."

"It isn't about that, not entirely," Alia murmurs. "Drea is right, however— it would be best if we took our business indoors, where it is warm and somewhat private." She looks at the house; her head cocks, then she twists the doorknob, tugs it open, and motions them inside.

Carolyn slips her phone into her hand as they pass, typing as she shrugs out of her jacket. She hands her jacket to Drea to hang up while she finishes sending her message.

Drea brought her mother to see me. We're coming upstairs. If there's any chance you and Nik could not be in the room for a bit, it would be good. I have no idea what they want from me.

Drea waits patiently for Carolyn to start up the stairs before she motions for Alia to proceed. "Is Heather around?" she asks, and as Carolyn's phone pings with Heather's response, she shares it with Drea.

Nik and I went to Minnisale's so we won't be home for a while. Planning on studying at the library later so we don't get distracted.

"'Distracted,'" Drea says with a soft, huffed laugh. "Wow, they have really—"

"Yeah, they're close," Carolyn says, not wanting to discuss the details. It's so different from how things are between Carolyn and Serina. If there is a "Carolyn and Serina"; she still isn't sure. It's apparently obvious enough that other people are noticing, but Carolyn doesn't know how to bring it up. Or if she should bring it up. Maybe she should just go with the flow and enjoy whatever it is they're doing while it lasts. She's certain that, eventually, she'll either do something wrong or Serina will realize that Carolyn's a bad relationship prospect. She hasn't had a lot of luck with significant others, after all. And that's without even addressing the question of Carolyn's sexuality.

The room is a mess when Carolyn walks in, Heather's things mixed with Nikita's and spread across the floor. Carolyn picks up what she can and tosses it on Heather's bed, then pulls out both desk chairs to offer. Drea grabs one and sits on it backward, but Alia shakes her head.

"I'd rather stand," she says.

And then silence.

Carolyn glances at Drea, then back to Alia. "I don't know what to say," Carolyn admits. "I don't know what you want."

"Dad isn't getting worse, but he isn't getting better," Drea says. "He's obsessed with the Shadow. He doesn't believe she's gone for good, and he can't believe that she's a Clan girl who Emerged and went on to kill Orson. He's positive that Mages are behind Orson's death, and that there has to be a reason it happened. And he's riling up the other elders in our community. Mom's the only thing keeping them sane."

"They are wary of Alaric and the potential for how his views will change our Clan leadership," Alia says. "And Alaric is creating his own alliances among the younger members of the Northeast Clan families. He is doing well." Pride is evident in her voice, in the smile that graces her lips. "But he is not the leader of our settlement yet. There are those who will agree with him, but they will be unable to find their voices in the face of the beliefs of Theobald and those who support him."

"It's a mess," Drea grumbles.

Carolyn and Drea talk often enough that Carolyn has heard some of this, but she doesn't understand— "What does this have to do with me?"

Alia's lips press thin, pursed as if she's swallowed a lemon. "In the absence of answers, Drea suggested that you might be able to offer choices. Potential directions."

Carolyn glances at Drea, then back to Alia. "You'd want me to do a reading for you?" she asks. She reaches for her bag, feeling blindly for her deck and notebook. "I can read the cards, but you have to be willing to see the opportunities they present. It won't work if you're resistant. The reading won't lock you into some kind of future, and it won't tell you what to do."

Alia nods tightly. "Drea said that you will give me things to think about. Perhaps you will offer a new way of looking at a situation, an approach we can't see because we are mired in tradition."

"It's worked for Alaric," Drea says. "Having Rory for a roommate and a best friend, he's been able to change his perspective. And I've got Carolyn." Her voice is firm. Decisive. "Clan isn't an island, and we can't pretend to be anymore. And I may not always like Dad, but I love him." Her voice wavers. "So, help would be good."

"And I will do my best to accept that help," Alia agrees. She doesn't sound enthusiastic, but Carolyn's used to Alaric's reserve around magic, so Alia's behavior doesn't surprise her.

"Okay," she agrees, taking the cards out and shuffling them, thinking through her options. "Divergent path. We'll do a reading in which I place two sets of three cards each. The two sets offer you two different, potential directions. You have to remember: these two options aren't your only possible choices, and they're not locked in. Just because one path has the potential to end well or to end in disaster, that doesn't guarantee that it will."

"I accept your terms," Alia says.

Carolyn wants to correct her—these aren't the terms of an agreement. But perhaps, to Alia, they are. So Carolyn stays silent and holds the deck out to Alia, who stares back at it as if Carolyn has offered her a venomous snake.

"You have to shuffle them," Drea says.

Alia shakes her head, then holds up her hand, palm out, toward the cards. "No. Thank you."

Fine. Carolyn can work with this. She starts shuffling again, moving slowly enough to invite interruption. "Tell me when to stop."

She shuffles overhand, and she has half the deck in each hand when Alia touches her fingers.

"Stop," Alia says.

Carolyn nods and places the cards from the hand Alia touched on the top of the deck. She moves closer to her desk, gesturing for Alia and Drea to get close as well. Alia remains standing, but Drea wheels the chair closer.

"Neither left nor right is inherently better than the other," Carolyn says as she lays the cards out. "Which is better lies in the interpretation, not the order. The three cards in each path represent the situation, the decision point, and the potential outcome." She smiles slightly. "And yes, that may mean that each path defines the situation differently."

Drea leans in to look at the cards without touching them. Alia holds herself perfectly upright, her arms crossed as if she might touch something by accident. Carolyn grabs the other chair and sinks into it, opening her notebook to jot down notes as she interprets the layout.

"One path is toward growth, the other toward potential ruin." Carolyn begins slowly, gesturing at the first reading. "In this path, we have the situation as a positive female role model—a woman who leads by standing side by side with her subjects. She's loyal and strong and willing to listen, looking to find a solution that will combine what is needed with what is wanted. She faces a dark time; her people are worried, tormented by what hangs above them. But she can bring everyone together and create a large force to push the darkness back. By doing this, she can achieve stability for her community, if only on a literal, physical level, but she must never forget that the darkness remains. Stability is a work in progress, and everyone must continue to work together lest their protections fail."

Carolyn doesn't look up, not wanting to see Alia's expression. She can hear Drea's sharp inhalation, but Alia is so silent that Carolyn thinks she holds her breath, waiting for Carolyn to be done.

"The other path is focused on masculine power, in the form of someone who rules with such an iron will that he has become domineering. He expects his decisions to be followed and allows little room for deviation. He is balanced at the junction of several paths, but he fails to decide among them. As a result, he could fall at any time, and his people will fall with him. Science and logic surround him, but he is unwilling to listen. His inaction threatens his security and freedom, and could destroy it altogether."

Carolyn bites her lip as she stops speaking. She reaches to gather the cards up, but Alia stops her with a touch.

"Please. I would like to look," Alia says.

Carolyn rolls the chair out of the way, letting Alia step close; Carolyn resists the urge to pull the cards away when Alia sniffs them. Drea's hand slips into hers, squeezing gently, and Carolyn lets it go, lets Alia explore the reading in whatever way makes her comfortable.

Alia straightens and turns, her arms crossed again as if they can gird her against the magic in the room. "I see," she says. "I believe I have heard what I needed to hear, and"—her expression gentles, her shoulders slumping— "it is no different from what I already knew in my heart."

"Mom."

Alia touches Drea's cheek, draws her close, and leans in to press their skin together, trading scents. "You and your brother are safe," she murmurs. "You will have your promised years. I will ensure that there is a community to return to when you are done. Now come. We should find your brother, and you two can show me where you prefer to eat here. I should have visited Orson more often. I will remedy that with you."

They leave, and Carolyn slumps in her chair. She needs to write this reading down; her cards may have had an extremely significant impact on the lives of an entire community, and very specifically on Theobald and Alia Herne and their place in that community.

She doesn't know how to process that.

"I think I just told Drea's mother to start a revolution," she murmurs to the empty room. She pulls her notebook close and starts to write, not only about the cards and what they said, but about her fears for the future that they implied.

Theobald Herne isn't going to like where this goes. Not at all.

33

It's strange how half her life seems to be filled with drama and decisions that impact people other than herself, and then there's Serina. Carolyn used to think of Heather as the quiet part of her life, but since Nikita stormed in, that no longer holds true. But Serina's a safe haven and, in the midst of unexpected ice storms, potential Clan rebellions, and the confusion of what Talent actually is, Carolyn keeps gravitating toward her.

With Serina, Carolyn can rest.

Serina attends Coven on Tuesday and whisks Carolyn away as soon as the meeting's done, taking her to Sweet Scoops for vanilla-drowned gummy bears.

On Wednesday, she's waiting outside of Carolyn's last class with take-out from Minnisale's, and they head over to the Madison Center, grab a table, and eat and study there. Carolyn loses herself in a debate essay for her psychology class, and by the time she has a solid first draft, her chicken parm is gone and she doesn't remember eating it.

Serina sits on the other side of the table, an organic chemistry book open in front of her and a pinched expression on her face as she stares down at it. Her hand hovers over a lab book, the tip of her pen not quite touching the paper.

"I forgot you were taking organic chemistry," Carolyn says.

Serina jerks back, lifting her pen quickly before it can mark the page. She exhales roughly, then closes both lab book and text. "Yeah. I skipped the intro chem classes and jumped straight into orgo. It seemed like a good idea at the time, but I regret it now."

"Kit did the same thing." Carolyn remembers how rough the first few weeks of freshman year had been, but how happy he was to be doing something new in chemistry. "He ended up getting through it okay."

"I know; he told me," Serina says. She carefully stacks her books, and because she seems to be cleaning up, Carolyn does the same. "It's actually how we met. I was having a rough start, and the professor suggested I talk to Kit. We went our separate ways after that, but I thought he was cute. And later, well…" She shrugs. "He's apparently known as some kind of orgo wunderkind." Serina closes the takeout containers and collects everything to toss into the nearest bin. "Everyone in the chem department knows him. The professor loves him."

Carolyn huffs. "He always says that he wishes people could see the rest of his personality instead of just thinking of him as 'the guy who's good at orgo.'"

"He loves it, that's obvious," Serina says. She doesn't bother putting her textbook in her bag, hugging it to her chest once she gets everything else put away. "He'll be a great doctor someday. He has a good way of looking at things."

She's right. Carolyn knows she's right, but it's awkward to hear Serina talk about Kit like this. It shouldn't be; Carolyn knows they dated. But she's become closer to Serina since then.

Maybe she's let herself get too close.

"You're fangirling," she murmurs, picking up her own bag and shouldering it, armor against her own confused thoughts.

Serina slides close to her, then bumps into her shoulder; Carolyn takes the nudge and starts walking, heading for the stairs. It takes a moment before Serina runs to catch up with her.

"I have short legs," Serina calls. "Don't walk so fast."

Carolyn slows when she reaches the bottom of the staircase, holding open the door to the outside so Serina can slip through. There's a light snow falling, the flakes coming just often enough to leave a spatter of dots on Serina's dark hair before they melt. They shine in the streetlights.

"I don't like him better than I like you," Serina says as they walk along the street.

Carolyn forces herself not to speed up and tries to avoid tripping as if the words are physical things under her feet. One foot in front of the other, navigating over and around the cracks in the sidewalk. It isn't slippery, not yet, but she thinks it won't be long before it is.

"Carolyn," Serina says, "are you mad at me?"

"No." Carolyn's a little angry at herself, though.

"Caro."

Carolyn stops, turns, and waits for Serina to catch up. Standing under the light, Carolyn watches the snowflakes drift down, alighting atop Serina's head. "You should wear a hat," Carolyn says.

Serina laughs. "A hat. That's what we're talking about? Carolyn..." Her voice drops low. "I didn't mean to upset you by talking about Kit. I know it's probably weird because I dated him, and now I have this kind of absolutely raging crush on you, and I don't even know if you like—me, girls, I don't know any of it. And I haven't asked because I'm a little afraid of the answer."

Oh. Well. That's blunt. And no different from what Nate said, nor from what Carolyn had thought might be happening. Had maybe hoped was happening.

Carolyn's mouth is too dry to form words.

Serina's gaze drops. "Oh, okay. Well. I guess—"

"Are we dating?" Carolyn blurts out.

Serina's head snaps up, her mouth hanging open.

Carolyn swallows hard. "Should we be dating? Is it too fast? Am I a substitute because Kit—"

"It's nothing to do with Kit," Serina says firmly. "It isn't. I'm not dating you because I can't date Kit. I mean. If we're dating. If it's anything to do with Kit, it's that he was the wrong twin all along. I just didn't realize it. And I really do still like him as a friend."

Carolyn isn't sure what to say. Her throat feels tight, her chest twisting with nerves. She holds a hand out, and Serina curls her hand into it, palm to palm, fingers interlaced.

Carolyn settles a little.

"I told you I like girls," Serina says softly. A snowflake catches on her bangs, melts, and drips onto her eyebrow. Carolyn reaches up with her free hand and brushes some of the snow away. Serina smiles, then says, "You've never told me if you like girls."

"I like you," Carolyn says. She knows how that must sound. She wants to explain that she's not turning gay for Serina, and Serina looks like she's about to say something, and— "I'm not ready to talk about how messed up my dating history is. It's complicated, and I'm still untangling it, but I like you. So that's one girl I like, and I think that's what matters right now. But I can't promise that being with me will be easy. I have a lot of hang-ups."

"I'm getting wet." Serina tilts her head back and sticks her tongue out at the falling snow. "Is the snow getting worse? You should walk me home. There must be a ritual for keeping dry in the snow, isn't there?"

Carolyn feels like she should have whiplash from this conversation. "You could ask Thorne about that; he's all about fire, right? I don't know a lot about ritual. Serina…"

Serina lifts their joined hands. "See this? Remember how I told you that I told Kit that I wanted to be with someone whose kisses made me tingle? Well this—just holding hands—this makes me feel warm all over, so much so that the snow melts as soon as it hits me. It's better than kissing Kit."

Carolyn laughs; her cheeks warm as something blooms in her chest. "You're ridiculous."

"I like you," Serina says. "I like you a lot, Carolyn Merrill, and right now I am really hoping that you like me back even a little bit."

"I do. Like you back," Carolyn agrees. "Is that enough for now?"

"Yes." Serina tugs, and Carolyn moves closer. It's awkward to hug in the cold. Their bags get in the way, and Serina's still holding her orgo textbook in one hand, but Serina is warm and it's comfortable for Carolyn to lean down and wrap her arms around her.

"When you do want to talk about it," Serina murmurs against Carolyn's shoulder, "I'm willing to listen. But I'm not going to push. This is okay. I just need to know one really, really important thing."

The warmth fades as Carolyn pulls back, worried. "What?"

"Can I call you my girlfriend?" Serina asks. She squeezes Carolyn's hand and grins as she starts walking, heading for Townhouse Row and tugging Carolyn along in her wake. "Because I have been dying to tell the world about my incredible girlfriend, except I wasn't sure if she was or not.

Despite the cuddling, snuggling, and handholding. And dating. Even my roommate has noticed the dating, and honestly, Becky doesn't pay much attention to me. She's not even there half the time."

"I don't think I've even met Becky," Carolyn admits. "What does she look like?"

"A Becky," Serina says.

That makes Carolyn think of nondescript girls with bland-colored hair that hangs straight, and probably bland eyes that don't even register, and she doesn't know why. She supposes it's the name, which feels very white middle class and late twentieth century, much like her own. "I guess I look like a Carolyn," she realizes. White. Tall and somewhat thin. Long brown hair.

"I like the way you look." Serina sways closer to her, and Carolyn lets go of her hand, reaching out to carefully put her arm across Serina's shoulders instead. "I think I've lucked out, getting to know this particular Carolyn."

"I'm glad you didn't get to know a different one and crush on her instead."

As jokes go, it's mild and ridiculous, but it makes Serina laugh, and Carolyn honestly thinks she could fall in love with that sound. But "love" is a word she is in no way ready for. It lingers in the corners of her mind, waiting for her to trip and fall. She remembers thinking that she was in love when she was sixteen, that she thoroughly and completely understood everything that love meant.

And she very vividly remembers learning that she was wrong.

When they reach Townhouse Row, they walk down the side for Douglass, ignoring SigPsiEp. At the door, Serina lingers before taking out her card to swipe herself in. "Do you want to come up?" she finally asks. "Not to, like—not that. Becky might be there. But we could watch a movie or something. Be kind of date-like. Now that we both know it's a date, and the handholding isn't as awkward."

Carolyn knows how easy it is to go too fast, how easy it is to go from comfortable to expected to involved. She knows the bright rush and heady sensation of tumbling into things.

They've been going fast, in some ways. She knows that. But it doesn't feel like she's rushing headlong.

She feels safe.

She lowers her hand from Serina's shoulder and grips the handle of the door so she can open it as soon as Serina swipes her card to unlock the door. "That sounds good," she says. "Lead the way. I'll follow."

34

RISKS ARE TERRIFYING, and Carolyn doesn't like taking more than one in a week.

At this point, she's lost count for this week, and it's only Thursday.

On the one hand, she has a girlfriend. A sweet, adorable girlfriend.

On the other hand, she has to convince Del to help with her final project. And while there are more than two months left in the semester, Carolyn feels an urgency to help Sam now. She needs to make this call.

After more than two years of silence, it feels strange to dial Del's number. Carolyn sits on her bed with her back to the wall. Nikita and Heather are curled together on Heather's bed, sharing headphones as they watch a movie on Heather's laptop. They offered to leave, but Carolyn asked them to stay. She knows that having them there is a crutch, but she also knows she might need Heather to help her feel even and safe enough to have this conversation. That thought pricks at her skin; she's irritated by how much she's let herself lean on Heather without learning how to handle her own emotions.

But this conversation isn't going to be easy.

The phone rings at least six times before Carolyn fully realizes that there's been no answer. She takes the phone away from her ear, puts it on speaker, and lets it ring twice more.

It's not going to voicemail, so she presses the "End Call" button. She drops the phone on the bed, then leans her head back against the wall with a *thump*.

"No luck?" Heather asks, her voice a little too loud.

Carolyn shrugs. It's not like it's time critical.

Lie.

Sam's been stuck in the facility for a long time, but clearly something has changed. Something's pushing him to try to escape now, whereas he was fine before. He begged for her help.

Her phone rings, the loud sound muffled by her comforter. She presses the button to answer, then hits the speaker, waiting a heartbeat before calling out, "Hello."

Heather glances over; Nikita touches the keyboard to pause the movie.

"Hi, Carolyn." Del's voice is light, but Carolyn hears the rustling of papers in the background. She's fidgeting. Even after all this time, Carolyn can imagine the way she moves things around, picking up papers and neatening piles to have something to do with her hands.

"Are you alone?" It comes out sharper than Carolyn means it to, the words landing heavily enough that Del laughs.

"Why, is this some kind of weird—? No, I'm not even going there," Del says. "Yes, I'm alone. No Shawn, if that's what you really want to know."

Carolyn cradles the phone in her lap, breathing through the tension in her shoulders. "Yes, that's what I really wanted to know. I don't want to talk to him right now, just you."

"Does this call have to do with him?" Del asks.

Carolyn licks her lips. There are so many holes in this plan, so many things she hasn't figured out and can't get data about. But she gets the feeling that Del's asking about an entirely different conversation, and this isn't that. Not really. Even if Shawn might have to be involved in the ritual. "Not right now, and not that way. Eventually we need to talk about him. But no. I'm calling about Sam."

"Oh." The sound of a chair dragged across the floor, squeaking as Del settles into it. "Did he contact you again?"

"He did. And I went to see him." Carolyn bends her knees and props her phone on them so she can wrap her arms around her legs and hunch over. "We talked, though he was only with me about half the time. I'm guessing that's better than usual."

"You didn't hurt him like I did," Del says softly. "I loved him. You know that, right? I didn't want to hurt him, or any of you, on purpose."

"I don't think what happened was solely your fault." Carolyn can't say that none of it was Del's fault. The more research she does, the more she thinks that she and Sam and Del might be on the same axis of Talent as Dreamwalkers, and their ritual probably enhanced their separate Talents to the point that they were catapulted into the Dreamscape. "That's all past, Del. We need to figure out how to unmake the problem."

"You think you know how to do that?" Del's tone puts up walls against the idea. Disbelief.

"I have enough pieces of the puzzle to put together a ritual that should work," Carolyn says. "With Pawel's help. I've sent him a pitch, and I'm meeting with him tomorrow, along with Kit and Kit's boyfriend."

"Kit has a boyfriend?"

"Soulmate, actually." It would be easy to shift topics, to skate away from the difficult things while rediscovering friendship and bonding around the good in their lives. Carolyn can't let that happen. "You can talk to him when we get together." For all she knows, Rory may end up involved; she's not sure why Kit's bringing him to the meeting, but there must be a reason. "That's not the point of this."

Silence for a long moment. Then: "I know."

Carolyn picks at the fabric of her pajama pants, waiting to see if Del has anything else to say. As the silence stretches out again, Carolyn gives in and breaks it first. "He was telling me about the Dreamscape. About what he sees when he's there." Del makes a small noise, and Carolyn interprets it as *go on*. "He's in a forest," Carolyn says quietly. "He's lost, and there are paths everywhere. He thinks it's your forest, and he thinks you've stuck him there."

"I've never seen a forest," Del says.

"You have the meadow. He knows about that, too. We were all there together." Carolyn glances at Heather and Nikita, who are clearly focused on her conversation. "But now he's in a forest, and he thinks that when we went into the Dreamscape, our Talents leaked out of us and into Shawn. But he's self-destructed since then because he was never meant to hold all that. And now…Sam thinks we need to find the right path to walk to get free. All of us together."

"In the Dreamscape," Del says. "You want me to put us into a Dream, then we walk some kind of path that'll bring us back to 'start.' Like senior year never happened."

"I don't think that's possible."

"Good. Neither do I." Del's words fall harder than Carolyn's, sharp and vicious. "Nothing is going to reset this, Caro. We did what we did. There was fallout. There's no magical reset button."

"That's not what we're looking for." Carolyn hugs her legs hard, the press of her thighs against her chest comforting. "Del."

"What." It's not a question. It's defensive, thrown up like another wall between them.

"You're helping Kit," Carolyn says. "You're helping Kit with that project he's working on with Rory."

There's silence for a long moment, long enough that Carolyn wonders if she needs to break it. "Rory," Del finally says. "Wait, he was holding hands with— Is that the boyfriend?"

"Please don't get sidetracked."

"I may have missed some information along the way, but hey, I'm not designing the ritual, so I'm not the one trying to account for interpersonal relationships," Del says glibly. "On the other hand, maybe that's where we went wrong in ours."

Oh.

She doesn't mean…

"Del," Carolyn says. "None of what happened was because Shawn—"

"You and Shawn fought," Del responds. "You fought just before everything happened, and when things went sideways, he was locked out of the Dreamscape and the three of us were locked in."

"That could affect a ritual," Heather murmurs, and Carolyn's heart skips. She'd almost forgotten they were still sitting there, listening to every word.

Carolyn licks her lips and picks at the fabric of her comforter. "Fine. When things went haywire, I was at least a little bit at fault," she mumbles. "We were all a mess. Don't forget Kit was outside the Dreamscape as well."

"And he didn't end up with less or more power after," Del says. "He wasn't affected. It's like everything skipped over him."

Carolyn chews on her lower lip. "Okay. Yes. Point taken."

"Okay," Del agrees.

Silence again. Carolyn's lost track of the conversation; Del has railroaded them so far off track that Carolyn isn't sure there's an easy way back.

So she'll have to take the hard way and be blunt.

"I need your help," she says. "Sam's getting worse. And it might actually be that he's getting better: he's reaching out, which means he's more in this world. But his behavior is making him a more difficult patient." Carolyn pauses for a breath. "I'm going to push for that ritual design to be finished when we meet with Pawel tomorrow. I want to go see Sam this weekend. And I want to get him out of there. I want this over. What happens after, I don't know. But I know we need to help Sam, and we need to do it now."

"So the four of us go to Sam," Del says slowly, "and I take everyone to meet him in the Dream, and then the five of us walk out."

Carolyn exhales. "Yes."

"What if I can't?" A soft hiccup from Del's side. "Carolyn, this isn't exactly a natural Talent that I've got control over. I'm a Mage. I'm not a Dreamwalker, and when I go to the Dreamscape, it feels like I change. Like I—like there's someone else inside of me. She knows how the Talent works, but she isn't telling me, and she isn't telling you, and I think she wants us to stay there. In her domain."

"You're not insane, Del."

"I'm not saying I am." More rustling as Del fidgets. "I'm scared, Carolyn. I'm terrified. I don't want to go there, and I don't want to help Sam more. What if this time you get stuck, or Shawn does, or we all do? What if we come out, and it becomes Shawn who can travel through pictures, and Sam gets his illusions back, and you end up with nothing? What if I make a mess of everything?"

"There are a lot of variables." Carolyn's notebook is on her desk, nowhere near her. Heather must have seen her look that way, because she slides off her bed, grabs the notebook and pen, and hands them to her. "And you know ones I haven't even thought about."

"Duh. I'm the one who's actually done this."

"Don't be snippy." Carolyn quickly scribbles down as much as she can remember. "Maybe the problem is that last time, we were five people sharing our Talents. Maybe this time we have to act as one person. We're better at rituals now. We're older, and we understand our Talents better."

"Maybe you do," Del mutters dryly.

Carolyn really doesn't. Her magic is still changing, and she feels like she's in Talent adolescence all over again. "We know how to work with variables," she corrects herself.

"What does your professor think?" Del's voice is small. Scared. It's hard to reconcile the vulnerable sound with the image in Carolyn's mind of this strong woman who always stood up to the world when Carolyn couldn't.

"I think he thinks I'm nuts," Carolyn admits. She has to tell the truth; they have to walk in with eyes open, aware of the pitfalls. "I think he's exhausted, Del. He's been fighting all of this since last fall, and it's so much more than this thing with Sam. This part isn't Professor Szczek's battle, but he's taking it on because it's related to the Shadows. Weird has become a way of life, and it's burying him. So if we can stop some small part of the weird, and maybe even understand it, I think he'll be on board. He wants to understand."

"And you think doing this'll help us—him—understand?"

"I think it'll be more data, and I think we need to know more." Carolyn glances at Nikita. "I think doing this will give us a fighting chance."

"Okay." The word is a soft exhale, and Heather's suddenly there, sitting next to Carolyn, one arm around her, a calming presence against the prick of insecurity caused by Del's cautious response.

"Okay?" Carolyn confirms.

Another low exhale, then Del whispers, "Okay. Fine. I'm in. Call me tomorrow for this meeting or whatever. Right now, I need to—" She cuts off, and Carolyn fills in a series of potential endings for that sentence, guesses which of those endings is the most likely.

"Tell Shawn," Carolyn says. "We'll need him there, too."

A soft huff from Del. "I will. I will." Quiet for two heartbeats, then Del says, "Carolyn?"

"Hm?" Carolyn says.

"Don't leave me behind."

Carolyn exhales, the air punched out of her. It hits her then what she's asked by requesting that Del take them into the Dreamscape. "I won't," she promises. "We won't leave anyone behind. That's the whole point of doing this."

"Good. Good." Another soft rush of breath. "I have to go."

"Goodbye, Del. Talk to you tomorrow."

Carolyn's left staring at the phone propped on her knees, the call ending as the phone flickers back to her normal background image.

"So that's it?" Heather asks. She leans with her hand behind Carolyn's back, her head tipped against her shoulder. She's comforting like a blanket, and the tension seeps from Carolyn's bones.

"Thank you," Carolyn says.

"Any time. You know that." The peace intensifies before it retreats, and as Heather sits up, Carolyn can breathe on her own. Heather crosses her legs and sits, looking at her. "Be careful, Carolyn. I'm pretty sure Del knows that place better than you do."

"Yes, and I know how weird Del gets when we go there," Carolyn says. At the Berman place, Del was a little like a dream herself. "I have an idea what we're getting ourselves into. Don't worry, Heather. We'll come back."

"Good. You're my best friend, and I don't want to lose you." Heather slips from the bed and heads back to her own to rejoin Nikita.

It's all set. It's going to happen. Planning, then attack.

Then rescue.

Carolyn has to believe they'll all come back. Any other outcome is too terrifying to contemplate.

WITH FAMILY AND FRIENDS

Eighth Position: Family & Friends

With family and friends...

Rarely does any person stand completely alone. This card helps the querent understand those who surround them. It is not meant to guide the querent's family and friends to any action, but rather to remind the querent of the people who love them so that they might understand how they and their situation are perceived. It may help the querent see support they had not expected. It may serve to expose treachery that lies hidden. The querent should take heed, look closely at this card's meaning, and try to understand how they fit with those around them and how their relationships may affect their current situation and goals.

Carolyn's Reading: Prince of Cups

A dark-haired man with a carefully sculpted goatee regards the querent. His eyes are narrowed, concerned. His clothes are fine, and a wand lies beyond the cup he holds. A scorpion crawls upon his arm, tail lifted. It may sting, it may not—the future is an enigma.

In any other position, this card would represent a specific person, likely someone mysterious or challenging or deceptive, in the querent's life. It is more difficult to interpret when applied from the outside view. The querent's loved ones may see the querent as the mysterious one, perceive them as having erected walls separating them. Alternatively, they may feel that the querent is concealing things from them, tricking them, or lying to them. In some cases, they see the querent as poised on the cusp of a decision between love and magic, where the scorpion represents the danger inherent in either choice. Select the wrong direction and the scorpion will sting. The querent's loved ones worry for the querent and hope they will be able to choose the best path.

Kit's Reading: The Empress (Reversed)

A woman, adorned ornately, sits quietly She is rich, yes, but it is nature that gilds her. She wears the stars on her head, their light at her ears. The Earth lies by her side, and a bird brings her fruit. She is the ultimate woman, representing nature amidst a vivid, beautiful landscape.

The traditional meaning of the Empress is that she represents femininity. She has wisdom and power, and she grants insight into all things natural and wonderful. She is growth and abundance, beauty and culture. But when reversed, these strengths grow dark. The querent risks lethargy or boredom, rejecting the bounty that the Empress can bring. In this position, reflecting the views of the querent's loved ones, it suggests that those around the querent believe them to be at risk of succumbing to the temptation of earthly things rather than rejoicing in their mystery and seeking their wisdom.

Alternatively, the Empress in the reversed standing can have a simpler meaning: that when the querent's loved ones look at the querent, they see femininity turned on its head, a denial of a feminine upbringing. Combined with the meaning of light and truth, in this manner it can be a powerful card for those who transition from the feminine to the masculine. It suggests that the querent's loved ones have accepted him for who he is.

35

PAWEL'S OFFICE IS crowded. He sits on his desk, and Rory and Kit have squeezed into one chair together. That leaves the chair behind Pawel's desk, which Carolyn won't touch, and the other, still empty, guest chair.

Carolyn stays standing, as does Del.

Pawel shakes his head and pushes at the guest chair with his foot. "One of you should sit," he says. "You're not at an inquisition."

"I drove here as soon as my last class ended, and I'm planning on driving again tomorrow," Del grumbles, her arms crossed like armor. Her dark braids fall across her shoulders, swaying when she shakes her head. "I don't need to sit. And why wouldn't I feel like I'm on trial? You're judging us."

"He's judging the project," Carolyn points out. She gestures to the chair, and when Del shakes her head again, Carolyn sits cautiously on the edge.

"He's judging our sanity," Kit mutters. He's on Rory's lap, Rory's hand resting against his hip.

When Carolyn looks at Rory, he looks back. It's not possessive or challenging, just a quiet, comfortable expression.

"This is normally when I'm at taekwondo," Pawel says. He kicks his heels, thudding them back against the desk like a quick drumroll. His jaw sets as he stills, and he crosses his legs with his hands on his knee to hold himself in place. "Conor's with Emily, so I'm set for childcare, but that doesn't mean I have infinite time. I've reviewed everything that Carolyn sent me. We're here because I'm not sure you're ready to run headlong into this."

"I don't think we'll get any more ready before Sam's in trouble," Carolyn says. She keeps remembering the sound of his voice, the way he shifted from lost or vacant to scared. She grips her jeans, tugging at the fabric. "I'm worried he's been there too long already." Her gaze drifts to Del. "I wonder if it could make him lose his mind completely."

"His mind's already lost. It's stuck there," she deadpans.

Carolyn isn't amused. "That's not what I meant."

Pawel stops them with a wave of his hand. "You think it's urgent, and that's why we're here. You have a plan of sorts." He glances at Rory, brow furrowing, but doesn't say anything more.

Everyone else's presence makes sense, but Carolyn doesn't know why he's there, either, other than that he arrived with Kit.

"We have a plan," she agrees. "Of sorts."

Pawel gestures *go on*.

"We're relying on innate Talents," she says. "The problem is, we can't be sure what will work and what won't, so we've worked some flexibility into the process. Sam thinks that because we all walked our path together back at the beginning, he needs all of us to be there now to walk the path again and get him out. He needs to come with us this time. So Del and I have to somehow transport ourselves, plus Shawn and Kit, into the Dreamscape. I don't know if that means physically—I think for me and her it does, but I don't know for certain about Shawn and Kit. Then we work together to find the right path out."

It sounds so simple when she puts it into words. Too simple.

Both of Pawel's eyebrows rise. "You realize I have two very important questions for you, right?"

Carolyn's gaze drops. She knows. She's not sure she has specific-enough answers to satisfy him.

"How are you getting in? And how are you getting out?"

"Getting in is Del's Emergent Talent. That's how this started. She's almost a Dreamwalker but isn't quite," Carolyn says. "We're relying on her to get us into the Dreamscape. Getting us to Sam is my responsibility. I'm going to have Kit do a few drawings—I already have one of Sam that I can use as a focus—and Kit can draw the forest as well, the place where Sam's mind is, or at least he can draw something representative enough that I can use it to focus my Talent to help us travel there."

"And getting out again?" Pawel asks mildly.

Carolyn's heart sinks. "That's the tough question. Sam thinks we need to walk the paths. He thinks I'm critical. I think we're going to find a path that reaches home, or I'm going to take out a picture, reach out, and travel us to someone sitting outside. I was thinking that should be you, Professor." She doesn't feel confident, but the trick is to act confident. To make Pawel believe her. Half of ritual is belief, after all. She has to believe it will work more than anyone else believes it won't.

Pawel's gaze shifts to Kit. "And how does your art figure into this?"

Something touches the back of Carolyn's neck, sending shivers down her spine. She twists to see Del behind her, fingers resting on top of the chair.

"Sorry," Del murmurs.

"It's okay." Carolyn reaches up, touches Del's hand, and encourages her to rest it on her shoulder as if they're still friends. As if it's still high school, and they're still close. Del clings to her, and Carolyn realizes that in this room, she's the only friend Del has. For a moment, she feels bad about not including Shawn, but Carolyn's not ready to deal with him. They'll just have to be here for each other, at least for now.

"Your art is magical?" There's doubt in Pawel's voice, and Carolyn realizes she's missed whatever Kit's said.

"Since when is your art magical?" she asks.

"It's not—" Kit cuts off, and Rory's fingers move along his hip in a soothing motion. "My art isn't itself magical," Kit clarifies. "My art isn't what opens Carolyn's gateways, or whatever she uses. That's her own Talent. My Emergent Talent isn't what the art does. It's creating it in the first place."

"I see," Pawel says. Carolyn can see the wheels turning in his mind, and it's obvious that Pawel doesn't see. Not at all. And he's still waiting for an explanation.

"We might never have realized if Rory hadn't supercharged me," Kit says.

Del snickers.

"It wasn't like that," Rory mutters. There's a clear undertone of *you don't know me* and *stop* beneath the words.

Carolyn squeezes Del's fingertips in a silent request for her to keep quiet.

"What did happen?" Pawel asks. He leans back, one arm over his stomach, the other bent as he tilts his head forward and pinches the bridge of his nose.

"It goes back to what Mattie—the Shadow—said to me when we first met," Rory says, his tone carefully even. "My innate Talent is that I can make Talent stop, and I used it against her. After I did, she said I was brimming with all the Talent I'd stolen. You know how I struggle with sharing energy with anyone in ritual. That's why I took part in Ángel's soul-mark ritual, so I could get some practice. But when Kit and I were together, and he was drawing, it was like my magic knew his. It poured into him, and I'm pretty sure we both lost time."

Kit reaches into his pocket and pulls out a folded, creased black-and-white photograph of Rory hunched over his guitar. But—it's not a photograph. Carolyn leans forward, and she can see the pencil lines that compose the sketch.

Pawel inhales roughly. "Okay. So. Your Talent is creating hyper-realistic art."

"And Carolyn's Talent is using art—and particularly my art—to travel," Kit says, gesturing between himself and Carolyn. "We're twins. Our Talents match, but they aren't the same. They complement each other."

"When this is over, I'd love if you'd consider making me a new Tarot deck," Carolyn suggests. She's not sure how Kit will take it, bringing this new, fledgling Talent back to their family heritage. When he grins, she's relieved.

"I'll think about it," he says, and she knows he means *yes*.

Pawel holds up both hands. "We're off track," he says, his voice tight. "Yes, it's important that Kit has a new Emergent Talent, and yes, it's important for the two of you to explore how your Talents interact. But right this second, you have a plan, and you want to implement that plan immediately, and that has to take precedence. I'm not certain—"

"Tomorrow," Carolyn says, because she knows she put it in the email. That's why Del's here now—to make sure they have the details in place. That's why Shawn's set to meet them at Sam's tomorrow, and it's why they need to finish this. Everything needs to be set.

"Tomorrow," Pawel says quietly. His shoulders slump. "Fine. We'll find a way to make it work. I'll get Emily to keep Conor overnight. Mac can handle taekwondo again. You're not doing this without me." His back straightens slowly until he's upright again, and he looks at each of them. "Is this only a rescue mission, or is this your final project?"

"This is my final project; I'll also research Dreamweavers and Soulstealers and how they relate to each other and potentially intertwine as Lineages," Carolyn says.

"It's only part of mine," Kit says, tangling his fingers with Rory's. "I'm working with Rory as well, and I plan to compare and contrast the two rituals and see what I can learn from doing so."

"I expect fully researched documentation," Pawel says. "Introduction, proposal, methodology, results, and conclusion." He slowly slumps again, and he sounds tired. "You give me the information, and I'll contact the institution and set this up. We'll leave from my house in the morning. Kit, can you get the art done?"

"With Rory's help, yes."

"I'll drive myself," Del says. "I know where we're going. We can caravan."

"Then I suppose we're done here." Pawel pushes his hands against the desk like he's going to jump down, then hesitates. Carolyn thinks maybe he'll say something else, and she stays put until he finally moves, sliding off the desk and reaching for a notebook. "Carolyn, can I get that information from you?"

"Of course." She catches Kit's eye as he rises. "Where are you two heading after this?"

Rory and Kit exchange a glance before Kit says, "Hayworth, but we need to stop by Douglass first."

"Wait in the hall for me?" Carolyn asks. "Del and I can walk with you."

She slips her phone from her pocket as they leave, bringing up the information Pawel needs so he can copy it down. His hair falls in his face; it's shaggy now, not the buzz cut he's worn as long as she's known him. His face is thinner, and his shirt is wrinkled, hanging on him.

"Are you eating?" she asks, and his pen skitters across the page.

Pawel tries to cross out the mark he's made but only makes it worse. His jaw sets as he finishes, then carefully sets the pen down. "I'm eating," he says. "Magic takes energy, Carolyn. You know that. And those of us who have magic to spare tend to be thinner. I should have thought of that when I met Rory. He has the build of someone whose power could be devouring him from within."

He's deflecting.

"Are you sleeping?" She tries again, and this time he simply picks up the pen and copies down additional information from her phone. He'll run out soon—all she has is the contact information for Sam's mother and for the institution where he lives. She can wait.

When he puts the pen down again, she takes back her phone and repeats, "Are you sleeping?" She crosses her arms and looks at him.

He opens his mouth, closes it, then rubs at the bridge of his nose with the tips of his fingers. "It's a sign of how exhausted I am that my first thought was to retort *you're not my mother*," he mutters. "What's sad is that I said exactly that to Mac earlier. The two of you. God." He inhales roughly, exhales in a rush. "I'm fine, Carolyn. I'm tired, yes, but there's a lot going on, and I need to keep you kids from doing something beyond your abilities. I need to keep you safe."

"When I took Introduction to Magical Studies, you said that you're considered an expert, but that you know you don't know everything," Carolyn says bluntly. "You said that you're still learning, and that for those of us who are Lineage, if we can teach you, you want to learn."

"You don't know more about this than I do," Pawel counters.

"Then we're all learning together." Carolyn shrugs. "Congratulations, Professor Szczek, you're taking an independent study in new Emerging Talents, as taught by Carolyn and Kit Merrill. You don't have to pay for the class or turn in a paper. And sadly, we don't get paid to teach it." There's one more thing he needs to hear, even if he's not going to listen. Again. "And you don't need to protect us. You can't, not and keep yourself safe and sane."

Pawel laughs sharply. "Funny thing, Mac said that, too. Not quite the same way, though. When I said 'you're not my mother,' she pointed out that I'm not her father, either, and that I needed to stop trying to parent the entire magical student body. Which is a sad thought, really. I'm not that much older than any of you."

Carolyn remembers her first day of classes at PHU, walking into Introduction to Magical Studies with Kit and seeing Professor Pawel Szczek standing at the podium. She hadn't been able to believe he was old enough to teach.

Now he looks like he's aged a decade in the last few weeks.

"Rest," she says gently. "I'll see you in the morning. But you need sleep, or we're going to crash on the way there."

He nods. "I will. And you—" He pauses, tilts his head, and smiles slightly. "You get the taekwondo speech. Whatever happens tomorrow, you're going to have to make a decision at some point. You've built in flexibility, but eventually you'll need to pick a direction. Whichever direction you pick, commit to it. Don't do anything half-assed. In taekwondo, you have to commit to the kick or you might miss. With magic, lack of commitment could be deadly."

That's a chilling thought.

"Got it," she says. "In the morning, then."

"In the morning," Pawel echoes.

36

WHEN CAROLYN CATCHES up to the others, Kit and Del are talking quietly about something, heads bent together. Rory stands nearby, his hands shoved in his pockets, his shoulders hunched against the cold. He watches Kit with a small smile, fondness in his expression.

Carolyn's happy to see it.

"Hey," she says. She motions at the road, and Kit and Del move out ahead, leaving Rory to shorten his stride to match Carolyn's pace.

He makes a sound that might be a laugh. "Hey. Is this the part when you get me alone so you can threaten to kill me if I hurt him?" His smile is wry. "I come from a huge, close-knit family. I'm pretty used to the concept of protective family members. And you're twins."

Carolyn considers him closely before shaking her head. "I don't think I need to, do I?" There's something about the way they are together—Kit's relaxed familiarity—that has set her at ease. "Are you the kind of guy who flits around from one boyfriend to the next?"

"Kit's my second boyfriend," Rory admits. "I was still dating the first when we found out we were soulmates. Or rather, when the spell resolved. It made things awkward, but we figured it out."

Because Rory brought it up, Carolyn's a little more comfortable asking about it. "How does the soulmates thing work?" She glances at Kit, walking ahead, deep in conversation with Del. "I'm not going to give you the shovel talk, but I really don't want Kit being forced into anything, either. He's— I worry about him. Neither of us has had great relationship experiences."

"The spell won't force anything," explains Rory. "It's like a beacon—an indicator that says 'hey, this person might be the perfect person for you.' It's supposed to be cast by people who are already involved with each other, who are already planning on spending their lives together. It's not supposed to work the way it did."

"So he got the mark involuntarily, but that doesn't mean there's something making the two of you to be together." Carolyn thinks of the horror stories people have written about magic since long before the Emergence. "You aren't going to get sick or pine forever if you're separated."

"I'd miss him." That small, fond smile again, as Rory watches Kit. "If he decides this isn't right for him, we can break up. He can leave. I can leave if I need to. There's nothing binding us together, nothing that says we have to do this. We could just be friends, and that'd be fine."

She can hear his hesitation. "But...?"

"Our magic meshes perfectly," Rory says. "It's not about the marks; it's the way our magic feels together. Like now that the floodgate's opened, I can feel his magic, and mine really wants to help his. When we're together, it's like a cocoon around us, locking us away from the rest of the world. It's comfortable."

Carolyn's curious if Kit's as comfortable as Rory, but that's a question to ask her brother another time. "So do you think you—?"

"It's not love," Rory says quickly, a flush high on his cheeks. "I mean, maybe it will be someday. I definitely like him romantically. A lot. He—he gets a lot of things. He listens to me. And he pays attention."

"Oh?" Carolyn's not surprised. Kit can be very thoughtful, and the idea of him spoiling someone romantically seems about right.

"I told him I wanted to spend a whole day watching movies and snuggling, and he brought over takeout and a projector." The flush staining Rory's skin intensifies. "He's sweet. I like it."

Carolyn smiles. "He likes you. He seems comfortable with you, and Kit isn't comfortable with many people."

"I'm comfortable with him, too." Rory shrugs, his gaze drifting to Kit again. "I'm glad about the soul mark now. I was angry, frustrated, and confused when it first happened. Kit and I were friends, and this was a whole level of stress we didn't need. I wasn't even sure if he liked guys." The slow smile starts again, until he's flushed and grinning, ducking his head. "Pretty sure it's working out, though."

He's adorable. He is absolutely adorable, and Carolyn is happy for Kit. "I'm glad. Can I see the mark?"

"Sure." Rory stops and turns toward her, pulling his sleeve up to bare his arm.

It's much bigger than the mark Kit showed her. Rory's ink is a double helix, curving around his wrist and up his arm, disappearing under where he has the sleeve shoved up. Between each strand there are smaller images, but she can't see the details in the dim evening light.

"It's impressive," she says.

"In order to encapsulate Kit's personality in one ink design, I needed an entire sleeve," Rory says. "Even the magic knows how complicated and intricate he is. It's also a song. I started feeling the beat of it as soon as the ink hit my skin. Maybe even before that."

It's an interesting way of putting it.

Someday she wants to look more closely at Rory's mark, at the path of images from by his hand to his elbow. She wants to jot them down and interpret them like a reading. Because that's what's on Rory's skin, she thinks. It isn't just a representation of Kit, it's Kit laid out in Prediction, as befits his Lineage. And it's perfect. She doesn't want to voice the thought, though. Kit wouldn't like it.

Rory rolls down his sleeve, then shoves his hands back in his pockets. "I was freaked out at first," he admits. "But I like it now. It feels like Kit."

They're approaching Townhouse Row, and Carolyn should take Del down one side toward the house while Kit and Rory go down the other. Alternatively, Carolyn could stick with Kit and Rory, following them into Douglass. She could stop in and see Serina.

That would be awkward.

Carolyn walks a little slower; Kit and Del have paused because they've reached the point where Kit would need to turn to go to Douglass with Rory. Del raises a hand, and Carolyn ignores the clear gesture to hurry up.

"What?" Rory asks.

"I was thinking that I could stop by your floor." Carolyn bites her lower lip, considering her words carefully. "Go up and see Serina. But I've got Del. I probably shouldn't. Besides—" It would mean explaining things to

Kit, and she's not sure she's ready. She's not sure Kit's ready, either, or even what, exactly, she'd be explaining.

Rory's brow furrows. "Besides what?"

"I'm dating Serina," Carolyn admits. "I haven't told Kit yet."

"Oh." Rory shifts, looking to Kit and then back to Carolyn. "You should tell him. I don't think he'll care. They broke up before he and I started whatever it is we're doing. As long as you're happy, I'm sure it's fine."

"Aren't there rules about not dating your brother's ex or something?" Carolyn asks.

"I would never date someone Thorne's dated," Rory mutters, shuddering. "We would not be compatible. He and I are very, very different. But other than in cases like that, I can't see why there would be some kind of rule about it. I mean, my dad dated my dad's twin before he and my dad got together."

"Come on!" Kit calls out, bouncing to keep warm, his hands shoved deep in his pockets. His beanie is pulled low over his ears, and even from this distance, Carolyn can see he's shivering.

And oh…she can also see someone excitedly waving, off to the left, hurrying to intersect them.

Serina.

Rory follows her gaze, then shrugs toward Kit. "You have about five seconds if you want to tell him before he sees. Because knowing Serina, it'll be completely obvious."

He's right.

Carolyn picks up the pace, and she gets to Kit when Serina is still a few steps away. He's watching her, unaware of Serina's approach.

"Are you trying to freeze us?" Kit asks as Rory moves behind him, wraps his arms around him, and pulls him close. "Mm, you're warm. Don't stop."

Rory laughs. "Wasn't planning on it, although it'll be hard to walk this way."

"Kit." Carolyn's throat is dry, her heart pounding with every footstep of Serina's approach. Del cocks her head, attention on Carolyn. "I—"

"Hey!" Serina pushes between Kit and Del, grabbing onto Kit's arm and going up on tiptoes to kiss his cheek. "You look like you're freezing.

Did Carolyn make you wait for me? Because while that's really sweet, she shouldn't have stuck you standing out here." Serina pats his cheek, then reaches up to pat Rory's as well before she lets them go. She opens her arms, and Carolyn opens hers automatically to take the hug, tucking Serina in close. When Serina reaches for Carolyn's head, she freezes as Serina frames her face and draws her close, but all Serina does is rub noses with her. It's so cute that Carolyn grins, her cheeks going warm. Serina tucks in close to her side, arm around Carolyn's back. "I'm really glad I bumped into you."

Del's gaze flicks between Carolyn and Serina, and her eyebrows go up.

"Oh hey, hi, I'm Serina." She leans forward, her free hand outstretched.

"Del," replies Del, taking Serina's hand for a moment.

"The high-school friend who does Dream things that interfere with Nikita. I've heard about you. Did we meet before? I can't remember actually meeting you, but sometimes things escape my memory."

"I've heard of you," Del says blandly.

Serina beams, squeezing Carolyn. "Awesome. 'Cause we're kind of a thing, I think, and I'm going to take that to mean that Carolyn really likes me. Carolyn doesn't talk about much; if I'm on her mind enough to talk about, that's good."

There's a sick twist in Carolyn's stomach as she looks at Kit.

Kit lifts one of Rory's hands and kisses his fingertips. "The fact that we both might be in vaguely healthy relationships at the same time is some kind of a miracle."

"Or a sign that the world is changing, hopefully for the better," Del says. "But your friend is right about one thing. It is way too cold to be standing on a corner chatting."

When she realizes everyone is looking at her, Serina coughs. "So. I could stop at Douglass to drop off my bag, then maybe come over to the house for a while? If you want? I mean, you've got Del there, and I don't know, maybe you have plans or something."

"You guys figure it out," Kit directs. He unwinds from Rory enough to hold hands, then tugs, leading Rory down the walkway to toward Douglass. "I'm going inside."

"We need to hit the road fairly early, but I don't see why we can't hang out," Del offers. "I mean, it's not like I care if we watch a movie and you two make out."

"We aren't going to be making out in front of you," Carolyn mumbles, her face hot. "We aren't—" She stops herself from saying that they aren't going to be making out at all, because that's a conversation for only her and Serina.

"We are not putting on some kind of lesbian performance for you," Serina says, her tone softer than the sharp words imply, "but you could tell me what you guys are doing, in case I end up with a surprise Carolyn in my room again."

"I'm not asking you to perform; I'm really not that into watching public displays. I'm just saying I don't care if you do or you don't." Del shrugs. She starts walking down the same path Kit and Rory took, and Carolyn hurries to catch up with her; she's pretty sure Del has no idea where they're going.

"Are you going to tell me what's happening?" Serina asks, joining her.

"Yes," Carolyn decides. It's what you do when you trust people, when you might need people to act as an anchor. And maybe if they'd told more people what they were doing in high school, they wouldn't be in this mess.

37

"Do you think this is going to work?" Shawn has his arms crossed, dark eyes narrowed under a furrowed brow. He stands in the hall outside of Sam's room as if he's been left there waiting for them.

Maybe he has been; Carolyn isn't the one coordinating this, and she certainly isn't the one talking to him.

Del runs her hand over his shoulder, down his arm, to his elbow. "I think it's our best shot, and I think Sam thinks it's our best shot. That means it's a shot we have to take."

Pawel approaches, one of the nurses in his wake. "We've got an hour, and Joshua here will be in the room with us the entire time. If Sam gets combative, Joshua will administer a sedative that will calm him but won't knock him out." There's a tension in his words; neither he nor Joshua look pleased, and Carolyn gets the feeling it's a compromise on both sides.

"The point is to wake him up, not knock him out," Shawn says curtly, pressing his lips together when Del squeezes his elbow.

"We need him to be calm enough that we can perform the ritual, but not actually unconscious." Del addresses Joshua. "Did Professor Szczek explain?"

"You might as well call me Pawel. My upper-level students generally do," Pawel mutters. "Not that you're actually my student, but at this point, the details seem moot."

Carolyn takes in a shuddering breath. She's standing in this hall, outside the room where she visited Sam not long ago. It feels familiar, but there's also a sense of unreality about it, like maybe this isn't actually happening. Maybe they're already in a Dream.

It's disturbing to think that maybe they've already set things in motion, and maybe they have no idea where real is and where it isn't.

She wraps her arms around herself and shudders. That's not a path she wants to go down. She has to be confident. Calm. Ready to do this, finish it, and get the hell out.

Del presses a hand against Shawn's chest, and from their expressions, Carolyn's missed something. Del pushes, and Shawn steps back, stopping when he's against the wall. "Get out of your own head, and don't act like a dick because you're feeling insecure," Del tells him, the words sharp. She seems more in focus, less dreamlike than the rest of the world. "Go into the room, Caro. I need to have a quick talk with Shawn, then we'll be in."

Shawn's jaw is set, but his familiar anger has been blunted by something. He looks up, then down and away, and Carolyn can't read the emotion in the movement.

Joshua opens the door, then stands to one side after entering, his scrubs a stark, dark slash of blue against the soft gray walls.

Sam looks up as they enter, his gaze unfocused, and that makes Carolyn feel even more detached from reality. Pawel still looks exhausted as he approaches Sam, one hand out as if he's approaching a wild animal. Sam doesn't move, even when Pawel sits on the edge of the bed next to him.

"Samuel," Pawel says quietly, and Sam doesn't turn.

Kit grabs one of the chairs in the room and sinks into it, sitting with his feet kicked out in front of him and his arms crossed. He pulls papers out of his pocket and flips through them.

Carolyn looks over his shoulder and takes in the images. There's a new one of Sam, based on pictures that Sam's mother sent of how he looks now. Older, and a little thinner, than when they were in high school. Sharper and more tired, as if fear eats him from the inside. Or maybe that's just Carolyn's interpretation based on the things he's said to her.

It could be both.

There are easily a dozen pictures of forests, each based on descriptions Del gave last night. They'd all spent the night together, Del talking while Kit slipped into a strange fugue and created image after image based on her words. There are even two with figures in them: one with Sam, and another with Sam and shadows in the distance.

The last one makes Carolyn shiver, and it's the one she reaches out for.

"Carolyn." The pleasure in Sam's voice makes her look up. He stands and comes to her, his arms open, and she takes the hug he offers. "Kit. You're both here." There are shadows in his gaze as he looks at Joshua, then back at the bed. He frowns to see Pawel, and the frown deepens when he sees that his door is still cracked open. "Are you both here, or am I dreaming? Are we going to find the right path?"

"We're going to find the right path." Del pushes the door open, and it bangs against the wall before Joshua catches it.

Shawn enters the room behind her; Sam comes to attention and takes a step toward Carolyn. "We're all here," Sam says.

Del's expression gentles. "And soon we'll all be there. If this goes as planned."

Sam's gaze drifts to Carolyn. "It will. I trust you."

She feels the pressure settle over her shoulders. "I'll do my best."

The room is small, and it takes some maneuvering to get into the formation they had designed for this ritual. Kit offers Sam a seat in the center of the room, and Sam's expression goes slack as he sits. Carolyn joins Del, Kit, and Shawn, spaced evenly around Sam; she's aware of Pawel and Joshua by the door, watching closely. Carolyn sets her right hand on Sam's shoulder, her left on Kit's shoulder. The others echo the same position, like they're forming a five-person dance formation.

During senior year, they'd fed their abilities into Sam. Touching him—that part is the same. But this time, they've also created a feedback loop. They want to feed energy into Sam, and they want to connect with him and travel to where he is. But they also want the energies to circulate, to feed each other. They must act as one.

Carolyn holds the image of Sam in the shadowy forest. It felt the most real to her when she touched it, matches what he told her, resonates; now, it's pinned between her hand and Sam's shoulder, directly in her vision.

"So what now?" Shawn asks; his voice disrupts her concentration.

"You shut up," Kit says sharply.

"Carolyn's Talent is traveling through illusions," Del says, tone carefully even. "Sam's Talent will intensify hers, if he's got any left. I'm hoping that when yours leaked out, Shawn, it went back where it belonged. I'm going to use my Talent at the same time as Caro, so when we travel, we go into the actual Dreamscape where Sam is. Then we have to get back out."

"How?" Shawn's fingers twitch against Carolyn's shoulder as if he's about to let go.

"Good question," Carolyn says. She looks across the circle to Del. "We'll figure that out when we get there."

"Your hour starts now," Pawel interjects. He has a list of acceptable and agreed-to ways of trying to shake them out of the ritual if it goes too long. Pawel is their failsafe, but he has no way of impacting what they do after they leave.

Carolyn's pretty sure that the only way out is to go through.

"Ready," Carolyn murmurs, and she focuses on the image in front of her.

The illusion blooms quickly, trees growing and filling the room, pushing everything away until the five of them are within the shimmering confines of an illusory forest. Pawel is no longer visible; the sounds of the hospital are far enough away that Carolyn can barely hear them.

"Now," Del whispers. She giggles, and abruptly the illusion becomes real.

Sam crouches on one knee in front of them, his head bowed. In the distance, shadows move in the darkness, and Carolyn catches glimpses of figures among them.

It's not welcoming.

They stand on a dirt pathway that appears oddly well-trodden, threading between the trees. It stretches off in either direction, and Carolyn can see forks beyond forks, a seemingly endless maze. Light streams through the canopy of leaves overhead, flickering but surprisingly bright along the path. Beyond the established way, in the depths of the forest, it quickly shutters into darkness.

Sam looks up. "Are you real?"

Del sinks to her knees in front of him, cradling his face. "Hell yes, Samson, and we're going to get you out."

"I don't think that's going to be easy." Kit catches Carolyn's fingers, gripping tightly. "There's not a sign that says 'Exit.'"

"I've tried all the paths. None of them lead home." Sam rises, shaking something unseen from his shoulders before he stands straight. This is the Sam of her memories, with all the strength and vitality of high school. His cheeks are fuller, his shoulders broader. He's more confident than the last time she spoke to him.

"One of them has to." Shawn starts walking to his right without waiting for them. "We have to try our options."

"There are a thousand options, Shawn," Sam protests, raising his voice without moving a step. "A thousand or more. I've been down every path."

"You said we had to walk the paths," Carolyn reminds him.

His gaze narrows. "You have to get us out."

"You said we all had to be here." She wants him to remember, wants to make sure they get this right because they may never get another chance. "You said everyone had to walk their path, even Kit."

Sam's gaze strays to the darkness beyond the path. "It's too dangerous to split up. We don't want to fall into the split."

"No one said we had to walk our paths alone," Del says. She hurries toward where Shawn waits, his energy barely contained. Carolyn suspects he would run if he dared, and she doesn't blame him.

This place gives her the creeps.

Del catches Shawn, swinging their joined hands. "Come on." Her voice is cheerfully singsong. She skips a few steps down one path, tugging Shawn with her. "Let's see where you need to go."

This place isn't merely creepy, it's downright disturbing.

"It's like a reading," Kit murmurs.

And oh, that's true. It's a pathways reading, with different choices like different cards along the way. Carolyn starts moving as Sam and Kit bracket her.

"Read the right pathways," Sam tells her. "Reach the final outcome."

Carolyn remembers reading for Shawn long ago. He'd wait for her to lay the cards out, then start to tell his own story based on the pictures. He'd bull ahead rather than looking at the meanings behind the cards, and he'd ignored half of what she said, picking and choosing the pieces that worked for himself.

Shawn is no different now. He drops Del's hand, moving ahead of her, denying Carolyn the chance to look for meaning, or even determine if this is a pathways reading. He barely pauses when the road forks, picking a path seemingly at random, and Carolyn barely has time to pay attention to the places around her, needing to move quickly to keep up with the pace he sets. She tries to remember the twists and turns but loses them in the dreamlike feeling of time jumping, pulling them forward. The faster Shawn moves, the more the scenery feels less like a layout and more like shuffling cards, sliding by in flickering images.

Sam seems to drag until Kit grabs Sam's hand and pulls him along so he doesn't get left behind. "We can't split up," Kit murmurs to Sam. "We're not leaving without you."

The Shadows grow darker, moving closer to the path.

"Shawn, I don't think this is the best—"

"We're going this way," Shawn says, determined. He chooses a left fork, between a flowering magnolia and a tall maple, then twists right into a long stretch of pine. Time slows down, and Shawn starts to run; the path narrows abruptly, forcing him to slow and giving them time to catch up. Carolyn blinks, and the world stops flickering, the surroundings stable again. The path has ended with a tall tree rising in front of them. The trunk is as wide as the path is narrow, blocking the way.

Shawn steps to one side, apparently planning to go around, but Sam grabs his wrist tightly.

"Don't go off the path," Sam cautions. "Don't let the split take you. The Shadows will consume you."

For a moment, Carolyn thinks Shawn is going to explode. But his gaze catches on something past Sam, and he steps back, shaking off Sam's hold. "Fine. We can't go around. And I don't think we're meant to go inside the tree. So, we're here. This is the end of the path. We go home from here."

"I don't see why we couldn't have tried to go home where we came in," Kit grumbles.

"Because we have the paths," Del tells him, patting the side of his face. "Don't you know that's why everyone comes here? We Dream to travel the pathways and find our way in the waking world."

Logical, yes, but the way she says it is chilling. Especially considering that Sam's been traveling these particular paths for years.

Shawn feels along the bark of the tree as if seeking a secret door. "How do we get out this way?"

"How do you know it's the correct path?" Del counters. She leans in, lips brushing against his cheek. "Maybe we should try another," she whispers. "There are so many ways we could go. We should try them all."

Carolyn brings out the picture of Pawel. "It's only the right path if it gets us back to reality," she says, focusing on his face.

She imagines him as he has been recently: scruffy and tired, with dark circles under his eyes.

The illusion fails to rise.

She tucks the papers back in her pocket.

"This isn't the final outcome," she says, and Kit smiles slightly.

"I've looked into other worlds," Sam mutters. "The worst of them want to come through to get you. The worst of them have been overtaken by Shadows and are little better than hell."

A great *crack* thunders from the sky and shakes the ground.

Kit grabs Carolyn, throwing them sideways as a branch crashes down. The trunk of the tree before them has split. She lies there, stunned, as Shadows spill out of the shattered tree, flowing across the path and disappearing into the forest.

Every spot they pass over succumbs to darkness, and the path is slowly consumed. The end is already gone, the tree a part of the darkest woods, surrounded by teeming movement.

"Change is beautiful," Del murmurs.

"Do you see?" Sam asks. "Even if we don't stray into the split, it might come for us. We have to find a way out."

Kit scrambles to his feet, pulling Carolyn with him. "Run!" he orders, and does just that.

Shawn, Sam, and Del race after them. Carolyn keeps pace with Kit easily, her feet moving in sync with his in a way they never would in the real world. The magic of Dreams, she supposes, her lungs burning from effort but never quite giving out.

The Dream has given way to nightmares, Shadows reaching out to graze the path, tickling their skin on the way by. Del's giggle echoes softly, and Carolyn isn't sure if she's hearing it or imagining it, and she isn't going to slow down long enough to figure it out.

Kit hesitates at every fork, and every time he chooses, it's exactly the one Carolyn would have picked. There's a sense of rightness as she travels with her twin, step by step down the same path, following the exact same movement. It's everything they had when they were younger. They have always been different people, but they have always, always traveled together despite their differences.

Kit hesitates at one fork, gaze shifting between the three options. He quickly looks away from the far right, and Carolyn's grateful. Just looking in that direction makes her skin crawl; there is nothing good that way. He looks to the left, and for a moment Carolyn catches a glimpse of a woman there, her image in reverse. The woman doesn't hang upside down, but rather her entire world has been turned on its ear, upside down and backward. When she turns away, the world rights itself again and a man stands there.

"The Empress, reversed," Carolyn murmurs. "Femininity rejected and masculinity accepted."

Kit takes a step toward that path, and she catches hold of him. "Not that way."

"It feels right." He takes another stubborn step, pulling her with him.

"I wonder what it would feel like, to touch a Shadow," Del muses. Shawn holds her close, keeping her from straying from the path.

In the distance down the center path, Carolyn sees two figures. One is a walking man, the other less clear, but both people are beckoning them closer. "Not to me," she insists. "I can see you down both paths, but I'm not on that one. If you go that way, I can't go with you. If we go to the right, we destroy ourselves. But if we go to the center, it's your path, but I'm with you. We're different, and together."

Kit wavers.

"Pick something before Del gets loose and goes chasing shadows," Shawn grits out.

"We need to leave," Sam insists, gaze darting around. "The paths are crumbling to darkness."

Their surroundings don't look different to Carolyn, but she hasn't been here long; she trusts Sam's assessment. She holds out her hand to Kit, palm up, and says, "Together?"

Kit places his hand atop hers. "Together," he agrees, and at Sam's insistent yell, Kit shouts, "Run!"

They race down the center path, and it grows lighter as they go. The tightness in Carolyn's lungs eases, and she breathes in, long and deep, before pushing forward again. They burst out of the forest into a meadow, the heavy scent of flowers and fresh grass almost overpowering. Sun beats down on them, thick and warm.

Del pulls away from Shawn and skips out, stopping to spin with her arms out, her braids swinging with the movement. "Home," she sings out.

"I've never been here before," Sam says. He crouches down, running his fingers through the grass.

"This is Del's Dreamscape. Her personal one." It's familiar in a way that Carolyn doesn't want to remember. "Del, can't you just—?" She stops; Del is ignoring them in favor of lying down on her back, starfished among wildflowers and grass.

They can't rely on Del.

Kit's staring at her like he's waiting for her to do something.

Sam looks like Carolyn holds the answers to everything he's ever wanted.

And Shawn lies down next to Del, watching her with wonder.

Carolyn supposes that he's never seen her like that before. None of them have, except for Carolyn.

"I promised to get her out of here," Carolyn whispers. "She knew she'd want to stay, that she'd get lost."

"Do you think this is the way back?" Kit asks.

Carolyn shakes her head. "Not exactly. But I think that if anywhere is thin enough for us to punch through and get out, it's here. We're with Del, and we're kind of in her mind. It's like when we went into Mattie's Dream, and I walked us out of there through an illusion. We're going to do the same thing here."

She takes the picture of Pawel out again.

"Sam, I need you to hold onto me," she directs. She doesn't want to risk him getting left behind; making sure he's the first through is the best way to prevent that. "Kit, as soon as I've got this working, I need you to get Shawn and Del over here. And be ready for an argument. I don't think Del will want to go. She's happy here." Like a child, she thinks. Innocent. Free. This is a place where the past never happened and the future doesn't loom. She can't blame Del for wanting to stay.

The meadow is bright, but she can see Shadows around the edges where the forest begins. They move, reaching into the light then retreating again. It's only a matter of time before they push inward, making the light smaller. And she wonders what that will mean for Del's mind, if it's possible for the Shadows to overtake her personal Dreamscape.

Focus.

"Don't let go," she murmurs as Sam holds her shoulder. He responds by wrapping his arms around her, heavy and solid against her back.

As she stares at Pawel's image, an illusion springs up. He's leaning forward, posture stiff and angry, mouth open as he says unheard words. "Pawel," Carolyn calls out, and he straightens, turning toward her.

"Carolyn?" he says, peering in her direction. His gaze narrows as he catches sight of her. "Where are you?"

She didn't think this through; she doesn't know how to open a gate or a doorway to send everyone through. "Dreamscape," she says. Sam's breathing is rough behind her, and she isn't sure if he can see Pawel. She hopes he can; it'll make this easier.

"The four of you disappeared, and Sam passed out," Pawel says curtly. "It's been an hour and a half and I've been arguing every minute of the last thirty to keep them from doing something to wake Sam up."

"Thanks." Carolyn can't be sure, but she thinks that's a good thing. On the other hand, if Sam's both there and here, she's pretty sure she needs to rethink the plan. "This is Sam behind me. I was going to send him through first, but I get the feeling that if he's already there, I need to bring him with me. I need to deal with the physical people first." She raises her voice. "Kit! Now!"

"Already here." Someone touches her arm, and Carolyn glances sideways to see Kit standing there, eyes wide as he looks past her. Shawn stands behind him, Del thrown over his shoulder. She has a flower in her hands and is picking petals from it, tossing them into the faint breeze.

"It's the only way she's leaving here," Kit says.

Carolyn nods. "I promised I wouldn't leave her behind."

"Now what?" Pawel asks.

Carolyn reaches out, and Pawel lifts his hand to match her motion. Carolyn feels it when she breaks the plane between here and there, his fingers solid on hers. He's more real than the world behind him, and she tightens her grip. "Here's how I think this will work. Kit, hold my hand, then take Pawel's free hand and go to him. Then Shawn, with Del. Then I'll bring Sam. Got it?"

"Got it." Kit nods sharply and does as she's described. Carolyn feels when he leaves the Dreamscape, like with his departure he sucks a bit of reality out with him. The illusion falters, almost falls away, and she feels a thick surge of the Dreamscape rushing into the space Kit left, threatening to swallow her.

Pawel's gaze is narrowed, lines deeply furrowed around his eyes. His fingers grip hers so tightly that they hurt. "I'm trying to help, but let's get this over with quickly."

Carolyn reaches blindly for Shawn, grabs him, and shoves him toward Pawel. As Shawn carries Del through, the illusion shakes again, and Carolyn goes to her knees, dragging Sam and Pawel down with her. Echoes reverberate inside her head, pounding. She closes her eyes against the pain, opens them again when Pawel snaps her name.

"I'm here," Carolyn says, looking at him. She twists in Sam's grip and wraps herself around him as he wraps around her in turn. "We're taking you home."

He smiles, leaning in forehead to forehead with her. "Thank you."

She steps forward, stumbling as Sam's weight disappears from her shoulders.

Pawel catches her, lowering her to the floor; she kneels, head bowed, eyes closed against the light.

She hears a shout, Sam's voice rising in the background. "I'm home!" There's the sound of flailing, of a struggle, Shawn yelling as Pawel pats Carolyn's hand and leaves her there. She can't do anything but try to breathe, struggling to get her body under control. It feels like she could sleep for a week. She leans back until she's sitting on the floor, half sprawled because her limbs won't cooperate.

"It worked," Kit murmurs, and she opens her eyes to find him crouched next to her, his hand behind her back to help her sit upright.

"Good."

There are raised voices and alarms, people calling for examinations while Sam protests. Carolyn can't separate the words into coherence. She presses her hands to her ears, tries to block them out.

"Just breathe," Kit says, and he does it with her. In-two-three-four. Out-five-six-seven-eight. Repeat. Repeat. Repeat.

In the corner of the room, Shadows coalesce, squirming in ways that remind Carolyn of the forest. She scoots backwards, farther from the darkness, and Kit turns, focusing on the same space.

"Did they follow us?" Kit whispers.

"You see it too?"

A figure forms and steps out. She looks so normal as she stands there, hands on her hips, surveying the room, then she looks down at Carolyn. She smiles, her mouth full of sharp teeth. "You people are noisy."

Mattie looks like any other girl about Carolyn's age who she might pass on the street: jeans and a T-shirt with a denim jacket thrown on over it and a phone in her hand. Mattie shoves the phone into her pocket and looks over at the nurse, Joshua, who is approaching quickly.

"She's with us," Carolyn says.

Joshua hesitates.

Pawel turns around, blinking to see Mattie standing there. "They want to examine Sam. We should take this into the lobby, perhaps." He hesitates, and Carolyn can see the wheels turning as he looks at Mattie. "Will he be safe?"

She shrugs. "I can't say. You people made a lot of noise. I felt the reverberations, although I was already on my way after Rory mentioned what you were doing. As long as I'm with you, I don't think any other Shadowwalkers will come."

"And if we leave Sam?" Pawel asks.

Mattie pushes past Joshua, edging up close to Sam. She has to wedge herself between another nurse and the bed, and Sam leans back as Mattie leans forward. She inhales roughly, seems to taste the air around him. Her hand rests lightly on his arm for a moment, then she withdraws. "He's nothing compared to what you've done. It lingers around him, but it's an aroma. Cologne. The trail leads back to you, and no one would bother with him when you're only a little farther down the trail."

"Can we trust you?" Carolyn doesn't want to ask it, doesn't like the way Mattie's expression darkens. "I need to know."

"Yes," Mattie says curtly. "I don't plan to eat you. If I did, you would never have seen me first." She tilts her head, lips pursed. "Besides, I'm a soul vegetarian now. Rory's family insists."

Kit makes a small, strangled noise. Carolyn thinks it might have been a muffled laugh.

Carolyn puts her hand on his arm and lets him help her to her feet. She still feels wobbly, as if every ounce of energy has been sucked out of her.

Mattie's gaze narrows as she watches Carolyn. "You've already spilled your cup. There's nothing left to drink right now."

"Good to know," Carolyn mutters.

She wants to check on Sam, but they won't let her near him. A nurse helps him lie back on the bed, and there are three staff members—four, counting Joshua—surrounding him. Joshua ushers Pawel, Mattie, Carolyn, and Kit out into the hall, where Del and Shawn already stand.

"They've gone to call his mom," Del says. She's tucked under Shawn's arm, her head tilted against his shoulder.

Carolyn crosses her arms, shivering. "Good. I'd hoped—I guess she didn't think it would work."

"We weren't working in known territory, and it's been years," Pawel murmurs. "No one thought it would work."

There's something in his tone that captures Carolyn's attention. "You didn't even think it would work."

He pushes his hair out of his face, then rubs his cheek. "No. I didn't. But I knew that you'd learn something from trying, and whatever you learned might help you find a solution. I didn't expect a home run on the first attempt."

"Instead you lit a beacon and begged to be eaten," Mattie muses. Her fingers trail over Pawel's shoulder. "You're not drained, despite what you fed to her. I felt it, that flow of energy. It was incredible. Like a chocolate fountain."

Carolyn shudders. "If you could please not talk about eating us, I'd appreciate it."

"Some people like—" Mattie cuts off abruptly and gives a dark look to Pawel. "Why did you do that?"

"Because whatever you were going to say, I don't think it'd be appropriate for the current location or audience," he mutters, his fingers pinched around the bridge of his nose. "There has to be a lounge here somewhere."

"It's a patient lounge, and it's this way." Del carefully disengages from Shawn and leads them down the hall into a wide room filled with comfortable chairs, tables, and sofas. There are other patients there; a few look up, curious, but they go back to their own activities quickly.

Pawel drops onto one of the sofas, leaning back. Mattie sits next to him, drawing her feet up. Carolyn doesn't want to be touched, so she finds a chair to pull over, waving Kit off when he tries to be near her. Shawn and Del manage to occupy the seat, and Kit ends up standing.

Mattie looks at Pawel. "You don't have to be afraid of me."

"I'm not afraid of you," he mutters.

"Yes, you are." Her tone is quiet, matter-of-fact. "I meant what I said: I don't plan to eat you. Any of you. I'm here to protect you because Rory warned me what you were doing, and I like Rory. He would be delicious, and I would still never eat him, therefore I can't eat any of you."

It's a strange and twisted kind of logic, but Carolyn follows it.

"I can feel them, you know," Mattie continues. "Pressing. Beating at the spaces around here. We should stay near the light." She looks at Carolyn, and Carolyn gets the feeling that she's leaving something out.

They sit for a long, long moment. Carolyn counts breaths again, her heart rate almost approaching normal. She feels like she can breathe easily, and she exhales long and slow each time.

"Are you going to tell me what happened?" Pawel asks, his head still tipped back and his eyes closed. The aura of exhaustion is intense. Mattie said she didn't think he's expended his resources, but he looks even more drawn than before. Carolyn hopes he's up for driving them back to PHU. She doesn't really want to try to transport them there through an illusion. She's not sure she could even bring one to life right now.

Carolyn drifts, letting Kit tell the story. His outsider view seems cleaner than her own, as if he could see Del and Sam more clearly than she could.

"I don't remember much," Del admits when Kit runs out of words. "I felt as if I had to go somewhere, and then as if I were home and I ought to stay there. I was angry when Shawn picked me up, but it was Shawn. So it was okay. I just—I wanted to be happy."

"I know you think you aren't a Dreamwalker," Pawel says, "but I think you could benefit from training, Del. I can put you in touch with someone."

"I'm not your student." Her words are rapid, angry—a quick burst of fight.

"I know."

Mattie pushes to her feet, then reaches across the space to grip Carolyn's wrist. Her fingers go tight, pressing in against her skin until Carolyn looks up. Mattie grins. "I need to pee," she announces.

"Fine," Del says, flicking her fingers. "Bathroom's that way."

Mattie stays where she is, holding Carolyn's wrist. "I need to pee," she repeats, firm and bright.

Carolyn's jaw sets, and she tilts her head. Mattie nods in shallow motion. "Right. Del, c'mon," Carolyn says, pushing roughly to her feet. Mattie catches her when she stands, and Carolyn wavers on her feet. "Apparently I am incapable of going anywhere on my own."

"Del, help us," Mattie orders.

Del frowns, then pushes her braids back as she stands. "Fine." She wedges a shoulder under Carolyn's arm, and Carolyn stumbles as they move forward. Del waits, taking Carolyn's weight, and Mattie carefully finds a better way to hold up her other side.

It's awkward, but they make their way out to the main lobby; there's a guest bathroom down the hall. Mattie opens the door, then closes it after Carolyn and Del and leans against it, tilting her head to listen. Then she sighs with satisfaction. "He wants to keep an eye on you. But he isn't ready to hear this."

"Pawel?" Carolyn asks.

Mattie dismisses Carolyn's words with a flick of her hand. "He won't understand. You two have been there. You're a part of it. It's in your souls already. He'll never be a part of it the way you are."

"Dreamwalking?" Del asks. She leans against a sink, arms crossed and jaw set. "I'm not—"

"Doesn't matter," Mattie says. "I want to talk to you about the Shadows."

Del looks away.

Carolyn shudders. "There were so many," she says.

Mattie nods and leans forward. "Do you know why?" she whispers.

Carolyn shakes her head. "It felt like they wanted to get to us. Like if they could, they'd attack. But as long as we stayed in the light, they couldn't reach us. If we'd stepped off the path—"

"—into the split," Mattie says sharply. "If you'd stepped into the split, they would have swarmed you. They're starving there, cut off from the worlds, feeding only on Dreamers. They are nightmares, and they will suck souls dry if they can reach them. And they are trying to escape, to crawl out of the split, to find their ways into worlds."

"Worlds," Del says slowly.

"Worlds," Mattie agrees. She gestures with her fingers spread wide, hands held out and palms down. "Every path, every fork in the road, makes another change, leads to somewhere slightly different. A thousand variations, and a thousand choices, make a thousand, thousand worlds and more."

"You're saying that the paths are ways between alternate universes?" Carolyn asks. It matches with her theory that Dreamwalkers might not actually walk through Dreams but instead travel between worlds. Like the place that Nikita has been Dreaming about.

"And the split lies between, filled with soulless creatures," Mattie says, "but there are cracks."

"In the split," Del says slowly. "Cracks in the split, so they can get out of there and into the worlds?"

"Yes." Mattie leans back, pleased. "You understand."

"Not exactly." There's so much information missing, and the biggest piece is: what do they do about it? "They're people, like you."

Mattie makes a small noise. "Not like me. Like I used to be. Emergence splits our souls, strips away our humanity."

"Why are they there instead of here?" Del asks. She pushes away from the sink, steps into Mattie's space, and jabs a finger in her chest. "You were here. You and others, and you killed someone. But Shadows are rare. Legends, really. So how are you here, and why are they there?"

"Once upon a time, there were people who didn't know that we could be healed, so they sought to exile us," Mattie says. "It worked. Mostly. Until now. And the ones who have been locked in the split have been starving since they were sent away. They hunger for souls."

"Were you one of them?" Carolyn asks. She tries to imagine being locked away and staving, mindless and needy. It starts her shuddering again, and she closes her eyes. It doesn't help; all she can see are the shadows reaching for her.

"I'm younger," Mattie says. "One of the others, he told me. He remembers being sucked out of his world. He remembers escaping through a crack into ours."

"Fine. So let's say we accept this information at face value." Del spreads her hands. "How do we fix this? How do we make sure that these Shadows don't invade our world and start sucking down every soul they find?"

"How do you know that leaving them trapped is the solution?" Mattie steps forward, shadows swirling around her. The lights are bright, but Mattie is a spot of darkness formed into solidity. "Think, Del. Think, Carolyn. We are people, too. Do not forget."

The shadows fade; Mattie disappears with them.

Carolyn stumbles forward and catches herself on the edge of the sink. She twists the water on and leans down, cradling water in her hands and splashing it on her face. "I want to sleep for a week," she mumbles.

"What do you think of what she said?" Del asks.

"I think I can't think yet," Carolyn admits. "But it fits in with what I've been studying, with what I need to know. Maybe Pawel knows something about whatever ritual was done, and when it was done. Mattie didn't exactly give a timeframe other than that it happened before she Emerged."

"Can I trust Pawel?" Del examines her hand while Carolyn grabs towels and dries her face.

"To train you, or find someone who can?" Carolyn asks. "Yes. I trust him. But he's stretched thin right now, and he feels responsible."

"Is that why he follows you around like a watch dog?"

Carolyn doesn't think it's that bad, but she can see where Del's coming from. "He cares about his students. Particularly those of us who are doing idiotic things."

Del rolls her eyes. "Fine. I'll try whatever he decides." She catches Carolyn's hand, and as Carolyn turns, she tugs her into a hard hug. "Don't be a stranger. I think we're in this together. Whatever this is."

"Okay," Carolyn agrees, her voice muffled by Del's hair. "I'll keep in touch. I promise."

"We'll figure it out."

Carolyn wants to believe her, but she gets the feeling this is bigger than they can handle. Right now, she'll take figuring out even one small part.

And they got Sam back, safe and sound. That's a win for today.

38

CAROLYN SLEEPS ON the way back to PHU. She curls against Kit's shoulder in the back seat, and her last thought before she slips off is that she hopes Pawel manages to stay awake.

When she finally wakes, she's propped against the side of the car, and Pawel sleeps next to her while Kit drives.

Kit kills the engine, twisting to look back at them as Pawel stirs. "I took over around Sturbridge," he says. "I was the most awake person in the car, and Pawel had to get back for Conor, so we didn't want to stop and stay at a motel." He raises his voice. "We're at your place, Pawel. Carolyn and I can walk from here."

Walking is the last thing Carolyn wants to do, but she recognizes that the bracing, cold air will at least help wake her up. So she nods, slowly unbuckles her seat belt, and climbs out, stretching to try to get blood flowing to her limbs.

She flinches when Pawel slams the door. Her head is still fuzzy, and sounds are too loud. "I can walk," she says in case anyone doubts it. She doubts it. But one foot in front of the other can't be all that hard, right? She takes a step and remains upright, so she supposes that's a plus.

"I'm good," Pawel says, waving Kit toward Carolyn. "You two go. Conor's with Emily, and if all else fails, I'll sleep on Emily's couch. It wouldn't be the first time." He starts up the walkway to the house next door to his own.

"C'mon." Kit hooks his arm through Carolyn's, and her next step is steadier with him by her side. "Let's get you home."

"Douglass," Carolyn corrects his assumption. "I want to see Serina."

Kit keeps walking, slow and steady, and Carolyn moves with him. She feels as if the world tilts on every step, but as long as she stays standing, it's okay.

"Does Serina know you're coming?" Kit asks.

That's a practical question. Carolyn would like to have an answer to it that sounds better than the one she has. "Probably not. Not exactly. I haven't texted her since before the ritual, but I told her I'd try to come by after we got back." She tries to use her free hand to get her phone, but she can't reach into the pocket where it is. She twists, and Kit stops moving to keep her from unbalancing herself. "I'll check my phone."

"I don't think that'll help," Kit catches her hands to stop her. "She knows you're coming, then, but not exactly when, and she has no idea that you're so exhausted that you're as good as drunk."

Carolyn parses through all that and nods slowly. "Sounds about right." She's pretty sure it won't matter. She knows Serina will be there to hold her. Let her lean on her. "Serina's cuddly."

"You really do sound drunk," Kit mutters. He fishes his phone out and sends off a text. "I told Rory, so he can give Serina a heads up or let me know if she's not in her room. Think you can make it that far?"

Carolyn crosses her arms, drawing herself up to her full height. "I am fine. It's the world that's spinning because someone sucked the magic out of it," she says as sharply as she can manage. She's sure it would be impressive if she didn't have to taste each word on the way out to make sure it's the right one. "Serina will make it better."

Kit smiles, huffs a soft laugh. "You really like her, don't you?"

"Didn't you?" Because this seems important to Carolyn, to make sure she really understands how Kit felt. Feels. Everything is so tangled up and confusing.

"Not as much as you," Kit admits. He starts walking, and she follows, no longer needing to cling to stay upright. "Rory, on the other hand…"

"You really like him?" Carolyn's found the cadence of her walk, not quite lurching, but the steps aren't smooth, either. She can feel the way the sidewalk rolls under her toes, the way the earth curves with every step.

"So far, yes." He smiles at her, a quick, bright grin. "I'm heading for Douglass to meet up with him; I'll walk you there."

Carolyn focuses on the walk after that. Her phone buzzes, but she doesn't try to get it out, not sure if she can manage that while moving forward. Thankfully it's not icy, and there are long stretches of sidewalk that have been cleared of lingering snow.

When they arrive at Douglass, Rory and Serina are waiting to let them in. Rory wraps Kit in a tight hug, his face pressed against Kit's hair, and Carolyn blinks to see her brother relax into the embrace. When they step apart, Rory picks up a bag. "I've already got my stuff," he says.

Carolyn doesn't reach for Serina, doesn't do anything but stand there feeling awkward and unhitched from the world.

Kit glances at them. "I'm going to Hayworth with Rory. Are you guys okay?"

"We'll be fine," Serina assures him. She steps closer to Carolyn, placing both hands lightly on her shoulders. "Won't we?"

"Okay," Carolyn agrees. She's lost the thread of the conversation and isn't sure exactly what she's agreed to, but she's with Serina, so she knows she's safe.

"I recommend a lot of sleep," Kit says, and it doesn't sound like a terrible idea, if only there were a bed handy. But Carolyn doesn't see a bed.

"All right, up we go." Serina catches Carolyn's hands, tugging her toward the stairs.

Oh yes, stairs. To the second floor. Where Serina's room is and where there happens to be a bed. For sleeping in. Nothing else. And, oh, that reminds Carolyn that there are things she should talk to Serina about. Maybe once they're in the room, except... "Becky?"

"She went home for the weekend," Serina says. "So if you don't want to share my bed—which would be totally okay, you know, I don't want to make you uncomfortable—I can sleep in hers, and you can crash in mine. You might get more sleep that way anyway. These beds are really small. I mean, how do people like Rory and Alaric share one without someone ending up on the floor?"

Carolyn remembers Drea talking about how Alaric and Rory sleep like Clan. "I think Rory sleeps on top of Alaric," she says slowly, nodding because the words taste right. "Yes. That. They probably take up less room that way."

"Does it bother Kit that his boyfriend sleeps with someone else?" Serina asks.

They crest the top of the second-floor landing, and Carolyn pauses, head tilted and brow furrowed. "Why would he?" she asks. "It's only sleep." It's funny how people get jealous. Like sleeping automatically means something else. Like touching means something else. Like there's only one way to be. She purses her lips. "Shawn got jealous. I didn't like it. He said mean things when he was jealous, and we argued."

"I don't think you want to have this conversation in the hall," Serina says quickly, tugging on Carolyn's hand again. Carolyn stumbles after her, finding her footing after a few stuttered steps.

There are people in the lounge, and something that smells good bubbles on the stove in the tiny kitchenette. Carolyn waves, and they wave back before Serina pulls her onward. They go around to the right, then to the right again, all the way to the end of the hall where Serina and Becky's room is tucked in the corner. Music spills out of the room next door, and Carolyn pauses, turning toward it curiously.

"Jackson and Patrick are loud," Serina says. She pulls her door open, motioning for Carolyn to go in. "We ignore it. It's funny; I figured the rock star would be the loud one on the floor, but no."

"Trish isn't loud either," Carolyn muses. Maybe it's because they're so public normally that it feels good to be quiet at other times. Or maybe it's just a mask. Everyone wears a mask, after all. She wore a lovely mask all through high school. She's avoided masks in college, until recently.

She can keep this new mask on, or she can let Serina see her.

She thinks she wants Serina to see her.

"Do you want to see me?" Carolyn asks, and Serina tilts her head. "The real me," she clarifies. "All of me."

"Please don't get naked when you sound like you're drunk." Serina digs through a drawer, then holds out a T-shirt and shorts. "The bottoms'll be really short on you because you're so much taller than me, but I want us both to be dressed when we wake up in the morning. No poorly thought-out decisions."

Carolyn looks at the bundle of fabric that Serina has shoved in her hands. "I didn't mean naked," she says. She turns around and starts changing while she's talking. "Shawn didn't know me. And I don't think he liked me, not really. But I like you, and it'll be easier if you know me than if you don't. And I know that's complicated and messy, so it's okay if you say no, and I'll put the mask back on. I can try to be that other me. She pretends okay sometimes, but it's uncomfortable and weird and I know I'm kind of broken most of the time. But I can try if that's what you want."

Silence.

Carolyn drops her bra on the floor, then pulls Serina's T-shirt over her head. It's soft and worn, and she suspects it's bigger on Serina than it is on herself. She tugs it down self-consciously, but it rides up again like a crop top.

When she looks up, Serina is staring at her, strangely silent, her mouth open in a small "O."

"I don't want you to feel like you have to wear any kind of a mask around me," Serina says. "Carolyn. Caro. I just want to know you, okay? Like, this is me. Scattered and kind of weird and I just…I mean…I don't know how to be any other way. And I really hope you're comfortable enough to be honest with me, too."

"Oh." Carolyn's knees feel weak, but there's no chair so she sinks down to sit cross-legged on the floor. "Okay."

Serina picks up Carolyn's bra, moves it out of the way, and sits next to her. "Okay?" she asks.

Carolyn nods. "Okay. I think. But you might not like me. Shawn didn't."

"I get the feeling that this story is going to end with me not really liking Shawn," Serina says, "but I'd like to hear it, if you want to tell me." She tangles her fingers with Carolyn's and leans into her shoulder, and Carolyn leans back. She likes the feel of Serina's warm weight against her. It's good. Comforting.

"You like kissing." Carolyn says, because that's going to be part of the problem here. She's come to terms with it, and despite what she told Kit, she knows it wasn't entirely about Shawn or the kumquats. It was about her. "I'm not a good kisser. And I saw you kissing Kit, and you really, really liked it. And I just—I don't think I can do that. When I think about someone—even you—putting their tongue in my mouth, it makes me panic."

Serina rubs a finger along Carolyn's hand. "All right. You don't like kissing. I'm fine with that."

"You want to tingle," Carolyn protests.

"I already told you that holding hands with you feels better than kissing Kit did," Serina counters. "If you're not ready to kiss, that's fine. If you're not ever ready to kiss, that's fine, too. If you want to make rules about kissing, or about anything else, that's totally fine, Carolyn." Serina lifts Carolyn's hand, pausing with it in front of her lips. "May I?"

Carolyn nods, and Serina brushes her lips lightly against the back of Carolyn's fingers before lowering their linked hands again.

Carolyn closes her eyes. She can feel sleep threatening to overtake her, but she wants to get this out. The words are there, now, just before the tip of her tongue. She feels like she could push them, force them to pass her lips. Other times, they're further away, harder to summon. She wants to tell Serina while it feels possible.

"We were all together today," she says. "We brought Sam back from where he's been stuck. And it's the first time I've been that close to Shawn since high school. Since the ritual that messed everything up. But we were already a mess before that. I told Kit that Shawn and I had broken up. I didn't tell him why."

"Do you want to tell me?"

Carolyn loves that Serina gives her the out. Lets her make her own choice whether to speak or not, rather than demanding more information. "Yes," she whispers. She breathes through the frustration and fear, ordering the words in her mind. She tries to wrangle them into neat lines, ready to march out and be heard. "It was a few things. Shawn was jealous. Always. He was angry when I spent time alone with Sam, or even with Del. He thought—he saw sex everywhere. He couldn't believe that I could hang out with someone and be physically close to them without ending up in bed with them. And because I wasn't in bed with him, at least not as much as he wanted, he was angry thinking that I might be with someone else."

Serina makes a soft noise, encouraging. She strokes Carolyn's arm gently.

"We argued all the time about it," Carolyn says. She turns her face toward Serina's shoulder, hides there in the crook of her neck. "One time, he asked if I was falling in love with Del. She was with Sam, and I said no, I wasn't. Not with Del. But that sometimes I thought maybe I might like girls, too." Carolyn hesitates, then continues, "He was the first person I admitted that too. And he said that if there were certain things—physical things—I wouldn't do with him, then he couldn't imagine I'd do them with a girl. So I couldn't be bi."

"He was wrong," Serina murmurs. She kisses Carolyn's forehead. "He really was wrong, and he didn't know what was in your heart. He couldn't."

"But I still don't—" Carolyn struggles, failing to find the right words. "I'm not sure I'll ever—and then you'll get angry. Just like he did. Because I'm selfish. It's not that I hate— It's that I—" She can't continue. Instead she burrows closer, kisses the small spot at the crook of Serina's neck, and tastes the salt of her skin.

Serina's breath hitches softly, and she exhales on a sigh. "Lemme try translating here," she says. "You think you can't be bi because you're not sure you want to be all-the-way physical with a girl. But you also didn't want to be all-the-way physical with a guy. Am I following right?"

It's more complicated than that, but Carolyn nods because none of that is wrong.

"And you think you're selfish because there are things you do like doing, and you're not ready to talk about that part yet," Serina continues, kissing Carolyn's temple when she nods again. "And you think that I'll end up like him, wanting more than you do and angry at you when you still don't want to."

"I don't want you to hate me because I'm broken. I want to move on, forget about how everything he said hurt me and how it stuck under my skin and still makes me question everything."

"If I say that I don't think you're broken, and I think you can totally fall in love with boys and girls even if you don't necessarily want to get physically intimate in all possible ways…does that help?" Serina touches her cheek, then waits until Carolyn looks at her. "Because right now—this? This is way more intimate than if we were both naked and groping each other. We can figure out what works for us together, and I'm okay with that. We just need to talk, because Carolyn, I really, really like you, and I want to give this a chance, and I'm hoping you want to do that, too."

Carolyn can feel Serina's lower lip quivering, and she's afraid Serina's going to start crying, so she does the one thing she can think of and presses her lips to Serina's. Close-mouthed and quick, a press of flesh together as if to seal a promise.

"I really, really like you, too," she whispers, hiccupping. "When I woke up in the car, I wanted nothing but to come over here so I could feel like how I feel when you're holding me. I want to let go of everything in the past. Sam's back. I don't think I'll ever need to talk to Shawn again, unless I have to because of Del. And Del and I might be friends again."

"Then why don't we move to the bed, because it'll be way more comfortable to hold you there." Serina stands and offers her hands to Carolyn, helping her stumble to her feet. "Leave the past where it is, and we'll start fresh. You and me—we'll figure out what works for us. It doesn't have to be anything like what works for anyone else. And don't worry about making me tingle, Carolyn." Serina frames her face, looking up at her with a soft smile. "You do that just by being you. And yes, I'm sappy, and I'm going to keep being sappy all over you until you realize that I mean it. Okay?"

Carolyn's hand shakes when she touches Serina's wrist; she kisses the palm of Serina's hand. "Okay," she agrees, even though she thinks there are still land mines, that Serina's going to step on them and they'll explode. But maybe that won't happen, or maybe Serina will be able to navigate around them.

Carolyn's willing to give them both a chance.

Through Hopes and Fears

Ninth Position: Hopes & Fears

Through hopes and fears...

Throughout the reading, the querent has faced the truth about the obstacles that stand in their way. This card simplifies the reading to clarify the two most basic paths that the querent may take toward their future: their greatest hope and their greatest fear. For some, this card may show one or the other, for others, the same influence may light both paths. It is for the querent to recognize this aspect of themselves and to acknowledge how it might change their route to their final outcome. They must face their fears and choose risks to achieve their hopes.

Carolyn's Reading: Princess of Swords (Reversed)

A young woman stands in full light, a bird of prey by her side ready to fight. She carries a sword but does not wield it; it has a flower where the hilt should be. She is graceful and dangerous.

This card is that of the right-hand woman in a position of authority. She is the trickster who aids the leader, the Mage who uses illusion and sleight of hand to bring about a coup. While she is not the leader, she is the instigator—the one who truly holds power and who has the intelligence and wit to see plans through.

However, she is also representative of the unforeseen—the chance that plans can fail, that cracks can widen and shatter until that which is stable falls to ruin. She can be frivolous yet severe, pushing forward her plans without thought for consequences.

This card draw suggests that the querent hopes for great success and fears that success will come with a price or may crumble a the last second. Take this card as a caution: look beyond the pretty face of any problem and see the truth behind the attractive exterior. Do not be deceived, and gains will be true.

Kit's Reading: The Queen of Pentacles

A beautiful woman stands partly bared to nature, pouring water from a jug into a flowing stream of pure water. The sun rises, flowers bloom, and birds take flight in the purity of her surroundings.

This is a card of the soul, of the melding of the energies that create a person as they travel through life. People are tempered by their experiences, and some moments burn hotter than others. Like a blade in a forge, there is always a chance that a soul will become harder, persevering through all, but there is also a chance to become brittle, easily shattered.

The querent fears that change will break them, that each new experience will weigh too heavily, and that they will be unable to manage the stress. The querent must reach within to find the hope of perfect tempering, must strive to not shatter into a thousand pieces. Find the blending that makes the soul bloom, and rejoice.

39

A WEEK AFTER returning from the sanitorium, Carolyn is still off-kilter. She finally feels rested, but the world seems dreamlike and not quite real. It's strange to text with Sam, to have him coherent and home and texting her back. Del has become a constant in her life, sending random photos of her campus and snippets about her life. They both fit back into Carolyn's days as if they've never been gone.

They have a group text as well, all five of them, as if it's still high school and they're discussing where to meet for lunch or what prank to pull. Carolyn's quieter there; she's not ready to interact with Shawn. She can keep Del and Sam as her buffers in that space, at least.

It's easier to see now, after years have passed, how set apart Kit is from the rest of them. He chats, yes, but his life has veered down a different path. Carolyn's not sure if she's on the same path as Kit, or if she's just pushed herself back onto the path with her old friends, or if she's found a new path of her own.

Heather is her rock amidst it all, and Carolyn leans on her in ways she hasn't allowed herself to since Nikita came into their lives. Nikita doesn't sleep in their room during that week, and Carolyn falls asleep each night with Heather's hand on her shoulder, lulling her to quiet. It's peaceful to let go and not worry about processing everything yet. Heather lets her temporarily forget, let's her put the more difficult emotions in a neat little box, waiting to be opened later. It won't work forever, but it lets her reach Friday without panicking. Classes are done, and Carolyn's sitting in her room with Heather waiting for Kit and Nikita to join them. Then her phone pings, and Carolyn's heart starts racing as she looks down at the screen.

We're here and checked into that same motel as last time. Are you sure we want to do this?

Heather places a hand on Carolyn's shoulder, and Carolyn breathes in the induced calm. She can almost imagine the lemon scent that Alaric always says Heather exudes, and she exhales slowly. *Yes*, she sends back. *I don't think it's that we want to do it. We need to. You need to hear what Nik has to say, and she needs to hear about what Mattie told us. The only way we're going to figure anything out—and keep the bad stuff from happening again—is to share as much information as we can.*

And if your friend Nik and I drag the entire town into the dreamscape? Del replies.

Heather's grip on Carolyn's shoulder tightens.

You won't, Carolyn types. *Nikita's under control when she's with Heather. And I'm not going to let you turn into Dream-Del again. We brought you back, and we'll bring you back again if we have to. No one gets lost.*

There's a knock on the door, then it opens and Nikita's there. Kit stands in the hall behind her, his beanie pulled low over his ears and his phone in his hand as he texts.

They're here, Carolyn sends. *We'll be there soon and we'll bring dinner.*

"Are we walking?" Nikita asks. "How far away is it?"

Kit glances up from his phone, brow furrowed and expression concerned.

"We borrowed Trish's truck." Carolyn digs into her jacket pocket to find the keys, brandishing them while attempting to get her jacket on. "Kit, you're driving. She says I'm too out of it this week, and Heather doesn't like to drive."

"I'm guessing I don't have a say in this," Kit mutters, catching the keys when she tosses them to him. "You know, I thought about going out tonight. Trying that 'dating' thing."

"But Rory's busy," Nikita points out. "He and Thorne are recording something or other. Demos, I think. They're trying to sort out which tracks are going to make the cut for the new album."

Carolyn hears what Kit isn't saying: that he doesn't want to stay on this path any longer than he has to. "Thank you," she says quietly. "I think we're close to finishing whatever we've started, and then we can move forward, right?"

Kit gets an arm around her shoulders when she approaches and squeezes her tightly. He's only a couple inches taller than her, but it's enough that he can kiss her temple easily. "It'll be better when we can start moving forward," he murmurs. "Even looking back will be easier then."

Carolyn nods, then motions toward the stairs. She leads the way to where Trish's truck is parked, and she pulls the seats forward so Heather and Nikita can climb into the back.

It takes Kit a little time to find the right settings for the seat—he's taller than Trish, but her legs are longer—then the truck comes to life with a roar. He drives carefully, staying far from the cars parked on the side of the road and avoiding the oncoming traffic. His jaw is tight and set, and he parks far from other cars when he reaches the motel lot.

Carolyn has the room number; they're on the first floor this time, and Del opens the door as they approach.

Heather clasps Nikita's hand, murmuring something as they walk together. Nikita lifts her hand, and Del waves back just as cautiously.

"I can do this," Nikita says, and she moves ahead of the others, Heather still connected to her but trailing behind. She reaches Del and holds out her hand. "Hi. Let's test this and see if we can do it."

Del looks at her warily. "All I'm going to say is that if we end up in a forest or a fragrant field, I'm over it." She clasps Nikita's hand and closes her eyes, wincing.

Nothing happens.

Nikita shudders, lets go of Del, and moves closer to Heather. "Okay, so, on my part it isn't easy, but I can hold on. It's like—I feel this weird sensation over my entire body, like I'm exhausted and wide awake and I want to explode outwards, and I'm pretty sure that's power. Maybe we should've called Rory, too."

"Still could," Kit offers, phone in his hand.

Del shakes her head. "I think we'll be okay. I'm a little light-headed, but I can focus. And I don't know if you noticed, but it's snowing."

Carolyn turns around and looks, and there are indeed snowflakes drifting through the air.

"It was supposed to snow tonight," Nikita says. "I don't think that's me."

Del steps back, then pulls the door wide. "Come on in before you get wet, I guess."

Shawn's in the way, standing just beyond Del, and Carolyn pushes past him to get to Sam. He already looks better than he did a week ago, and when he captures her in a hug, his grip is strong and sure.

"You look good," she murmurs, her face pressed against his.

"I sent you pictures," Sam tells her.

"I didn't believe them." They only added to the sense of unreality this week. She touches his face, feels the smoothness of his skin. "I needed to see you in person. I'm glad you came."

"Can we get down to business? Because I feel like my skin could crawl away on its own, and I'm blaming proximity to Nikita," Del snaps. She crosses her arms tightly and leans against Shawn, who wraps his arms around her.

"Seconded." Nikita's found a spot on the bed, Heather sitting next to her. She has Heather's hand tight in her grip, so tight that her knuckles are pale and Heather's fingers are darker. Heather brushes over the top of their clasped hands, and Nikita's grip eases.

Everyone looks to Carolyn, and she's not sure how she's ended up in charge but apparently she is. "We need to talk about the split," she announces, even though she feels like she's in uncharted territory on this topic, "and we need to talk about Nik's Dreams, and how the forest intertwines with everything. And how traveling works, and what it means for us." She gestures between herself, Nikita, and Del. "I think we're each using different aspects of the same Emergent Talent. We were all Mages before: Weather Witch, predictive, and Del's generalized magic. Something's changed, and I think everything's tangled together."

"We're probably affecting each other, too," Del comments. "Especially when we're together."

"But it started before we three met," Carolyn points out. "For you, it started almost three years ago, and for me, who knows when it really started, but it became noticeable just a few months ago. And Nikita changed when she came to PHU. That's why we need to talk."

"Fine." Sam moves forward. "Let's start with the forest, and the Shadows."

"The Shadows are in Nikolai's world, too," Nikita points out. "They're everywhere there, and they're dangerous to the Talented people. Between them and being hunted by humans, Talented people are in danger, and Nikolai's on the run."

Del's gaze goes sharp. "Okay, no, let's start with a clearer explanation of that. Who's world?"

Nikita fidgets, patting and stroking along Heather's hand. "When my weather magic goes haywire, I'm usually asleep. We thought it meant I was having nightmares, which turned out to be true. I've started remembering the Dreams recently. In those Dreams, I'm someone named Nikolai, and he's on the run. He's got this whole life, and I keep seeing him—being him, really. It's easier when I'm with Heather. I don't panic, so I don't cause storms, but I still Dream, and it's like I'm there."

"And his world?" Del prods.

"Chaos," Nikita says. "A decade ago, it was overrun by Shadows. They started attacking people with Talent, and that brought magic out in public. The humans blamed the magical people for what was happening with the Shadows, so they started attacking them, too. People with Talent have retreated—at least, I think that's what's happened. I only know what Nikolai thinks about or what he and Seth talk about. But Nikolai and Seth are on the run. They're going from safehouse to safehouse, trying to find some kind of settlement that I think is near here. A safe community so they can fight back."

"So you're Dreaming some other entire life, in another world," Del says slowly.

"That sounds like events happening in one of the Shadow-infested worlds outside of the forest," Sam says. "I saw a lot of those when I was trying to find my way out. More of those than normal ones, but that could have been because of the paths I chose."

"Or it could be that the Shadows are escaping from the split, like Mattie said, and some worlds have more cracks than others to let them in," Del murmurs.

It sounds logical to Carolyn. And disturbing. "What keeps our world from cracking? How do we know Nikolai and his world are real?"

"We go there," Kit says. He leans forward with his elbows on his knees. "We see if we can open some way to that place, and we go. Just like we did to get to Sam."

"They weren't in different worlds," Carolyn points out.

"Won't know if we don't try," Kit retorts. "It's worth a shot."

"You want to go directly there, not through the Dreamscape?" Del asks. She slumps when he nods. "Good. The split—that's all the spaces off the path in the Dreamscape. My space—my field—is safe. And the paths seem safe as long as you don't stray off of them."

"I saw people disappear into shadow," Sam confirms. "They were there, on the path ahead of me, then they veered off and—"

"—fell into the split," Carolyn finishes. "That's what Mattie said not to do."

Sam nods. "Exactly. The thing is, the paths keep getting smaller, and there seem to be more Shadows."

"More people without souls," Del says. "Why?"

"Do you think that if we go to Nikolai, I'll stop Dreaming about him?" Nikita asks, shifting the topic abruptly. She grips Heather again, and Heather's expression is drawn and pained. "Because if I stop having those nightmares, then I'll stop worrying about him, and my power will stop going out of control, and things can go back to normal. So I'm in for Kit's idea of going there."

Kit rises, grabbing his bag. "Why don't you and I go outside and talk about that place? I need a good description of it."

The door slams as Kit and Nikita exit, Heather following quickly after.

"I don't think it's the same," Del says quietly.

"I don't think it'll hurt to try," counters Carolyn, "and Kit can get the sketches done quickly. Maybe we'll still end up going through the Dreamscape. Either way, I think it'll take all of us to do this again. And we'll need to be ready for it tomorrow." When Shawn starts to protest, Carolyn shakes her head and cuts him off. "You guys can rest here tonight."

"We'll be fine," Sam says.

"You could stay here if you want," Del offers, pointing at the other bed. "Platonically, obviously. Pick whoever you want to crash with, and we can talk tonight."

"No, I think—" She cuts off. She feels jumpy and anxious. She wants to spend time with Serina. She wants to see her, let her know what's going to happen and what they're going to try. "I need to relax tonight before we do this, and as much as I miss how we were together before things went upside down, staying here won't be relaxing."

"I understand." Sam opens his arms and wraps her into a warm hug. Del does the same after, her braids heavy against Carolyn's cheek.

When they separate, Shawn stands there, his hands in his pockets as he watches her.

Carolyn isn't ready to hug him.

"Can we talk?" Shawn asks.

Carolyn drops her gaze, turns away slightly. She pulls out her phone and sends a text to Serina. *I'm about done here. I'm going to walk over to see you. Be there soon.*

She puts her phone back in her pocket, keeping her gaze and her tone even when she looks at Shawn. "Sure. Let's go outside and talk."

She's not ready for this, but then, she doesn't think she'll ever be ready. And if they can have clear hearts and minds tomorrow, they'll probably be better off.

Doesn't mean she's happy about this conversation, though.

Kit's nowhere in sight when they get outside, although Trish's truck still sits where he parked it. As Carolyn approaches, she realizes that Nikita and Heather are sitting in the truck, in the back. She pulls open the driver's side door and leans in, doing her best not to pay attention as they untangle themselves.

"Where's Kit?"

Nikita shoves her hair out of her face. "He walked back to Douglass so he could get started as soon as possible on making the art with Rory. He left the keys with us. We didn't want to go back inside. Are you ready?" Her gaze shifts from Carolyn to Shawn, and her brow furrows.

Carolyn shakes her head, all too aware of how close behind her Shawn stands. "Not yet. I need to talk to Shawn first, then I'll drive us back. You guys stay warm, and I'll go do this."

The keys are sitting on the driver's seat, so she grabs and pockets them, then closes the door to give Nikita and Heather some semblance of privacy. When she turns around, Shawn's too close, and Carolyn steps sideways to put space between them. "This isn't a conversation I want to have with anyone listening," she says, walking back to the motel.

"I don't think they're going to eavesdrop," Shawn says.

"It's not that." Carolyn stops when she gets back to the motel room. She wants to lean on something, have something to hold her up, but she doesn't want to feel trapped between Shawn and the wall. She leans her shoulder against it, standing sideways so he has to do the same to face her. "I don't think Del and Sam will go out of their way to listen in, either. I just don't feel like being aware that we have an audience."

"Right." Shawn stands in front of the door, his arms crossed and his legs slightly spread. He looks combative. Stubborn. It's familiar, and it makes her skin crawl. "Are you ever going to talk to me again?"

"We're here right now," Carolyn says. "Talking." She knows that's not what he means, but she wants him to say it, wants him to have to state that he actually understands what's wrong.

Shawn scowls, mumbling something under his breath.

Carolyn tilts her head. "What was that?"

"I didn't mean to hurt you," he grinds out, and the words punch the air out of Carolyn's lungs.

"But you did," she says when she can breathe again.

"I know."

She stands there, hugging herself. He knows he did damage; that's one step. She's still not sure he knows how or why it happened. "Do you?" she asks quietly. "Do you even understand what you did?"

"I made you uncomfortable." The words are slow and steady. Rehearsed enough that Carolyn wonders if Del's been coaching him, and if she did, how she knew what Shawn should say.

"You didn't want to take 'no' for an answer," she replies just as slowly. Carefully. Needing him to hear every single word she says.

"I didn't force you to do anything." Quick this time. Defensive, throwing walls up between them, denying his culpability even as he apologizes for it. "I had no idea—"

"I didn't know myself," Carolyn replies, tone sharp. She teeters, wobbling in place, stance brittle as though she could be blown back at any moment. "I didn't even know—I didn't know that kind of sexuality existed."

His gaze narrows, and he takes a step forward. "You thought you were bi," he says.

She takes a step back, maintaining the distance between them, making sure she has room to retreat. "I am bi," she says firmly. "Romantically. Sexually…that's a different story. I hate kissing. I didn't want to have sex then. I'm not even sure I want to have it now."

"You certainly liked it when I—"

She raises a hand to cut him off before he can dig up old arguments, use worn phrases as knives against her. "It's complicated," she says, and she feels down to her bones the impossibility of putting her feelings into words. "There are things I like the idea of, and things that make me feel cold. There are things I think might be okay, but not right now. And things that are okay when I do them on my own, but not when I do them with someone else. And I don't know how to encapsulate it except that I might be gray asexual. Or demisexual. I'm not sure either of those really, truly fits, but I know I'm something and it's not…it's not allosexual. I may not have the words for it yet, but the point is—I said 'no,' Shawn."

"Whenever it involved what I wanted," he grumbles. Another step forward, and she holds her ground this time, looking at him as he says, "Whenever it involved you, you were fine."

"It's a control thing, sometimes," she admits. "The point is, you shouldn't have—"

"We were both young and stupid," he says flatly.

Her mouth snaps shut when he interrupts her. She stares at him, confused and hurt once more. "I can't argue with either of those points," she says, "but neither absolves you. Any five-year-old knows that 'no' means 'no,' and we were seventeen. So no, I'm not sure I can forgive you for how fucked-up our relationship was. I can't forgive you for the things you said that made me feel guilty for how I felt about sex, nor for making me doubt how I feel about people."

"I had no idea—"

"Doesn't matter." She doesn't want to let him finish another excuse. She licks her lips. "It doesn't matter what you did or didn't know. Maybe we could've figured it out together. Or maybe you thought girlfriend equaled sex, and I thought boyfriend equaled love, and we were both really, really wrong. And when it blew up in our faces, it also blew up everything for everyone we cared about."

Shawn frowns, hands slowly dropping to his sides. "You think we were what went wrong with the ritual?"

"I think we weren't cohesive by then," Carolyn says, the words welling up because she's been mulling this over for a while now. "We'd broken up, and we'd said we could still be friends, but I lied about that. I didn't want to touch you, and I didn't want to share energy with you, and my reluctance could have put cracks in the ritual. But I couldn't say it then because if I had, I'd have just proved everything you'd said about me. That I was cold. Unwilling to touch. That I couldn't bridge the distance between us. I tried to be who I was supposed to be, and I cracked us wide open."

Shawn stares at her, his brow furrowed in deep confusion. "I don't understand how you can say that you don't like—"

"Stop." She can't take this anymore. "Just—I get it, you don't understand. And you don't need to understand; it's been a long time since we were together. But you need to accept it. You need to accept that I'm not broken, and if you say I am, I swear to God I am going to punch you."

He takes a step back, raising his hands. "Look, I didn't mean—"

"Yes, you did." She's not yelling; she's stating a fact. "You thought we should, so you thought I should, and when I didn't want to, you thought we should anyway because maybe I just didn't get it. Maybe I'd like it if we tried. I didn't want to push my limits that way. I should have been better about saying what I needed to say other than just saying 'no.'" She looks him in the eye as she says, "And you should have been better about listening to what I did say and asking questions when you didn't understand me."

"Fine." Shawn lowers his hands, finally taking one small step back. "I'm the evil one in this scenario. I get it."

Carolyn laughs; she can't help it. It's so far from funny that she wants to cry from the stress, but doing that won't help anything right now. "I'm not saying you're evil," she says. "Although yes, I did think you were for a long time. But I realized you were operating under the impression that we were having an entirely different conversation than we were. I didn't have the words to get you on the same page as me. And I'm glad we broke up, and it's taken me a while to realize that it's okay that you're with Del because you're probably not hurting her. You guys are more compatible than you and I were. I'm glad you've both found that. But I can't give you absolution for what happened between us, and I can't completely stop being angry about how you made me feel about myself. Okay?"

Shawn's jaw is tight, his shoulders hunched, and Carolyn wonders what Del's said to him. What she may have figured out.

She steps forward and touches his forearm. "If you want to try to understand my side of the conversation, read up on asexuality. That might help you understand a little."

A soft cough.

When Carolyn turns, Serina is standing there. Serina wiggles her fingers in a small wave and comes forward to wrap her arms around Carolyn and cuddle in close.

"Hey," Serina says.

"Hey." Carolyn leans down, and they brush noses. When Carolyn looks back at Shawn, he's watching them carefully. "Shawn, this is my girlfriend Serina. Serina, this is my ex Shawn. We're trying to figure out how to be friends again." She doesn't say that it might not be possible; she has to make the effort. For Del, and for Sam.

Serina keeps her arms wrapped around Carolyn. "I'd say nice to meet you, but Carolyn's upset, so I can't." She shrugs, making a face. "Maybe next time. I am really glad Caro's made up with her high-school friends, and I'm glad she yelled at you. I'm kind of falling in love with the person she's become. She's pretty amazing."

"She'll never sleep with you," Shawn mutters.

"We sleep together all the time," Serina says cheerily. "It's awesome, because honestly, is there anything better than waking up snuggled in bed with someone warm who you really like? I don't care if she never wants to have sex." She wriggles her fingers in the air as if to dismiss the thought entirely. "It's not like it's a big deal."

The door opens; Shawn jerks in place, then turns around as Sam steps out. Shawn grabs the door before it can swing closed and heads into the room without a word.

"Am I interrupting something?" Sam watches the door close behind Shawn, turning back once it thunks shut.

"I don't mind the interruption," Carolyn says. Serina rubs her back, and Carolyn relaxes by inches, slowly letting go of the tension from her shoulders and unclenching her hands. It feels good to have Serina pressed up close to her, supporting her.

"Del's been telling me your theory about how everyone's abilities changed after high school," he says. He points, and Carolyn sees a bench down by the vending machines. She's relieved to have a chance to sit; her legs are shaking.

Sam continues speaking after they're settled. "I know I said some things while I was trapped that support your theory, but now that I'm out, I don't necessarily think you're right."

Carolyn clenches and unclenches her hands. "It makes no sense for me to suddenly have illusion Talent," she says, looking down at her fingers.

"It does if you're Emerging," he says. He takes her hand in his and turns it over. When he touches her palm with his finger, a flame flickers to life, burning without heat. "I still have my illusions. You didn't steal them."

"What about Shawn taking my power?" Carolyn asks. "What about how overpowered he was after the ritual, and how he's lost everything now?"

Sam gestures, and the fire turns to light. He sends it up, and it bursts overhead in a silent sparkle of fireworks. "I think it's a natural progression that was sparked by the ritual," he says. "My illusions were suppressed in the Dreamscape, so I thought I'd lost them. Now that I'm back in the real world, I'm not stuck in a nightmare anymore."

"And the rest of us?" It makes a kind of sense, but Carolyn's still not sure.

"I think it was always there, but the ritual sparked it inside of you," Sam says. "Shawn's burnt himself out, but it's probably temporary. I think his magic will come back eventually. Your illusions aren't like mine, and

Del—well, we sent her into the Dreamscape, and we all know how that turned out."

Carolyn closes her eyes and is quiet for a long time. "I'm glad you're back," she finally says.

"I'm glad I'm back, too. I'm going to be in therapy for a while; it's still hard to convince myself to sleep," Sam admits. "But even therapy is better than being stuck inside that place a moment longer. Thank you for coming to get me."

"Any time," Carolyn says, and she means it. When he hugs her, she lingers over the contact, grateful to have him back.

"Did you guys figure out what you wanted to figure out tonight?" Serina asks. She wrinkles her nose. "I know you said you'd walk over, but I decided to come meet you. Any excuse to see you a little longer. I passed Kit; he was heading back to campus. So I figured you guys were done?"

Carolyn stands slowly, offering a hand to Serina and feeling settled when she takes it and stands as well. "We're as done as we're going to be tonight," she says. "We're doing a ritual tomorrow. I'll tell you about it on the way back. Heather and Nik are waiting in the truck."

"Okay. I'll wait there, too. You say your goodbyes." Serina leans up to press a kiss to her cheek.

Sam stops her, one hand light on Serina's shoulder. "Hey," he says, voice low. "It's good to meet you. Keep being good to Carolyn."

Serina's smile is bright. "I fully intend to."

"Are you set?" Sam checks in with her as Serina walks away.

Tough question. It's been an emotionally loaded night, but Carolyn feels like she's gotten a lot off her chest. Like she can finally let go of things and move forward. "I'm on the right path," she says, and she steals one more hug before stepping away. "I'll see you tomorrow when it's time to go down the next rabbit hole."

40

THEY SQUEEZE INTO the motel room again on Saturday morning after an early brunch. Rory was with them at first, but he left Kit with a kiss as he headed off to the library to do some research. Serina, however, sticks close to Carolyn, refusing to leave.

"I don't think we need Rory's energy," Kit says when Serina checks again whether Rory should be there. "He'd overpower me, and that would unbalance the ritual. We have the art, and that's what's important here."

"This is…" Nikita smooths the pieces of paper she has spread out on the bed. "These are chilling," she admits. "It's like seeing my memories in black and white. You've really captured the aura of how I felt. Like, I didn't tell you anywhere near this much detail, and it's still all here."

Carolyn picks up the picture of the safehouse Nikita had described. It's little more than a cabin in the woods, canned goods open on the table, a fire in the fireplace. A young man sits in a chair by the table, his head half turned toward the viewer. The picture looks as if it's been drawn from the point of view of someone talking to him. His glasses are tilted and look oft repaired, sliding down on his nose. His cheeks are round, his body heavy beneath a baggy T-shirt. His brow is furrowed, his mouth open; he's been caught mid-sentence.

"That's Seth," Nikita says, tapping the picture. "You've captured him perfectly. I think he's Nikolai's Heather. He even looks a little like her."

The glasses. The short, round build. The faint freckles. Seth's not smiling in the image, but Carolyn imagines his eyes would crinkle like Heather's do, lighting up. Even his hair seems to have that same tight curl, close against his head then frizzing out because it's long and unkempt. Heather's curls soften to a halo she tries to keep pulled back; Carolyn remembers her saying it's easier to keep it long, the weight tugging the curl straighter, than to take care of it short.

"Now what?" Shawn sits on the other bed, his back against the wall, his knees drawn up, and his arms crossed. He's still defensive, staring at Carolyn like she's a puzzle he has yet to figure out.

"Now we decide exactly how we're doing this." Heather lays a hand on Nikita's shoulder, then slides it to idly rub at the nape of her neck. "How we can be safe about it. I'm not ritualistic, in general, but I know how rituals are supposed to work."

"Should we talk to Pawel?" Del gestures toward campus, and Carolyn's struck by the easy familiarity with which she says his name.

"How are you getting along with him?" she asks.

Del rolls her eyes. "We've been talking constantly. He hooked me up with some Dreamweaver dude near my campus, and I've started talking to him, too, but we haven't met up yet. Your professor is fascinated by anything he doesn't understand, isn't he?"

"That's why we don't tell him," Kit says quietly. "Right, Carolyn?"

They all look at her, and she wonders again how she became their ringleader. Shawn's lips are pursed and thin. Sam's waiting for her to speak, his expression open and encouraging, his body leaning toward her from where he sits on the edge of the bed. Del picks up another piece of art, looking at it, silently waiting. Heather continues to toy with Nikita's hair.

Kit coughs.

Oh. Right. She needs to speak.

"We can apologize later," Carolyn says. "He'd say no. He'd say we're not prepared, and he'd be right."

"What about the Shadows?" Del asks.

"Rory texted Mattie; she'll be around somewhere, but we won't see her," Kit says. "That should keep any others from coming after us."

"Right." It seems everything's set except the final plan. "Then I guess we need to get started. Nikita, is that the best picture of Nikolai's home?" Carolyn asks.

Nikita lifts the one of the safehouse and hands it to Carolyn. "Yes. It's exactly like I've seen it when I'm Dreaming of being Nikolai. Do you really think you can get us there if it's an entirely different world?"

Maybe. She doesn't know.

Carolyn takes the picture gingerly, looking at it. It feels like Kit's art; it feels almost as if it's a part of her, as if she can reach inside of it and bring out the reality. She glances sideways to where he stands close, watching her.

"You're right," she says. "Our Emergent Talents are definitely linked. Mine isn't right without yours."

He squeezes her around the shoulders. "We're twins," he says as if that's all that matters, and she supposes it is.

She leans her head against him for a moment, basking in their closeness. Then she carefully disengages. "We probably shouldn't touch, in case I lose control and go through unexpectedly."

"Do you have a way back?" Serina asks. She stands with her hands clasped behind her, rocking on her toes. She looks like she wants to stand by Carolyn's side, as if she's doing everything she can to stay in one place.

Carolyn reaches into her pocket and pulls out her wallet. She opens it to show the small collection of sketches there—her own room, Serina, Serina's room, Kit, and a few other portraits, including one of Pawel. She organizes them, putting them in the order she thinks she's most likely to try to use them. Her own room is on top because it's familiar, and Serina's and Kit's portraits are after that because they're expecting her to reach out to them. Pawel is next, in case she needs extra, pure power pushed into the connection as they did when they brought Sam back from the Dreamscape. Then she folds the pictures and puts them away again.

"I'm set," she says.

They give her space but stand close enough to grab onto her. Carolyn holds the safehouse sketch loosely in her hands, and the illusion rises bright and quick, expanding to surround them.

Sam slides off the bed, turns in place, and reaches out to touch the table that has sprung into existence next to him. His hand passes through. "It's just an illusion," he says.

"Probably a good thing since we're standing in the middle of it," Del points out. "Last time she swallowed us with an illusion, we traveled through it pretty damn quickly."

Carolyn reaches forward, but there's no sense of pushing through, no feel of a barrier breaking. "It's just an illusion," she agrees. "I can't go through it. I can't get from here to there."

"Maybe I can help." Sam's beside her before she can reject the idea, his hand over hers. She feels the strength of his power, and the illusion grows brighter, stronger. It flickers like there's light streaming in through the tiny window of the cabin, sun sparkling against the aged wood.

It's hyper-realistic, but it's still not real. Carolyn can't touch a thing.

She shakes her head. "It's not working." She puts her hand over the picture, and the illusion drops abruptly. "That's not our way in."

Out of the corner of her eye, she sees Shawn's shoulders sag. "Good," he mutters.

"Do we talk to Pawel now?" Heather asks. Her hand cups the nape of Nikita's neck, and she bites her lip in concentration.

"No," Nikita says. She looks at the picture, wiggling her fingers to silently ask for it, but Carolyn's loathe to let it go. "Maybe I need to be involved. It's my Dreamscape, right?"

Carolyn looks from Nikita to Del. "I'm pretty sure that letting you make Dreams into reality is a bad idea," she says. "Isn't that how Dreamwalkers make entire towns disappear?"

Nikita drops her hand. "You have a point. But it is my space we're trying to get to."

"Maybe we should go about it differently." Del pushes between Nikita and Carolyn, reaching for both of them. "Maybe you can't just barge through the walls between one world and another. And maybe letting that other world—one filled with Shadows—into this one directly is a bad idea. So let's go through the Dreamscape." She nods at Kit. "The forest. You have pictures of it already."

"Several," he agrees, pulling out his sketchbook. "I have the extras from when we went to Sam, ones without him in the picture."

"I still need to be involved because it's my world we're going to," Nikita says stubbornly.

"I'm not saying you shouldn't be." Del looks at Heather. "But we don't want to drag everyone along. I need to be involved because we're talking about physically going into the Dreamscape, not bringing it here. And we need to be careful about the split."

"I have to go because I'm opening the portals," says Carolyn. "Plus someone needs to keep you on the path. Dream-Del likes to go skipping off wherever."

"Should I come to carry her out?" Shawn asks. His arms cross more tightly, and Carolyn can read the fear in his expression. It's strange to see him scared.

Carolyn shakes her head. "I think we need to keep the group to a minimum." She looks at Nikita and Del, then raises a hand between them. "Just us. Just the weird Dreaming travelers. Right?"

Kit hands her a sketch of the forest, and she holds that out to them. Del gets her fingers on the edge, but Serina steps in between Nikita and the sketch before Nikita can touch it.

Serina puts her hands on Carolyn's shoulders. "Wait."

Carolyn lets go of the sketch, leaving it in Del's hands. "What?" she asks as her hands come up to Serina's shoulders, matching Serina's gesture as she holds on.

Serina slides her hands up to Carolyn's head, then pulls her down so they can lean forehead to forehead. "Are you sure this is safe?" she whispers. "I'm worried for you. What you did last week exhausted you, and it's so soon. Can't this wait?"

Carolyn closes her eyes, thinking of last night's snow and the worry every time a storm blows in that Nikita is going to bury the Northeast again. "We've got Del here now," she whispers. "We've got Heather to help keep Nikita from losing control. I've got you to anchor me. I'm coming back to you and Kit. Don't worry. I need you to hold down the fort here while we're gone."

"If you go there—really go there, not just in your head—then Heather won't be with you," Serina points out. "Nik will be on her own. You'll all be on your own."

Carolyn shakes her head. "We'll be together. And I think we'll work well together. Nik's and Del's Talents intertwine; we already know that. And we'll make mine fit between them. It'll work out, and we'll see if we can get to Nikolai's world and stop our Nik's nightmares."

Serina presses a thumb against Carolyn's jaw, and Carolyn opens her eyes. Serina's so close she can feel every breath washing over her skin, warm and sweet. Serina shifts, and she rubs their noses together. "Be safe," she whispers, then steps back.

As safe as I can be, Carolyn thinks. "I will be." Carolyn hopes it's a promise.

Nikita stands next to Del, holding on to the sketch. Carolyn touches it as well, and she can feel power thrumming through her. Del and Nikita lift their free hands to rest on Carolyn's shoulders. The illusion rises without her asking it to, the forest building around them. She hears a shout in the distance, and the scent of pine floods her nose. The noises from the motel room dim, and there are murmurs in the shadows off the path.

Del turns to look, and Carolyn grabs her, not letting her stray.

"We're really here," Nikita says.

Carolyn nods. It's only the three of them, exactly as she'd hoped. "We're really here," agrees Carolyn. Del pulls against Carolyn's grip, but Carolyn holds on tighter. "We need to stick together."

Something flickers in Del's eyes. "There are so many paths to follow," she says, her gaze drifting from Carolyn to the paths that spiral away from them. "We need to move."

"We need to move in the right direction." Carolyn tries to orient herself. She turns in place, Del moving with her; they're standing at the junction of easily a dozen paths, some darker than others. Shadows linger to the sides, farther away than before but making their presence known as movement amidst the darkness. She doesn't feel the rising panic this time. "It's different," she says. "Sam panicked, and we panicked. He was in a particular place, not here. So we don't need to panic."

"What are those?" Nikita edges in close, shoulder to shoulder with Carolyn.

"Shadowwalkers," Carolyn murmurs.

"The split," Del answers cheerfully. "They live here, and we could go out among them—"

"No." Carolyn cuts her off, holding on tight before Del can dance away.

"We're here for Nik's path, remember."

Del's expression clouds. "Nikita's path is the same as ours. We'll end up in the meadow and go home."

"I don't think it is, or that we will. We're starting somewhere else entirely."

"Of course," Del says. "We have to because we're in Nikita's nightmare. How else are we going to find our way out?"

Nikita laughs sharply. She takes a step forward, then turns around and faces a different path. She tries seven times, and on the eighth she takes a second step, closer to that particular path. "We're not looking to get out of my nightmare," she reminds Del. "We're looking for the path in."

"And you think that will be your path out," Del counters. She closes in on Nikita, and Carolyn has to follow close behind because she refuses to let go of Del. Del reaches out with her free hand to pat Nikita's cheek. "Nightmares never truly end for people like us," she murmurs. "We're always dreaming."

That's a truly disturbing thought. "We need to focus on finding our way to reality," Carolyn says firmly. "Either ours or Nikolai's. His first."

Del pulls her hand free of Carolyn's. "I'll stay with you," she says. "There's plenty of time to play later."

Carolyn's tempted to reach out and grab her again, unsure if she can move fast enough if Del decides to dart away. But Nikita's heading down the path, and Del is following her, so Carolyn has no choice but to hurry to keep up.

"Don't stray off the path," Carolyn tells Del, trying to sound authoritative.

Del giggles. "Right. Don't go into the split. Don't worry. The Shadows want to come home to play. It'll be fine."

Also not a comforting thought

Nikita traverses the pathways in a methodical way, much as Kit had. When they come to a junction, Nikita pauses and considers each option carefully. The paths seem more divided than before, the choices more varied.

"It feels bigger," she says.

"It's different for everyone," Del replies. She has one hand out, fingers skipping lightly against the bark of the trees within reach of the path. "No two people walk the same path."

"I thought you said you'd never been here before Sam."

Del smiles slightly, the corners twisting up into a dark smirk. "I hadn't. I just know. This is where I belong. The meadow is my safe space, but this…this is my world."

"We're going to talk about this when we're home," Carolyn mutters. "And I swear I am going to make you promise never to return here."

"Can't do that," Del singsongs, skipping until she's caught up with Nikita, who is considering which option to take out of four branches. She hooks her arm in the crook of Nikita's elbow and points. "That one."

Dimly, Carolyn can see someone else on the path; they duck under low branches and pick their way over high roots and through thick underbrush. They're not the first person she's seen, but they're certainly the closest.

Nikita stares, watching as that person veers away, taking an unseen branch. She shakes her head. "No, not that one. That's not for us." She turns and strides down the rightmost path.

Carolyn is pleased that Nikita chose the same path she would have, if it were her at the junction. On the other hand, given what Del said about paths being different for everyone, she wonders if they are seeing the same options, or if they see alternate choices—paths the others can't take.

No, she saw the same path as Kit; he almost took it, the one that didn't have space for her on it. Being together means they must see the same paths. Being together gives them choices they might not otherwise have.

At each junction, their options dwindle from an average of five down to two, and Nikita's choices grow more certain as the paths narrow. The Shadows move, reaching out, and something tickles at Carolyn's legs and arms.

She tries to stay at the center of the path, grabbing Del when she strays sideways.

"It's getting darker," she says.

Nikita pauses, looks over her shoulder. "It's pretty damned dark where Nikolai is, so that's probably about right," she says. "I really want to rescue him, Carolyn. But how could I rescue him and leave the whole rest of that world in trouble? Is that right to do?"

"It's an ethical quandary," Del replies. "Think on it deeply. Who knows, maybe deciding wrong will break the entire multiverse."

"Please stop with the less-than-cheerful thoughts," Carolyn says, shivering.

"Who says that's not cheerful?" Del's voice is quiet, all hints of giggling gone. "Maybe the multiverse needs to be broken. Maybe the problem is that it exists."

Carolyn opens her mouth to reply, stuttering to a stop because she has no idea what to say. She adds it to her mental list of things to look into later; she can't deal with it now.

"This way," Nikita says, heading down a tiny pathway that Carolyn hadn't noticed until Nikita took it.

They duck under a heavy overhang of branches, and the tickling sensation of darkness closing in increases. It's a shortcut, Carolyn thinks, a way across the split without quite falling into it. It's no less dangerous; they're within easy reach of the Shadows. She's not sure why they don't grab on, why they slink away after touching her. It's another piece of data, but she doesn't even know which mental bin to stick it in.

They emerge from the dark canopy into a small clearing. There's a wide path stretching away to their left, and three paths to their right. When Carolyn turns, the small path they were just on has melded with the rest of the forest, invisible to her eyes.

Del hums under her breath, swaying in place. "Haven't we been here before?" she sings, then lapses back into a quiet hum.

Nikita turns toward the right-hand fork; as she lifts her hand, Carolyn pushes forward, getting in her way. "Not that way," she says. "That's destruction."

Nikita's gaze narrows. "Why?"

"I was here," Carolyn tells her. "We were here when we got Sam out. Kit and I actually stood right here, and we looked at these paths. I remember that knot in that tree; it was next to the path that leads to destruction. The place we just came from didn't exist then, and I can't even see it now, so you took us on some kind of shortcut to get here. Your path and ours have intersected."

"Huh." Nikita rocks back on her heels, crosses her arms. "So. Which path did you choose?"

Carolyn points. "That one. Kit could have taken either, but that's the only one that's meant for me."

Nikita's head tilts, considering. "And that led you home?"

"It leads to my meadow," Del whispers. "Which is home, yes."

"We could get home from there." There are shades of home in this conversation, and Carolyn's starting to wonder exactly where Del's mind exists on a day-to-day basis. Or if the answer to that is multiple locations, like *here* and *there*.

Nikita pushes past Carolyn, moving to the start of the rightmost path. She holds up a hand, reaches out slowly, then withdraws quickly. "You're right. Not that one." She turns in place, frowning as she looks at the remaining two paths from this fork. She moves again, finding the one spot where she can see them equally, and stares for a long time.

Carolyn's not sure what Nikita sees. This time, Carolyn can see nothing to differentiate the path, except a vague feeling that one is wrong and the other is right. But Nikita stares with her brow furrowed as if she's watching entire lifetimes play out in front of her.

Del sighs loudly. "Just choose."

Nikita raises a hand, pointing to the one Kit would have taken had Carolyn let him. "Nikolai is this way."

Carolyn doesn't like it, but she has to follow as Nikita marches down the path.

The path grows darker. The trees sink down, branches hanging heavily over their head. But Carolyn smells a familiar scent, and after a moment, Del seems to notice it as well. She skips forward, calling out, "We're almost there!"

Nikita and Carolyn have to run to keep up, stopping when the path ends in a field.

Del stands there, shoulders slumped, hands hanging at her side. Aside from thin strips of grass that meander like pathways through the field, flowers carpet the ground. The smell is overpowering, sickly sweet.

"This isn't my meadow," Del grumbles.

"No, but it's like your meadow. And Nikolai's world is like ours." It makes Carolyn think that her Talent could work from here, that she can punch through to his world. She brings out the picture Kit made of the safehouse and holds it in front of her as she moves a short way down the grassy pathway.

It takes no effort to bring the illusion up; it snaps into being around her, and she can smell old coffee, the damp scent of mildew, and a crisp, cold breeze whistling through cracks in the walls. She holds out her hand, and the image flickers, her fingers cold in the air on the other side.

Nikita stands next to her, looking around. She crouches next to the chair where Seth sat and looks at the crumbs on the table. "We could be here," she whispers wonderingly.

"We can go if you want," Carolyn says. "I can travel there from here."

"Do you really want to go to a world where you don't belong? How would you get back?" Del asks idly. "It took all three of us to get here. I don't think you can cross on your own."

Carolyn has a theory about that, about why Dreamwalkers are called "walkers" and not "weavers" even though Pawel thinks the latter term is more accurate. She also thinks that, despite their prior plans, this isn't the time or place to test that theory.

"If you stay here, I can get back to you," she says. There's an image of Del buried in her wallet. "I'm going to take a quick look, then when I reach out to you, you can bring me through here."

"How?" Del asks, blinking in confusion.

"Not something I can explain because I've never been on the receiving end of it, but Serina and Pawel had no problem helping me," Carolyn replies. She hopes the metaphysics doesn't change because Del's in the Dreamscape, not the real world.

"I want to go," Nikita says, gripping Carolyn's arm. She sidles in so close that Carolyn can't move without her. "I want to see where Nikolai is."

It's a bad idea. But there's no sign of Nikolai himself; she suspects this is a place he passed through while Nikita Dreamed about him, and that he's since left.

Maybe it'll be okay.

But she feels worse about this idea as every second passes. Nikita is shivering next to her, vibrating with excitement. "Fine," Carolyn says, and she reaches out to breach the space between the meadow and Nikolai's world.

As soon as her fingers break through, darkness swarms. Something grips her wrist and yanks, and she stumbles; only Nikita's grip on her other arm keeps her in place. Carolyn shouts as darkness rises and pushes through the small opening, shadowy tendrils sliding along the length of her arm to make it wider.

"No!" Del yells, and she pulls on Carolyn.

Carolyn is the rope in a tug of war, and the grip through the gateway feels as if it will suck the energy out of her soul. She sags, exhausted. Nikita and Del give one more strong tug, and Carolyn tumbles backward into the flowers. The illusion crumbles as scent explodes outwards, and Carolyn starts to sneeze.

Nikita crouches next to where Carolyn lies on the ground, one hand on her shoulder. "I think you got their attention," she whispers, leaning close. "The Shadows are coming."

When Carolyn looks up, Del stands between them and the teeming darkness that moves closer with every heartbeat. Del has her hands out, murmuring something under her breath. Carolyn gets the feeling that without her, they'd be overrun.

Carolyn comes up to a crouch, ready to stand and run. "I can't leave Del behind. I promised."

"We don't have a path," Nikita says. She's right. The Shadows are between them and the path from which they entered this field.

There are no pathways.

Shit.

Carolyn closes her eyes, turning slowly until she sees a break between the trees. The darkness there isn't completely black. "There," she says. "You start running. I'll grab Del."

"How do I know where I'm going?" Nikita asks.

"Think of home," Carolyn orders. "Just like Dorothy—there's no place like home. Now go!"

She jumps to her feet, not watching Nikita. The Shadows shift and move, seemingly torn between keeping their attention on Del and chasing Nikita.

Carolyn needs to break the tableau or Del will be stuck here.

She wraps a hand around Del's wrist and tugs sharply. When Del turns, eyes wide, Carolyn pulls until she stumbles forward. "Come with me. We have to go."

Del nods, and they both run.

They overtake Nikita, and Del pushes past her, crashing between the trees to break their path. She finds small spaces that magically grow wide enough to let them through, tumbling from moment to moment, scrambling over fallen logs, ducking under the overhanging limbs. Carolyn doesn't stop to think, just grabs onto Nikita's hand and follows Del, trusting that she knows where to go.

When they burst into the meadow, all Carolyn feels is relief. She trips over nothing, stumbles into Del's arms, and looks up at her.

"We need to go home," Carolyn says.

Del smiles. "I am home."

Darkness spills in around the edges of the meadow, and Del shouts at the Shadows as they flow toward them.

There's no time to argue. Carolyn reaches into her pocket, and the illusion comes to life before she's truly seen the picture. Kit stands before her, mouth opening when he sees her. She thrusts an arm toward him, and he reaches for her at the same time. Reality snaps in around them when they clasp hands, and she shoves Del toward him.

"Nikita!" she shouts, reaching for Nikita, helping her go through the illusion.

Kit passes Nikita into Heather's waiting arms, and Carolyn throws herself forward. She feels the Shadows' touch as she goes, and she collapses in exhaustion against Kit, crumbling to the floor when he can't hold her dead weight.

She closes her eyes, waiting for her heart to steady.

"Ten fingers, ten toes," Del says.

"How's your head feel?" Carolyn asks, not sure if Del will truly understand the question.

"Given that my alternate-reality Dreamscape was just taken over by darkness, pretty decent," Del mutters. "Give me a few days. I have a feeling that's going to affect me."

"We were there," Nikita says, talking to Heather. "We found Nikolai's world, but the way in is blocked by Shadows."

"Who chased us straight into my brain," Del adds.

Carolyn exhales. She untangles herself from Kit and sits up; Kit's hand remains on her shoulder. Shawn and Sam hold Del on the bed, and Nikita is curled close to Heather.

The trip took a toll, which isn't surprising.

This may not have been their best idea.

But she thinks they've learned something, if she can only step back long enough to figure out what. They might even have a way forward. She just needs to think about what Del said, about what they saw. She needs to put it all together.

And they need to do one more thing, she thinks. Because they might need help.

"Now it's time to talk to Pawel," Carolyn says, and no one disagrees.

THE FINAL
OUTCOME

TENTH POSITION: THE FINAL OUTCOME

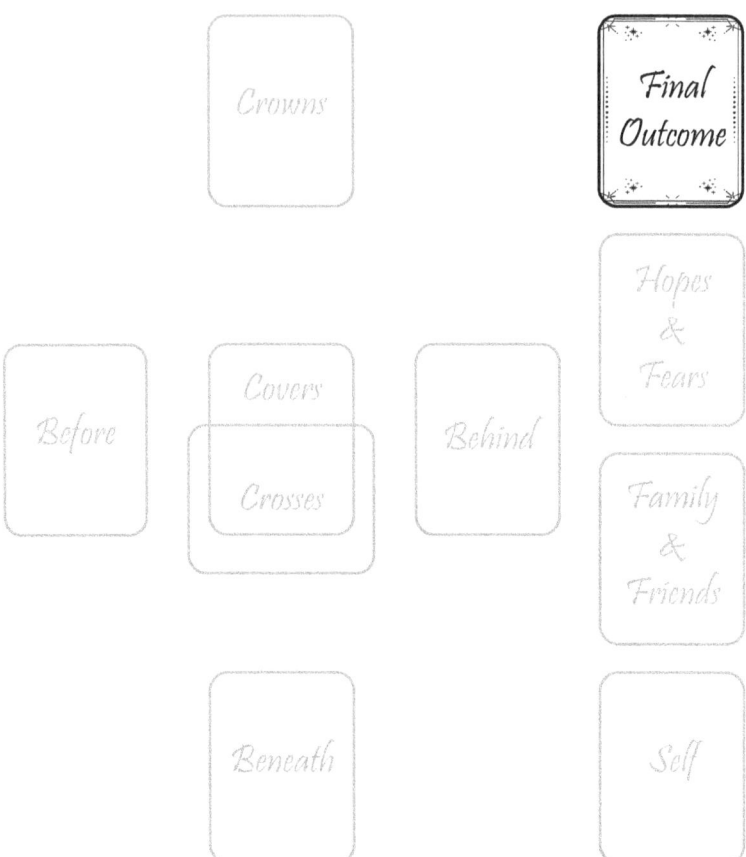

...THE FINAL OUTCOME

Eventually, the querent comes to the end of the path. This card shows the end result of the querent's efforts to achieve what they have been striving toward: the climax. This is how the story resolves. If the card drawn reflects an outcome that the querent desires, then the querent can take guidance from this card and the entire layout may reach this result. If the card drawn shows an outcome that the querent would prefer does not come to pass, then the querent can take guidance from that as well, gaining insight on how to avoid difficulties, find a new path, and achieve a new outcome.

This is the finality, although it may not be the end of the story. If the querent so desires, a new reading may be cast with this conclusion as the focus to divine further clarity.

But in this moment—this is when the current story ends.

Carolyn's Reading: The Three of Cups (Reversed)

A couple is united by the shore of a lake, entangled in perfect harmony. The colors are warm, the embrace passionate yet gentle, and three cups around them overflow with abundance.

The querent will have their happy ending, although because the Three of Cups is reversed, the conclusion may not be as perfect as they desire. This is a card of high emotion and satisfaction, as well as one of family, both blood relatives and found community. When the story ends, the querent will find happiness with those around them, and they may find love as well.

This card may also mean consent—freely given and accepted. It is a card of communication, of understanding what one's partner(s) desires and needs to truly be happy.

The caution inherent in the card's reversed position is that the querent may go beyond pleasure into excess, and thus they should take caution to ensure that they keep to moderation. This card cautions wariness: the querent may find themselves in over their head during emotional situations. Communication is important to ensure comfort with their partner(s) and their family.

Kit's Reading: The Nine of Cups (Reversed)

The sun shines upon a couple who appear united in the innocent passion of a sweet kiss upon the forehead. They are surrounded by nine cups filled to the brim without overflowing. It is a picture of the moment of sweet harmony.

This card, as a final outcome, suggests that the querent will find emotional victory. They will achieve what they have sought and discover the blessings of their path. It is a card that requires the querent to be open, to accept that which is freely given in order to find their happiness. They may need to rely upon intuition and emotion to see beyond the practical and discover the true harmony that they seek.

Reversed, this card also suggests that the querent must acknowledge that there will be mistakes. "Perfection" is rarely truly perfect. There will always be new things to learn, new joys to discover, and new heartaches to mend. While something may be meant to be, that doesn't mean it will happen effortlessly. Rejoice in what is given and take pains to make achievements grow truly blessed and great.

41

CAROLYN KNOWS THEY need to talk to Pawel, but no one actually wants to reach out to him. Carolyn and Heather end up with Kit, Nikita, and Serina in their room for the night. Exhaustion helps them sleep, and Sunday morning, they meet up with Del, Shawn, and Sam at Teas Please for breakfast.

Only then does Carolyn finally get in touch with Pawel, and they make plans with him for the afternoon. Unfortunately, Del and the guys will have to leave before the meeting time, but Carolyn promises to catch them up and keep them informed.

By the time they reach Pawel's house, Carolyn almost feels like the world is real around her again, that the prior day's adventures were the dream.

She knows that it's all real, but it's almost too surreal to believe.

"You shaved," she says as soon as Pawel opens the door.

He reaches for his chin and rubs his fingers along the smooth jawline as if he hadn't realized. "It was getting scruffy. I had to either trim it properly or shave it off, and I don't own a beard trimmer."

"You look like you've taken five minutes to take care of yourself," she says.

He pulls the door open and ushers them inside. The living room looks as if an entire library unloaded its shelves onto every spare surface. Carolyn recognizes several books from the special collections room. "They let you take those out of the library?"

Nikita makes a beeline for the couch, clears herself a small space, picks one of the books up at random, and looks through it.

"I donated them, so yes." Pawel scrubs a hand through his hair. He may be clean-shaven, but he's still in his pajamas despite it being afternoon, and his hair is still shaggy and long. "They belonged to me before I officially gave them to the library, so they trust me to take care of them. I've been doing some reading."

"We've been doing some experimenting," Nikita says, glancing away from the book in her lap. She holds it up. "This is an interesting view on weather witchery, but not useful to the problem at hand."

"Do we know what the problem at hand is?" Pawel picks up books and places bookmarks in them, then stacks them neatly on the table to clear the rest of the couch. Heather sits next to Nikita as soon as there's space, and Serina pats the space beside herself in an overstuffed chair, silently suggesting that Carolyn join her. Pawel stands with the last few books in his hands; Carolyn can't tell if he's uncertain or merely distracted by a stray thought.

Carolyn really wants him to be sitting for this. She points to the remaining chair, and he sits.

"We went into the Dreamscape," she says quietly. "Again."

He leans forward, elbows propped on his knees, head in his hands. His fingers grip his hair; they're white from pressing. "Why?" he asks, voice muffled.

"Because of me," Nikita says. She sets down the book, closing it neatly then adding it to the top of one of the stacks Pawel created. "Because I started remembering my Dreams. And because, after their trip into the forest with Sam, Del and Carolyn thought that my Dreams might be an actual, different world."

"So Del was involved too. Did it occur to you that the two of you could have set off..." Pawel's tone is flat as his voice trails off. He's speaking to the space hidden by the curl of his body, and his fingers dig into his scalp. Carolyn can hear each of his rough breaths.

"We were safe," Carolyn says. "As safe as we could be. Yes, there were Shadows. No, we didn't know exactly what we were doing, but we knew that there were different worlds along the pathways in the forest. And we knew that if we tried, we could find Del's meadow and come home from there. So we had knowns as well as unknowns."

"Thank God for that," Pawel mutters.

"We found Nikolai's world," Nikita says. "We found it, and Carolyn opened an illusion to it. We could have gone there, and we didn't."

"What kept you from it?" Pawel lowers his hands slowly and looks up at them. "You've gone down every other path of insanity, why not that one?"

"I knew I couldn't open a doorway from here to there directly, and I didn't want to get stuck there if I couldn't open an illusion from there to return home," Carolyn says. Serina's hand touches hers, and Carolyn grabs on, holding tight. "It wasn't a conscious thought at the time," she says, correcting herself. "Nikita wanted to find Nikolai. His world is dark. Very dark. But as soon as I opened the illusion and breached it with my hand, darkness and Shadows came through. Something grabbed me, and I broke free, but they chased us, so we panicked and ran. We found some kind of shortcut across to Del's meadow. We went off the path," she continues carefully, ideas that have been in the back of her mind coming together. "The gateway to Nikolai's world was in a field similar to Del's meadow, only more…dead. Flatter. Which makes sense, since the Shadows have overrun his world. When we tried to run, there were no paths out, so we crashed through the space between his field and her meadow. And it was…it wasn't easy, but it seemed like they were close together."

Serina squeezes Carolyn's hand. Carolyn closes her eyes, tilts her head against Serina; Serina gently combs her fingers through Carolyn's hair, and Carolyn loves the feeling. It's soothing.

Pawel holds up a hand, and everyone falls silent. "One"—he holds a finger in the air—"you've been Dreaming of someone named Nikolai."

"I haven't been Dreaming about him, I've been Dreaming that I am him, living in a kind of post-apocalyptic world where the Emergence went really badly," Nikita explains. "He's on the run with Seth; they're trying to find a safe haven."

"Who—?" Pawel cuts off, then he waves his hand in the air as if scrubbing that train of thought away. "How similar are his world and ours?"

"Except for the 'being hunted' thing, very, I think," Nikita says.

"Alia Herne is bedrock," Pawel murmurs. "The Shadows cross between the worlds, and they're in the split. Souls are trapped in their own Dreamscapes. And you Dream of his world and only his world, yes? Most Dreamers I'm familiar with have varied Dreams. They projected and took others with them to many places. But you seem almost…twinned."

"What if the two worlds are twinned?" Serina asks. When Pawel looks at her, she shrinks toward Carolyn. "I'm not a Mage, so this isn't exactly something I know a lot about, but when they were talking about it, it sounded like there are a lot of worlds, but that these two are like…super similar or something. Maybe that's why Nikita's Dreaming about this one person specifically. Because they're entwined realities."

"And if the Emergence happened at the same time in both…" Pawel murmurs.

"…then maybe the Emergences are also linked." Serina grins. "It's a theory that makes sense."

"It does, it does." Pawel reaches for something on the table, then stops with his hand mid-air. He frowns, pushes to his feet, and moves around the living room until he finds a notebook and pen. He stops to scribble in it.

"I didn't Dream about Nikolai last night," Nikita says.

Pawel's pen stops scratching. "What?"

Nikita licks her lips. Heather kisses her temple; Nikita smiles and turns to kiss Heather slowly. There's no passion in it, only a sweet press of lips as they smile against each other.

Serina coughs, and Carolyn hides a smile against Serina's shoulder.

Nikita turns back to them, flushed. "I've been remembering my Dreams for a few weeks now," she says. "But last night, I don't remember Dreaming about Nikolai. I didn't wake up, I didn't freeze anyone, and there wasn't any weird weather. I just slept."

"Maybe because we were all there?" Serina asks, and Nikita shrugs.

"Maybe," she agrees, "or maybe something happened. I'm worried. There was that swarm of Shadows, and Nikolai had been in that safehouse recently. What if they caught up with him?"

"Or the Shadows coming through somehow forced the two worlds farther apart." Pawel scribbles more notes. He points at Nikita with his pen. "That could be to your benefit, Nikita. If the worlds are becoming untethered, then your Emergence might slow and become controllable."

Nikita shakes her head. "I don't want that. I think Nikolai needs help, and I'm sure I've been Dreaming that I'm him for a reason. That's why I wanted to try to go to him. If he needs help, then I need to help him."

"What makes you so certain that you can help?" Pawel asks. "You could end up as trapped as he is. And if you are him, but from another world, I can't even imagine the complications that could arise from you and he being in the same place."

"Doesn't matter. I have to try." Nikita rises, and Heather stands with her. She rocks back on her heels, crossing her arms. "I can't go there on my own," she says, "and I'd like help from Carolyn and Del again because I think that's what we need to do. We need to get to Nikolai and help him, and that's when the Dreams will end. When his world stops giving me nightmares, I'll stop having trouble controlling my weather Talent while I sleep. Plus, saving his life seems to be pretty important. We're talking about a real person whose life I see in my head. I can't just say he's not my responsibility and ignore him."

"I'll investigate," Pawel agrees. He sets the notebook down and lays the pen neatly atop it. It starts to roll, and he catches it, then fidgets with it until it's placed perfectly. Only then does he turn to face Nikita. "I'll talk to some Dreamwalkers I know and see if there's any precedent for how your Talent has manifested."

"I think the matrix I was developing around Shadows, myself, Del, Nikita, and other travelers might help," Carolyn offers. "You've already got those notes."

"Mm." Pawel's gaze flits to the door, then back to the books. Carolyn gets the feeling he isn't really with them anymore, that he's already halfway buried in his research. "I can see the appeal in investigating the alternate worlds. But if the split surrounds them, and it's filled with creatures—with people, with Shadowwalkers who mindlessly suck our souls—then going there may not be a viable option." He shakes his head, gaze clearer when he looks at Nikita. "I will research what I can, and we can meet again."

Nikita purses her lips. "I get the feeling that for Nikolai, at least, this may be time sensitive."

"I understand." Pawel turns away, and it's a clear dismissal. Carolyn isn't even sure he remembers that they're in the house.

"Do you need help with Conor?" she asks.

His shoulders go stiff, and he shakes his head without turning around and sifts through piles of books, obviously seeking one in particular. "Emily has him and will get him to school tomorrow. Don't worry, she'll bring me something to eat." He waves them toward the door. "Go on. You don't need to mother me again."

Carolyn is fairly certain that him saying that goes to prove that he does need help—that he'll forget to take care of himself while buried in his research. She'll have to let Mac know what's going on. Someone needs to make sure Pawel's okay.

Serina touches Carolyn's elbow, and she realizes that Heather and Nikita are already heading out the front door. Carolyn turns to follow Serina, fingertips tangling with hers as Serina reaches for her hand.

"If you want to come over for a little while, we could go back to my dorm," Serina says. She pulls on her mittens and tugs her hat down over her ears, then waits while Carolyn does the same. "I think Becky has a study group, she's got some massive exams this week."

"Don't you have a big orgo test?" Carolyn doesn't know anyone else currently taking orgo, but it's midterm week, and she remembers even Kit being stressed about it their freshman year.

"Not 'til Wednesday," replies Serina. "I'm ready for everything else, and I can take a night off. If you want to take a night off with me." Her soft smile is uncertain, and Carolyn hates that she's made Serina worry about every single little step around her.

"I want to take a night off with you." Carolyn frames Serina's face with her mitten-covered hands and leans down while Serina looks up. She kisses Serina's forehead, then rubs noses with her. "So yes, I'd love to go back to Douglass with you."

Serina smiles and kisses the tip of Carolyn's nose. "Good," she says.

42

THEY BUMP INTO Becky on their way up to the second floor. She waves cheerily and wishes them a good evening, then tells Serina that she doesn't expect to be back until after midnight. Serina takes Carolyn's hand and leads her through the hallway, past the room that always seems to be thumping with loud music and into Serina's room in the corner. The door closes, and the music fades to a muffled *thud-thud-thud*. Serina pulls out her phone to send a text, and by the time she drops it on her desk, the volume's lowered until it's barely audible.

"Pat's gotten better about turning down the music," Serina comments. "On the other hand, the rest of us have gotten really used to hearing his music. It's funny when he plays stuff from Rory's band. I've heard Thorne sing along when he comes over."

Carolyn shrugs out of her jacket, tucks her hat and mittens into the pockets, and drapes it over the back of Serina's desk chair. She turns in place; the bed is the only good place to sit. Climbing up, she ends up with her back against the wall, her legs stuck out straight and crossed at the ankles, while Serina putters around, digging behind Becky's bed.

"Aha!" Serina brandishes a remote. "I knew it wasn't lost forever. I'll admit, it's been helpful not to have the distraction while I'm studying. I'd say that Becky hid it on purpose, but after watching her try to work the TV manually so she could watch her favorite show on Friday, I'm pretty sure it was accidental. She's addicted," Serina confides as she crawls across the bed to kneel next to Carolyn. "She's some kind of superfan, and I think she might be famous on the internet. Like, she writes loads of fanfic, and her blog is way popular, but I don't think anyone knows it's actually her. I read some of the comments on her stuff, and people really think she's good."

"I think that's more than I've ever heard anyone say about your room-mate," Carolyn admits. She moves her arm to the side when Serina taps her, and she waits while Serina straddles her, settling in comfortably. Carolyn's hands automatically fall to Serina's hips, and it's nice being able to look her directly in the eye.

But. They're…

Carolyn licks her lips, heart speeding up uncomfortably. She flexes her fingers. "Um."

"Any time you're uncomfortable, you say 'stop,' and we stop," Serina says. She leans forward, and they end up forehead to forehead. Her hands are on Carolyn's shoulders, and her thumbs lightly glide over her throat.

It feels surprisingly good.

"Is this okay?" Serina asks, and Carolyn nods because so far, yes, it's fine.

Serina leans in and lightly brushes her lips against Carolyn's. A close-mouthed press, flesh against flesh, as Serina slides her hands up to cradle Carolyn's face. Slow kisses, over and over, without trying to press more deeply.

"Still good?" Serina whispers against her mouth.

"It's not bad," Carolyn agrees.

Serina draws back; Carolyn blinks in surprise as Serina's brow furrows. "But is it good?" Serina asks. "I don't want to be shown your mask, Carolyn. I don't want you to pretend because you think I want something."

"I'm not pretending." Carolyn's fingers tighten on Serina's hips. She tries to smile even though her heart is hammering and her nerves are rising. "It's not bad. I want to keep trying. I'll tell you if there's a problem, I promise." When Serina stays where she is, still wary, Carolyn repeats, "I promise."

Serina leans forward again, using her hands to tilt Carolyn's head. She kisses along Carolyn's jaw, back to a spot behind her ear; the feeling leaves Carolyn gasping in surprise. She feels Serina's smile. "Good?" Serina asks softly.

"Yeah. Good."

Serina hums against her skin and kisses down the line of her neck to her throat, then into the hollow. She nips gently, and Carolyn shudders. "I felt that," Carolyn mutters, a familiar thrum warming her body.

This. This is why she's broken. Because it's not consistent. Because she wants to lie back and take and not give. Because she does feel desire and arousal and hunger.

Shit.

"Stop," she says, her voice hoarse. She raises her hands between them, pushing Serina away, only afterward realizing where that means she's grasped. She looks at her fingers against Serina's shirt, feels the softness beneath them, and jerks away. "Sorry."

"For saying 'stop'?" Serina shakes her head. "It's okay. Do you want me to move?" She sits back on her heels, lifting part of her weight from Carolyn's lap. Her tan skin is flushed, and Carolyn swears she can hear her heart beating rapidly. Or maybe that's her own heart. She reaches out, unthinking, pressing her palm down on Serina's chest to feel the rapid-fire thumping. Serina brings her hand up, covers Carolyn's with her own, and smiles.

Warmth floods Carolyn's cheeks. "I don't want you to move."

"Is it okay if I stop kneeling?" Serina asks. "I can stay this way, but my knees are starting to hurt."

Carolyn slowly drops her hands to Serina's waist and tugs. "It's okay." She feels like there's something she needs to say, but she can't find the words. Her head is swirling, and her body is warm, and she doesn't know what to do with her hands. What they're doing feels too complicated. Communication is important, but using language seems impossible.

She slips her hands under the back of Serina's shirt; Serina sighs, and Carolyn presses them against warm skin. When she tugs, Serina shifts so she's sitting with her heels behind Carolyn and her knees bent, and then Serina hunches forward and lays her head against Carolyn's chest, curling in close.

It's as if they're wrapped together in a cocoon, and it's warm and comfortable. Carolyn rubs small circles into Serina's skin, and slowly their heartbeats ease into a slower, calmer, synced pace.

"I'm sorry," Carolyn whispers again.

Serina huffs. "I said to say 'stop' if you needed to stop. If it's any consolation, I have no idea what I'm doing, so I'm pretty open to any possibility."

Carolyn's mind supplies a surprisingly strong stream of possibilities, all of which leave her warmer than before. "Um."

Serina pats her chest. "Slow," she says. "We'll take it slow."

"I liked when you bit me." Carolyn manages to push the words out, cheeks heating at Serina's soft chuckle. "What? You bit me. You can't laugh at me for liking it."

"I'm not. I liked biting you." When Serina pulls back, her grin is wicked. "You taste good. Your skin is all salty-sweet, and I liked the little sound you made, and honestly, if you keep making that sound, I'm going to just tingle from head to toe uncontrollably."

"Oh." Carolyn isn't sure what to do with that statement or how it fits into her view of the world. "I don't know what we're doing."

"We'll figure it out." Serina nuzzles close again. "And if you say 'no on-the-lips kissing,' but let me kiss you everywhere else, I'm good. I know you said you think you're selfish, but maybe that kind of works for me."

"It won't forever," Carolyn mumbles.

"Maybe not, but maybe it will." Serina tilts her head and kisses Carolyn's jaw. "How about we talk about that when we get there. For now, we'll keep stumbling forward with what's good, okay?"

Carolyn's body feels tight and hot and awkward, and for a moment, she wonders what Serina would think if she walked away to try to calm down on her own. She chews on her lip so hard it hurts. "I know you said that if I'm never ready to go all the way, you're okay. But I'm not exactly sex-repulsed. I'm just—sometimes nothing feels good. And sometimes I don't feel right reciprocating, it makes me feel panicky. Sometimes everything feels great right up until the moment that I want to run away and finish on my own. My psyche is messy."

"People are messy, and that's okay." Serina sits back and looks her in the eyes. "I'm not going anywhere, Carolyn. If you tell me that we're going to have sex by talking to each other from separate rooms and that's it, I'm okay. If you tell me that we're only going to cuddle for the rest of our lives, that's also okay. If you tell me you want to just take, that's cool, too. We'll figure it out. I swear, I'm good, and if I'm ever not good, I promise we'll talk about it. But I need to know that if you're ever not good, you'll also talk about it. No matter what. Because I'm kind of maybe actually falling in love with you, Carolyn Merrill, and I don't want to lose this chance."

"Oh. Oh, wow." Carolyn's heart punches a huge *thump* in her chest, and she pulls Serina closer, hugging her hard. "I don't—I'm not sure what to say."

"You don't have to say it back," Serina mumbles, her voice muffled by Carolyn's chest. "I know I'm probably pretty early on saying that, but it's what I feel, and I want you to realize this isn't some, like, little crush or something. I really feel a lot of feelings for you. Intense feelings. And I'm kind of confessing this all to your breast right now, so maybe can I move a little?"

"I think that I'll always be able to travel to you." Carolyn tries to relax her clutching hold on Serina, and her hands slide down Serina's arms as she pulls back. "You're my anchor. You're always here. You're always a place of calm for me. I can cling to you during a ritual even if you're not there."

"That's pretty intense." Serina smiles softly. "I like it."

"Do you want to—?" Carolyn stops, struggling to put into words what she's offering. "Can we lie down? We can keep figuring things out if you want."

Serina's smile broadens to a bright, cheerful grin. "I'd like that. A lot."

She lets Carolyn guide them until they're stretched along the bed, and she lets Carolyn set the pace. Slow and easy, with soft touches and occasional flashes of skin. Carolyn's heart is thudding, her skin tingling. Her body sings with every hushed sigh from Serina, and she loses track of the passing of time.

Her phone chimes several times in rapid succession, jolting them from the pleasant fugue. Serina reaches past Carolyn to where the phone lies on the desk, bringing it back for her. They lie back, shoulder to shoulder, looking up as Carolyn unlocks it and brings up her messages.

I've found a reference to something interesting, Pawel sends. *There are rumors that someone performed a ritual years ago to seal something against Soulstealers. Which is intriguing in that they were thought to be only a legend. I'm going to investigate. If I'm not back by the time classes return to session, you and Kit can work independently, and I will expect your papers by the end of the semester.*

"I don't like the sound of that," Carolyn mutters. Serina kisses her shoulder, snuggling close as Carolyn types up a response.

Take care of yourself, she sends. *Eat. Drink. And please plan before doing anything. Tell me you have it all thought out.*

She half expects him to send back that he's the professor and the expert. But no.

Not really, he says, *but I will take care.*

It's not comforting because she realizes that his response means that he knows they're on shaky ground. No one's an expert, and no one knows where they're going. She can only hope he gets to wherever it is safely.

Winging it is the theme of the day. She hopes Pawel has his own anchor, like she has Serina.

43

Carolyn appreciates the break from the independent study that Pawel's investigation provides. After the intensity of the past couple months, it's strange to go for a whole week without seeing him. They won't see him again until after spring break at the earliest.

"Stop thinking so loudly," Kit says. He's cross-legged on her bed, still in his coat even though his hat and mittens are discarded next to him.

"Your boots are dripping water on my bed." Carolyn throws a folded sweater at him. He catches it as he stretches out his legs, his boots hanging over the bed's edge so that the muddy water will drip down the side of her comforter instead.

He drops the sweater into her half-packed spring break bag. "Better?"

"A little." She digs in her drawer and counts out enough pairs of underwear and socks for the week, then adds two extra pairs of each. She has no idea what they'll be doing all week, but she knows they're going to a farm that's also a magical community, and she knows it's in Burlington, which is even colder and snowier than PHU.

It'll be great.

"So…" Kit draws out the word, and when Carolyn walks over, he's sitting back on his hands, staring up at the ceiling. He glances at her while she shoves the socks and underwear into her bag, then looks away again.

"So?" she prompts.

"I tried casting the cards this week," he says. "I mean, after everything that's happened and all the changes in our Talent, I figured you'd ask if I'd tried recently. And I wanted to do it for the independent study because that's where we started out."

"And?" Carolyn turns her back to him on purpose, giving him privacy rather than hovering over him as she waits for an answer. She'd like to think she's improved as a sister, learned to give him more space. It hasn't been easy, but she's trying.

"It was gibberish," he says. She hears a soft *thump*, and as she glances back, he's lying on the bed, his arms spread. He starts to lift his feet, but she coughs, and he drops them again over the edge. "I tried doing a reading for myself," he says, "and I tried doing one about me and Rory. Both were incoherent. I couldn't even follow the story. And considering how the last few weeks have gone, I've got some idea of just how insane the story can get. People going into the Dreamscape. Shadows coming to eat us. Really weirdly complicated relationships. But…nothing. It was like I'd given the deck to a random five-year-old and told them to toss it in the air, then tried reading the random patterns in how the cards fell."

Carolyn bites her tongue, resists the urge to say that they can see the patterns in anything, find the paths and stories to tell. Nothing's truly random.

"Speaking of complicated relationships—"

"Smooth, Caro." There's a soft laugh in his voice. "How are things with you and Serina?"

They'd spent last night curled around each other in Carolyn's bed, warm and cozy under the comforter, trying not to hear the way Nikita snores when she's not having nightmares.

It was nice.

"Good," she says, all too aware of how her cheeks are hot. "The more time I spend with her, the more I like her. She's definitely not Shawn."

"That's good. The more I think about Shawn, the more I want to punch him," Kit says dryly. "He really did his best to fuck you up, didn't he?"

"Can we just say 'high school sucked' and leave it at that?" Carolyn asks. She's not over it, but she's ready to leave it in the rearview mirror. "We were young. Out of all of us, I think you actually had your shit together the best. I'm still figuring myself out. And now, you and I both have found something good."

"Rory's good, yeah. And I wouldn't say I've got myself figured out, but I'm definitely getting there." Kit waves hand in the air. "How is it that we're both dating freshmen? It's like—I had no idea what I wanted, but Rory's exactly it. We're so different, but everything feels good with him. I like hanging around with him. And his band—I'm not even sure what to do with them half the time. Stormy hugs. A lot. And Thorne's…well he's Thorne. He's dialed back in my direction, but he's in overdrive everywhere else. And Rory's like this calm in the storm. This safe haven, a place where I can always go."

Carolyn remembers waking up in her little cave of warmth this morning, feeling Serina's kiss against the nape of her neck. "Yes," she murmurs. "That's it exactly."

"Do you think it's possible to fall in love with entirely the wrong person, someone you were never even looking for?" Kit muses.

"I think if you're falling in love with him, then he's entirely the right person, and you simply didn't know where to look. You're lucky you tripped over him."

"Literally, thanks to Shane." Kit laughs and sits up. "Are you ready?"

"Almost." Carolyn shoves things deeper into her bag, finding room for a few more T-shirts and two more pairs of jeans. She adds a pair of long-sleeved shirts on top, then two hoodies over that, then two pairs of boots. She's trying to figure out how to put in an extra three shirts when Kit stops her.

"They have laundry," he points out. "It's only a week."

"I don't want to put anyone out," Carolyn replies. She shoves the final shirts into her bag, then grabs a second bag and puts in the two bottles of wine Mac picked up for her to bring as hostess gifts. "I feel like we're already invading because there are so many of us going. And Rory barely knows me—"

"But you're Drea's Big, and Alaric is Rory's roommate, not to mention that you're my actual twin."

Twins. They've been two of a kind their whole lives, and now they're finally finding their own paths. Carolyn thinks about how one path in the Dreamscape had Kit without her, how that path ultimately led to Nikolai's world. She turns to Kit, leaving the bags on her bed even though she should be grabbing them and getting out the door.

"Are we good?" she asks. "I mean with each other. Things have changed so much in the last couple months. I feel like we've splintered in some ways. We've always been 'the predictive twins,' and now we're—I don't know what we are."

"We're Kit and Carolyn." Kit slides off the bed, wraps his arms around her, and pulls her in to a warm, solid hug. "You're still brimming with predictive magic. The cards love you, and now you've got this little traveling Talent as well. And I've got art, which feels really right when I do it, especially when I do it for you. It's not predictive, but it's still connected to our family history, and I'm happy with it. We're still on the same path. Even if we diverge, we'll always be here for each other. Our paths connect, Caro. We're good. We'll always be good."

"And if I help Nikita save Nikolai?" Carolyn asks. She squeezes Kit, then lets him go so she can shrug into her jacket and grab her bags. Kit pulls on his hat and mittens, tugging the hat low enough that his hair almost covers his eyes.

He grins. "You'll need me for art, and you might need Rory to help me art or to help you turn up or turn down someone's Talent. You should think about keeping Drea and Alaric involved, too, because Clan will be useful in a place like Nikolai's world. And we'll all be careful of the Shadows and make sure we don't get lost in the split between worlds." He holds out a hand to her, and Carolyn takes it, squeezing before they let go. "We'll do this together. I'll always have your back, and you'll always have mine. We're twins. Nothing can come between us."

The door pushes open, banging with a *thud* against the wall.

"Sorry," Drea says. "This place is kind of dead right now, isn't it? I figured some of the sisters would be around for break, but it looks like most of them went home."

"Or they went on road trips, or they're out, or they're staying elsewhere, like Cass." Carolyn shoulders her bag. "Are we ready to go?"

"Corbin's bus should be here soon, and Rory and his bandmates are waiting in the common room downstairs at Douglass, so yeah, I think we're ready," Drea says. She holds out a hand, and Carolyn passes her the bag with the wine, bottles clinking. "Serina's still packing, if you want to go try to help her hurry up. She said something about getting a slow start this morning."

Late wakeup, and a lazy start because they hadn't wanted to crawl out of the warmth. Heather had packed the night before, and she and Nikita were off to Nikita's room before Carolyn and Serina even stirred. In the dark of a quiet room, Carolyn had lost time while she and Serina snuggled.

Carolyn smiles softly, brightening. "It was worth it," she murmurs. "Serina is definitely worth it."

Kit nudges her toward the stairs. "Fine, then go help her get moving now that you've made her late. It's vacation time."

Time to relax and forget about the Dreamscape, about traveling, about the split. Time to just be themselves. They need this, and Carolyn's more than ready to enjoy every second of it.

"You're right," she says, heading for the door. "I'm ready. Let's go."

About the Author

Tris Lawrence has been writing since she was a child, filling notebooks with the worlds, dreams, and voices from inside her head. She declared in sixth grade that she wanted to be a writer, promptly started drafting her first novel in seventh grade, and never looked back.

Tris has always been fascinated by the way people work: how their relationships fit together, how they interact socially, how they learn and discover. She has read avidly her entire life, devouring mysteries, romances, science fiction, and fantasy novels, and as an adult still loves all of these genres. Her favorite stories center on people who are learning or discovering new things, and coming-of-age stories top that list, which is how Pine Hills University came to be. She wants to share stories of people who are learning how to relate to each other, how to adult, how to college, and how to just be. She hopes to share stories about diverse characters with representation of everything she wishes she could have read growing up, and she hopes that these stories will touch the lives and hearts of those who read them.

When not writing, Tris is a wife, a mother (to two children, two cats, and a dog), a knitter, a system administrator, a black belt in taekwondo, an avid reader, and a music aficionado. Sleep, she claims, is optional.

Links

Bluesky: tryslora.bsky.social
Dreamwidth: tryslora
Facebook: trislawrencewrites
Mastodon: wandering.shop/@tryslora
Patreon: tryslora
Pillowfort: tryslora
Tumblr: welcometophu

Titles by Tris Lawrence

Warm Anything You Want

Welcome to PHU

Twinned Trilogy

> **Book 1:** Commit to the Kick
> **Book 2:** Missed Fortunes
> **Book 3:** Into the Split

Side Stories

> Best Friends AND…
> if it's meant to be
> Just Let Me Lose Control
> Live Like There's No Tomorrow
> so he won't fly away

Books and short stories in the Welcome to PHU 'verse available at

- https://duckprintspress.com/about-duck-prints-press/creators-we-work-with/authortrislawrence/
- https://welcometophu.tumblr.com/
- https://www.pillowfort.social/community/WelcomeToPHU/

Anthologies including Tris Lawrence

Add Magic to Taste (author contributor)
He Bears the Cape of Stars (author contributor)

About Duck Prints Press LLC

Duck Prints Press LLC is an independent publisher based in New York State. Our founding vision is to help fanwork creators navigate the complex process of bringing their original works from first draft to print, culminating in publishing their work under our imprint. We are particularly dedicated to working with queer creators and publishing stories and artwork featuring characters from across the LGBTQIA+ spectrum.

Support Duck Prints Press on Patreon!

Find us online at our website https://duckprintspress.com/ or on social media:

Bluesky: duckprintspress.com
Bookshop.org: duckprintspress
Instagram: duckprintspress
itch.io: duckprintspress
Patreon: duckprintspress
Pillowfort: duckprintspress
TikTok: @duckprintspress
Tumblr: duckprintspress

Goodreads: https://www.goodreads.com/user/show/129902473-duck-prints-press-llc
Storygraph: https://app.thestorygraph.com/profile/unforth_duckprintspress

If you enjoyed this story, don't forget to leave us a review!